FOR ALL OUR SINS

FOR ALL OUR SINS

A Tracy Brubaker Mystery

John Carter Stell

The Tracy Brubaker Mystery Series

#1 The Big Nap
#2 Crossed Stitch
#3 Murder Me Twice
#4 Practice to Deceive
#5 Gun in White Satin
#6 Murders and Acquisitions
#7 Poisoned Candi
#8 Thread Killer
#9 The Lady in the Cake
#10 The Witness with the Waggly Tale
#11 Last Turn of the Cheek
#12 Seasons Bleeding
#13 For All Our Sins

Library of Congress Control Number: 2022900818

ISBN: 9798401281678

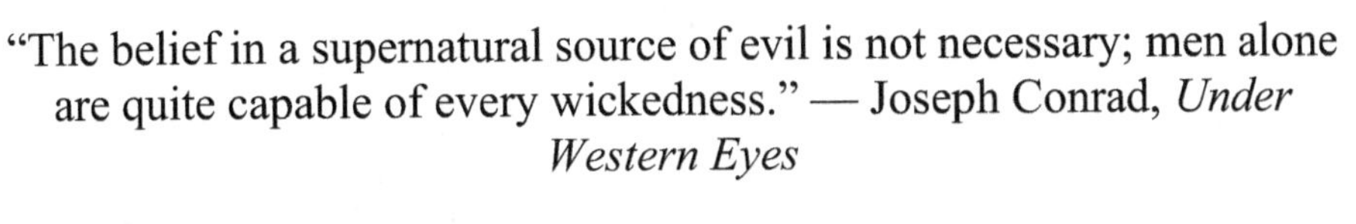

"The belief in a supernatural source of evil is not necessary; men alone are quite capable of every wickedness." — Joseph Conrad, *Under Western Eyes*

PROLOGUE

"The 911 call came in at 2:37 a.m.," Detective William Culpepper began. "The caller reported hearing a single gunshot from this residence. Officers arrived at the scene at 2:42 a.m."

"How'd they get here so damn fast?" Detective Jim Lucas asked.

"They were headed in this direction in response to an earlier call. A prowler had been reported in the area. Dispatch just rerouted them here; sent out another unit to the earlier call."

"Ah."

"Officers arrived and, after failing to get a response, entered the home. The front door was closed, but unlocked, and the alarm was not engaged. They found the victim — Cynthia Lydecker — dead upstairs in her bed."

"Cause of death?"

"Single gunshot wound to the head seems to be the cause. The ME is still upstairs."

Lucas was surveying the first floor of Cynthia Lydecker's two-story Baltimore City home.

"Doesn't look like robbery," he told Culpepper. "This place is spotless."

"So's the upstairs. I swear, Jim. It looks like this guy came in, walked up the steps, shot the victim, and then just left. Very smooth."

"A professional hit? Is that what you're thinking?"

"Not sure."

"And no sign of forced entry?"

"No."

1

"Sounds to me more like a close, personal, friend — or closer. Unless of course you think Ms. Lydecker went to bed leaving her front door unlocked and forgetting to set her alarm."

"Well, I checked her purse, medicine cabinet, and bedside nightstand. No signs of birth control pills or condoms."

"Meaning what? You don't think she had a boyfriend?"

"Doesn't look like it. No men's clothes anywhere — nothing."

"Maybe she had her tubes tied and is in between men. Maybe she had a girlfriend."

Culpepper blinked. "Yeah…maybe…I guess."

Lucas was now standing in front of a wall adorned with framed eight by ten photographs. Most of them had Cynthia Lydecker smiling for the camera, standing next to someone doing the same. Lucas let his eyes scan the images.

"These don't appear to be boyfriends," Culpepper said.

Lucas looked at his partner with a mild scowl. "I figured that out myself since more than half of these are with other women."

"Oh, sorry." Culpepper cleared his throat. "She — Cynthia Lydecker, I mean — was quite the philanthropist, huh? All these photos seem to be from a benefit of some kind or another."

"Yeah," Lucas murmured.

"I guess everyone has their causes."

"Sure," Lucas agreed. "And there's usually a reason why they have the causes they have."

A heavyset figure was now making his way down the stairs. Lucas and Culpepper turned.

"Done up there, Doctor?" Culpepper asked.

"Yes," Dr. Derek Shahey answered. "I think your victim was asleep when she was shot."

Lucas put his hands on his hips. "So, no other signs of violence to the body other than the shot?"

"None that I could see. It appears someone came up behind her, put a gun to the back of her head, and pulled the trigger. I'm thinking maybe .38-eight caliber."

"Bullet's still in the body?" Lucas asked.

"Yes," Shahey nodded.

"Time of death?"

Shahey looked at his watch. "Well, it's 3:40 a.m. now, and body temp tells me less than two hours but more than one. I'd say between two and two-thirty is a good estimate."

Lucas sighed. "Thank you, Dr. Shahey."

"You'll have my report by late afternoon," Shahey said while he moved towards the front door.

Lucas blinked. "What's that about?" he asked Culpepper.

"What do you mean?"

"Shahey sounds as if he's making this one a priority."

"He probably is."

"Why's that?"

Culpepper looked at his partner. "Don't you know who Cynthia Lydecker is — was?"

"Uh…no. Should I?"

"Jesus, Jim. Her father is Alastair Conroy."

"Owner of the Jolts?"

"Baltimore's first professional basketball team in years…"

Lucas rolled his eyes. "Marvelous. No wonder she could afford to be such the philanthropist."

"And her ex-husband is Edward Lydecker, one of Annapolis' favorite sons."

"A politician."

"House of Delegates."

"Jesus Christ!" Lucas practically screamed. "So, now I'm going to be dealing with the rich and would-be powerful? I *already* hate this case."

"Sorry. It could be somebody killed her to get back at her father or ex-husband."

"Why the hell would someone think her ex-husband even cared being he's her *EX*-husband?"

Culpepper sighed. "I don't know. I'm just saying the suspect pool could be pretty big."

"I haven't heard any rumors about corruption regarding the Jolts or Lydecker. Have you?"

"No."

"Well, I wouldn't go sharing your initial thoughts with the father and former husband if I were you."

"No, of course not."

Detective Lucas was looking as if he wanted to spit. Culpepper looked as if he was about to be spit *on*. But the latter was saved by the arrival of uniformed Officer Blanc.

"Detective Lucas," Blanc said. "I think we may have located the murder weapon."

Justin Wilmont was in his pajamas and more than ready to go to bed. His Monday night — now Tuesday morning — was usually rather peaceful. Maybe he should never have made that call about a prowler.

"Look Mr. Wilmont," Lucas said, starting to get irritated with the whiny potential witness, "I appreciate you've told the other officers. But I really need to hear your account of events given what we found in your trash can."

Wilmont grunted. "Fine! But I intend to call someone about this! Why you people can't just talk to each other—"

"Start with what you were doing just before you heard the noise, please."

"Noise? Racket you mean."

"Racket, then," Lucas muttered.

"All right. Monday night I work until about midnight."

"Where?"

"I'm the maître d' at *Brussels*."

"…Sounds way above my pay grade."

Wilmont looked Lucas up and down. "Probably. We close at 10:00 p.m. but after clean-up and close-down, I'm usually not leaving until 12:00 a.m., and I'm home before 12:30."

"So, you got home around 12:30, more or less. What did you do then?"

"What I always do. I watch the late-night talk show monologues that I've recorded. And then maybe watch some of the guest interviews if they seem worth it. But so few people have anything worth hearing these days."

"I'm sure. What distracted you?"

"It's about 2:25 a.m., maybe a little earlier. I'm sitting here and then I hear this noise. I've heard it before: the sound of some punk ass knocking over my trash cans. So, I get up, turn on the porch light, and then look out the window."

"And please tell me *exactly* what you saw, Mr. Wilmont."

"This person was in the process of picking up one of my cans, which he must have knocked over. I thought he might have been some drunk or something. So, I just banged on the window, figuring he'd take off like some frightened squirrel. And that's what he did."

"What did this person look like?"

"I didn't really get that good a look."

"Just do the best you can, please."

"Very well. He — if it was a he — was dressed in black or dark blue. He had on a knit cap and gloves too! He definitely had gloves on."

"Could you tell how tall he was, or what race he was?"

"No. He was hunched over and then he started running. And I never saw his face at all. It was dark of course and he may have had that covered too. I just got a bad feeling — the way he was dressed. I thought maybe he robbed somebody and hit my can while running away."

"Was he carrying anything that you noticed?"

Wilmont blinked. "No; no, I can't say I remember him having anything — in his hands anyway."

"And you called 911 at about 2:28 a.m.?"

"That sounds right."

Lucas looked at where Justin Wilmont was seated while watching his television programming. Both chair and set where in the family room whose bay window provided an almost unobstructed view of the street.

"Did you have any lights on or was it dark except for the light from the screen?"

"Dark. I prefer it that way."

"Mm."

"I heard they found a gun in there. Is that true?"

"I'm sorry, Mr. Wilmont, but we'll be taking your one can and all of its contents. Crime lab will want to go through it thoroughly."

"Oh. Well, that's fine I guess, as long as I get the can back. You can just throw the rest of it away when you're through with it."

"Of course."

"Now is that all, officer?"

"Detective," Lucas corrected.

"Is there a difference?" Wilmont asked snidely.

"And how long have you been working as a busboy again?" Lucas snapped.

"I'm not a — oh. I see. Well, *Detective*, is that all?"

"Just one more thing. Did you notice if any of your neighbors saw this person?"

"I couldn't tell you. It's usually rather quiet around here."

"All right."

"Now, *is* that all?"

"For now, Mr. Wilmont. We'll be in touch if we have any more questions."

"I'm sure."

"Good night, Mr. Wilmont," Lucas said, starting to turn.

"Good *morning*, Detective," Wilmont corrected.

Lucas ignored him and motioned for the two officers and his partner, Culpepper, to exit Wilmont's homestead. Soon Wilmont was alone so he could resume his early Tuesday morning routine.

"Look, guys," Lucas began as the officers approached their vehicle. "I hope you didn't take any offence at my busboy analogy in there. I was just trying to make a point with that pissant."

"No offence taken, sir," one of the officers responded. "We understand."

"Good. Nice work tonight — or this morning rather. Lab people should be here soon to collect the can and gun."

"Yes, sir. We'll stay here."

"Thanks." Lucas smiled pleasantly at his efficient comrades and then started making his way to his own car, with Culpepper at his side.

"You really think they need to take the whole can, Jim?"

"Sure. It's procedure, isn't it? Maybe this person put something else in there. Maybe he left prints on something."

"Witness said this guy was wearing gloves though."

"Yeah; sure." Lucas sighed.

"What is it, Jim? You seem more annoyed than usual."

Lucas scowled at Culpepper. "Bill, let me ask you something. Doesn't it seem odd to you that the call reporting the gunshot came *after* the call about someone getting rid of the gun? Shouldn't it be the other way around?"

"Uh…sure. I guess. But you're assuming that gun we found is the murder weapon."

Lucas looked at Culpepper with something akin to contempt. "You're kidding me, right? Please don't tell me you have any doubts that that's the murder weapon."

Culpepper, now tired of his partner's attitude, glared at him. "No, I don't."

"So?"

"Well, maybe the other caller was nervous; debated about calling or not."

"For nine minutes? That's quite a long time if you ask me."

"Maybe."

"Maybe, huh? Then let me ask you this. Would you please take a look at this neighborhood and tell me what you see?"

"I'm sorry?"

"Just turnaround and take a good look."

After he had done so Culpepper asked, "What's your point?"

"What do you see? Tell me exactly what you see."

Culpepper frowned. "A bunch of houses."

"And?"

"A bunch of trash cans."

"Right. And how many people do you see? How many houses have lights flickering in their windows?"

Culpepper sighed. He didn't like this game or whatever it was. "None, I suppose."

"Exactly. A quiet street with plenty of dark houses and trash cans to choose from. And yet our prowler not only picks the one house that had its owner obviously awake and watching TV, but he also knocks the damn can over, so he gets noticed." Lucas pointed at Wilmont's window. "Look!"

Culpepper obliged and noticed that instead of going to bed, the witness had turned his large screen monitor back on. The set's glow was clearly visible.

"Shit, Jim. You're right."

"Uh-huh. I'm telling you, Bill. I hate this case already. Hate it."

"I hear you," Culpepper said sincerely.

"And there's not a doubt in my mind that the lab will be able to trace that gun."

"Speak of the devil…"

Lucas turned to see a forensic team van approaching. He watched it pull up next to the uniformed officers, who then started explaining what was needed.

"Let's go talk to Sergeant Graham," Lucas muttered. He's no doubt wondering where the hell we are with this."

"Sure."

Lucas just grunted as he opened his car door. His stomach was now feeling upset. He hated this case already with all his being. And the damn thing had barely even begun.

"She had been divorced from Edward Lydecker for about four years," Culpepper was telling Sgt. Graham. "The two got married just out of college. So, they were together for 14 years give or take."

"Why'd they split?" Graham asked.

"Not really sure. But my understanding is that it was as amicable as a divorce can be. Both had money. And there were no kids."

"I don't see this guy killing his ex after four years, do you Jim?" Graham was looking at Lucas, who by now was feeling quite sick. "You okay?"

"Sure," he lied. "As for the victim's ex, it doesn't seem likely. But there could be reasons we don't know about."

"And this gun," Graham continued. "What do we know about that?"

"No prints," Culpepper continued. "And there was some half-assed attempt to obscure the serial number. But Nico thinks he can lift the number. He's working on it right now."

Graham turned and seated himself at his desk. "You both know who Cynthia Lydecker is, don't you?" After both detectives nodded, Graham said, "So I don't have to tell you I'll be getting calls hourly for updates."

"Yes, sir," Culpepper said timidly.

"Since her divorce, Cynthia Lydecker has been seen at more charity events than you could count. She's on the boards of the state's most visible nonprofit organizations. So, our work on this will be front page news from this day forward. Don't be surprised if you see her nickname all over the place."

"Nickname?" Lucas asked with apprehension.

"Saint Cynthia."

"Oh, for God's sake…"

"Listen, Jim. I'm serious. You need to be playing you're 'A' game here. Am I clear?"

"You're clear."

"All right. When you find out whom that gun belongs to don't stop to tell me. Just get him and tell me afterward. Now, why don't you two show your faces to Nico just to remind him we're all still waiting?"

"Yes, sir," Culpepper said.

Lucas just looked at his partner — his new, just assigned to the Northeastern District partner. God, how he hated this case.

"Gun's registered to a Keith Entwistle," Nicodemus Papa told the anxious detectives. He then handed them a sheet from his printer. "There's his address.'

"Thanks, Nico," Culpepper said.

"Yeah," Lucas added.

"We're checking his prints now with respect to the trash can and its contents. We'll let you know what we find."

"All right," Lucas said, stifling a yawn. He looked at Culpepper. "I guess we'll go wake up Entwistle."

Culpepper smiled and nodded. "I'll call Maggie and get her to run the background on this guy."

"Yeah, you do that."

Lucas turned and moved quickly, while Culpepper thanked the technician again before catching up to his partner.

On the way to the car, Culpepper called Detective Maggie Bristol. Soon after they had started their journey, he told Lucas, "Maggie says Entwistle's clean."

"No surprise there. We're not dealing with some pro here, what with knocking trash cans over."

"I guess not. Entwistle *is* married though. I'm thinking affair."

"Affair?"

"Sure. To get in the house the perp had to have a key and know the alarm code, right? Now who else but a close relative or boyfriend would know the alarm code?"

"Uh-huh."

"Maybe he wanted to end it and she didn't, or she did, and he didn't."

"Stop getting ahead of yourself, Bill. Let's hear what Entwistle has to say."

"Sure."

Culpepper looked at Lucas a few more moments before turning his attentions elsewhere. Suddenly the view outside seemed much more interesting. It was well known throughout the department that Detective Jim Lucas was getting more unpleasant to deal with by the day, apparently brought on by his ex-wife's remarriage. There were probably other reasons too. And Culpepper was getting tired of playing the gosh-golly-gee new partner. It was just a strategy he developed so as not to come off like some hot shot know-it-all. So, Culpepper decided to keep his mouth shut for the rest of the trip to the suspect's Anne Arundel County home.

It was almost 7:30 Tuesday morning when the detectives parked in the Entwistle driveway. Lucas quickly exited and looked impatiently at Culpepper, who twice tried closing his door, prevented from doing so by the seatbelt that didn't retract properly.

"Sorry, Jim," Entwistle mumbled after succeeding on the third try.

Lucas just turned and headed toward the front door. He rang the bell and then withdrew his identification to have it at the ready. The door was opened by a man in his bathrobe.

"Keith Entwistle?" Lucas asked.

"Yes," Entwistle said cautiously.

After Lucas introduced and identified himself and Culpepper he asked, "May we come in please, Mr. Entwistle?"

The homeowner looked at them confused. Then he said, "Of course," and unlocked the screen door. "May I get you some coffee?" Entwistle inquired after the investigators had entered and the door was closed.

"No, thank you," Lucas answered for both himself and his partner.

"Okay. What is it you want?"

"Do you own a Smith and Wesson 637 .38 Special?" Lucas asked.

Entwistle blinked. "I own a gun, yes. It's a Smith and Wesson."

"Can you show it to us please?"

"Uh…sure. It's upstairs, I think. Just follow me."

Entwistle looked from Lucas to Culpepper and gulped. They were both looking at him intensely. He wanted to ask what this was about but decided not to. Instead, he turned and started towards the stairway. After everyone had entered the bedroom, Entwistle pointed towards his closet.

"It's in there."

"Fine," Lucas nodded.

Entwistle gulped again, and then moved towards the closet doors. After he pulled them open, he shoved his hand under a heavy comforter that sat on the top shelf. He then withdrew a zippered case and, after holding it in his hands a few moments, looked at it curiously.

"What's wrong, Mr. Entwistle," Lucas asked.

"It doesn't feel right," was the answer.

"Would you mind opening it for us?"

"Sure." Entwistle unzipped the case, and then stared, looking confused. "I don't understand. This is where we keep it."

"We?" Culpepper dared to ask. Lucas thankfully seemed to take no issue.

"My wife and I."

"Where is your wife?" Lucas asked, reassuming the interrogation duties.

"At a conference — in Virginia. She should be back later today."

"She wasn't here last night?"

"No. She stayed over because the conference was all day Monday and resumed early today."

"So, you were all by yourself here last night," Culpepper commented.

"Yes." Entwistle took a deep breath. "Now, can you both please tell me what all this is about? Did something happen to Katie?"

Lucas' turn again. "Katie's your wife?"

"Yes."

"Do you know a woman by the name of Cynthia Lydecker?"

Entwistle appeared to think a moment. "No, I don't think so. Why?"

"Have you ever heard of her?"

"I said I didn't already."

"You said you didn't know her. But she was something of a celebrity so maybe you know the name."

"I'm sorry, Detective… What was your name again?"

"Lucas."

"…Detective Lucas. I never heard of her. Now, please. What's going on here?"

Lucas sighed. "Earlier this morning between 2:00 and 2:30, somebody fatally shot Ms. Lydecker with *your* Smith and Wesson, Mr. Entwistle."

The civilian's face registered panic and horror. "Oh my God! I don't understand."

"Neither do we. When was the last time you saw your gun?"

"What? Oh. I'm not sure."

Lucas sighed. "You're not sure?"

"We got that gun a few years ago for protection. But we moved to a better neighborhood not long after and I just put it in the closet. I kept meaning to look into selling it but…"

"Are you saying you haven't laid eyes on your gun for a few years?" Culpepper asked skeptically.

"No. But the only time I saw it was if we needed something from the closet shelf and had to move things around. But I can't be absolutely sure when the last time I saw it was."

"Did you ever loan it to someone?" Lucas inquired calmly.

"No! Of course not!"

"Who knew you had it and where you kept it?"

"I'm not sure. Lots of people, I guess." Suddenly Entwistle's eyes widened. "Oh my God! Of course!"

"What is it, Mr. Entwistle?"

"The burglar must have taken it!"

"Burglar?" Lucas and Culpepper asked almost simultaneously.

"Yes! Last Wednesday night, my wife and I were at dinner. We got a call from our alarm company that our house alarm had gone off and it turned out someone had broken in."

"Really," Lucas said, raising an eyebrow.

"Yes. But it didn't look like he ever left the first floor. What I mean is nothing in the bedroom was even touched; my wife's jewelry was all here. It didn't even occur to me to check the gun."

"What did he take?" Culpepper asked.

"Our Blu Ray player and some movies; my beer."

"Your beer?" Culpepper chuckled.

Entwistle glared. "Cops who took the report figured it was kids and they ran off not too long after the alarm sounded."

"All right, Mr. Entwistle," Lucas said flatly. "Why don't you give me the name of the detective who handled your break in, and I can follow up with him or her."

"Sure. I have a file I'm keeping with all the paperwork. I haven't finished the insurance company stuff yet though."

"That's fine."

"I have it all downstairs in the study. Should I get it now?"

"We'll follow you down."

Lucas let Entwistle exit the sleeping chamber and then he followed, with Culpepper getting to play caboose. After the detectives were given their peer's name, they thanked Keith Entwistle and promised to be in touch.

The partners had just finished fastening their seatbelts when Culpepper asked, "What do you think, Jim?"

"We'll see if there's any evidence that Entwistle knew the victim."

"That's not what I meant. No way was it the thieves who took that gun."

Lucas sighed. "I agree. They would have just grabbed the case, not taken the time to remove the piece."

"Yeah. Pretty convenient timing of the burglary too."

"We'll follow up with Detective Mitchell and see what she thinks. Could be there have been other break-ins in the area just like this one."

Culpepper sighed. "I still think Entwistle was screwing that girl."

Lucas cleared his throat. "Bill, let me tell you something. Don't get in the habit of reaching conclusions before you have all the evidence. And even then, try to keep an open mind. I've leapt to the wrong conclusions a few times in my career and luckily somebody was there to make things right. At least, I hope there aren't other people doing time they shouldn't be because of me."

Culpepper looked at Lucas quizzically. "My gut tells me this guy is guilty."

"Funny. I thought Entwistle looked genuinely surprised that his gun wasn't where he thought it was. Obviously, one of us is wrong."

Culpepper shook his head and sighed. Now he was starting to hate this case too, although not for the same reasons as Lucas. "Well, I guess you're right about the first piece of business being seeing if they knew each other. But if they were having an affair that might not be too easy to nail down."

"There should be something: phone records, restaurant receipts, gift purchases…something."

"I guess."

Lucas didn't say another word. *His* gut was telling him there was something very wrong about this. Very, very wrong. What it was exactly, he couldn't be sure. All he could be sure of was that he was going to hate this case even more before it was all over; hate it with a passion. Sadly, the only thing in his life that he had any passion *for* was this very job. But did he have enough left to get him through this case? He'd learn the answer to that question soon enough, even if it weren't the answer that he hoped it would be.

PART I: FORGIVE US OUR TRESPASSES…

Chapter 1

"What name do you give your child?" Father Mathias asked the smiling couple.

"Peter Xavier," they told him.

"And what do you ask of God's Church for Peter Xavier?"

"Baptism."

The celebrant continued with the ritual. But Tracy Brubaker Shane's eyes remained fixed on the newest member of her family. She was cradling the sleeping infant in her arms, while her husband Brian held their two-year-old daughter Nicole in his. Eight-week-old Peter finally stirred when the priest splashed his little noggin with the font's water. He opened his eyes and saw his mother, figured everything must be all right since she was smiling at him, and promptly resumed his nap.

Peter Xavier Shane had been born November 19 of last year. But because of the holidays his parents had scheduled his christening for the second Sunday in January, the 13th. Peter's godparents were Jack and Emily Bronski, whose 12-year-old daughter Jenna was Tracy's godchild. Tracy hadn't seen her close friends the Bronksis very much since their move to North Carolina almost three years ago. Despite the distance though, Tracy had very much wanted Jack and Emily to take on the roles. They had eagerly accepted.

Tracy's *other* godchild was one-year-old Kenneth Tanner, son to Tracy's sister-in-law Crystal Shane and her husband Elias Tanner, Jr. It was only fair since they were godparents to Nicole. Tracy had hoped having Crystal and Elias at the mass would somehow help keep the antsy Nicole calm. She did love having one-sided conversations with her cousin Ken. But Nicole had spent all morning — and all mass time — alternating her attention-seeking between her own mother and father. Even the snacks being offered by Nicole's grandmother, Violetta Brubaker, weren't doing anything to settle the child down.

Now Nicole was clinging to her father as the family stood in front of the gathered church goers. Father Mathias, having completed the baptismal rite, asked the congregation to welcome Peter into the Catholic community. Nicole smiled broadly at her father as she joined in the applause.

"If you don't sit still Nicole, I'm going to have to take you out," Brian told his daughter not long after they'd returned to their pew.

Nicole shook her head. "I want to hold baby," she complained.

"Baby's asleep right now. Let Mommy hold him."

"I want to hold Mommy," Nicole protested.

Tracy, overhearing her daughter, smiled and carefully passed the newborn to Brian, who in turn placed Peter in Violetta's arms. Nicole smiled and practically leapt into Tracy's lap.

"Calm down, Nicole," Tracy said gently.

"I want to go home," Nicole whimpered.

"Soon baby girl," her mother assured her.

"But baby got his bath."

"Hush, Nicole," Tracy reiterated, now rising along with the rest of the assembly.

Nicole just grunted and pressed her face into Tracy's shoulder. Brian shook his head. Suddenly the prospect of Nicole missing her afternoon nap due to the planned celebration wasn't very appealing. As much as he was looking forward to the day's activities, Brian Shane was looking forward even more to them being over with. Peace and quiet were such rare commodities these days.

"Can I hold him?" Jenna Bronski asked her godmother.

"Sure," Tracy smiled. "I just fed him so he might spit up a little. He does that sometimes."

"Because of the air he swallows. That's okay. I'll just put the burp cloth over my shoulder."

Peter looked briefly at Jenna as she took him. Then he looked back at his mother.

"Hi Peter," Jenna said as sweetly as she could. "I'm Jenna."

Emily Bronski soon sat down next to Tracy and hugged her. "Great job there, Tracy B," she said. "He's a handsome devil."

"Thanks, Em. Did you get enough to eat?"

Emily grabbed her stomach. "Oh, my yes! Probably got more than that."

Tracy chuckled. "Take some leftovers with you anyway. Jack's parents probably have room in their fridge."

"Are you kidding? They stocked up when they learned we wanted to stay the weekend. And we've hardly made a dent."

"Hey girlfriends!" Crystal Shane said loudly as she approached Tracy and Emily.

"Crystal Pain!" Emily said while coming to her feet.

"Oh, shut up!" Crystal responded. Then she hugged her insulter firmly. "I haven't missed you at all."

Emily laughed as she sat. "I've missed you less."

Crystal sat down. "God, would you look at us? Moms. Responsible people. Yuck!"

"I always knew you'd get the brass ring, Crystal," Emily told her.

"I thought I'd end up a hippie."

"Tracy should have been the hippie."

"Hey! What's that supposed to mean?" Tracy asked grinning.

"You were always Ms. Peace and Love."

"Me? I don't think so."

"She's still Ms. Peace and Love," Crystal said.

"Oh please. More like Peace and Quiet — at least, that's what I'd like."

Crystal and Emily chuckled. "Good luck with that," the former told her.

Emily looked at her friends. "I'm so proud of you two. One's running a multi-million-dollar company and the other has her own law firm. I'm just a lowly pediatrician."

"Dr. Bronksi," Crystal said, shaking her head, "if you can convince Jackie boy to move back here you would have three new patients instantly!"

Emily shook *her* head. "I wish we *could* move back here. But Jack is still running things at the branch and Jenna's doing so well in school."

"Jenna's beautiful," Tracy said. "And she seems so mature for her age."

"She has to be," Emily said with some regret. "Jack and I have worked our share of late hours and depended on Jenna to help out with so many things. We're so proud of her."

Crystal wiped her eyes. "If you wenches make my cry, I'm going to be *so* mad at you. How in the *hell* did your kid get to be 12 years old, Emily?"

The fussing that suddenly was heard redirected the ladies' attentions.

"I think Peter wants his mother," Jenna said, moving towards Tracy.

"Thanks, Jenna," Tracy replied, taking back her son.

"Hey kid," Crystal grinned. "You're growing up *way* too fast."

Jenna smiled shyly. "Mom says that all the time too."

"Well, don't be in a hurry to grow up. Remember to enjoy this time of your life, like I did."

Emily looked at Crystal. "When did *you* become the wise sage?"

"I've always been wise. You just never listened to me."

"I think trying to get us all to go skinny dipping in the fountain by the school may have had something to do with that, Crys," Tracy giggled.

"You cowards," Crystal grunted. "That was the time in our lives when we could have done something like that. Now I pull muscles just taking off my shoes."

Everyone laughed, even Jenna.

"Yes," Tracy added, "every young woman should have a disorderly conduct charge on their record."

Crystal frowned. "The cops would have been *thanking* us and then taking us out to dinner." She looked at Jenna. "Jenna dear, take it from your Aunt Crystal. If you ever have the opportunity to—"

"You can stop talking *right* now," Emily interrupted.

"Hey! I was just going to say, always take an opportunity to spend time with friends."

"Does Peter need a change, Tracy?" Emily asked. "Cause I *smell* something."

"Ouch," Crystal said. Then more laughter followed.

"He *does* need a change," Tracy said.

"Let me find Brian," Crystal offered.

"I can handle it," Tracy said. "Brian's letting Nicole run around somewhere to burn off her overabundance of energy."

"I'll come with you, Aunt Tracy," Jenna said as she picked up the diaper bag.

"Okay, Jenna. There's a changing station in the rest room."

Jenna just smiled and then followed her godmother out of the private banquet room.

Emily turned to Crystal. "Crystal, are all those things that I read about Tracy true?"

"What *things*?"

"People have tried to kill her."

Crystal frowned. "Yeah, unfortunately."

"Dear God."

"Tell me about it. I try to get her to quit. But she won't."

"But she has kids now."

"I know that. *She* knows that."

Emily sighed. "What can we do then? Should *I* try talking some sense into her?"

"Good luck with that. Now, I'm not the best example of a Catholic girl you'll find. But the only thing I can think to do is pray for her."

Emily gulped and then nodded. "I really should visit here more often and make time to see you guys."

Crystal Shane just looked at her friend. "Yeah, we *all* should try to do that." She looked in Tracy's direction. "You just never know when you won't be able to anymore."

Tracy Brubaker Shane was splitting her workday between her home office and the one she had in Owings Mills. Her two associates — Neal Bennett and Tyler Wannamaker — were doing a fine job keeping up with things at the office, with the help of the extraordinary Rebecca Dietz. Modern technology had made communication with her employees and clients quite painless. And having her stay-at-home-dad husband and live-in mother to help with the children was a stress reliever too.

Tracy was preparing to leave for work mid Monday morning. She had nursed Peter and pumped some additional milk for his future consumption. Next, she bid everyone *adieux*. Brian however decided to follow her to her car.

"How late do you think you'll be?" he asked.

"Not sure yet. We have a meeting with a potential client and Neal has some things he wanted to go over. But I'll try to be home by 7:00 p.m."

"I think I'll build a fire tonight."

"You think it's safe?"

"I was thinking after Nicole went to bed."

Tracy smiled. "We could cuddle."

"It's been so crazy with the holidays, and you going back to work already, and then the whole baptism thing."

"I know, Brian."

"We haven't had a chance to just sit and talk; we both are so worn out by the end of the day."

Tracy embraced him. "A fire sounds nice."

"I'll see you tonight," Brian whispered in her ear. "I love you."

"I love you more," she responded as usual.

As she opened the door to the garage Brian gently touched her shoulder. Then he watched her get into her car and back out of their driveway. He closed the garage and mudroom doors when he could no longer see her.

"Dad-*dy*? Where *are* you?" a voice called out.

"Coming, Nicole," he answered. Now *his* workday would begin in earnest too.

Tracy greeted everyone cheerfully as she entered her suite of offices. They returned the salutation in kind. She had barely gotten settled when Tyler Wannamaker entered her private office.

"Tracy, can we talk?"

"Sure, Ty. Everything okay?"

"Actually, it isn't. Can I close the door?"

"Sure."

Tracy looked at Tyler with concern as he secured the room and then stood behind the chair in front of her desk.

"I'll just come out and say it. I need to take a leave of absence."

"Why? What's going on?"

"It's my family. My family needs my help."

Tyler Wannamaker had been with Tracy now for just over a year and a half. He had been hired to help with the ever-increasing client list, and he had been an excellent choice. Tracy may not have been as close to him as she was to Neal and Rebecca, both of whom had been with her since she started her firm. But she liked Tyler Wannamaker very much. And she could tell he was truly upset.

"Sit down," Tracy said. "Sit down and tell me what's going on."

Tyler gulped, nodded, and then sat down.

"It's bad, Tracy. I mean it's very bad."

Now Tracy felt herself getting upset. "It's okay. You can tell me."

"You've heard about the Cynthia Lydecker murder."

"Oh yes. It's all over the news all of the time."

"Well, they just made an arrest."

"Oh?"

"Yes. My brother-in-law."

"*What?*" Tracy exclaimed.

"Yeah. Katie just called me. Well, not 'just.' But I have to go down there."

"Of course, Tyler; of course. But why do you have to take a leave of absence?"

"Why? Isn't it obvious? Katie wants me to defend him. And you don't generally take on murder cases. And this one…God…this one is going to be…"

Tracy took a deep breath. "Tyler, just relax a moment. Are you saying you want to disassociate yourself from the firm so you can defend your bother-in-law?"

"Yes. You don't want to get mixed up in this, Tracy."

"Why not? Do you think your brother-in-law killed that woman?"

"God no! Of course not! Keith would never do something like that!"

"Okay, okay."

"Sorry."

"It's all right. Do you think it's a good idea for you to get involved? Being so personally involved…"

"…Says the woman who defended her sister-in-law."

Tracy blinked. "Touché," She sighed.

"Katie is eight years younger than I am. She's always looked to me to help her out of everything. And of course, I always did. I probably always will. So, the idea that she'd want someone else to help in this…Well, Katie just wouldn't hear of it."

"Mm."

"She's going to need all the help I can give her. That Lydecker woman's father is richer than God. Her ex-husband is rumored to be on his way to DC at some point. You understand what I'm telling you?"

"Yes, Tyler. You think your brother-in-law has already been convicted."

"Hasn't he? This is going to get ugly before all is said and done. And I'm ready to get ugly too. And you don't 'do' ugly."

Tracy sighed. "I actually met Cynthia Lydecker a couple of times."

"You did?"

"She was on the board of one of the charities we do work for. I met her at some social functions."

Tyler shook his head. "This is all so insane. He didn't even know this woman."

"He told you that?"

"Katie said he told *her* that."

"Mm."

Tyler stood up. "I have to go. They're waiting for me."

Tracy stood up too. "I'll go with you."

"What? No. That's not why I came to see you. You've been through enough hell—"

"Don't sass the boss, Tyler. Let me at least talk to him. The both of us will talk to him."

Tyler sighed. Then he snorted and smiled. "I guess if we argued some more it wouldn't do any good."

"I just want to talk to him," Tracy said.

"Yeah, and you love to talk, don't you?" Tyler grinned.

"Let's go. You can drive though. *That* I'll let you do with no argument. I can make my calls while in transit."

Tyler shook his head and then opened the office door, with Tracy following right behind him. After informing Rebecca of the sudden change in schedule, the attorneys were on their way to see just how ugly things were looking for Keith Entwistle.

"This is Tracy, Keith," Tyler Wannamaker told his brother-in-law. "She's here to help."

Entwistle managed a smile as he shook Tracy's hand. "Ty talks about you all the time," he told her.

Tyler frowned. "He's exaggerating. I do mention some of the cases you've cracked."

"You go on and on about them though."

Tracy cleared her throat. She never could take compliments very well. They always seemed to embarrass her.

"Look Keith, obviously Ty is very concerned about you. He of course wants to help, and I want to help him. So can you tell us why they arrested you and any other details you know of?"

Entwistle nodded. "It's the gun mostly. That woman was killed with *my* gun."

"I already knew about that," Tyler told Tracy. "Katie told me about the cops' first visit after Keith told her about it."

Tracy nodded. "And how did the killer get the gun?"

"My house was broken into about a week and a half or so ago. They must have taken the gun then."

"They?"

"Whoever broke in. I guess it could have just been one person."

"They just took some movies and alcohol," Tyler added. "They probably found the gun and then sold it to somebody."

"Okay. So, there's an explanation for the gun. What else is there?"

"Fingerprints."

"At the murder scene?"

"Not exactly. You see this guy tried to get rid of the gun in somebody's trash can. The police told me they found my prints on some trash inside the can."

"Oh," Tracy said, making notes in her small spiral-bound book. "Is that it?"

"No," Entwistle sighed. "Because of the gun and prints they got a search warrant."

"What were they looking for?"

"A set of keys."

"Car keys? House keys?"

"I don't know. I think both."

"And did they find them?"

"Well...no..."

Tracy breathed deeply. "What *did* they find, Keith?"

"I swear I don't know how it got there," Entwistle said, looking at Tyler.

"How *what* got *where*?" Tracy asked.

"They found a key to this Cynthia's front door somewhere in my sock drawer."

"They found it yesterday," Tyler told Tracy. "I was out of town as you know so I couldn't be there when the warrant was served."

Tracy shook her head. "The police went looking for keys in a sock drawer?"

"The whole idea is that he would have hidden them."

"Mm," Tracy murmured. "So, just how well did you know her, Keith?"

"What?"

"How well did you know Cynthia Lydecker?"

"I didn't."

Tracy studied Entwistle a moment. "You didn't know her?"

"No. I keep telling the police that. They think I was having an affair with her, but I wasn't." Entwistle looked at Tyler again. "I've *never* cheated on Katie!"

"So, you're saying somebody planted that key in your sock drawer?" Tracy asked.

"I guess so. How else could it have gotten there?"

"Mm." Tracy looked at Tyler. Then she looked at Entwistle. "All right, Keith. You're going to meet with a District Commissioner soon and he'll explain the charges, talk about the possible outcomes, and all kinds of legalities. Tyler can be there with you. Normally you might get bail at this initial appearance. But because it's first-degree murder you're going to need a bail review hearing instead. Most likely that will be tomorrow."

"Jesus…"

"Tyler can help you with that too. I already have things scheduled for tomorrow."

"Okay."

"I want to talk to Tyler for a few minutes."

"Sure."

Entwistle looked at his brother-in-law. Tyler looked at Tracy, confused.

"I'll be right back, Keith," Tyler told him. "It'll be all right."

"Okay." Entwistle watched apprehensively as the attorneys left him.

"What's wrong?" Tyler whispered as soon as they had exited the holding room.

Tracy looked at him. "What's wrong? He says he didn't know her."

"And?"

"In spite of the key they found."

"So what? Somebody obviously planted it there."

"They did? Why?"

"To frame him, of course."

Tracy sighed. "Tyler, why would somebody frame a person who didn't even *know* the victim? Usually, a person who's framed has a motive to harm or kill the person who's been harmed or killed. *That's* what makes a frame so appealing. Why would someone frame someone else who had *no* connection with the victim? It makes no sense to me."

Tyler stared at Tracy a few moments. "You think he did it, don't you?"

"I didn't say that. I just don't know, Tyler."

"Do you really have appointments all day tomorrow? Or did you just say that because you concluded Keith killed that woman and you're done?"

Tracy folded her arms. "Let's not talk about this anymore here. Let's wait until we get back to the office."

Tyler shook his head. "I don't believe this."

"Go be with your brother-in-law, Tyler."

"And what will you do?"

"I'll get a cab back to the office. I do have a meeting later today. Pop your head in my office when you get back."

Tyler looked at the floor, and then back at Tracy. "Tracy, there's no way Keith did this. You'll never convince me he did."

"I'm not going to try to. I'll see you later."

Tyler was soon by himself in the hallway. He realized several people were staring at him. He just shook his head and went to rejoin his awaiting brother-in-law.

"What do you think, Neal?" Tracy asked her associate in a behind-closed-doors meeting.

"Right now, it's all circumstantial. Any witnesses to an affair?"

"No," Tyler said. "At least, there don't appear to be."

Tracy was drumming her fingers on her desk. "It's very strange," she said finally.

Her associates both looked at her. "What is it?" Tyler asked excitedly.

"Why did he presumably dump the gun but keep the key? It's very strange."

Tracy was leaning back in her chair, staring at the ceiling. Tyler wasn't sure if her response was to his question of if she was just thinking out loud.

"I don't understand why he wouldn't have tossed the key too. It would be such any easy thing to do."

"Exactly!" Tyler said with a smile on his face. "Are you starting to believe me now?"

She looked at Tyler. "I'm still having a problem understanding why someone would frame Keith if he didn't know Cynthia. Unless…"

"Unless what, Tracy?" Tyler was now standing next to Tracy, who was still seated.

"…Unless Keith is the real target here."

"What?" Neal asked. "What does *that* mean?"

"Cynthia Lydecker is dead; that's true. The gun used to kill her belonged to Keith Entwistle; that's also true. And everybody is going to busy themselves wondering why Keith would kill Cynthia."

"Okay," Neal said slowly.

"But what if we should be asking who might want Keith to go away for a long time?" Tracy stood up suddenly, causing Tyler to move back and almost trip over himself. "Let's say for the moment that Tyler is right about Keith: he's innocent and he didn't even know Cynthia. So, why would somebody pick him? Answer: because he's the one the killer is really after. So, while everyone is looking at motives for killing Cynthia, what we should really be asking is who has it in for Keith?"

Tyler looked at Neal. Then he looked at Tracy. "I can't imagine why anyone would have it in for Keith. He's just a small businessman. There's not much intrigue in catering."

Tracy sighed. "Tyler, I've just spent the last couple of hours trying to reconcile the facts with your strong, personal feelings about Keith. Now it's quite possible that he did know her and is lying about it. But that doesn't mean that he killed her." She looked at her associate.

"Oh, so now you think he *was* having an affair, is that it?"

"Think about it. Would he admit to such a thing in your presence? If he wants your help, do you think he'd tell you he was cheating on Katie?"

"He'd never cheat on her."

Tracy sighed again. "This is why you need someone who can be more objective, Tyler. Now, if the police find out about an affair, then

Keith's had it. If you can get him to admit it, then we can move forward with the idea someone knew about it and framed him because of it."

"I just can't believe it," Tyler growled.

"Then the only other reasonable option here is that Keith is meant to go down for this because he's the real target — unless either of you gentlemen have another thought."

Tyler put up his arms. "I'll talk to Katie. Maybe there are some things going on that I don't know about."

Tracy twisted her lips. "Maybe *I* should talk to her. She might be more forthcoming."

"Maybe we should see her together. And then if she wants me to, I can leave at any time."

Tracy smiled. "That sounds like a plan. You were probably going to see her after work, right?"

"Yes. In fact, she's waiting for me now."

"Fine. I'll follow you."

Tyler smiled. "Okay. That should be fine."

Neal folded his arms. "So does this mean we're taking this case as a firm?"

Tracy looked at Neal. "Maybe, if Katie can help make more sense of this."

"That will put us right back in that spotlight you keep telling me you hate, boss."

Tracy moved towards Neal and put her hand on his shoulder. "Neal, if Tyler is right about Keith, then someone is hurting his family. And Tyler is *our* family. You get me?"

Neal grinned. "I get you."

Tracy looked at Tyler. "Come on, Ty. Let's go talk to your sister."

Chapter 2

Katie Entwistle embraced her brother as he came through her door. She then smiled at Tracy and shook her hand vigorously.

"I'm so glad to finally meet you," Katie told her. "Ty has told me so much about you. And I've read about all those cases of yours — the ones that made the papers, I mean."

Tracy smiled and blushed. "Thanks. I don't know what else to say."

Tyler grinned. "My sister's a fan of yours."

Katie chuckled. "I'm an admirer, that's all."

"Thanks just the same," Tracy said appreciatively.

"Can I get you something to drink? Ty knows he can serve himself."

Tyler scowled while Tracy just said, "No thank you."

"Well, let's all go sit down then," Katie said as she turned towards the living room.

"Have you eaten anything?" Tyler asked her.

"Don't start, Ty. I don't need that right now."

Tyler and Tracy exchanged knowing glances and then joined their hostess on the couch.

"What do you do?" Tracy asked Katie.

"I'm a lawyer too; employment practices. My life isn't as exciting as yours or Ty's is."

"Were your parents also lawyers by any chance?"

"Mom and Dad?" Katie chuckled. "Oh my, no. Ty was the first in our family to go into law. I kind of followed *his* lead. Dad was a dentist; he's retired now. And Mom was his main hygienist."

"They're both in elder care now," Tyler said somberly.

"Dad just couldn't stop smoking," Katie commented angrily, looking at her brother. "It's *his* fault Mom got it too."

Tyler looked at Tracy. "They both have respiratory issues. They need regular looking after. Katie's convinced Dad's secondhand smoke is the cause of Mom's problems."

Katie frowned. "And you *don't?*" Katie sighed and then looked at Tracy. "I'm sorry, Tracy. You're not here to hear all about *that*."

"It's all right," Tracy reassured her.

"I wish it were. But it's not, is it?" Katie stood up from the sofa. She paced a few moments, then looked at her female guest and smiled. "But if you're going to help us then I know things will be okay."

"Gee thanks," Tyler mumbled.

"Really, Tyler," Katie scolded. "That ego of yours…"

Tracy couldn't help but grin. She had witnessed similar exchanges between Brian and Crystal.

"Well," Tracy said, "let's focus on Keith for the moment. I'd like to ask some questions about him if I may."

"Oh certainly," Katie said as she sat back down. "Ask me anything."

"Ty mentioned your husband is a caterer."

"Yes. He has his own company, Whistler's Cooking."

"Just him?"

"Him and two friends of his: Barney Schultz and Ian Tapper. They all own it, and they have some employees. They also contract additional help for larger jobs."

"Equal owners?"

Katie thought a moment. "No. Keith owns half and the other two each own a quarter. He put up most of the money to get things started and he *is* the best cook."

"That's why she married him," Tyler mused. "Katie never was a good cook." His sister ignored him.

Tracy grinned. "At some point during all of this I *must* sample his wares."

The siblings laughed. "Absolutely," Katie said.

"Have there been any problems with the business of late? Or wouldn't you know?"

"What kind of problems? You mean lawsuits or something?"

"Anything really."

Tyler cleared his throat. "Tracy's trying to find out if someone has it in for Keith."

Katie looked at Tracy, confused. "I don't understand."

Tracy sighed. She wished Tyler hadn't said what he said so soon. "Tyler assures me that Keith is telling the truth about not knowing the victim."

"Of course, he didn't."

"Well, I told Ty that Keith must have been framed then; there's no way around that. But it doesn't make sense to me that a person would frame someone with no connection to the victim, unless the endgame is really about who's supposed to take the blame."

"Oh," Katie said.

Tracy frowned. "I'm sorry. My theories can be abstruse sometimes."

Tyler grinned at his sister. "Hard to understand."

"I know what abstruse means," Katie snapped. "I was just trying to think of who might want to hurt Keith. There's nobody."

"The business is going well then?"

"It's fine. There were some problems a few years ago when the economy was all over the place but it's fine now."

"Perhaps Keith had problems with someone else — former customer or employee, for examples."

Katie shook her head. "Nothing like that. At least, Keith never said anything."

"Keith's kind of laid back," Tyler told her. "Nothing ever seems to bother him. My sister is the drama queen. She should have been an actor."

"Things bother Keith," his sister corrected. "But he's not going to tell *you* all about it. And would you just knock it off, Ty? You're not funny."

Tracy sighed. She looked at Tyler. "Maybe there's another possibility."

"What's that?" he asked.

"Maybe Keith was just convenient to set up. Maybe this killer knew both Cynthia Lydecker and Keith, even though they didn't know each other. And this person knew about Keith's gun."

"And just helped himself?" Tyler asked. "That doesn't sound right. Why not just buy a gun off the street?"

"Mm. Good point. It *does* seem Keith is supposed to take the fall for this."

Katie stood up once again. "I know what you two are thinking. You both think Keith was sleeping with that Cynthia person."

Tyler stood. "That's not true, Katie. I've always liked Keith. You know that."

"That doesn't mean you don't he think he was cheating on me."

"Fine. For the record, I don't."

"Not only that," Tracy added. "But this Cynthia Lydecker doesn't strike me as the kind of person who'd have an affair with a married man."

Both Tyler and Katie looked at Tracy.

"Why do you say that?" Tyler asked.

"The things people have been saying about her since her death; dedicating her life to helping others. How can someone in the spotlight so much be able to carry on such an affair? Why would she want to do that knowing if she were found out, it could negatively impact the work she's done — her *life's* work?"

Tyler smiled broadly. "There, Katie. You see. Tracy believes Keith too. So, there's no need to be standoffish with either of us."

Katie sighed and returned to her seat. "I'm sorry," she said, looking at each of her guests.

"It's all right," Tracy said.

Katie looked at her hands. "Do you think Keith will make bail?"

"Hard to say," Tracy answered quietly. "I think the SA may push for no bail in this case."

"I bet Pankow is golfing buddies with Ed Lydecker," Tyler tersely said. "Maybe even Al Conroy."

Tracy frowned. "I know Art Pankow pretty well," she said firmly. "He's a good SA and he's not one for politics."

"Oh, come on, Tracy," Tyler said disbelievingly. "He's no different than the others, at least in headline cases like this."

"Does Pankow like you Tracy?" Katie asked her.

"What? Oh — I guess so."

"Then maybe you should be at the bail hearing instead of Tyler."

"Hey!" the brother said.

"Look, Ty. If you go in there with an attitude it can't be good for Keith. Tracy seems to be on good terms with the state's attorney so maybe that could work in Keith's favor."

"I wouldn't count on that," Tracy cautioned. "Art and I get along fine but I didn't mean to suggest he does me favors right and left."

Katie sighed. "I still think it couldn't hurt."

"Tracy's schedule is already booked up tomorrow. So, you're going to have to settle for second best."

"Jesus, Ty," Katie said angrily. "You call *me* a drama queen. Just knock it off already. *You're* the one who told me how good she is."

"Katie," Tracy said, ready now to leave. "I'm afraid Tyler is right. I have some appointments tomorrow that I can't really cancel. People have already rearranged their schedules for me. If I could move things around, I would. I'm sorry."

Katie nodded her head. "I understand."

"I told you Tracy just started working at the office again," Tyler added. "She's already going out of her way to be here tonight."

Katie smiled at Tracy. "I hope you don't think I'm being ungrateful."

"Of course not. Your husband's in trouble and you're worried. I understand."

"Ty said he wasn't sure if you'd let him take leave to help us. Will you? Please?"

Tracy looked at Tyler. "Well, maybe Ty will let *us* help *him*. He wouldn't have to take leave."

Both brother and sister smiled broadly. "You'd do that?" Katie asked excitedly. "I'd never be able to thank you enough!"

"I like to take care of my family," Tracy said smiling also. "Speaking of which, I really need to go."

"Oh! Of course!"

Katie stood up. And when Tracy did so, Katie hugged her.

"Thanks for coming over. Thanks for believing in Keith."

"Sure," Tracy said.

"I'll walk her to her car," Tyler volunteered. "Then I'll be back for that dinner you promised me."

Katie grinned at her brother. "That's why you're really here, isn't it? And after insulting my cooking abilities, no less."

Tyler said nothing as he followed Tracy out the door.

"Were you being totally honest in there?" Tyler asked Tracy as she opened her car door. "Are you really now thinking Keith is innocent?"

Tracy sighed. "I'm thinking Cynthia Lydecker isn't the kind of person to get involved with a married man. It amounts to the same thing, I guess."

"She could have gotten involved with him before she realized he was married."

Tracy shook her head. "If that were true there'd be no reason to keep the relationship secret at that point. She'd get suspicious if he were trying to keep things quiet. And the police don't seem to have solid evidence about any affair. It's just guesswork by them at this point."

"All right. I guess that will have to do then."

"I really do need to go now, Tyler. We'll talk tomorrow at some point."

"Sure. I can't thank you enough for everything you've done."

"I haven't done anything yet," Tracy smiled. "Goodnight, Ty."

Tracy pulled her vehicle's door shut and backed out of the driveway. Tyler chuckled as she left, and then returned to collect his promised meal.

"I'm going to explode," Tracy said as she entered her home. "I need to either feed Peter or pump right now! Is he awake?"

"I think so," Brian answered. "I just put him down a few minutes ago while I…well, nature called."

Tracy chuckled. "When did you feed him last?"

"An hour or so ago."

"Good. Let me try him first and then we'll talk while I pump."

Tracy was moving hurriedly to the bassinet where her son lay. The nursing mother was full of milk thanks to her unplanned meeting, which had thrown off her schedule. Peter smiled at his mother and was soon enjoying fresh sustenance.

Violetta came into the living room where Tracy and Peter were seated.

"I thought you were going to be home at a reasonable hour," she scolded her daughter.

"Emergency meeting, Mom; it happens."

"And I suppose you didn't eat anything. How is the baby going to get what he needs if his mother doesn't?"

Tracy sighed. "You said the same things with Nicole and she turned out just fine. You can't say she lacks energy."

"You can't keep running around like this all the time."

"Mom, I'm not really in the mood for this tonight. Could you just write it all down and I'll read it tomorrow while I'm on the toilet?"

Violetta stood up. "Oh, you difficult child!"

Tracy rolled her eyes. "Yeah, Mom. I know."

The angry grandmother turned and headed up the stairs to her bedroom. She passed Brian who was coming down. He joined his wife on the couch.

"What's wrong with Mom?"

"Guess."

"You two had a tiff."

"Ding ding ding ding ding."

Brian chuckled. "Sorry, love."

"When did you change him last?"

"Just after he ate."

"Mm. He's asleep. I'll take him upstairs and put him to bed. Then you and I can talk in the kitchen."

"Sure. Should I warm up something for you?"

"No. I need to pump first. Then I'll eat."

"All right."

Brian gave Tracy a quick kiss before she headed upstairs. Before coming back down Tracy stopped to kiss the sleeping Nicole, who didn't stir at her mother's touch. Bonkers, the family's Irish setter who was also Nicole's roommate, licked Tracy's hand a few times as she petted his coat. Then it was off to the kitchen to join her husband. Brian listened as Tracy brought him up to date on the day's events.

"It occurred to me on the drive home that maybe Cynthia Lydecker did meet Keith Entwistle at some point."

"How?"

"He caters, right? Cynthia attends various social functions, right? Isn't it possible that Keith's company catered one of these functions?"

"Yeah; I guess that's very possible."

"I'm hoping I can get a list of Keith's customers and/or a copy of his calendar. And then compare all that to Cynthia's itinerary. I'm sure the police and SA's office are doing that already."

"You'd think they would have nailed down motive before making an arrest though."

"I agree. But according to Tyler and Keith, the police haven't indicated they have anything solid. The truth is, though, with all the circumstantial evidence they have, they may not need to."

"You could argue in court Entwistle was framed, couldn't you? Point out the police have no evidence of a relationship."

"I was thinking about that too. And that could be risky."

"What does that mean?"

"Put yourself in the position of a jury member, Brian. The defense is arguing that her client was framed. What are you going to be thinking?"

Brian stared at Tracy a moment. "Give me a hint, maybe?"

"All right, fine. If *I* were a member of the jury, I would be wondering why the killer picked the defendant to frame. There'd have to be a reason, right?"

"Of course."

"And if I'm the SA, I'd make sure to question the investigating detective about what Keith said regarding his relationship with Cynthia Lydecker."

"But you told me he said there was no relationship."

"*Exactly*, Brian. And then, as SA, during closing arguments, I would point out the defendant both claims to have been framed for the murder *and* that he didn't even know the victim. And then I'd ask those 12 reasonable people if that made sense to them. You see?"

"And you think all 12 would conclude that Keith is lying, and that since he is lying, he must have killed her."

"All 12? Probably not. I'm thinking best possible outcome for the state is a mistrial."

"Well, then I don't see the problem with arguing he was framed. A mistrial means Keith goes home."

"Maybe; maybe not. If the SA finds 12 people who are in the mood to punish *somebody* for Cynthia's murder, he could get a conviction."

Brian sighed. "So, what are you going to do?"

"Take things one step at a time. Tomorrow I'd like you to research Keith's company, Whistler's Cooking. Check for any lawsuits or complaints against them. Katie said they were clean but maybe Keith wouldn't have alerted her to any problems. Then, see what you can find on Keith and his partners. If any legwork needs to be done, I'll contact El."

"All right."

"And if you confirm that Keith and his buddies are nothing more than honest businessmen, then we'll have to refocus on Cynthia."

"Saint Cynthia."

"Mm. It could be she was killed not because of anything she did but rather who she was."

"How's that?"

"Her father owns the Baltimore Jolts and they've made the playoffs the last few years. He's rolling in the dough. And her ex-husband is a state delegate. Maybe that's worth looking into."

"Maybe," Brian frowned.

Tracy had by now finished her breast pumping. "Could you make me a plate while I soak my pump parts and store the milk?"

"Sure; no problem."

"I think I want to get into my PJs before I eat. I might be too tired to do that later."

"Quite a day, huh?"

"Quite."

Tracy kissed Brian before she headed upstairs. She returned to find a plate of boiled chicken, roasted potatoes, and string beans waiting for her. She poured herself a glass of milk before sitting down. Brian sat down next to her.

"Warmed up enough?"

"It's perfect. Thanks, honey."

"Mm."

"Is something wrong, Brian?"

"Nah."

"Come on, Brian. What is it?"

"I'm just being cynical."

"Cynical about what?"

"This Cynthia Lydecker."

"What about her?"

"She seems too good to be true."

"Why do you say that?"

"She spends most of her time doing charity work. Even her ex-husband doesn't seem to have a bad thing to say about her, which makes you wonder why they split up."

"*He* could have done something."

"I realize that."

"So, what are you saying? You don't think it's possible Cynthia is the person everyone thinks she is?"

"Don't *you* think that's possible? Most people have a skeleton in their closet. I know I have my own."

"And what's *my* skeleton, Brian?"

"I haven't figured that out yet."

"Oh, you're cute," Tracy grinned.

"I'm serious though. I'd get Elias to take a good look at her too. Just don't buy into the public image."

Tracy frowned. "Jeez, Brian. What'd Cynthia Lydecker ever do to *you*?"

"I never said she did anything to me. But somebody had it in for her. And you seem to want to look at everyone else but her as to the reason why."

"That's not really true. El will take care of that."

"Yeah, I guess."

Tracy shrugged her shoulders and then resumed eating. When the plate was clean, she rinsed it off and put it in the dishwasher. Then she wrapped her arms around the still-seated Brian.

"Honey?" she cooed.

"Yes?"

"Could you do something for me?"

"Do what?"

"Brian, could you…would you…wash…my…*pump parts*?"

He chuckled. "Sure."

"I'll probably be asleep when you're done. So let me kiss you goodnight now."

Brian turned his neck so he could oblige. He watched Tracy ascend the staircase before returning to the sink. He stared at the container of soapy water that held bottles, breast shields, valves, tubing, and membranes. He grabbed the scrub brush and started cleaning out the bottles; he rinsed them out and placed them on the specially designed drying rack. Then he cleaned the rest of the parts and put them on the rack also. When he had finished, he dried his hands and sat down at the kitchen table.

Brian shook his head. Cynthia Lydecker, formerly Cynthia Conroy. He gulped. He was going to have to tell Tracy at some point. He was going to have to tell her about him and Cynthia. It really shouldn't be bothering him this much, but it was. *He* could tell Tracy some stories. *He* could spin some yarns about Saint Cynthia. Saint, his ass. Brian looked toward the steps. He wished Tracy hadn't gone to sleep. Maybe he would tell her tomorrow morning. No, this conversation would be more than just a casual one and the mornings were much too hectic. And after eating breakfast she'd want to go into the home office and be left alone until she was ready to leave for the day. Damnit! That was the thing about skeletons. They could make so much noise when they wanted to — especially when they wanted out.

Chapter 3

Tracy was trying to get out the door Tuesday morning. She had a conference call in less than an hour. But Peter was crying and didn't want to be put down; Nicole had knocked over a pitcher of water and the mess remained; Brian was currently out back with the dog; and Violetta was upstairs changing Nicole out of her now-wet clothes. Tracy opened the back door.

"Brian! I really need you!" she called.

"All right; I think Bonkers is done."

"He has to be."

As soon as Brian came in, Tracy handed him Peter and explained things. "When Mom's done give her Peter and you clean the water off the floor."

Brian looked at the kitchen floor. "Uh, Bonkers is helping with that right now."

"Oh! Supreme! Well, clean up what he leaves. And Nicole needs to be reminded not to climb up on the chairs. But it *was* an accident, so don't be too hard on her."

"Fine."

"I *really* need to go. If there's any traffic, I'm going to be late for my call."

"Go then. But Tracy…"

"Yeah?"

"We need to talk about something tonight. It's nothing to worry about or anything. But we really should talk."

Tracy blinked. "Okay, Brian. I'll try to avoid any last-minute meetings."

"Please do."

Tracy looked at Brian a few more moments and then exited the house. Brian watched her back out of the driveway.

"Look Grammaw!" he heard Nicole say. "Bonkers cleaned mess!"

Brian turned and smiled. Then he looked at his sad-looking son and pressed his forehead against Peter's. "I miss Mommy too," Brian whispered.

"Congratulations, Ty!" Tracy said enthusiastically after hearing the news. "I wish I could have been there."

"Maybe not. Not everybody was pleased with the news. There are still some rather angry people around here right now."

"Can Keith post the bail?"

"Yes; my sister's taking care of it."

"Okay. Do you want to take the rest of the day off to be with your family? It's all right if you do."

"Thanks, Tracy. But I was hoping to come back and talk to you about where we go from here."

"When's the preliminary hearing?"

"February 12. Say, I have some interesting news for you."

"Even more? I can't wait to hear it."

Tyler laughed. "We'll soon see. Jim Lucas is the primary on this thing."

Tracy blinked. "Is he really?"

"Yup. He was here today. He asked me at one point if you'd be joining me."

"Oh," Tracy sighed.

Detective Jim Lucas. He had worked several cases Tracy had been involved with during the last five or so years, including those of her husband and sister-in-law. But instead of him getting irritated with her for regularly proving him wrong, he had grown attracted to her, even to the point of kissing her during a vulnerable moment for each of them. The display had shocked her; he had apologized repeatedly. But they hadn't really seen each other for a year and a half. They almost did, however, when Tracy was hospitalized last year after a failed attempt on her life. He had stopped by to check on her. But she learned about that only later.

"So, what about tonight?" Tyler asked again.

"I can't tonight, Ty. Why don't you be with your family instead and I'll meet with you and Keith first thing tomorrow here — which for me is 10:00 a.m."

"Okay, that's fine."

"How's the press over there?"

"Pulling at us from all directions. It's nuts."

Tracy chuckled. "Tell Katie and Keith *not* to watch the news. They won't learn anything, and it will only upset them."

"I'll do that."

"See you tomorrow then, and congrats again."

"Thanks, boss. Goodbye."

Tracy stared at her phone. It was a new phone — a Christmas gift from her husband. He couldn't stand seeing his wife with an antiquated flip model anymore. So, he had gotten her that smartphone she had avoided getting for so many years. She admittedly liked some of the things she could do with it. But there was also too much she could do with it that she didn't need to be doing with it. She pursed her lips as she started texting Brian the news of Keith Entwistle's bail. It wasn't long before Brian sent his response: "Old news." Where was the symbol for sticking out one's tongue again? She had used that one *a lot*.

Tracy placed the now-asleep infant in the crib, which was at the foot of her and Brian's bed. Peter would be up in four or five hours for his late-night snack, so Tracy slid under her covers looking forward to sleep. Brian came into the room after dropping Bonkers off in Nicole's room, and then readied himself for bed and joined her. Tracy smiled at him.

"So, what did you want to talk about?" she asked pleasantly.

Brian sighed and sat up. "Cynthia Lydecker."

"Oh."

"Remember when you asked me if Cynthia Lydecker ever did anything to me and I said 'nothing'?"

"Sure."

"Well, that's not exactly true."

Tracy, who had been drifting off, wasn't any longer. She sat up in the bed and looked at her mate. "What are you talking about?"

Brian looked down at Tracy's hand; actually, he was staring at her wedding ring. "She took something from me. Well, that's not exactly true."

Tracy gulped. "Brian, please just tell me."

He looked at her. "She was my first, Tracy. You understand?"

Tracy's back stiffened. She was at a loss for words for the moment. Suddenly she looked down too.

"So," she whispered. "You and Cynthia, huh?"

Brian sighed. "She was a senior and I was a freshman. I had just lost my mother. And since our dads were both members of the city's wealthy set, I was already getting invited to parties by upper classmen who knew who I was. Maybe you don't want to hear this."

"It's okay. I get the impression you want to tell me about it."

"I'm not doing this to hurt you, Tracy."

"I know that. I know that, honey."

Brian took Tracy's hands. "Well, I was feeling so down that I decided what the hell? And I and a buddy of mine went to one of the parties. It had booze; so, I had some. And I met Cynthia there too."

"She was a senior you said."

"Yeah. She had come with some of her friends. And…we hooked up."

"She was your first, huh?"

"Yeah, but I clearly wasn't hers."

"I see."

"She knew she had life made. She spent most of her senior year weekends partying. But she and I didn't last very long. My grades started slipping and my dad freaked out and suddenly I wasn't going out anymore. Cindy found someone else, no problem."

"And that was it?"

"Yeah. I really didn't go to too many parties the rest of the year and Cindy was gone when the year was over. I never saw her again. I had heard she got married right out of college. But by that time, I had someone very special in my life."

Tracy couldn't help smiling. "Do I know her?"

"Look, Tracy. I guess it was only a matter of time until something like this happened. Your star is rising in this city and your clientele isn't just the poor and downtrodden anymore. The City's wealthy tend to be a close bunch in some ways. So of course, you'd eventually come in contact with someone I know — or once knew."

"I guess."

"It's just so weird hearing what a great person she is when I knew her as the wild party girl who cared only about herself."

"People mature, Brian. People change."

"Yeah, I guess. So, are you mad at me? What are you feeling right now?"

Tracy sighed. She looked at Brian and smiled. "I'm wondering since you had all those pretty rich girls to choose from why you picked me."

"Oh, Tracy, not that again."

She shook her head. "I'm just kidding; trying to break the tension."

"Are you hurt?"

"No, Brian. I knew you had been with other women before me."

"I wish I hadn't."

"It doesn't matter now anyway. We're together and we always will be."

"Yes. We always will be."

She embraced him tightly. "Then we don't have to talk about it anymore. I love you."

"I love you more."

"No, you don't."

Brian chuckled. "I won't argue with you."

"You're learning finally."

Brian pulled back so he could kiss her. "Let's make love, Tracy. I know we're both tired, but I miss you."

She smiled. "Tired? Who's tired? I'm not tired. Let's just try not to wake up Peter."

"I'll try," Brian whispered. "But I might not be able to contain myself."

Tracy just grinned as they kissed again. And Peter continued to sleep in ignorance while his parents enjoyed their bliss.

Tracy actually arrived before 10:00 Wednesday morning. Keith Entwistle and Tyler were already at the office. Tracy had them all gather in the conference room.

"First thing we should discuss in the preliminary hearing," Tracy began.

"They have means and opportunity," Tyler said quickly.

"The gun could have been stolen during the burglary," Tracy commented.

"And the key they found?" Tyler asked.

Tracy frowned. "Well, it stands to reason if someone *took* the gun then they could have *put* the key in the drawer at the same time."

Entwistle looked at Tyler and then at Tracy. "You really think that's how it got there?"

"I do. Whoever broke in didn't want you to think they'd been in the bedroom. Maybe it wasn't so much the gun they didn't want you to notice was missing but rather they didn't want you checking your dresser drawers too closely. If they'd taken any of Katie's jewelry you certainly would have thoroughly checked the drawers. You might have found the key."

"So, they didn't have Keith and Katie's alarm code but didn't know of any other way to get the gun," Tyler mused. "They make it look like kids broke in for beer and that player."

"I think that's quite possible," Tracy agreed. She looked at Entwistle. "So, you see why I'm so adamant about learning if anyone had a beef with you, Keith? This person wanted the police knocking on *your* door."

Entwistle sighed. "I wish I could think of someone. But I can't."

"It doesn't have to be recent," Tyler added. "It could go back a few years."

"That's a good point," Tracy agreed. "This thing took some planning. He had to know that you and Katie were out dining, and your home was empty the night of the burglary. He had to know about Katie's conference the night of the murder. And then there's the gun of course. He would have to coordinate all of this with whatever he knew about Cynthia Lydecker. He would have had to know Monday was the night the trash was put out for Tuesday pick up. So, who knows how long it took for everything to come together for him? You see?"

Entwistle nodded. "Who could hate me so much?"

"The only thing missing is a solid motive for you," Tyler said to his brother-in-law. "Tracy made a good point about that. Framing you makes little sense without a motive."

"Keith," Tracy said, looking at him intensely. "Are you sure you never met Cynthia? Did your company ever cater an event she hosted or attended? Did she ever interview your company to cater an affair even if you didn't get hired? Do you maybe contribute to charities she sponsors or endorses? Can you think of anything like that?"

"I'd have to talk to Barney and Ian about some of that. Ian takes care of most of the bookings."

"Okay," Tracy smiled. "Then that's *your* homework, Keith."

"What about looking at who might have it in for Cynthia?" Tyler asked his employer. "Could we get Elias to look into that?"

"I guess it's not too soon to do that," Tracy answered. "The ideal situation would be to find someone that knew both Cynthia and Keith here. That's what I'm hoping we find."

"Okay," Tyler sighed.

Tracy again looked at her client. "I'll let Ty go through the mechanics of a preliminary hearing with you, Keith. I'm thinking if they have any proof of a relationship, they'll bring it up February 12 at the hearing. Meanwhile, I'll see if I can chat with an old friend about things."

Tyler grinned. "You really think he'll talk to you?"

"He may feel like he owes me one," Tracy said. "But enough said about *that*."

"Gotcha," Tyler responded. "Thanks, Tracy. I'll talk to Keith about the prelim right now. So, I guess you can get back to your other work."

"Very well, gentlemen. I'll bid you both *adieux*."

Tracy stood and left the conference room. Entwistle looked at Tyler.

"I like her, Ty."

"So, do I. And she's definitely your best bet."

"But I'm still nervous as hell."

"Look, Keith. Everything will be fine. You're innocent, right?"

"Of course, I'm innocent."

"Then Tracy will find out who really did this. That's what she does. Try and remember that. Okay?"

Entwistle snorted. "It's easy for you to be so damn calm. You're not the one going to jail if she can't…"

"Easy? Watching my sister go through all this is easy, huh? This isn't easy for any of us, Keith. Remember that too."

"You're right; I'm sorry."

"Forget it. Now let's talk about the hearing."

Tracy decided she'd stop at the Northeastern District of the Baltimore City Police Department prior to going home. If she knew Detective Jim Lucas, he'd be working overtime on the Cynthia Lydecker murder. She obtained her visitor's pass and found Lucas working diligently at his desk.

"Hi, Jim," Tracy greeted.

Lucas looked up. "Hi, Tracy. How've you been?"

"Supreme. And you?"

"All right. Congrats on your son."

"Thanks. He's a cutie."

"I bet."

"Can I sit down?"

"Sure."

Tracy seated herself next to Lucas' desk. "I never did get to tell you how thoughtful it was that you came to the hospital."

"What?"

"When I got hurt last March."

"Oh," Lucas said, after a few moments. "I was near the hospital, so I thought I'd stop in."

Tracy smiled. "Well, I still think it was nice of you to ask about me."

Lucas nodded and looked down at his desk. "I guess you're here about Cynthia Lydecker."

"Yes. What am I in for with this?"

"In for?"

"Just how sure are you about Keith Entwistle being your man?"

Lucas blinked. "Most people seem satisfied I guess."

"Most people, huh?"

"Yeah."

"Are you one of the most or the few?"

Lucas grinned slightly. "Let's just say we moved too quickly for my liking on this."

"Is Cynthia's father making things uncomfortable for everyone?"

"You might say that."

"Well why do *you* think more time was needed?"

Lucas sighed. "I really shouldn't be talking to you about this, Tracy."

"Come on, Jim. Anything the police have will have to be disclosed eventually; most of it will come out in a few weeks at the prelim hearing. And your opinion certainly isn't anything official."

Lucas looked at Tracy skeptically. "Oh really? You wouldn't call me on any doubts I had when I was on the stand?"

Tracy twisted her lips. "We can make today off the record. If I betray that then you know never to trust my word again."

Their eyes met long enough that Tracy started feeling a tad uncomfortable. Lucas looked away. "Everyone thinks your client and the deceased were having some affair. Nothing's been found to support that though. I think we should have waited until we knew one way or the other."

"Keith denies an affair."

"I'm sure he does."

"Anything else about the facts that bother you?"

"Have you seen the details of the 911 calls?"

Tracy shook her head. "I probably won't get that until this thing is turned over for trial."

"Mm. Well, you'll soon learn the call about the gun being found in the neighbor's trash can came before the call about the shot being fired. There's nine minutes between calls."

Tracy nodded. "That does sound a little weird."

"And we can't be sure where the call about the shot came from. The number belongs to a prepaid cell, so we don't know who made the call. I don't like that either."

"An anonymous caller, huh."

Lucas chuckled. "I guess you're rubbing off on me Tracy, or at least I'm starting to think like you."

Tracy grinned. "What does that mean?"

"Just that it was way too easy to find that gun and trace it."

"So, you think Keith was framed too."

"I didn't say that," Lucas corrected.

"Then what *did* you say?"

"That we moved too hastily to arrest Entwistle. He could still be our guy. We just might not have the right motive for him."

"Ah," Tracy said. "So, with the physical evidence most likely sufficient to get through the hearing, Art is hoping the motive can be locked down between now and the trial."

"I don't know *what* Pankow is thinking. You have questions for him you know where the state's attorney office is."

"Sure, Jim."

"That's all I can really tell you. Sorry."

"It's okay." Tracy sighed. "You seem down, Jim."

"Down? I guess that's one word for it."

"Anything I can do?"

Lucas again met Tracy's eyes. "No, Tracy. There's nothing you can do."

The attorney sighed and then stood. "Thanks, Jim. I hope you feel better soon."

"Sure. I guess I'll see you in a few weeks at the hearing. Or will your associate be handling that?"

"I'll probably handle it."

"See you then."

Tracy took a deep breath as she left Lucas staring at his desk. It was pretty clear to the attorney that Jim Lucas was still dealing with his feelings for her. There was no doubt in her mind that he talked to her *because* of those feelings. As a result, she felt sorry for him as well as guilty about taking advantage of the situation. But this crush or infatuation or whatever it was couldn't last forever, could it? Tracy hoped not. She didn't like it. She liked Jim Lucas, but she didn't like knowing she made him uncomfortable, even if it was all his own doing. Tracy felt a little down herself as she started her car's ignition and headed home to her family.

"I have inside information," Tracy told Brian as they dressed for bed.

Brian grinned. "Wow, you have your own Deep Throat, huh?"

"This isn't Watergate," Tracy chuckled.

"But there *is* a politician involved; it's no secret to whom Cynthia used to be married."

"Good grief, Brian. I wish I hadn't said anything."

"Too late now, babe. So, what is it about the 911 calls?"

"For now, this stays between you and me, right?"

"Sure."

"It will come out at the trial if not the preliminary hearing, but the calls were out of order with the events. And I think that Jim thinks the call about the shot was made to make sure the gun was found."

"But the one guy had already called about the prowler I thought."

"Yes — but the prowler couldn't have been *sure* that this Wilmont would call the police. So, after he dumped the gun, he made the second call. You see?"

"And that implies he knew the police would start interviewing witnesses in the area and learn about the disturbance."

"Right. The question is whether or not this was a good or bad thing for the killer."

"What do you mean?"

"I kind of already told you. My insider is bothered by the call sequence. If Wilmont hadn't made the call everything would have worked out."

"Then I guess it is a bad thing for the killer then."

"I don't know, Brian."

Tracy's husband sighed. "Now what are you talking about."

"It's something my insider said to me, I guess. He said maybe they have the right guy but the wrong motive."

Brian thought a few moments. "Wait, I thought you just said this Deep Throat thought your client was framed."

"Stop calling him that."

"Fine, but my question still stands."

"I'm not sure. I just know this case is starting to give me the creeps."

"Jesus, not again, Tracy."

Tracy folded her arms. "Something is really off about this whole thing. Keith says he didn't know her. But somebody thought he'd make a great fall guy. Why? Cynthia has spent the last four years or so of her life doing good works, despite what you told me about her teen years. Yet someone killed her. Why? I have it on good authority even the investigating detectives aren't sure what's going on here."

"Terrific."

"Even if it turns out Keith's company catered an event that Cynthia attended, what is that going to prove? I keep telling myself that I believe Keith about the affair. But that's more because Cynthia Lydecker doesn't seem the kind of person who'd have such an affair. I don't *know* Keith."

"No comment."

"But maybe she and Keith could have had their affair years ago; maybe *that's* what led to her divorce."

"We can do some research on that."

"Yeah, we should. But let's for argument's sake say there was an affair. Why wait so long to kill her?"

"You mean Keith or the ex-husband?"

"Either one of them really."

"How would the ex have gotten a key and the alarm code? You'd think she'd change both of them after the divorce."

"I don't know. I have more questions than answers at this point."

"All right. No need to get testy."

"I'm not testy."

"My mistake."

Tracy frowned. "Any luck on the Whistler's Cooking research?"

"Just the basic data. I checked the Maryland Department of Assessments and Taxation website for some info, which I emailed to your business address."

"Yes, I got that. I'm sorry I forgot to say thank you, honey."

Brian smiled. "No problem. As far as the state is concerned, the business is in good standing. Nothing has turned up with respect to lawsuits or complaints as of yet. But I didn't really get much of a chance to dig into that today."

Tracy smiled. "Our little rascals distracting you, huh?"

"A smidge."

She sighed. "I think I should get some sleep. I need to catch up after last night."

"Me too. Nicole had me help her build every puzzle she owns today."

Tracy grinned as she laid her head on her pillow. "You're such a good Daddy."

"I try," Brian grinned in return as he joined his wife. "How's returning to the office been, other than exhausting I mean?"

"Okay. The days fly by since there's so much to do. And I love seeing my office family again."

"But…"

"The same thing as always, Brian. I miss my own family. Does Nicole ask about me?"

"Sure, she does. I tell her you are at work and that you'll be home and that makes her happy. You get that great big hug and smile when you get home, don't you?"

"Sure. It might be my favorite part of the day."

"You should call me if you're ever feeling down. I can bring the kids over to visit."

"I might take you up on that."

Tracy smiled and gave Brian a good night kiss. Closing her eyes, she tried to shut out thoughts of Keith Entwistle and the charges against him. It wasn't easy. Brian had confirmed Keith's supposed victim had some things about her past she may not have been proud of today. And now Tracy found herself wondering if Entwistle had skeletons in his closet too — and if they were armed.

Chapter 4

When Keith Entwistle returned to his place of business Thursday, he had company. Tracy Brubaker Shane wanted to meet with her client's partners — Barney Schultz and Ian Tapper — especially the latter, since Keith Entwistle had confirmed Tapper booked most of their jobs. The company was headquartered not too far from the Entwistle home. Not surprisingly the building was mostly an enormous kitchen. Entwistle entered through the rear and started giving Tracy a tour of the facility.

"A lot of times we'll get a job where there's a kitchen available. So, we'll do most of the cooking there. But there's always prep work we can do here. If the job site doesn't have what we need, we'll do all the work here and transport the food in warming containers."

Tracy nodded. "How many vans do you have?"

"Two right now. We're looking at getting a third one."

Tracy surveyed the equipment: large ovens that would make her mother envious; multiple refrigerators; commercial mixers, blenders, a dishwasher, pots, and pans. And there were also the three preparers making use of it all.

"Presentation is of course important," Entwistle continued. "Psychologically, food that *looks* delicious tastes better."

Tracy breathed deeply. "What is that I'm smelling, Keith?"

Entwistle grinned. "Ty told me you enjoy a good meal. So, I thought I'd have a snack prepared for you since we're in between breakfast and lunch."

"Snack?"

"Large stuffed mushrooms — a specialty of ours. And you can also sample our crab dip; our clients rave about that too."

Tracy blinked. "Keith, you are officially my favorite client of all time."

Entwistle started laughing. "Come on. I'll show you the rest of this place and then we'll all meet in our presentation room."

Tracy just nodded. Despite a hearty breakfast, her mouth had started watering and her stomach was rearranging its contents to allow for additional room.

"Over here is where we store our table settings. And then over there is where we keep our linens. And there's also a closet for cleaning supplies." Entwistle stopped moving. "I guess that's it really. What would you like to do first?"

"Eat."

Entwistle started laughing again. "I love it. Hopefully, you'll remember us if you want to have an office function."

"I'm mad Tyler never mentioned what you did for a living before."

Entwistle was now smiling. "Ty is more of a traditional meat and potatoes guy. He doesn't go for more — how shall I put it? — specialized preparations."

"Silly man," Tracy said, gulping. "If it's okay, Keith, I'd like to meet with each of your partners one-on-one instead of together."

"Sure; that shouldn't be a problem."

"But you'll let me know when my snack is ready, right?"

Entwistle shook his head laughing. "I love it! I'll make sure you're disturbed."

"Supreme! Can I talk to Ian first?"

"Follow me."

Tracy obliged when Entwistle turned and started moving towards the front of the building.

Ian Tapper was seated at his desk when Tracy and Entwistle entered. He stood and smiled. Tapper was dressed casually and on the tall side; not quite as tall as Brian — maybe an inch or two shorter. He was balding but there was no attempt to disguise this fact. The black hair remaining was neatly coiffed. Tapper also had something of a stomach; it reminded Tracy of how she looked during month five of her second pregnancy. But how could she blame him given the aromas that were in the air?

"I'm so glad you're helping Keith, Tracy," Tapper said after the introductions and handshakes were done with. "I've heard about you."

Tracy smiled and blushed slightly. "Tyler and I will of course do what we can."

"Tracy would like to talk to you, Ian. Would that be okay?"

"Of course. We can talk right now."

Entwistle grinned. "Vanessa and Georgina are preparing something for our guest. You may be disturbed briefly."

Tapper chuckled. "I hope they're making enough for two."

Tracy gave Tapper a mock look of horror. "I was hoping to take any leftovers home with me."

"Yeah, Ian," Entwistle said. "Let Tracy get her fill. She's a working mom with two small kids at home. She needs her energy."

Tapper just nodded and sat down. "I suppose I could restrain myself this *one* time."

"I'll leave you two then," Entwistle said as he exited, closing the door behind him.

Tapper stared at the shut door a moment, and then he turned to Tracy. "Keith's brother-in-law works for you?"

"Yes," Tracy answered pleasantly. "Almost two years now."

"Nice people," Tapper said quietly. "I just don't understand all of this."

"Neither do I. What I was hoping you could help me with concerns past jobs. I'm trying to see if Keith and the victim — Cynthia — had any prior contact."

Tapper snorted. "The news people have stopped just short of saying they were having an affair. It's ridiculous."

"Why do you say that? I mean you're his friend so of course you'd stand up for him. People who don't know Keith might be skeptical."

"Look. Keith busts his butt doing this; we all do. We have loans to pay off for nearly everything on top of all the other expenses. Then he goes home to his wife. He's crazy about her. He's just not the type to cheat. And given his wife's temperament, I'd be afraid for him if he did."

"I hear you. Could you maybe pull up your calendar and we could go through it?"

"Oh, sure. This is all confidential, right?"

"Of course. I'm interested only in seeing if you catered a function Cynthia Lydecker may have attended."

"She did a lot of charity work, didn't she?"

"Yes. Have you guys worked anything like that?"

"Let's have a look," Tapper said as he swiveled to face his computer. "I have our entire six-year history in here. We do mostly smaller venues though: anniversary parties, bar mitzvahs, engagement parties, graduations, and things like that. We've only recently started taking on larger jobs."

"That's a good thing though, right?"

"Keith and I think it is; Barney is still undecided. You see, the bigger the job, the more help you need. Barney's afraid we'll bring on the wrong help one day and that will be the end of us."

"End of you?"

"Once case of food poisoning would probably ruin us."

"I see."

Tracy blinked. Before she even heard the knock on the door, she turned her head. The aromas had arrived before the food itself; they must have snuck in through the door's cracks.

When Tapper heard the raps, he said, "Come in!" with much enthusiasm. A smiling young woman was soon pushing a cart into Ian Tapper's office. "Meet Vanessa," Tapper told the now starving attorney.

Tracy smiled as the cook-turned-deliverer brought the food to her. "You have my eternal thanks and gratitude," Tracy told Vanessa, who in turned smiled gratefully and looked at Tapper.

"Go ahead and try one," Tapper insisted.

Tracy reached for a small plate; she didn't need to be told twice. The top level of the cart had a tray of four stuffed Portobello mushrooms – *jam-packed* mushrooms; the kind you couldn't just pop into your mouth. That's why Tracy also picked up one of the small forks that was right next to the plates. She cut off a generous piece and placed it on her tongue. She closed her eyes and chewed. "Heaven," was all she said.

Tapper and Vanessa laughed. "Try the dip too," Tapper insisted.

Tracy looked at the cart's second shelf, which had a large bowl of warm crab dip and a tray of toast points and thin crackers. Tracy used the spoon provided to spread the dip on one of the crackers. Again, it all went directly into her mouth with no hesitation.

"So good…" Tracy commented.

"Thank you," Vanessa smiled appreciatively.

"No, thank *you*, Vanessa," Tracy corrected. "I love my crab dip spicy, just like this. And that was Italian sausage in the mushrooms, right?"

"Yes," the cook answered.

"And the cheese you used had a kick to it too."

"It's Keith's own recipe," Tapper said. "So is the crab dip. He takes traditional recipes and adds his own tweaks."

"He has nice tweaks," Tracy said, enjoying another bite of the mushroom.

"I'm so glad you enjoyed it," Vanessa said.

Tracy grinned. She found herself staring at Vanessa's bracelet. It was a simple chain with four ruby-red rhinestones.

"I like your bracelet," Tracy commented. "It's beautiful."

"Thank you," the cook responded. "It's my favorite. I don't usually get to wear—"

Tapper cleared his throat. "Thank you, Vanessa," he said as a dismissal. "You've done excellent work, as usual."

Vanessa blushed slightly and bowed, and then left her employer and his guest. Tracy, whose mouth was now too full to thank the woman again, smiled and nodded. She took a napkin and wiped her hands.

"Well Ian, if I know of anyone who ever needs a caterer, I'm sending them here."

Tapper laughed. "I'm so glad you enjoyed the food."

"*Enjoyed*?" Tracy asked. "That implies that I'm done. I'm still *enjoying* your food. I'll eat while you look."

Tapper again cleared his throat. "You don't mind if I…"

Tracy chuckled. "Of course not. I can't eat all of this myself."

Then the interviewee smiled and relocated one of the mushrooms to another plate. They both ate and investigated in silence.

"Nothing, huh?" Entwistle grunted. "I was afraid that was the case. I didn't remember any job like the ones you were looking for."

"It's no problem, Keith."

"I wish I hadn't wasted your time."

"Wasted my time? Good grief, Keith. I just had some of the best food I ever tasted. If that was wasting my time, I should waste more of it."

Entwistle laughed. "Thank you so much."

"Maybe I could be lawyer to caterers in the tri-state area."

"Don't go exclusive just yet, Tracy. I still need you."

Tracy grinned. "I'm just funning. But I really do mean it, Keith. The food was supreme, and I thank you. And my two-month-old nursing son will be thanking you later."

Keith Entwistle looked at Tracy for a few moments. "Tyler was right about you."

"I'm sorry?"

"You're not like what I thought a lawyer would be."

"Oh," Tracy said sheepishly.

"I'm sorry. That was a stupid thing to say."

"It's okay. I know you meant it as a compliment and appreciate it. But you probably know I don't handle murder cases on a regular basis. At least, I try not to."

"Yes; Tyler told me about that too. He thought you might not take my case."

Tracy smiled. "Well, I *am* taking it."

Entwistle shook his head. "Katie is beside herself. I think she's more upset about this whole thing than I am."

"I'm sorry."

"I think she's wondering about me now."

"Wondering?"

"If I had an affair with Cynthia."

"Oh. What has she said or done to make you think that?"

Entwistle shrugged his shoulders. "Nothing, I guess. It's probably just the stress of the whole thing. She can be such the drama queen sometimes."

"I'm sure it's not easy for any of you."

Her client sighed. "Would you like to talk to Barney? He's here now."

"Sure."

"Now, Barney may not seem as warm and outgoing as Ian. But he's a very nice guy."

"I'm sure he is."

"He's our financial partner. He can tell you all about budgets, figures, long-term plans, and that sort of stuff."

"I get you. You're the one with the gifts in the kitchen; Ian schmoozes and keeps the clients happy, as well as pursuing new ones; and Barney is the businessman."

"Excellent summary. But Ian and Barney also are at home in the kitchen. That's how we met."

"Oh! How *did* you meet by the way?"

"We were all taking a cooking class. Our instructor liked us — or rather, what we were doing in the class. One night we all went out for drinks, and she suggested we open a restaurant together. We all kind of laughed at the idea but the more we thought about it, the more we started talking about the possibility. But none of us liked the idea of a restaurant. We all seemed to be of one mind on catering being a possibility though."

"Awesome. I love hearing stories like that. You meet a person or persons one day, and without meaning to, you start on a new journey together. Life is just filled with moments like that."

Entwistle nodded. "I met Katie at one of our earliest jobs. It was an office party her company was having. She made it a point to meet the cooks because she enjoyed the food so much. She and I hit it off."

"Was it the stuffed mushrooms or crab dip?" Tracy grinned.

"As a matter of fact, it was the crab dip she really liked."

"Then I completely understand."

Entwistle chuckled. "I'd never cheat on her. Never."

Tracy nodded. "Let's go bug Barney now. And then I have to get going."

"Sure," the client agreed. "This way, Tracy."

Barney Schultz studied Tracy a moment after Entwistle introduced and left them. Tracy smiled, her hands folded on her lap.

"This whole thing with Keith is nonsense," Schultz said finally. "But I don't know how I can help you. I know very little about Keith's personal life."

"But you're his friend as well as partner, right?"

"Of course. But he wouldn't tell me about an affair if he were having one."

"Affair?"

"That's what everyone is thinking, right?"

"I don't really know, Barney. There's no evidence that I'm aware of to support such a belief."

"Of course, there isn't."

Tracy cleared her throat. "I had some of your jumbo stuffed mushrooms and crab dip earlier. They were beyond delish."

Schultz nodded. "They should have made the smaller caps for you."

"I guess I'll have to come back then and try those too. What I won't do for my job."

Her comment seemed to break the ice. Schultz smiled. "What can I do for you, Tracy?"

"Just some general things, I guess. I'm working all kinds of possible theories, the details of which I won't bore you with. How's business going, for starters?"

"Just fine. My partners in fact want to take on larger clients."

"Isn't that a good thing?"

"Maybe; maybe not. Larger clients mean large cash outlay and larger risk — and not just monetary risks. Reputation is very important in this business. You really can't make a mistake."

"That doesn't seem fair. Everybody makes mistakes."

"Fair or not, it's the reality of the situation. One bad entree, or one botched menu, or whatever, and the word can spread, especially if it's for something more public. People can post whatever they want wherever they want whenever they want."

"Oh, I see. Private parties and whatnot are fine. But moving towards the spotlight makes you uncomfortable."

"I suppose you could put it that way. But Keith and Ian want to move in that direction."

"I've been to plenty of catered events in my career, Barney. And I'm being completely honest when I say the food I tasted today was exemplary. There's no reason why you guys shouldn't be better known."

"I appreciate you saying that. But it still makes me nervous."

"Change does that. But things are always changing. At least you have friends to change *with*."

"Yeah; sure."

"Has the company ever been sued? Is that one of the reasons you're nervous about growing?"

"Sued? No. We've had some complaints — not many — that we were able to work through. Usually that just means we reduced their bill. Sometimes a face-to-face meeting and apology was enough. We really have been fortunate."

"How about problems with employees? Or people you contracted with on larger jobs?"

"We had a worker's comp claim once thanks to a wet floor."

"What happened?"

"We all clean up at the end of the day. One of our preparers wasn't paying attention and slipped; broke his arm when trying to stop his fall."

"Yikes."

"Yes. We were sorry to lose him."

"He quit?"

"Yes. Things got a little testy. It really was his fault for not paying attention. But he had worked a full day and was naturally tired. He thought about suing us but ultimately the insurance company settled everything."

"What was this man's name?"

"Herbert Geist. But that was two years ago."

"I'm sure it's nothing, Barney. But I like to be thorough. Some people unfortunately aren't very forgiving; they hold grudges."

Schultz nodded. "Yes; I guess you have a point there."

"Any problems with vendors?"

"No. We pay our bills on time."

"How about your competition — any hostilities there you're aware of?"

Schultz smiled. "Just what kind of business do you think we're involved in here? We have competitors sure, but we view each other more as colleagues."

"Oh; okay."

"We would never go after a competitor's employees or try learning a proposed fee so we could underbid it. In fact, Keith once helped another company when one of their trucks was in an accident. He arranged it so they could borrow some of our equipment. That's the kind of person Keith is."

"Mm. When did this happen?"

"Oh, that was even before the Herbert Geist thing. Ask Keith; I'm sure he could tell you more about it than me."

"Okay. Thanks Barney."

"I just can't believe whatever's going on has anything to do with the company."

Tracy nodded. "It wouldn't seem so. But Keith having such a good reputation is a big plus for us. Character *is* important. And both Keith and Cynthia were people of character from everything I'm learning."

"True; very true."

"I guess that's it for now. Maybe if you think of something you'll let me know." Tracy stood up.

Schultz did likewise and said, "I will. And if you think of more questions, please call me."

Tracy smiled as she handed the partner a business card. "Thank you, Barney. I can find my way back to Keith's office."

"I should go with you. He could be in the kitchen. We have a birthday party tonight."

"Oh; thanks."

Schultz had been right. Tracy found Entwistle consulting with someone on what Tracy believed were pastries. "I'm going to head back to the office now, Keith," the attorney said when the consultation had ended.

"Okay," Entwistle smiled. "Don't forget this." He held up an insulated food bag that obviously contained Tracy's uneaten cuisine. "You can just return the bag at some point; I trust you."

"Would you refill it?" Tracy winked.

"Absolutely," Entwistle laughed. "I love it!"

Tracy accepted the fancy doggie bag. "Thanks, Keith. All client meetings should be this supreme."

"Thank *you*, Tracy. Don't hesitate to call me if you need anything."

"Sure. Good luck on your party tonight. I know someone who'd accept leftovers, no questions asked."

Entwistle laughed again as Tracy smiled and headed towards her vehicle. She was definitely warming up to Keith Entwistle. She refused to believe someone with his abilities at making taste buds so euphoric could be a murderer.

"Don't warm them up in the microwave," Tracy told Brian. "Use the oven and just set it on warm."

"Okay."

Tracy turned to her mother. "You have to try these, Mom."

"Try what?"

"Stuffed Portobello mushrooms. They have Italian sausage and garlic in them, among other yummy things."

"Eh," Violetta grunted with little enthusiasm — and maybe a little jealousy.

"Good grief, Mom. I'm not planning on having you replaced as head chef here or anything. Just try a little."

"Maybe I'll try."

"And there's crab dip too; spicy. We'll warm that up too."

Violetta Brubaker shrugged her shoulders. She really didn't like a stranger's food occupying *her* oven.

The Whistler's Cooking leftovers served as the appetizer to Thursday night's dinner. Nicole looked at the two strange, circular-shaped objects on the serving dish.

"Want some honey?" Tracy asked her.

Nicole looked at her curiously and didn't answer. Tracy cut the mushrooms in two, giving each herself, Brian, and her mother one of the four halves. After the family graced, Tracy watched Brian sample the goods.

"Wow," Brian said. "This *is* really good."

"Told ya."

Nicole looked at her father. "I want some," she said.

"She's not going to like it," Violetta opined while she ate — and secretly enjoyed — her own portion.

"I'll just give her a little to try, Mom."

"I want some," Nicole reminded everyone.

Tracy chuckled as she took a sampling from the remaining half. She put it on Nicole's tray. Nicole smiled as she lifted the fork that her mother had prepared for her. She put the contents in her mouth and started chewing. And just as quickly the food came right back out again.

"I don't like it," she grumbled.

Violetta made an "I told you so" face while the parents just laughed.

"Not too much wasted," Tracy said. "Who wants to split this last half with me?"

"Me!" Brian said quickly, which caused Nicole to laugh.

"Yucky," Nicole insisted.

"Yummy," her mother countered. "And there's still the crab dip to try. But it's spicy so I don't think you'll like it."

Nicole scrunched her nose. Tracy made the child a plate of more tame fare: boiled chicken, white rice, and corn. Nicole had no further complaints. After dinner, Tracy was nursing Peter on the couch when Brian sat next to her.

"That food was really, really good."

"I know. I was only kidding Keith about letting me take the leftovers home, but he handed them to me as I was leaving. I wasn't going to be rude."

Brian chuckled. "Of course not. And I appreciate you sharing all that with me."

"It was a tough decision."

Brian kissed her cheek. "I wonder how Peter will handle spicy stuff."

"We'll soon see. Nicole never had a problem. Is Mom putting Nicole to bed?"

"Reading to her."

Tracy smiled. "That's awesome. It's so great having Mom here."

"It is."

"Are you guys doing okay with Peter and that whirling dervish upstairs?"

"Just fine."

"I have to admit I'm taking a real liking to Keith Entwistle. He seems like a good guy."

"Any ideas then why someone framed him?"

Tracy sighed. "Not really. I'm afraid it's time to start looking closely at Cynthia Lydecker."

"I guess."

"Did you want to talk to me anymore about her? I'm okay with it if you do."

Brian smiled at his wife. "Not really. I only knew her a few months, such as it was. I didn't keep tabs on her."

"Okay. I suppose though this will all have to wait until after the hearing now. If the SA or police have some theory about a motive, hopefully they'll share it. Otherwise, I'm going to have to convince Alastair Conroy and his daughter's close friends to talk to me."

"I thought you had Elias to do that for you."

"I think I should handle it for this case. Mr. Conroy will probably need kid glove handling."

"No doubt."

"I'm curious to know if he thinks his daughter would have an affair with a married man."

"Oh, speaking of which, the Lydecker divorce was a no-fault divorce. They lived apart for a year and then got their absolute divorce."

"Oh. So, they've probably been living apart for five years then."

"I guess."

Tracy sighed. "Strange. What happened? Did they just get tired of each other?"

"Only Ed Lydecker can answer that question now."

Tracy frowned. "Yes. But I get the feeling it's a question he wouldn't want to answer."

"…Which of course means you're going to ask it."

Tracy grinned. "You know me so well, Brian. That's why you're my fella."

Brian looked at his wife warmly and stroked her cheek. He didn't need to say anything to confirm his feelings about her. She knew how he felt. And that's why he was starting to feel nervous. Tracy had seemingly dismissed the possibility that Keith Entwistle's occupation played a role in the murder. That meant she was moving into much more treacherous terrain. Politicians rarely gave the clear and concise answers people were hoping to get when they asked their questions. And this was a murder case. *Nobody* wants to answer questions in a murder case. Edward Lydecker would not be greeting Tracy with gourmet food. He might not greet her at all. That could be a mistake on his part; Tracy rarely took no for an answer. And that could be Tracy's mistake. Mistakes of course can have future value — *if* you're around to learn from them.

Chapter 5

Tracy and Tyler Wannamaker entered the courtroom with Keith Entwistle walking between them, Katie Entwistle behind. Arthur Pankow was already at his station. Tracy saw Detective Jim Lucas waiting to testify. Everyone took their seats shortly after Judge Claudia Daley took hers.

"We'll be calling only one witness," Pankow addressed the court. "I ask that Detective James Lucas please be sworn in."

As expected, Pankow established that the murder weapon belonged to Entwistle and that a key to the victim's home was found in his residence.

"Detective, was there any physical evidence that placed Mr. Entwistle at the scene of the crime?" Pankow next asked.

"Yes," Lucas answered.

"What evidence is that?"

"We found Mr. Entwistle's fingerprints on some trash from Mr. Justin Wilmont's trash receptacle."

"This trash with the prints: was it in the same trash can where the murder weapon was found?"

"Yes. Mr. Wilmont had only one trash can out that night."

"I see. Could you tell the court please, Detective Lucas, exactly where you found Mr. Entwistle's fingerprints?"

"They were found on a box that once held frozen chicken."

"Anywhere else?"

"No."

"Did Mr. Wilmont say if that was his discarded box of food?"

"No; Mr. Wilmont said he didn't purchase any frozen fried chicken. He said he avoids fried foods of all kinds."

"So, what did you conclude from this, Detective?"

"We figure Mr. Entwistle knew it was trash collection the next day and that he thought he could hide the gun by first stuffing it in the box, and then putting the box in the trash can."

"Why do you say that, Detective?"

"Mr. Wilmont said the prowler — the person he saw by his trash can — was wearing gloves. And there were no prints on the gun or remaining cartridges. So, the fingerprints must have gotten on the box earlier. They must have already been on the box when Mr. Entwistle grabbed it that night to hide the gun."

"I see. Were there any other person's prints on this box?"

"No," Lucas answered.

"Thank you, Detective. The state has no further questions."

Tracy sighed. She had some ideas of how to poke holes in most of the State's seemingly persuasive circumstantial evidence. And there had been no mention of motive. But she hadn't quite yet figured out how to address the fingerprints. She remained seated.

"Do you have any questions, Mrs. Shane?" Judge Daley finally asked.

Tracy looked at Tyler, and then at Entwistle. She stood.

"Yes, Your Honor." She looked at Lucas. "Detective, isn't it true that the Entwistle's had their house broken into the Wednesday before the murder?"

"Yes; that's true."

"Isn't it possible that my client's gun was stolen that night?"

"It's possible."

"And as for this key you mentioned, there's no way of knowing if that particular key was used to open Cynthia Lydecker's door the night of the murder, is there?"

"No."

"You mentioned the reason for the search warrant was to look for a set of missing keys that belonged to the victim."

"Yes."

"Did you find this missing set of keys at my client's home?"

"No."

"Have you found them at all?"

"Not as yet, no."

"The victim had an alarm system, correct?"

"Yes."

"So, is it your — or the State's — belief that whoever entered Ms. Lydecker's home that night knew the code to the alarm?"

"Yes, that's our assumption."

"Did you find evidence in my client's home he knew the code, such as a piece of paper with the code written on it, for example?"

Pankow rose. "The absence of such a thing proves nothing; people memorize codes all the time."

"Their own codes, sure," Tracy countered. "But other people's they don't use all the time?"

"You can answer the question," the judge said. Pankow returned to his seat.

Lucas cleared his throat. "We didn't find the code written down. But we didn't go through every piece of paper in the house either."

"Fair enough, Detective. Did you go through every piece of paper in the trash can?"

"Excuse me?"

"Mr. Wilmont's trash can, Detective. I assume you tested everything in there for prints."

"Oh. No, we didn't find the code written on anything."

"Did you find that odd, Detective, that the killer would get rid of the gun but not the alarm code?"

Again, Pankow rose. "Mrs. Shane is assuming the code was written down on something. There's no evidence to support that."

"Move on, Mrs. Shane," the judge ordered.

Tracy sighed. "Detective, let's next talk about this box of chicken. Did you ask my client if he purchased this brand of frozen food?"

Lucas blinked. "No. But his prints were on it."

"So? Maybe he merely touched it at some point. He *does* work in the food industry after all."

"I doubt your client would buy generic frozen chicken for his business, Mrs. Shane," Lucas said testily.

"So, you can offer no evidence that my client purchased this chicken, is that correct?"

"His prints were on it."

"That just means that he touched it, Detective."

Pankow, for the third time, stood. "Mrs. Shane is badgering the witness, Your Honor."

Tracy glared at Pankow. "I'm not 'badgering.' I'm trying to ascertain just how much work the police did to prove my client once had that chicken in his freezer."

"We get your point, Mrs. Shane," Judge Daley said. "Any more questions for Detective Lucas?"

Tracy looked at the witness and sighed. "No more questions." Tracy returned to her seat.

The judge didn't even wait for Pankow to finish standing. "I find sufficient evidence against Mr. Entwistle to proceed to trial. How's a late July trial date for everyone?"

"Fine with the State, Your Honor," Pankow answered quickly.

"Fine with the defense," Tracy added, without much enthusiasm.

"Fine. I'll see everyone Monday, July 22. We can schedule any motions another day."

Tracy and Tyler again looked at each other. Neither was really surprised. Tracy looked at Entwistle. "Do you even *have* fried chicken in your freezer anywhere?" she whispered. "Being a chef, I can't see you buying frozen chicken."

"Katie might, I guess," the client grumbled. "I don't know."

"But it was your prints that were on the box," Tyler reminded him.

Tracy blinked. "Hey, that's right! Detective Lucas said that only Keith's prints were on the box. If that chicken box had been in the house freezer, what are the odds that Katie's prints wouldn't have been on it too?"

Tyler nodded. "Great point! But then how did Keith's prints get on there?"

Tracy twisted her lips. "We'll just have to work that out. My first guess is that the killer somehow got Keith to touch the box. Or Keith touched it at some point somewhere and the killer snatched it."

"Good Lord," Tyler murmured. "This guy did some planning."

"It sure looks like it," Tracy agreed. It was then that she noticed Katie Entwistle standing silently behind her, Tyler, and Entwistle. Tracy gulped.

"I'm sorry Katie," Tracy said.

"It wasn't Tracy's fault," Tyler quickly added.

"I know," Katie said quietly. "Can we just leave now?"

"Sure," Tracy answered.

"Should I come home with you guys?" Tyler asked.

"No," Katie said firmly. "I just want it to be Keith and me right now."

"All right," Tyler said.

"First we have to get through the mob," Tracy added. "I'll do the talking."

"I don't mind doing some talking," Tyler said angrily.

"You'll have time for that later. Let me take today."

"All right," he grunted.

The Entwistles left the building with the two attorneys serving as bookends. Tracy wasn't surprised when the first microphone shoved in the couple's faces belonged to Shirley Hammersmith of WFFE television.

"Do you think your husband is innocent?" was the reporter's first question.

"Of course, she does," Tracy snapped. "My client isn't answering any questions at this time."

"Well how do you feel about the rumor that the SA won't be making any plea deals in this case?"

"That's a coincidence since we won't be accepting any plea offers ourselves."

"Are you worried, Tracy, that defending the person who killed such a pillar of this community could hurt your reputation?"

Tracy shook her head. "There's so much wrong with that question I don't have time to address it. Now will you please leave us be?"

Shirley Hammersmith grinned at the annoyed attorney and turned off her microphone.

"We're just getting started here, Tracy," she whispered. The journalist then left as requested.

Tracy sighed. She and Shirley were definitely not friends. In fact, this particular reporter downright disgusted her. So now this case disgusted her a little more too.

"I want to find out everything about that chicken box," Tracy began.

Neal chuckled. When Tracy glared at him, he said, "Sorry. It just sounded funny."

"Uh-huh. I want to know where they sell that kind of chicken. Then we'll see if we can get Keith to retrace some steps."

"Got it," Neal said.

"And now we have to tackle the unpleasant task of Cynthia Lydecker herself. What did she do to make someone want to kill her? As distasteful as it may sound, we're only going to get that answer if we start digging in the dirt."

"That's not your style, Tracy," Tyler said.

"We have to do this in this case, Ty. To help Keith we have to find someone who wanted to hurt her. Wouldn't you agree?"

"Sure," Tyler sighed. "I'm pretty good at that sort of thing; at least I used to be."

"I thought that was with witnesses mostly," Neal said.

"Mostly; but sometimes victims, too."

"Dead ones?" Neal asked him, a slight tone of contempt present.

"All right, Neal," Tracy interrupted. "Let's not go there. Neither Keith nor Cynthia seemed the type to make enemies, but here we are. It's Cynthia who's dead so let's focus on her."

"I'm on it," Tyler said.

"What about the ex-husband?" Neal asked her.

"There's definitely something there," she answered.

"How can you be so sure? What do *you* know about troubled marriages?"

Tracy frowned. "Very funny. It just seems weird to me that as soon as she gets divorced Cynthia becomes a full-time philanthropist. Why? Wouldn't being married to such a person have been good for Ed Lydecker's political career? Why did he let her go?"

"She could have decided to do that *after* the divorce."

"I know that. But this woman went hardcore, Neal. There has to be a reason. So, I want to talk to the ex, the father, and one or two of Cynthia's closest friends."

"Good luck with that."

"I don't think I'll need it, smart guy. If any of them had told the police about an affair with Keith, it would have been brought up today. It's a rock-solid motive. So, they all must be wondering the same thing everyone else is. Why did Keith supposedly do this?"

"Sure, they are. But that doesn't mean they'll want to talk to *you* about it."

"Quit being such a cynic, Neal. Don't be a bummer, Bennett."

The bummer shook his head. "I think you're confused about me. I'm just trying to be the Voice of Reason here."

"You must have laryngitis then."

Neal frowned. "Oh, that's funny, Tracy. You missed your true calling. With jokes like that you could be the opening act for The Sylvia Plath Comedy Tour."

Tracy folded her arms. "What's that, Neal? You have to leave now? Oh, that's too bad. Goodbye, Neal."

"Yeah. Goodbye."

Neal turned and left his perturbed employer. His zinger obviously stung. Of course, she had fired first. He figured they'd call today a draw.

"Hi, El," Tracy greeted the senior Elias Tanner. "How's life?"

"I knew you'd be calling," Tanner chuckled. "There's some footage already showing up of you leaving the courtroom with your client."

"Whoopty doo."

Tanner sighed. "Seriously though, Tracy, you're really in for it."

"I'm always 'in for it,' El. It's just a matter of degrees."

"Prepare to be boiling this time around."

"Oh, you're cute," Tracy chuckled. "Are you up for dirty work?"

"Come again?"

"Cynthia Lydecker. Why did someone want her dead?"

"That is the big question, isn't it?"

"Yes. Somebody handed Keith Entwistle to the police on a silver platter. But they forgot to put sauce on the goose."

"*What?*"

"In this case the sauce is the motive, as in there isn't one."

"Not for your client anyway."

"Exactly. So, I need you to find out everything you can about the victim. Who was she before she became Saint Cynthia? Why did she and her ex split up? I know we're headed toward tabloid-type territory here but *dems da breaks*."

"Uh-huh. And you have to feel bad for Arthur."

"Art? Why?"

"He really needs to make the affair part of the record. But by doing that he might soil Cynthia Lydecker's reputation. That won't sit well with her father."

"Ah. Maybe that's why he didn't say anything about motive today."

"Maybe."

"But El, Keith denies any affair. And I believe him."

"Really."

"Yes. Everyone I talked to — people who know him well — say he wouldn't do something like that. And Cynthia doesn't seem like that kind of person either. So, I'd bet my last dollar that there's some other reason for all of this."

"Mm. You may very well be right."

"So can you start looking into her background with the tools available to you?"

"Sure."

"I'll try lining up some interviews with family and friends. My angle will be that Cynthia wouldn't hook up with a married man, so everyone has this all wrong. If people agree with that, I might get lucky in speaking with some of them."

"You might. It doesn't hurt that you have a reputation of getting your clients cleared."

"I suppose. But I don't want to come off as arrogant or overly confident. Most don't like that in other people, in general, and in lawyers, especially."

"I realize that. Also remember who Alastair Conroy and Ed Lydecker are. They made their careers by being able to manipulate people; to get their own way. They're not, ahem, the usual suspects."

Tracy chuckled. "So, they might be immune to my charms?"

"What were you saying about over confidence?"

"Very funny."

"Look. I know you hate when I say this, but I'm going to say it anyway. Please be careful, Tracy. There's something very *cold* about this murder; something matter-of-fact; something efficient. I can't quite explain it."

"I know what you're saying. We don't seem to be talking crime of passion here. But don't worry. I won't be doing any interviews at the stroke of midnight."

"Can I make another suggestion?"

"Sure."

"Don't let these people you talk to know you care so much. Try to be as businesslike as you can. Make it seem like it's just a job for you. Am I making sense?"

"Sure, you are. I'm like that when I'm in court."

"I know you are. I'm asking you to be like that when talking to these people."

"...Because you're afraid I might talk to the wrong person: someone who wouldn't like that I care too much."

"Yes. Can you do that for me?"

"I can try. But it's not who I am."

"I know. Anyway, I'll start looking into things on my end."

"Thanks, El. You be careful too."

"I will. See you soon."

"Bye for now."

Tracy sighed as she put the receiver down. Tanner's request sounded easy enough, but Tracy knew fulfilling it wouldn't be. If only she could make herself feel as she did after Neal irritated her — *that* would keep things frosty. Who was she kidding though? Even if she tried to play Tracy the Snowman, she'd still have that jolly soul of hers threatening to shine through. But enough of this internal debate for now. It was close to quitting time, so she'd soon be out in the cold anyway. But that was fine since her ultimate destination was the warmest place on earth.

Tracy was seated at the kitchen table stirring her hot cocoa. Brian had made it for her while she was nursing Peter to sleep. It was just the marrieds awake now in the Shane household. Brian was next to Tracy with his own cup of chocolate.

"Art didn't even approach me with a plea offer," she told her husband. "I think they're going to be hardcore on this one."

"You can fight pretty tough yourself, love."

Tracy smiled. "I might have to."

Brian stood up and started massaging his wife's shoulders. "Why don't you just let Tyler handle this thing? He has plenty of experience. Use it."

"I know what his experience is, Brian. I don't want him just spouting out accusations at any and all witnesses hoping something sticks. And I don't care that it's worked for him before. I can certainly understand wanting to do everything possible for his family. But I want the firm to keep its reputation."

"Okay. Just a suggestion."

Tracy reached back and patted Brian's hand. "And I appreciate it, honey. But having me on this allows some degree of detachment. And of course, Jim and I have a history."

"Jim?"

"Detective Lucas."

"Oh right."

"That feels *so* good, Brian."

Brian kissed the top of Tracy's head. "I can continue upstairs if you want — full body massage."

Tracy chuckled. "Uh-huh."

"I mean it. I can feel how tense you are."

"Am I really that bad?"

"That's a loaded question."

"Oh, good grief." Tracy grabbed Brian's hand. "Sit down now so I can see you."

"Okay."

After Brian sat, Tracy said, "You know what's really weird?"

"What?"

"El and I talked about it today — how dispassionate this murder was. This guy just came into the house and shot Cynthia while she was asleep."

"Yeah; pretty creepy."

"Right. But to get in the house this guy had to have a key and the alarm code. That suggests someone close to her. You see the contradiction?"

"I guess so."

Tracy's eyes widened. "Hey! I just realized something!"

"What?"

"Assuming she changed the code after her ex-husband moved out, that means whoever had the code had to be someone in her life going back no more than five years: the four yours she was divorced plus the year she was separated."

Brian smiled and nodded. "That's a good point."

"I wonder if she spent time with someone during that year before the divorce. Maybe this other person is who inspired her to become Saint Cynthia."

"You really are hung up on that, aren't you?"

"I'd like to know the reason behind it, yes."

Brian sighed. "Well, try and take advantage of all your resources on this thing."

"I am. I'm not going solo on this."

"And don't forget you have people here waiting for you every night."

"I won't," Tracy said quietly.

"Tomorrow when you come home, I want us to talk about something other than this case."

Tracy looked at Brian, confused. "I thought you liked hearing all of this. You *are* still a firm employee."

"I do and I know I am. It's just sometimes I need a break from it."

"Okay. What should we talk about instead?"

"I don't know."

"You don't know."

"How about we go on a date? Just you and me. Every day you come home after a long day, and we talk about the kids all through dinner. After you have your mom time and put them to bed, we talk about your cases. Weekends it's mostly chores and more mom time."

"But Peter has his nursing marathon at bedtime."

"Then let's go out Saturday afternoon."

Tracy smiled and stroked Brian's cheek. "I'd love to go out with you Saturday afternoon. Were you thinking a meal, or did you have something else in mind?"

"I'll give it some thought."

Tracy stood. "Done with your cocoa?"

"Oh, yeah."

Tracy took the mugs and brought them to the sink, rinsed them out and placed them in the dishwasher. Then she smiled at Brian and rested her arms on his shoulders.

"Let's go upstairs so you can work on my back. I think there're some tight muscles that need attention."

"Then I'll loosen them," Brian grinned.

"And we can talk about our date too."

"Sure."

The couple soon retired for the evening, and from their bedroom they could hear the outside rattles being caused by a particularly aggressive February wind. Perhaps it wanted to be let indoors to escape the cold, envious at having heard about the rising temperature inside. But it could make all the noise it wanted; there would be no entry. Both Tracy and Brian had already gotten their second winds for the evening. So, there was no need to let in a third.

Chapter 6

Despite Elias Tanner, Sr.'s thorough efforts, the motive behind Cynthia Lydecker's murder remained a mystery — at least to Tracy.

"Other than her parents' divorce when she was six," Tanner began Monday morning, "her life was pretty normal, relatively speaking, as the daughter of Alastair Conroy: private education all the way through college, a few mildly scandalous headlines when she was a teenager—"

"What kind of headlines?" Tracy interrupted.

"She was caught drinking underage at a few parties; cops busted her for having a fake ID."

"Ah."

"She married Ed Lydecker right out of college in June 2000."

"Big ceremony?"

"No ceremony. She did things like you did."

"Got married in an office? I wonder how her father felt about that."

"Don't know."

"You'd think she'd have wanted the wedding day of a princess. Her father could have afforded it."

"She did seem to behave like the spoiled rich girl up until that day."

Tracy sighed. "It sounds strange to me. Anyway, what else do you have in your notes?"

"According to court records, she and her husband officially separated in May 2014; they were officially divorced July 2015."

"A no fault divorce."

"Correct."

"What did she do exactly for the 14 years she was married to Lydecker?"

"Played the supportive spouse from what I can tell. Lydecker got elected to the House of Delegates in 2006 at age 29. Before that he worked for Baltimore County government. Now he serves on the Civil Law and Procedure Subcommittee of the Judiciary Committee."

"The Judiciary Committee? Oh boy."

"I hear you."

"Lydecker comes from money too, right?"

"Yes. So, while Cynthia earned a bachelor's degree in business administration, she didn't really use it until after her divorce when she started her own charitable organization with help from her father. The official name of the entity is The Lydecker Crime Victims Foundation, Inc. They basically help anyone and everyone who's been a victim of any sort of crime: domestic, assault, rape, as well as helping families of murder victims in the form of money and/or counseling."

"Jeez," Tracy murmured. "I wonder if someone took issue with her helping a crime victim."

"Like a wife beater, for example?"

"Yes. Was there any evidence that Cynthia was ever a crime victim?"

"Not that I could find. But she could have been, obviously, and just kept it quiet or never even reported it."

Tracy rubbed her palm over her lips. "You know, El, this no-fault divorce sounds like butt-covering BS."

"Think Lydecker abused her?"

"Possibly. If such a thing came out, his political career would most likely be over."

"But why would she agree to cover for him?"

Tracy sighed. "I don't know. Maybe, despite everything, she still loved him. Or maybe he promised to donate to her foundation; encourage his pals to do the same."

Tanner paused a moment and then said, "You think he killed her?"

"I don't know. Why would he wait almost four years to do that? I wonder if something happened. Has he remarried by any chance?"

"He's actually engaged. The fiancée's name is Debra Dooley."

"Cute. What does *she* do?"

"Owns her own advertising firm. Her ex-husband is Judge Reginald Dooley, a family court judge."

"Holy crap. So, I guess Lydecker somehow met her through his work on the subcommittee; maybe he and the judge were pals. Maybe he and the judge's wife were even more. How long has the judge been divorced?"

"Last summer."

"Wow. Cynthia's ex and Debra sure got engaged quickly, didn't they?"

Tanner chuckled. "I can certainly see what I can find on Lydecker if you want. But nothing came up on him initially, just PR stuff saying how wonderful he is for the state. As for the former Judge and Mrs. Dooley, you wouldn't find them making headlines unless there was a very good reason for it."

"Check them out please, El. *If*, and I do mean *if*, Ed Lydecker abused Cynthia and she found out he was getting remarried, maybe she threatened to tell the fiancée."

"I suppose that's as good a theory as any."

"If there was abuse, I wonder who Cynthia would have turned to — a close friend, a place such as the House of Ruth, maybe."

"If she turned to an organization, we'll never know it. All of that is confidential."

"I realize that. I want to get permission to look at the crime scene. Maybe there's something in Cynthia Lydecker's personal records that could help with that. I'm also curious to see if Ed Lydecker contributed any money to his ex-wife's charity."

"You'll have to subpoena the Foundation's records for that."

"If the SA's office did, then that shouldn't be a problem for us. But I'll revisit that later. One more thing and then I'll let you go."

"What's that?"

"From what you could find, who was Cynthia's closest friend?"

"Cheryl Whittaker."

"Got it. Thanks again for the report, El."

"Sure thing. You'll get an email with everything soon. I'll be in touch."

"Bye, El."

After Tanner and Tracy ended their call, the attorney leaned back in her chair. All she could think about was the name Tanner had relayed to her. It wasn't much longer before Tracy went searching for Cheryl Whittaker's contact information.

"We'll just talk in my office," Cheryl Whittaker said while shutting her door. Tracy took a seat in front of Cheryl's desk after thanking her host. "The cops said you'd probably be talking to me," Cheryl continued. "I'm surprised you called this soon, though."

Tracy smiled at the dour-looking woman across from her. "I'm sorry, Cheryl. But the fact of the matter is I didn't know Cynthia Lydecker and neither did my client. So, I'm at a loss as to why someone would want to hurt her. I figured you were the best person to talk to."

Cheryl sighed. "I guess."

"Cynthia never mentioned Keith Entwistle to you, did she?"

"No. I don't know him."

"I don't think Cynthia knew him either. Your friend certainly didn't seem the type to have an affair."

Cheryl shook her head. "No. Cindy hadn't been with anyone since the divorce."

"How long were the two of you friends?"

"Lord; 20 years I guess it was. We got assigned as partners in a college computer class we were taking. We were juniors."

"So, you knew her before she got married, huh?"

A smile snuck across Cheryl's lips. "God. Her and Eddie — a couple of real party animals, those two. I had no idea it was serious between them until she called me."

"Called you?"

"Yeah. She and Eddie needed a witness. Eddie's pal couldn't do it, so she called me. God."

"She never told you in advance she was getting married?"

"Not a hint of it. I thought she was putting me on."

"Did you like Ed Lydecker?"

"Eddie? He was okay. He was fine. Do you know what he does now?"

"He's a politician."

"Perfect for him. He always could talk you into anything he wanted you to do."

"Really? Like what?"

"Oh, have another drink; go to this party or that one; blow off this class to do that. Know what I mean?"

"Sure. Did you and Cynthia hang out a lot after she got married?"

Cheryl hesitated before answering. "Well…yeah."

"What's wrong, Cheryl?"

"Nothing really. It's just that Cindy changed after she got hitched.'

"Changed how?"

"Well, she stopped partying and really settled down. I think she was actually depressed."

"Depressed about what? The marriage?"

"I'm not sure. I thought maybe she was trying to get pregnant or something and wasn't having any luck. I stopped drinking altogether when *I* got pregnant."

Tracy smiled. "How many kids do you have, if you don't mind me asking?"

"Three sons; four if you count my husband."

Tracy chuckled. "I hear you."

"Mark's a great father but he can behave like the boys sometimes. You have kids?"

"A two-year-old daughter and a three-month-old son."

Cheryl smiled. "That's great. I had my boys in my twenties two years apart. My oldest is 14 now; his brothers are 12 and 10."

"I didn't get married until I was 32," Tracy commented.

"I'm glad I didn't wait until then. I wouldn't have had the energy." Both women laughed.

"Cindy never had kids, right?"

"No," Cheryl sighed. "I'm not sure if it was because she didn't want to or if it was medical. I stopped bringing the subject up at one point."

Tracy folded her hands on her lap and took a deep breath. "Cheryl, I know you'll think this is none of my business. But I'm only asking to help me understand your friend. My question is do you know why she and her husband broke up?"

Cheryl pursed her lips. "You're right. That *is* none of your business; and none of mine either." She looked to her side. "But the truth is I have absolutely no idea why they divorced. I remember calling her at her house one day and she told me matter-of-factly that Eddie moved out and it was over between them. And then she added she didn't want to talk anymore about it. And we didn't — ever."

Tracy shook her head. "Did you two spend any time together in that year they were apart?"

"Sure. She'd come over and have dinner and play with the boys. Then we'd talk. Sometimes she'd start crying, and then I'd start crying. I could tell she was hurting but she wouldn't tell my why."

"I see. Do you know why she started her foundation?"

Cheryl again met Tracy's eyes. "No. But it's the best thing that ever happened to her — at least after the divorce. She was pretty happy the last couple of years since everything was going so well for her."

"I know she did a lot of good."

"She did. She even got Eddie to help her."

"Oh. She and Ed remained friends?"

"Yeah, it seemed like it. She wanted to get victim's rights bills or something like that passed. Eddie tried to help with some of that."

Tracy nodded. "I didn't realize all that. That's pretty amazing."

"It is, isn't it? I was so proud of her. Everyone was."

"Yeah. I saw how the press dubbed her Saint Cynthia."

Cheryl snorted. "She hated that."

"Hated the moniker?"

"Yes."

"Do you know why?"

"Not really."

"Can I ask how you know then that she hated being called Saint Cynthia?"

There was another sigh. "I just remember the two of us were having a good time and then I brought up reading the Saint Cynthia thing. She just looked at me and asked me never to call her that. She said her nickname was much more appropriate."

"Nickname?"

Cheryl blinked. "Yeah. I used to call her Cyn."

"Mommy!" Nicole yelled.

"What?" Tracy blinked. "Oh, I'm sorry sweetheart. Did I stop reading again?"

"Yes!"

"I'm sorry. I guess Mommy's not feeling very well tonight."

"Are you sick, Mommy?" Nicole asked. She got on her knees and leaned against her mother's shoulder. "Poor Mommy."

Tracy smiled. "I'll be all right."

"Daddy should take you to the doctor."

"I just need some sleep, sweetie."

"You should get an ouch."

"I don't need an ouch."

"Then why do I get an ouch?"

"I got my ouches when I was your age. When you get to be a Mommy you only need an ouch occasionally."

Brian came over to the couch. Nicole looked at her father.

"Mommy's sick."

"Really just tired," Tracy added quickly. "I can't seem to finish this story."

"Too many big words?" Brian teased.

"Very funny," Tracy frowned.

"You read, Daddy," Nicole ordered.

"Yeah, *Daddy*," Tracy agreed. "We left off where the elephant has just discovered the sneaky fox has made off with the fruit basket."

"Mean fox!" Nicole said harshly.

"It was supposed to be a welcome home gift for Mrs. Monkey, who just had a baby."

Brian frowned. "An elephant managed to assemble a fruit basket?"

"He used his trunk, Daddy," Nicole explained.

"Oh."

Tracy handed Brian the tome. "Now sit down and read to us," she instructed.

"I thought you were going to bed."

"I want to know how it ends."

"Read Daddy!"

"All right, all right," Brian said as he tried to find the proper starting point.

Nicole was now seated in between her parents. She liked her special time when it was just her with them. Peter had already been placed in his crib for the night.

"Now let's see," her father said. "Where is my present for Mrs. Monkey? asked Emmerich Elephant. 'Filchy Fox took it!' Portia Possum exclaimed. 'Oh, that naughty fox,' Emmerich Elephant grunted. 'Ozan Owl will hear about this!'"

"He's the boss of the forest," Nicole told her father. "I want an Ozan Owl."

"You do?"

"He's cute."

"We already have a boss in this house, pumpkin," Brian smiled.

"I know. But Mommy's at work all day."

Tracy couldn't help what came next. So, she covered her mouth and started laughing, laughing heartily. Brian glared at her, thinking she had told their daughter to say what she had just said if anyone ever asked.

Brian cleared his throat. "Anyway, it's the lion who is king of the forest."

"The jungle," Tracy corrected, still chuckling.

"Whatever."

"There's no lion in the story, Daddy."

"Of course, the Cowardly Lion *did* sing that song about being king of the forest," Tracy mused.

"What?" Brian asked.

"Never mind."

"Book!" Nicole shouted.

"Yeah!" Tracy seconded.

Brian looked at them. He chuckled and then picked up the trail of Ozan Owl and Filchy Fox and the rest of them. He wanted to keep his bosses happy.

"Cyn, huh?"

"Yes, Brian, as in, thou shalt not…"

"I got it, Tracy."

"Don't backtalk the boss."

Brian folded his arms. "I plan on having a nice talk with Nicole tomorrow while you're at work."

"Oh, good grief. Anyway, Cynthia must have felt guilty about something. I wonder what sin she committed — or thought she committed anyway."

"Maybe she cheated on her husband," Brian smirked.

Tracy narrowed her eyes. "I think it something's much more interesting than *that*. She did a whole lifestyle change."

Brian got into their bed. "Her ex-husband probably knows the reason."

"Most likely," Tracy agreed while joining her husband. "And if he does, he's not talking."

"What?"

"Their marriage ended, Brian. If Ed Lydecker were innocent with respect to their breakup, he would have played the supportive, understanding spouse and tried to help his wife through whatever was bothering her. But they split. So, either he couldn't deal with his wife and her secret and cut her loose, or he's involved in whatever it is too."

"Terrific."

"I found out something else too. Lydecker is engaged to the ex-wife of a judge. Her name is Debra Dooley. I wonder if Keith Entwistle knows her."

"And Lydecker found out about Keith through this Debra…"

"Maybe."

"Uh-huh."

Tracy sat up and stared down at her horizontally positioned husband. "Politicians, judges, a rich sports-team owner, a troubled victim with a secret — I love it!"

Brian frowned at his grinning wife. "Well, I *don't*. The more I learn about this the more I think Cynthia Lydecker was the victim of a hit or something."

"Arranged by whom, Brian?"

"I don't know. Take your pick."

"Filchy Fox?"

Brian frowned again. "I'm serious, Tracy."

Tracy rubbed Brian's chest. "I know you are, honey. I have El looking into things for me and if he finds something I hope we can take it to the authorities."

Brian reached up and stroked Tracy's cheek. "Time for bed, boss lady. I really don't want to talk about this anymore."

Tracy smiled sympathetically as she rested her head on Brian's chest. "Brian, if you could be a forest critter character in *The Great Crime of Faraway Forest*, what would you be?"

Brian started playing with his wife's hair. "That's easy. I'd be the one married to the owl."

Tracy chuckled. "So, I'm Ozan Owl, huh? You're typecasting."

"If you go by Nicole, I am. So, what would you be if you weren't the owl?"

"I don't know. Maybe Frieda Fish."

"Figures," Brian chuckled. "She swims around all day looking for something to eat."

"Ha ha. She seems to be the happiest character in the book. She doesn't worry about anything. She has faith that her next meal will somehow be provided for her, and it always is. I wish I could have that kind of faith and not worry about everything."

"Be careful what you wish for, love. One day Frieda might not realize there's a hook attached to her meal, and it could be her last."

Tracy looked at Brian and him at her for a few quiet moments. Filchy Fox had seemingly stolen their tongues.

Both Neal Bennett and Tyler Wannamaker had alarmed looks on their faces after Tracy updated them.

"I'll ask Keith about Debra Dooley," Tyler volunteered.

"Don't tell him anymore than you have to, Ty. I don't want him drawing any conclusions or thinking we've found something when we may not have. Have you been reinforcing our request that he not talk about this case with anyone?"

"So much so that he's annoyed by it."

"Supreme!"

"We have to tread *very* lightly here," Neal added. "Ed Lydecker is one of the good guys: doesn't smoke, doesn't drink, and doesn't make the news unless it's the good kind."

"You know him, Neal?" Tracy asked.

"Just what's reported about him. He just seems a good guy to me."

"He may very well be. But there's something wonky about that divorce and I won't be happy until I know what it is."

"They were both public figures; well, Cynthia was the daughter of one anyway. Maybe they handled things that way so neither could be dragged through the mud."

"Maybe. But don't you think we should find out?"

Neal sighed. "As long as we're discreet about it."

Tracy looked at Tyler. "Any feelings to share on the matter?"

"I think you're both right. But it'd be really strange if Lydecker ends up being involved in this."

"Why's that?"

"He is very hard core about guns. He introduced legislation that would require additional restrictions for would-be gun owners if they had people under 18 living in the household."

Neal looked at Tyler. "Hey that's right. He wanted additional safety training and some kind of assessment."

"Assessment?" Tracy asked, wanting clarification.

"He wanted assessments done to make sure there weren't problems in the family. If you had small children, he wanted it that much more difficult for you to bring a gun into the house."

"Good Lord," Tracy said. "No way *that* ever had a chance."

"Give it time, Tracy," Tyler said. "If gun violence keeps on growing, you can bet Maryland is one of the places where radical laws have a chance of getting passed."

"But the government coming into your home, Ty? That's a dangerous precedent."

"Social workers can do that. It's all about the children, Tracy."

Tracy frowned. "I hear you. But we're getting too far afield here. Let's all get back to work now. I'll let you both know what, if anything, El finds out."

Both her associates nodded and then left the boss' office. It was no secret to anyone who knew Tracy Brubaker Shane that she loathed guns. She had no problem if someone wanted to buy one for protection. But she personally would never own one. Furthermore, no child of hers would be allowed to play at friend's house if the parent or parents were gun owners. She had made this clear to Brian in no uncertain terms, and she had no problem asking the question. Of course, Nicole and Peter were presently too young to be sent off to play at someone's house without Tracy or Brian there with them. But one day they'd be old enough. And there was no way Tracy would be changing her mind about this in the future.

So, Edward Lydecker didn't like guns either. Was it really about, as Tyler had said with some sarcasm, the children? Or was it just a political move for a man who had greater ambitions and wanted attention? Was Tracy letting her own personal distaste for politicians cloud her objectivity? Was she too willing to cast Lydecker in the role of villain? Maybe. But there was something off about that marriage. Tracy felt it. And her gut instincts usually proved to be right. She was, after all, as wise as Ozan Owl — at least in her daughter's eyes. But *this* owl was facing something much, much worse than a thieving fox. Brian was right that she should watch her step. Otherwise, she might one day look up and see the vultures circling.

Chapter 7

"I've gone through everything Arthur Pankow's office has sent over thus far and there's no indication of motive," Tyler Wannamaker told Tracy.

"Their whole case is circumstantial then?"

"Yes. I can't believe they're moving forward with this thing."

Tracy shook her head. "I guess it was a toss of the coin and Keith lost. Anything else in there besides the gun, the key, and lack of alibi?"

"They have his prints on the trash."

"Oh right, the box of frozen chicken."

"Tracy, I don't see how we can explain everything without saying Keith was framed."

"But we've talked about the risk doing that, Ty. Art could turn around and point out the unlikelihood someone would frame Keith if Keith's claim of not knowing the victim is true."

"But the State has no evidence he knew her. We can counter with *that*."

"What we have here is the makings for a hung jury or acquittal. What puzzles me is why Art hasn't made a plea offer. That isn't like him — especially with *this* evidence, or lack thereof."

Tyler started pacing. "He's getting pressure no doubt. It's Salem, Massachusetts — *1692!*"

"Easy there, Ty," Tracy said cautiously. "I don't think Keith will be convicted. We'll play up the politics, wealth, and pressure angles all during the trial. We only need one juror to agree with us."

Tyler stared at Tracy. "So, we're just going to wait until the trial then? It's only May. We have two and a half months until then. I don't know if Katie can make it, never mind Keith."

Tracy stood up, approached her associate, and placed her hand on his shoulder.

"I didn't mean to imply we are going to do nothing. In fact, this afternoon we're being allowed into Cynthia Lydecker's home. El and I are going."

"I didn't realize that."

"You've been busy, and I didn't want to get your hopes up in case we don't find anything."

"Can I come?"

"I'd rather you didn't. I need you here and you're no fan of Jim."

"Lucas is going to be there?"

"They don't want the defense roaming around the house unsupervised. What if we made a 'discovery'? Everyone knows your relation to the accused."

Tyler sighed. "You're right. I'm just finding it hard to focus."

"I understand. Believe me, I do. I'll let you know what we find as soon as I get back this afternoon. Okay?"

"Sure," Tyler smiled. "I know you know what you're doing."

"You didn't offend me. We're good."

Tyler nodded and returned to his office. Tracy could empathize with him. Around this time five years ago Brian had been arrested for the murder of his father. But his ordeal was over in just over a week's time — at least, the one related to his arrest. Tracy knew better than anyone it was impossible to forget a parent was murdered. At least when Keith was clear of this, he wouldn't have *that* particular memory to deal with. Of course, the memories he did have would be plenty.

It was just after 2:00 p.m. when Elias Tanner, Sr. and Tracy arrived at Cynthia Lydecker's home. Tanner had picked the attorney up for lunch before proceeding to their rendezvous with Detective Jim Lucas. Lucas was waiting for them with his arms folded. As the defense team approached, Lucas offered each his hand.

"Good to see you again, Elias," Lucas said. "How's retirement?"

Tanner grinned at Tracy before answering. "I'm not sure yet. I'll have to let you know."

Lucas smiled at Tracy and just said her name softly. Then the three of them entered.

"Just you Jim?" Tracy asked as he closed the door.

"Yeah. I guess they trust you guys."

"I would hope so," Tracy grinned.

Lucas moved towards the foyer wall. "This is the alarm box here. You enter the same code to turn it on and off. If you enter the wrong code or no code at all, the company will call you through the speaker here."

"Oh, it's connected to the phone line?" Tracy asked.

"Yes."

"I didn't see in what Art sent about the time the alarm was turned off."

Lucas shook his head. "The Lydecker woman didn't have that feature. So, we don't know when she turned it on and someone else turned it off."

"That's unfortunate," Tracy mumbled.

Lucas moved from the foyer and towards the staircase that led to the second floor.

"When the first officers got here all the lights were out on the first floor. So, they had to use flashlights." Lucas pointed at the carpeting. "They swear the carpet was spotless, just like the rest of the house."

"She kept a tidy place," Tanner said.

"Exactly. But you'd think someone would have left some kind of mess behind."

"You mean from their shoes?" Tracy asked.

"Yes — something they picked up from the pathway or street. But there was nothing."

"They could have taken their shoes off, or worn something over them," Tracy opined.

"They must have," Lucas agreed. "This guy was no idiot."

Tanner and Tracy exchanged glances, and then Tracy looked at Lucas.

"But it was pretty idiotic the way he disposed of the gun. Wouldn't you agree?"

Lucas didn't answer. Instead, he said, "Let's go upstairs to the bedroom."

Lucas turned and started climbing the steps. The other two followed.

"The coroner thinks she was asleep when she was shot," Lucas said as everyone entered the bedroom. "She was on the left side of the bed even though she had the king-size thing to herself."

"She probably spent 14 years on that side," Tracy said quietly. "I guess she hadn't broken the habit."

"I guess." Lucas moved so he was now standing next to where Cynthia Lydecker had been the night she died. "She was facing towards the opposite side. So, the killer shot her in the back of the head. And then he left." Lucas faced Tracy and Tanner. "And that's pretty much all we can be sure of. If the killer took something, we don't know what it is. She has a little office downstairs that's as neat as the rest of the place; nothing seems to be missing. She had some valuables in a wall safe and they are all accounted for. We checked with her insurance company and her father." Lucas sighed.

"What about fingerprints?" Tanner asked.

"Wasn't that report in what Pankow sent you guys?" Lucas returned.

"El hasn't seen all the things the SA has turned over."

"Oh. Well, obviously your client's prints weren't found anywhere in the home. And all the prints we could lift we matched up with friends and family of the victim. They're in Pankow's report."

"How about places where there should have been prints but weren't?" Tracy asked.

Lucas shook his head. "Impossible to really answer that. My bet is the killer wore gloves. We were able to lift Cynthia's prints from the alarm code keys so this guy was very careful."

"I bet he was. One wrong keystroke and the alarm company is calling."

Tanner frowned. "But if she had the alarm on when this guy entered, wouldn't it have made some noise before being turned off?"

"You can barely hear it from the bedroom, Elias," Lucas answered. "We checked. She probably never even heard it."

"How the hell did this guy get the code?" Tracy asked showing her frustration. "She changed it after the divorce, didn't she?"

"She did," Lucas confirmed.

"And the locks to the house were changed too?"

"Yes."

"She doesn't seem to have trusted her ex all that much."

Lucas gulped. "She probably didn't want him showing up suddenly to pick up something he forgot to take with him."

Tracy sighed. "I'm sorry, Jim. I guess I shouldn't have said that."

Lucas smiled. "Don't worry about it. I'm over my ex-wife."

"Can we just walk around the rest of the house?" Tanner asked.

"Sure."

Lucas moved towards the hallway and Tracy and Tanner followed. There wasn't too much left to see on the second floor. There were two other bedrooms that were mostly empty except for the closets, which held clothing meant for much warmer weather than January — the last month Cynthia Lydecker was alive. There was a fourth room that had exercise equipment, an audio system set-up, and a thirty-two-inch flat screen television mounted to the wall.

"I guess she could watch TV or listen to tunes while sweating," Tracy mused.

Lucas opened the room's closet. "And there's a mini-fridge in here stocked with water."

"Is there an attic?" Tanner asked.

"Not one being used for storage, if that's what you're asking."

Tanner nodded. "All right then."

Soon the trio was in the basement. Lucas pointed out the laundry room, a storage closet filled with unwanted bric-a-brac and boxes being kept for the more fragile items being used elsewhere. The rest of the subfloor was empty.

"I guess Ed Lydecker used to have some sort of setup here," Tracy mused aloud.

"Pool table," Lucas responded. Tracy just nodded.

Tracy, Tanner, and Lucas returned to first floor. Tracy found herself drawn to the pictures adorning the wall next to the staircase.

"Something ain't it?" Lucas asked her after a few moments.

"Yeah, it is. Did you track all these people down?"

"Each and every one of them. All of them had good things to say about her."

"I'm sure they did — Saint Cynthia and all that."

"Mm."

"I recognize some of these people from the other news coverage they've received."

Lucas was standing with his arms folded next to Tracy. "She's got almost everything covered: child abuse, battered women, homeless shelters, drunk-driving victims, widows and orphans, and on and on."

"She seems to be fond of black-tie events where the tickets are mighty expensive."

"And silent auctions too. She organized quite a few of those."

Tracy shook her head. Then she folded her arms and turned from the display. "I just don't understand this. I can't figure it."

"It's probably the simplest explanation."

Tracy frowned at Lucas. "An affair? They were so perfectly discreet that after all these months you haven't turned up anything? Come on, Jim."

Lucas looked at her and then at Tanner, who was now standing next to Tracy.

"Elias here can tell you I can't say anything on the matter. Bring up your skepticism in court."

Tracy clucked her tongue. "Can we see her office? It's on this floor, right?"

"Yeah. There's a study in the back. Follow me."

Once in the office Tracy moved towards the desk, where she expected to find a computer. "No laptop?"

"We have it."

"Of course. Going through emails and correspondence, hoping to find a love letter or something."

"I guess so."

"What about appointments? Did she keep everything electronic, or did she have something handheld?"

"Handheld. We have the current one but there're some old ones in the filing cabinet. She kept them with her personal tax stuff."

"Recordkeeping for Uncle Sam, huh?"

"I suppose."

"Which cabinet?"

Lucas moved towards a black, three-drawer filing cabinet that sat on the floor next to the desk. He pulled it open.

"This stuff is only for the last four or five years — since she's been single."

"She doesn't have copies of the joint returns?"

Lucas blinked. "No. Her ex-husband has all that. Why do you ask?"

Tracy smiled. "I can't really tell you. Defense strategy and all that."

"You going after Ed Lydecker?"

"Should I?"

Lucas frowned. "If you want to see the old records subpoena them."

"I will."

Lucas looked at Tanner, who was pretty much just observing Tracy. The he returned his eyes to the attorney.

"Anything else, Tracy?"

"Can I take some pictures of Cynthia's photo wall? Brian got me this new gizmo for Christmas, and the only pictures I've taken are of my kids. And my dog. Maybe of Brian too."

Lucas chuckled. "I guess that'd be okay. But their names should be in the witness statements Pankow gave you."

"I hope Art isn't planning to bring all these people to the stand."

"To work up outrage over the murder you mean?"

"Exactly. They can't have anything germane to say with respect to the murder."

"I'm sure you'll get the witness list when it's ready."

"It's going to be a short list."

Lucas looked at the floor. Tracy sighed and then took her pictures. She and Tanner then moved towards the exit.

"Thanks, Jim," Tanner said as the detective locked the door.

"Yes, Jim," Tracy added. "Thanks very much."

"Sure," Lucas said.

After everyone was standing by Tanner's auto Tracy said, "I guess I'll bother Art now."

"I'm sure he can't wait," Lucas responded.

"Oh, you're cute."

Lucas grinned at Tracy and then looked at Tanner. "Elias, can I talk to Tracy privately for a few minutes?"

"Sure," Tanner answered, looking mildly confused.

Lucas moved away from Tanner's vehicle and towards the front door. Tracy followed.

"What's up?" Tracy asked.

Quietly he answered, "You think the motive for this goes back a few years, maybe has something to do with her marriage to Lydecker?"

Tracy frowned. "Why do you think I think that?"

"Good Lord, Tracy," Lucas sighed. "Why else would you want old appointment books and who knows what else?"

"I have to keep my options open. But I can't discuss details with you. I'm sorry."

Lucas rubbed the back of his head. "You and I should talk."

"What do you mean? We *are* talking."

"I mean we should talk outside the office."

Tracy took a deep breath. "What are you talking about?"

"We can meet for dinner. That's innocuous enough, right?"

"What?"

"In a public place of course. I'm not talking about some romantic meal, obviously."

Tracy shook her head. "That's not a good idea."

"It's not what you're thinking. I just want to talk to you."

"Jim, I can't."

"Because you think I'll try something with you?"

"Well…no…not really."

"Then what's the problem? It's mostly a business meeting anyway."

"I'm sorry?"

"Think about it. We should talk. Your client's in big trouble and I might be able to help."

Tracy blinked several times. "What's going on?"

"Call me if you change your mind about dinner. If you get uncomfortable during the meal you can always just leave." Lucas looked towards Tanner. "Elias is waiting for you. You better go."

Tracy nodded and turned. During her walk to Tanner's auto her emotions started mixing together — a pinch of anger for the man who seemingly still had feelings she could never return; a dab of frustration for the detective who refused to admit even *he* didn't think Keith Entwistle was guilty; and a touch of sympathy for the lonely male who maybe just wanted someone to talk to. But the main ingredient was intrigue. What exactly did Jim Lucas know that she didn't? How could he help her client? Before she entered the car Tracy looked at Lucas again. He just nodded in return and watched her leave when Tanner stared pulling out of the driveway.

While en route to Tracy's office Tanner asked the obvious question. "What was that about?"

"Not sure," Tracy said tersely. She wasn't going to share her personal anecdote about Lucas with Tanner — or anyone else for that matter. Only her husband and sister-in-law knew what happened. But Tracy hadn't told either of them the name of her would-be paramour. "But I'm pretty sure Jim doesn't think Keith is their man."

"He told you this?" Tanner asked sounding surprised.

"Not exactly."

"Then what did he exactly say?"

Tracy sighed. "I don't want to talk about it."

Tanner stole a look at his passenger. "What's wrong?"

"Nothing's wrong."

Tanner sighed. Something was obviously bugging her, but it was just as clear she had no interest in sharing it. So be it then. Tanner said nothing more about the matter for the remainder of their trip.

Tyler Wannamaker appeared stunned. "You think we have a cop on our side? Wow. Maybe I was wrong about Lucas."

"I can't give you specifics, Ty. It's just a feeling I have."

"All right. I'll get working on those subpoenas right away. What exactly do you want?"

"All her appointment books, calendars, and the like, whether electronic or concrete. I want to know what she's been doing and who she's been seeing since her separation. That's really it for now. Then I want to start making a list of Cynthia's friends in those photos on her wall. I took some pictures with my phone."

"You want to talk to them all?"

"I don't know about all of them, but certainly the ones she's known the longest. They may have some insight into why Cynthia did what she did."

"Why do I get the sense you don't think it was out of the goodness of her heart?"

Tracy grinned. "It's not that, exactly. The change was just so radical. Maybe she looked at her life and decided she wanted to help other people. It could be as simple as that. Or there could be another reason."

"All right. Anything else you need me to do?"

"Not right now. When we get those calendars, we'll go through them *thoroughly*. Save your energy for that."

"Sure."

"It's late and I have to get home. Peter needs his dinner."

Tyler smiled. "Sorry. Didn't mean to keep you."

"It's all right, Ty. I'll see you tomorrow."

Tyler practically skipped out of her office, which caused Tracy to giggle. He needed some good news and she seemed to have given it to him. Her merriment however soon gave way to confusion. What was she going to do about Jim Lucas? She had hoped he had moved on with respect to his feelings for her. But she knew he hadn't. It made her extremely uncomfortable. But there was little she could do about it. And *that* made her angry.

Tracy's remixed emotions stayed with her during her drive home. Once home, she tried to be as pleasant as she could be and appear unoccupied. After tucking Nicole in, she took Peter with her into the bedroom while Brian took out Bonkers. Violetta had already retired to her own quarters.

When Brian reentered the bedroom, he saw Tracy seated on the mattress nursing Peter. He smiled at them.

"Shut the door, would you?!" Tracy snapped.

Brian obliged. "Easy, Tracy. Everyone's in bed. There's nobody roaming the halls."

"I know that. But still…"

Brian shrugged his shoulders. After he changed into his PJs, he joined his wife and son on the bed.

"What's wrong?"

"I like my modesty."

"Come on. That's not it and you know it. What's going on?"

Tracy sighed. "It's this case, Brian. I'm sorry I took it out on you."

Brian rubbed her bare shoulder. "It's okay; I figured it was that."

"See any news coverage about us today?"

"No. Wait until we get closer to the trial date though."

"Yippee."

Brian smiled and kissed the same shoulder. He told her, "Peter's going to be crawling any day now. He keeps getting on his hands and knees, and rocking. Even Nicole was cheering him on today."

Tracy smiled at her son. "My little boy's growing up and I'm not around."

"Sure, you're around," Brian quickly countered. "You've put in a couple of late nights, but you've been here the weekends."

"Do they ask about me?"

"Yes. Well, Nicole does. Peter can't talk yet. But if someone mentions your name or Mommy, he looks around for you. He knows who you are."

Tracy looked appreciatively at her husband. "He's done," she whispered. She then carried Peter to his crib at the foot of the bed, gently eased the babe onto his mattress, put her pajama top on, and laid down next to Brian, her head slightly touching his shoulder. "I love you," she said quietly.

"I love you more," he responded.

"You think any of your old girlfriends still love you?"

"What?" Brian asked, turning his head.

"Would that make you feel good, or would that make you feel uncomfortable?"

"What are you talking about?"

"What if you ran into an ex of yours and she professed to still love you. Would that be a boost to your ego, or would you feel bad for her?"

"Tracy, did you run into an old boyfriend or something?"

"No."

"Then where is this coming from?"

"Let's just say it's related to this case. The issue came up."

"Oh."

"So, what's your answer?"

Brian sighed. "I guess I'd feel a little of both. I'd be flattered on the one hand. But if she thought we could get back together I'd suddenly feel very awkward."

Tracy repositioned herself so she was looking at Brian. "I know you've told me you really never loved anyone before you met me."

"That's the God's honest truth, Tracy."

Tracy smiled. "But did anyone tell you she loved you? Present company excluded, of course."

Brian frowned. "Do we really need to talk about this?"

"I'm curious."

"Now you're Curious Cat, are you?"

"Very funny. Well?"

"A couple, I guess."

"A couple? So that would be two."

"Maybe three."

"Three?"

"I didn't keep count."

"You didn't have a little black book or something with all your girlfriends' names and emails?"

"I wasn't putting together a 'white pages,' if that's what you're implying."

"So, what did you say when they admitted their true feelings for you?" Tracy batted her eyes.

"Thank you, I guess."

"You said 'thank you' after she expressed her true feelings? Wow, classy."

"What was I supposed to say?"

"I don't know. So, you never said 'I love you, too' even if you didn't really mean it?"

"You mean did I lie to them?"

"A white lie to spare her feelings…"

Brian blew out loudly. "Maybe."

"Oh, really."

"You just said a white lie would be a kind thing."

"I never said that."

"You did!"

"That was just a way you could have justified not being honest. I never said how I felt about it one way or the other."

Brian scowled. "Tracy, this is nuts. I don't care what the reasons are. I don't like talking about this."

"Why not? I'm not mad about any of it."

"Good. Because you have no right to be mad about any of it. We're talking ancient history here: Brian B.T. — Before Tracy."

Tracy chuckled. "Calm down, honey. You don't have to be embarrassed by your life as a stud."

"I never said I was a stud."

"Three women professing love before I came along? You weren't even 20 yet. Face it, Brian. You were a stud."

"Now stop that."

"Why? Why does it bother you? I really want to know."

Brian sighed. "Because it was for all the wrong reasons, that's why."

"What does *that* mean?"

"Look. You know my mom died right as I was starting high school. People knew it. Women knew it. Women who knew who my father was knew it. And a lot of them were very attractive. And I was vulnerable."

"And they took advantage of the situation?"

"They did. I did too sometimes. It made me feel good and it made me feel good about myself — at least for a while. And then Crystal heard the rumors."

"Rumors?"

"About me and my…you know."

"Abilities."

"Something like that. It just got out of hand. One time I slept with this girl who had a boyfriend who wasn't the nicest person in the world. He found out and came after me with a knife. But he was a punk and a hit him good and hard."

Tracy gulped. She hadn't realized the wounds that would be opened by her good-natured teasing. "I'm sorry, Brian. I didn't know."

"I really didn't *want* you to know. I'm not proud of any of it."

"I'm sorry."

"Actually, that whole incident was good for me. I wondered about the next guy. He might not be a punk and he might have a gun, and all over a person I didn't care about, nor her me for that matter. It was a wakeup call, and I changed my attitude about girls and sex and all of that." Brian smiled at Tracy. "I decided the next girl I wanted in my life would be a nice girl. And I talked to Crystal about this because we were pretty tight during those years after Mom died. And not too long after all of that happened, she introduced me to you. And then it was Brian A.T."

Tracy smiled and kissed him. "I always knew Crys set us up. But she refuses to admit it."

"I think she was afraid you might think that's the only reason she befriended you. But she's always liked you."

"I can never be mad at Crys since it's because of her that I'm with you."

"Then you're a better person than I am. I can always find a reason to be mad at my sister."

They both started laughing. And then they both started kissing. But everything was all right because Brian had closed the door earlier. So, their privacy was assured. Life with Tracy had been very good for Brian Shane — and would continue to be. That's why he had no desire to revisit his past. He'd rather save his desire for much worthier pursuits.

Chapter 8

It was two weeks before Tracy's request yielded results. Now — with less than two months until the trial — she was in her conference room going through a stack of Cynthia Lydecker's personal calendar books. Elias Tanner, Sr. was with her, making a list of every name and place that the victim had entered into the volumes. There were 14 notebooks to scour, although the main focus was on the ones that encompassed the period from her separation until her death. Tracy started with 2014 since that was the year Ed Lydecker moved out of his home.

"It's weird, El," Tracy said as she started reviewing May's entries.

"What is?"

"The month Cynthia and Ed broke up I reunited with Brian — sort of, anyway."

"Oh."

Tracy said nothing further until she was done with the planner. She looked at Tanner. "She was seeing a priest."

Tanner looked up from the list he was compiling. "A priest?"

"Yes. I have to look in the earlier books to see when it started. But from January through September, she was visiting a Father Crowne."

"How often?"

"It varied. In the first half of the year, it was twice — sometimes three times — a week. But in June it went down to once every two weeks. The last time she saw him was in the first week of September. After that, nothing."

"That *is* interesting."

"And there's even more. Cynthia's divorce attorney of record was a Scott Lamb. But in August she had an appointment with another attorney, Edie Thorpe. I know of her. She's does a lot of work with nonprofits. So, I'm guessing Cynthia went to see Edie about starting the Foundation — or at least making initial inquiries. There was another meeting in October and another in December."

"So, after she starts on her path to the Foundation, she stops seeing this Father Crowne."

"Yes."

Tanner sighed. "I hate to state the obvious, but you're not going to get any details about anything from a priest and a lawyer."

"Sounds like the beginning to a bad joke," Tracy frowned. "Did *you* find anything interesting?"

"Not sure. I'm almost through 2018 and she had at least five lunch meetings with her ex-husband. The two of them seemed quite chummy."

"Mm."

"Some of the names I recognize — people or places with lots of money."

"Fundraising efforts no doubt."

"I'll check 'em all out."

"Thanks. There's one more name in here I'm curious about."

"Oh?"

"Yes. Cynthia had a meeting with a Kimberly Acosta in October. It's the only appointment with her I could find. But what's interesting is that Cynthia has an exclamation point after the name. It's the only time she did that, at least in 2014."

"Okay. I'll check on her first."

"I'll move on to 2015 and then we can break for lunch. Then I'll go back to 2013 if 2015 didn't provide anything of interest. And I have to take a pump break."

"Sounds good to me," Tanner agreed.

The two exchanged smiles before returning to their work. When all was said and done, they had compiled a list of over one hundred names. Tanner sighed loudly.

"Sorry," Tracy said sympathetically. "But it's probably not as bad as it looks."

"It isn't?"

"Focus first on the names neither of us has heard of. I highlighted those names in yellow for you after I merged our lists. And we can put the names of Cynthia's family and friends to the side for now too. If they turn up on Art's witness list, we'll of course talk to them at that point."

"Sounds good to me."

"I know we'd be wasting our time trying to talk to Father Crowne but find out about him anyway. Maybe he's just a priest who helps out couples considering divorce."

"All right."

"You know, when I talked to Cynthia's friend Cheryl Whittaker, she told me Cynthia said her nickname was appropriate."

"Nickname?"

"Cyn. Get it?"

"Yes, Tracy."

"So, what sin did Cynthia commit that caused her to think her nickname was apropos? And does it have anything to do with her seeing Father Crowne? You can see a possible connection, can't you?"

"I think, technically speaking, divorce is a sin in the Catholic Church, unless they got an annulment."

"I guess she could have been wrestling with that. But divorce is usually *not* a sin if there's a very good reason for it, like if you're an abused spouse."

"But it was a no-fault divorce. And we checked and found no indication Cynthia ever filed a complaint against her husband for any reason."

"I realize all of that. But that just makes me wonder more about everything."

"I can see that."

Tracy scowled. "Whatever. Do me a favor and check on that Acosta woman first. Then move onto the others."

"It's that exclamation point that has you curious, huh?"

"Yup."

"All right," Tanner smiled. "Give me a goodbye hug and I'll be off."

Tracy chuckled and then obliged. "Thanks for helping today, El."

"Thanks for lunch."

"Least I could do."

Tanner released the attorney and then exited the conference room. Tracy, in turn, relocated to Tyler Wannamaker's office.

"How's it going, Ty?"

"They have no case."

"They think they do."

"For everything they have we have a reasonable explanation. Well...except for the fingerprints."

"The fingerprints on the frozen chicken box."

"Right." Tyler stood and handed Tracy a series of photographs of the incriminating poultry container. "Now in his statement, Justin Wilmont — the trash can owner — denies that's his trash. And Keith and Katie say they don't buy frozen chicken. So how did Keith's prints get on that damn box? If we could provide an explanation for *that*, we could win this. We might not even have to present a defense."

Tyler watched as Tracy sat down and started going through the photos. She stopped at the one which featured a blow up of the area where the fingerprints were found. Not surprisingly they were on the perforated flaps where one would open the box. Tracy moved the picture close to her. Then she looked up at Tyler.

"Did you find anything that said where this chicken was purchased?"

Tyler blinked. "Uh...no. That's a popular brand so it could be purchased anywhere. It wouldn't help the prosecutor's office tracking that down. Who'd remember someone buying a box of chicken?"

"But it might help *us*," Tracy said standing. "You see these?" Tracy asked while pointing to a series of numbers and figures on the box lid.

"Sure."

"Do you know if you could track down where this chicken was purchased using this code?"

Tyler blinked. And then he smiled. "I don't know."

"Then let's please find out. It may not amount to anything but..."

"You don't have to explain yourself. I'll find out."

"All right," she grinned. "Anything else?"

"Not really. Still no motive from what I can tell."

"Do you need help going through all of this?"

"Not right now. Truth is I've already been through everything once."

"Okay. Then I'll leave you be."

"Hey, what about those appointment books?"

"Oh! El's going to check out some names. I'll let you know if he finds anything."

"All right."

With a nod, Tracy left Tyler's office and returned to her own. She started massaging her eyes. They were tired from all the reading they had done thus far today. *She* was tired and she wanted to go home. Life had other plans, however.

"Arthur Pankow is on line one, Tracy," Rebecca's voice announced.

"Thanks, Beck," Tracy responded in customary fashion as she picked up the receiver. "Hi, Art," she greeted.

"Tracy," Pankow said somberly. "We need to talk."

"About what? Keith Entwistle isn't interested in a plea, and I didn't think you were either."

"Can you stop by my office on your way home? I'll be here late."

"Your office isn't on my way home. What's this about?"

Pankow sighed. "Trust me, Tracy. I wouldn't waste your time. Should I expect you?"

Tracy looked at her watch: 4:53 p.m. She sighed. "All right. I should be there by 6:00."

"Good. I'll see you then." The line went quiet.

Tracy twisted her lips. A trip into the city during rush hour? Not Tracy's idea of a fun commute. But her curiosity had been piqued. She was now Curious Cat again.

"Have a seat," Baltimore City state's attorney Arthur Pankow told her. He closed the door to his office and then sat at his desk. "How's the family?" he smiled.

"Waiting at home for me. Forgive me for being bitchy. But I'm really tired and would really like to be home right now. So please, what's this about?"

Pankow took a deep breath and leaned forward. He opened a file on his desk. "Things have cooled down a bit, so I thought it was time to talk plea."

"No way."

"You need to hear what I have to tell you."

"And what is that?"

"You ever heard of George Finnegan?"

"Uh…I don't think so. Should I have?"

"He used to be an investigator for the SA's office. We had to stop using him several years ago."

"Why's that?"

"We think he was taking bribes not to report what he found."

"You *think*? You could never prove it?"

"No. It could have been gross incompetence of course. But there were too many instances where he should have found out and reported things to us but never did."

"Bribed by the people you were prosecuting?"

"We think. But in some cases, he possibly sat on exculpatory evidence that would have *helped* the defense."

"Good grief. So, this Finnegan dude was just out to line his pockets, huh?"

"It happens sometimes. In George's case he had college tuition and his wife's medical bills to pay. Someone probably reached out to him and once he started, he couldn't stop."

"Why would he sit on exculpatory evidence though? You don't think someone in your office wanted a conviction that badly, do you?"

Pankow sighed. "The case I'm referring to involved a rape victim with a wealthy husband. We think Finnegan approached the husband telling him the accused might go free, but he could make sure that didn't happen."

"For a price…"

"Yes. But we never really had any evidence against him. And no one would ever admit to paying him. So, our only option was just to let him go. He didn't put up much of a fight."

"I don't remember reading about that. I guess you were able to keep that quiet."

"We dealt with it on a case-by-case basis. We couldn't do anything about the people who were freed but we did help get new trials for the *possibly* wrongly convicted."

"Okay. But what does he have to do with Keith Entwistle?"

Pankow looked at Tracy a few moments. "George Finnegan's body was found early this morning in an auto junkyard. He was found in the trunk of his own car. According to the missing person's report filed by his wife, he disappeared last November."

"Geez. He'd been in that junkyard since November?"

"We're not sure really. It's possible. The owner of the place couldn't be sure either. Given how little the car was damaged he swore he'd have noticed the car if it had been there any length of time."

"And just how *did* the car get noticed?"

"Anonymous caller reported a smell coming from the trunk."

"An anonymous caller, huh? That has a familiar ring to it, pardon the pun."

"It happens."

"Fine. But I still don't see what his has to do with my client."

"I'll tell you. Just before I called you, I got a call telling me the results of the ballistics."

"Oh. He was shot and then his body dumped in the trunk, huh?"

"That's how it looks. We matched the slug that killed Finnegan with another one — specifically the one that killed Cynthia Lydecker."

The blood left Tracy's face as her eyes widened. *"Keith Entwistle's gun killed Finnegan?!"*

"There's no doubt about it. Now, since Finnegan vanished in November, I'm assuming that's when he was killed. So, this idea that Entwistle's gun was stolen during the burglary doesn't wash. It had been used in an earlier homicide."

Tracy stood up. "You can't for a minute think this gets presented at the trial, Art!"

"Why not?" Pankow asked, rising.

"Because Keith isn't on trial for Finnegan's murder! To bring that up would be prejudicial beyond belief!"

"If you argue that his gun was stolen during the break in, I have every right to challenge that!"

"Not that way you don't!"

"Listen! I was trying to do you a favor here. You better talk to your client and see if he changes his story. I've no doubt you believe in Entwistle's innocence but even *you* have to admit to having doubts now."

Tracy seethed a few moments more before starting to settle down. "All right; fine. But don't think for a second this gets introduced during Keith's trial. No way."

"Just talk to your client. Then give me a call if he wants to talk plea."

Tracy would later think she should have said "thank you" to Pankow for the heads up. But she was so angry at present that she just turned and left his office. Once in her car she dialed Tyler Wannamaker.

"Hi," her employee greeted.

"We need to talk to Keith pronto," Tracy said immediately.

"Why? What's wrong?"

"I'll fill you both in soon enough. Call him right now and see when we can meet. Then call me right back."

"Okay. Can't you—"

"Just call him, *goddamn it*!"

"All right. I'm dialing now."

"I'll be waiting. Goodbye."

Tracy tossed her phone on the passenger seat and started shaking her head. She had known all along something was off about this whole alleged set up. Arthur Pankow was right. She *was* having doubts. And without meaning for it to happen, the image of Jim Lucas came to her mind's eye. Not too long ago he wanted to meet her for dinner to discuss some things, off the record, of course. She had not yet taken him up on his offer, and he had not followed up. But now…

Tracy's phone started humming. She grabbed it. "When can he meet us?"

"He needs to finish something at his office and then he'll be heading home. Give him an hour he said."

"All right. Meet me there in an hour then."

"I'll be there. Now can't you please tell me what's going on?"

"Tyler, do you really trust your brother-in-law?"

"What? What kind of question is that?"

"Look, Ty. Even if Keith isn't guilty of murder, what if he's guilty of something else? Are you going to be able to visit your sister for friendly get-togethers if certain unpleasant truths come to light about Keith? Everyone has skeletons in their closet."

"Tracy, what in God's name are you talking about?"

"I'll see you in an hour. If you have lingering doubts about Keith, you may want to stay with Katie while I talk to him."

"Are you deliberately trying to piss me off?!"

"Goodbye, Tyler." The call was over.

Tracy sighed as she debated what to do next. First thing should be to call Brian and tell him she'd be late. So, that's just what she did. Then she thought the hell with it and started making her way to her client's house. Who'd really care if she were early? She sure as hell didn't.

By the time Tracy arrived at the Entwistle home, she had calmed down some. She was starting to feel guilty over how she had treated Pankow and talked to Tyler. Being overtired sometimes brought out the worst in her. But she would deal with all of that later. Tracy could see lights were on in her client's home, so she exited her vehicle. She hadn't taken two steps from her auto when Tyler Wannamaker's vehicle turned into the driveway. As he approached her after closing his car door, she could see the troubled expression on his face.

"Let's go, Ty," was all she said to him.

And then they both moved towards the front door. Katie Entwistle opened the door promptly after hearing the bell. Once inside Tyler's sister offered everyone coffee. Both attorneys declined.

"Keith is upstairs changing." Kaite informed them. "He smells like an eggroll." Katie chuckled at her own comment. Neither Tracy nor Tyler could manage even a slight smile.

"Maybe we should talk in private," Tracy told Keith when he finally joined everyone.

"What do you mean?"

"I'm here as your attorney, Keith," Tracy said somberly.

"Okay. But I still don't understand why you think we should talk privately. It's just Katie and Tyler who are here."

Tracy sighed. "Did you know a George Finnegan?"

"Who?"

Tracy repeated the name. Tyler then asked, "Wait, you mean that guy who used to work for the SA?"

"Yes," Tracy answered. "You've heard of him?"

"Sure, I have. There was some scandal, and he was forced out. There were all kinds of rumors. I think some cases he was involved with were reopened. But whatever was going on never impacted the firm I was with, so I can't really be sure of the true facts."

"Mm."

"But what does Finnegan have to do with any of this?" Tyler asked.

Tracy felt a sense of déjà vu. "His body was found this morning in the trunk of his own car. He was shot. The police think he was killed back in November, around the time he went missing. But the most salient point is that Keith's gun was used to kill him."

Tyler, Entwistle, and Katie exchanged glances. Then — as if the implication suddenly hit him — Tyler sat down on the living room sofa. "Jesus," he muttered.

"I don't understand," Entwistle said.

"It means your gun probably wasn't stolen the night of the burglary," Tracy said flatly. "It must have been taken earlier."

Entwistle shook his head. "I don't know; I just don't know."

Katie Entwistle moved towards Tracy, so they were face to face.

"What exactly are you saying here?" she asked the attorney accusingly.

Tracy looked at the distressed spouse and gulped. "I don't quite know if I'm *saying* anything. But since that break in must not have been when the gun was stolen, I don't know if it's just a coincidence, or if it was just used as a cover to plant the key."

Katie stepped back and then turned to look at her husband. Then she again looked at Tracy. "You think he killed her, don't you?"

"I didn't say that."

"You didn't have to." Again, Katie looked at Entwistle. "Well? Are you just going to stand there like a moron?"

"Katie…" Tyler scolded.

"What? What Tyler? I don't hear *you* saying anything."

"You're making too much of this," Tyler continued.

"Am I?"

Tyler looked at Tracy. "If someone managed to get hold of a key to Cynthia Lydecker's home as well as learn her alarm code, then this same person could have gotten Keith and Katie's code and stolen the gun. Right?"

Tracy looked at Tyler, and then she sat down. "You know…Tyler makes an interesting point."

"What do you mean?" Entwistle asked.

"Maybe it was Finnegan who made the key copy, got the alarm codes, and got the gun. He used to be an investigator after all. He meets with whoever hired him to get all that stuff, and then this same person shoots Finnegan dead with your gun."

Tyler looked at Tracy. "So, when he broke into the house, he planted the key then."

"Maybe."

"But if he had the code to the house why break in at all?" Tyler countered.

"Maybe Finnegan didn't get a chance to tell this guy the code. Maybe this guy got nervous and shot him before getting everything he needed."

"Sounds impossible to prove," Tyler murmured.

"Finnegan would have to have gotten two keys made. The one he left at Keith and Katie's house, and the one he used to open Cynthia Lydecker's door that night."

"I guess so."

"I wonder if Finnegan had a favorite locksmith."

"I'll add that to my list," Tyler said with some enthusiasm. "If you're right Tracy, why do you think Finnegan was killed?"

"Any number of reasons. He could have threatened whoever hired him. Or maybe this guy didn't want Finnegan around when things started happening. Finnegan would have been in an excellent position to blackmail him."

"Okay; that makes sense."

Tracy sighed. "I forgot to mention one other point. Finnegan's body was found courtesy of another anonymous caller."

"Like the one who heard the shot!" Tyler exclaimed.

"Exactly. I wonder why he chose this particular moment to make that second call."

Katie was now scanning the room, looking alternately at Tracy and her brother. "I don't believe you two," she said finally, shaking her head. "Are you listening to what you're saying? I mean…Jesus."

"Katie, just—"

"Oh, shut your damn mouth, Tyler! Do you really think there's some vast conspiracy out there to frame Keith for murder? This person hired this other person and then killed this other person so that this and that and…Bullshit! Why don't we just admit it?!"

Entwistle glared at his wife. "Admit *what*?!"

"You were screwing that woman!"

"NO!" the spouse protested.

"And then you killed her and then you screwed up in a different way!"

"NO KATIE! I swear to *GOD* I didn't—"

"I DON'T BELIEVE YOU!" Katie screamed. Then, in tears and red-faced, she turned and headed towards the stairway. Everyone heard a door slam shortly after she had reached the second floor.

Entwistle looked at his brother-in-law. "I didn't do this, Tyler. I swear to you. I didn't do any of it. I didn't cheat on Katie, and I didn't kill anyone. I *swear* it!"

"All right, Keith," Tyler responded. "Katie will be okay. You know how she gets. Tracy was right. I should have just let the two of you talk."

By this point Tracy was once again standing. "I'm sorry about all of this, Keith. Arthur Pankow told me about Finnegan just a couple of hours ago and wanted me to talk to you about it. He's open for a plea."

"A plea?" Tyler asked incredulously. "That's *bullshit*! Somebody who used to work for *his* office ends up dead, and before there's any chance to investigate, they want Keith to take the fall for that one *too*? Christ…"

Tracy sighed. "I guess it could be that. Or it could be that since they have a weak case, they thought a plea was their best chance."

"Sorry, Tracy," Tyler grunted. "I think *I'm* righter than you are about this."

"We should go," Tracy said after a few moments of silence. "Let Keith and Katie have some time. Hopefully, she'll be okay."

"All right," Tyler agreed. He looked at his brother-in-law. "Call me if you need anything. You know how Katie can be sometimes. I'm sure she'll calm down."

"Yeah," Entwistle said, with little conviction.

Tyler gave him a slap on the back and then moved towards the door. Tracy followed.

"I'm sorry about all that in there," Tyler said meekly as the attorneys moved towards their respective autos. "I can't believe Katie blew up like that. She must have been having doubts this whole time."

"This can't be easy for her either. Does she blow up like that often?"

"Not really. Well, now and again, I guess. When she was little, she did that a lot." Tyler smiled. "She was spoiled."

"Ah."

Tyler let out a sigh. He looked at Tracy and folded his arms. "I wish you had told me this in advance, though."

"Sorry. But I wanted to see in person how this all played out."

"And you think I would have given him a heads up if you told me ahead of time?"

"I don't know. I'm tired; this case is driving me nuts; and then Art drops this bombshell."

"Yeah; okay. So, what next?"

"I'm going home and see my babies. We can talk more strategy tomorrow — after I tell Art we're not interested in a plea."

"Okay, fair enough. I think I'm going home and having a few drinks. If I'm late tomorrow, you'll know why."

Tracy chuckled. "See ya then."

Tracy entered her car, and as was her habit checked her phone for messages or texts. Elias Tanner, Sr. had called. Against her better judgment she decided to return his call.

"Hi, El," she said with little enthusiasm.

"Are you all right there, Tracy? You sound down."

"I'll tell you about it tomorrow. What's up?"

"Kimberly Acosta. Should we talk later?"

"No! What is it?"

"Well, the first thing to know is she's dead."

Tracy wasn't feeling so tired anymore. "What happened, El?"

"You remember the Blizzard of 2016? The City got about thirty inches dumped on it."

"Sure."

"Kimberly Acosta was trying to shovel her car out when a driver lost control of his car and hit her. She died from the injuries."

"Oh my God."

"Yeah. She was 68 years old and lived by herself."

"68? Did she have some medical issue that maybe Cynthia was trying to help her with?"

"Not from what I could tell. I mean she was shoveling snow, right?"

"Yeah; right."

"But there's more. I figured you might want to talk to some family or friends of hers in the hopes they knew what she and Cynthia talked about. Now this might not be anything. But it might be more than a coincidence."

"You have my full attention."

"Kimberly Acosta had a daughter named Jeannine. Jeannine died in April 2000 when she was 20, a junior in college."

"How?"

"Hit and run. From what I could find — and there could be more to find — the belief is that she was hit by a drunk driver."

"Oh my God…"

"No arrests were ever made. Now, I'll follow up more with this tomorrow during the workday. All I know for sure is that for some reason Jeannine Acosta was walking back alone to her dorm from a party — and probably drunk — when she was struck. According to some less than sober witnesses the car that hit her never stopped."

"El, what college was Kimberly Acosta attending at the time?"

"The same one Cynthia Lydecker was."

"And two months later Cynthia marries Ed."

"Uh-huh."

"I wonder if they got married thinking it was a way to protect each other."

"Possibly."

Tracy took a deep breath. "Oh, El, is this it? Is this why she thought Cyn was an appropriate name?"

"It sure does sound like a strong possibility, doesn't it?"

"El, if we're both thinking the same thing, then it's very likely Ed Lydecker is involved in this. He and Cynthia partied hard together according to Cheryl Whittaker."

"I guess there could have been more than one person in that car."

"And Cynthia had a meeting with the victim's mother all those years later. What do you think they talked about?"

"I'd be afraid to guess."

"This has to be it, El. This must be the skeleton in the closet. This must be why someone killed Cynthia Lydecker. And if she did confess what she'd done — or been involved with — to Kimberly Acosta, then Kimberly could have told someone else. Either that, or someone was afraid who else Cynthia might confess to."

"How do we even begin to prove it?"

"Believe me, El, I'll be thinking about that very thing every waking hour from now until we *do* prove it. And we *will* prove it. I guarantee you that."

Chapter 9

"You think Ed Lydecker is behind all of this, don't you?" Brian watched as his wife nodded. "Why would he do that after all this time?"

"Maybe because of his engagement. We know Cynthia and Edward were meeting regularly. What do you think they were talking about?"

"And what about this Finnegan person?"

"Lydecker works on the judiciary committee, Brian. He most certainly heard about what Finnegan had done — the kind of person he was and the potential damage to prior convictions."

"So, he hires Finnegan and then bumps him off when he has no further need for him."

"Sure; potential problem eliminated."

"But why would he want Finnegan found? Wouldn't it have been better to just let the guy rot?"

"First, I'm only assuming Lydecker made that call about the body. Maybe he didn't. But let's say he did. He could be getting antsy over the case; maybe he figured finding Finnegan would motivate the SA's office; he knew what the ballistics would reveal. Their case is purely circumstantial."

"All right. What about Keith and his gun then? How did Lydecker pick him?"

"I'm still working that out. But we know about Lydecker's involvement with gun control measures. I wonder if he had access to actual gun ownership records."

"And picked Keith's name out of a hat?"

"Of course not. But once I find out how he *did* pick Keith, he's *done.*"

Brian sighed. "You better be careful how you do that. If you're right…"

"You don't have to say it, Brian. Lydecker killed Finnegan on the *chance* he'd be a problem down the road. You don't have to tell me the kind of person I'm dealing with here."

"Uh-huh. What's your next move?"

"Well, El is going to find out everything he can about the hit and run. I'm hoping he can review the case files. I'm going to see what anti-drunk-driving organizations Cynthia worked with. I think that'd be her charitable purpose of choice."

"But that won't really prove anything."

"Right now, I'm looking for links in a chain. Apart they may not mean anything but put them altogether and you've built a fence. You see?"

"I think so."

"I'm tired, Brian. My adrenaline has left me, and I just want to sleep."

Brian chuckled. "All right, love."

He kissed Tracy goodnight and then straightened the covers. They were both on their backs, staring upward. Tracy however was quickly asleep. Brian was anything *but* relaxed. How could he be? It wouldn't be long before the theory she was assembling made its way back to Edward Lydecker. She wouldn't be able to keep everything a secret until the trial. Of course, maybe she wasn't right about this. She couldn't be right *all* the time. But this thought didn't ease his fears. Yes, he was afraid. He had felt it too: something especially cold about this whole thing. Summer may be just a couple of weeks away. But there was a definite chill in the air.

The next afternoon Rebecca Dietz announced, "Jim Lucas in on line two for you, Tracy."

Tracy thanked her assistant and then greeted her caller. "How are you, Jim?"

"Hanging in there. You've been busy."

"Always."

"Word is making the rounds that Elias Tanner put in a request to review case files in a 20-year-old hit and run."

Tracy was quiet for a few moments. The fact this was already being talked about was *not* good news.

"Why is someone watching El's every move?"

"It's not like that. Somebody sees an old friend and chats a bit, and then passes the information along to another friend."

"So, El is old friends with someone in the records office or something?"

"Tracy, we need to talk. I mean it."

The attorney sighed. "Jim, I told you already. I don't think it's a good idea."

"Why not? I'm not going to try anything. I want to help."

"Why?"

"I'll tell you all about it at dinner."

"Good grief. What am I supposed to tell Brian? I don't think he'd like me having dinner with another man."

"Tell him you're meeting a confidential informant. You wouldn't be lying."

"Can't you just tell me what's going on *now*?" Tracy asked after a few moments.

"I have a feeling you'll be calling me by this time tomorrow."

"What the heck does *that* mean?"

"Think about my offer. I really am just trying to help. Goodbye."

"'Bye."

Tracy was soon drumming her fingers on her desk. Then her stomach muscles started tightening. She called Elias Tanner, Sr. and told her about Lucas' call.

"What do you want me to do?" the PI asked.

"Be careful. Be *extra* careful. I think we're all being watched."

"Forgive me, but that sounds a bit paranoid."

"Jim Lucas thinks I have a reason to be."

"When did you and Jim become such pals?"

Tracy gulped. "We've worked on some cases together — on opposite sides of course. But we respect each other."

"Respect, huh?" Tanner asked skeptically.

"What else would it be?" Tracy challenged.

Tanner sighed loudly. "It won't be until next week that I can look at the Acosta hit and run file."

"Is that normal to have to wait like that?"

"It's a cold case. I'm going to meet with the original investigator if I can. It will take a few days to organize that."

"Oh, okay. But I still say be careful."

"I will. You do the same."

It wasn't long after Tracy and Tanner ended their exchange when Rebecca put through a call from Arthur Pankow. And Tracy knew before she even reached for the receiver that this was going to be bad news for Keith Entwistle.

"Hello, Art," Tracy began. "I'm sorry I didn't call you back about the plea. I've had a rough day."

"Then *I'm* sorry, Tracy. It's about to get rougher."

"Just say it, Art," Tracy said, dreading his news.

"Cheryl Whittaker was in my office not too long ago. I'll cut to the chase. She told *me* that Cynthia Lydecker told *her* about her affair with your client."

Tracy remained stone faced. With her free hand she covered her eyes and then started rubbing her forehead. "Cynthia and Keith were having an affair," she repeated somberly.

"According to Cheryl they were. She wanted to keep it quiet for fear of what it might do to Cynthia Lydecker's reputation."

"She'd have her halo rescinded."

"I guess. Anyway, she said she couldn't keep it quiet anymore. So of course, I'll be adding her to our final witness list. So, here's the thing, Tracy. I'll give your client until the end of the day tomorrow to accept the State's offer: life sentence with possibility of parole. That's the best he gets. Otherwise, it will be life with no parole when the jury comes back with its guilty verdict."

Tracy said nothing. She was shaking her head.

"You still there?"

"Yes. I'll talk to Keith. Things sure have been going your way these past few days, haven't they?"

"Domino effect. Word got out about Finnegan and Cheryl probably got scared."

"That Keith might kill her too?"

"His gun killed two people. That's a fact."

"I'll be in touch, Art. Bye."

"I'm sorry, Tracy. But it was only a matter of time before this happened."

"Before *what* happened?"

"You picked the wrong client to defend."

Tracy said nothing. She put the receiver down. She then went into Tyler Wannamaker's office to give him the beyond-awful news.

Keith Entwistle — sans the missus — was in the conference room of Tracy Brubaker Shane & Associates Attorneys at Law within the hour. His anger was obvious.

"She's *lying*!" Entwistle shouted.

"Why would she do that, Keith?" Tracy asked.

"How the hell should I know?!"

Tyler was glaring at his brother-in-law. "You've really done it this time, Keith."

"Ty, I swear—"

"Just stop it, Keith. Just shut your goddamned mouth!"

"It *is* possible," Tracy began, trying to remain calm sounding, "that she's scared."

"*Scared?*" Tyler repeated sarcastically.

"If the SA's office has sold her on the idea that Keith is guilty then the discovery of Finnegan's body may have frightened her. Maybe she was afraid Keith would think Cynthia told her about the affair."

"There was no affair! I didn't even know that woman!"

"I realize that. I'm just giving a reason why she might lie. She's afraid she might be next, so she wants you locked up."

"Forgive me if I don't feel sorry for her," Entwistle snapped.

"All right, Keith. Art Pankow says if you plead to first degree murder by end of business tomorrow, you'll be eligible for parole. Otherwise, he's going for life with no parole."

"*NO!* No way! I didn't do this!"

Tyler shook his head. He looked at Tracy. "They got him. All they needed was a motive and now they have it."

"They have *one* witness, Ty. And unfortunately, we'll have to go after her."

"Damn straight!" Entwistle agreed.

"You want to vet her, Ty? I'm working some other aspects right now."

"You bet I will," Tyler answered.

"Maybe *she* killed Cynthia!" Entwistle offered. "She's lying to cover for herself!"

"How'd she get your gun, Keith?" Tyler asked skeptically.

"You know," Tracy mused, "she might have known the alarm code to Cynthia's house given how close they were. And she would have been in a position to make a copy of Cynthia's key. Maybe she *is* involved in this — although I'm not sure what her motive would be."

"See, Ty! Tracy still believes me!"

Tyler just continued glaring at Entwistle. Then he threw up his arms.

"All right Keith. I guess I should be feeling sorry for you. Katie...God, how is she going to handle this news?"

"I won't tell her just yet."

"You have to," Tracy said firmly. "It won't be long before the press finds out about this, and you don't want Katie finding out *that* way."

Entwistle shook his head. "Christ. I had just gotten her calmed down over the Finnegan thing."

"I'm sorry, Keith," Tracy offered.

"Can you be there with me when I tell her? You can explain why that woman might lie."

"Sorry, Keith. I can't tonight."

"I'll go with you, Keith," Tyler said. "I can try to explain things."

Entwistle smiled weakly, and then practically collapsed into the chair nearest to him. "Why is someone doing this to me?" he asked aloud. "I don't understand."

"Are you sure everything is all right with the business?" Tyler asked. "Isn't there anyone you can think of who has something against you?"

Entwistle shook his head. "I don't go around trying to hurt people or make them mad. I'm not that kind of person."

Tyler started nodding. "Yeah. I know you're not." He sighed. "I just don't understand this either."

"So, you believe me too, Tyler?" Entwistle asked hopefully.

His brother-in-law smiled. "Yeah, Keith. I believe you."

"Thank God. Thank God…"

"You two should probably tell Katie about this as soon as possible," Tracy told them. "I really don't have anything else. I'll let Art know your answer tomorrow. That may buy us some time."

"What do you mean?" Entwistle asked.

"If they think your mulling the plea offer over, they will probably remain tight-lipped. Once they know your answer though I'm sure the news will break about Cheryl Whittaker's claim."

"They'll want to poison the jury pool," Tyler said. "They'll want people to make up their minds about you *now*. And jury selection begins in a couple of weeks."

"Let's not focus on that right now," Tracy sighed. "The thing to do instead is make sure Katie is still on your side. When the time comes to make a statement regarding the affair, I want Katie standing next to you Keith, holding your hand. You get me?"

"Yes."

"All right. You fellas scoot then. I have some calls to make."

"I'll follow you home," Tyler told Entwistle. And then the fellas scooted.

After Tracy's first call was done, she made her second. "I'm afraid it's going to be another late night, honey," Tracy told her husband. "I'm sorry."

"Should we put Peter to bed?"

Tracy sighed. "Yes. I'll pump when I get home."

"Okay. You working at the office?"

"No. I have a meeting with a confidential informant."

By the time Tracy had arrived at Hooligan's House, Jim Lucas had already started his dinner. And he had had a few drinks too.

"Hi, Jim," Tracy said when she had reached his booth.

"Hi," Lucas smiled. "Have a seat."

Tracy did so. "I've never been here before," she said, trying not to appear as nervous as she felt.

"I don't come here too much myself. But I figure nobody will notice us. That wouldn't be good."

"I guess not."

"Want something? I wasn't sure if you'd be eating or not, so I went ahead and ordered. They have good sliders."

"I'm okay."

"Well, I did get you a glass of water, although it looks like the ice has melted."

"It's fine."

Lucas sighed. "Try not to be so nervous. I'm going to behave myself. And you can leave any time you want to."

Tracy smiled weakly. "Thanks for the water," she said as she reached for the beverage.

A server approached the table. "Get you anything?" she asked Tracy.

"No, thank you."

"I'll have another Rum and Coke," Lucas said.

"No problem sweetie." The waitress left them.

Lucas looked at Tracy. His arms and folded hands were now on the table. "Hell of a thing about Cheryl Whittaker, isn't it? I wasn't expecting that."

"Neither was I," Tracy responded glumly.

"I didn't think you would be. But I figured I should call you first — before Arthur did. I wasn't sure I'd be able to get a hold of you afterwards. I'm sure you've been very busy the last few hours. I'm just sorry you didn't take me up on my offer earlier."

"Why *did* you call me, Jim? I still don't really understand why you did."

Lucas looked at Tracy, hesitating to answer. But when his drink arrived, he took a long sip and said, "Well, I guess it's because I'm in love with you."

Tracy sighed loudly. "Oh Jim—"

"Don't worry. I know you'll never return the feelings. I wish I could just send them packing. But I can't. So, there it is."

Tracy looked at the table. "You have to. I like you and I want us to be friends. But I don't like the idea that you're…It makes me uncomfortable."

"I'm sorry."

"You don't even *know* me. How can you be in love with me when you don't even know me?"

"I know enough about you, Tracy. I know your smart and your funny and you have a good heart. And you're incredibly beautiful."

"Please don't—"

"I don't meet too many people like you given what I do. The job makes you cynical and skeptical. You're always wondering if people are being honest with you. But I never had any doubts with you. Even if I thought your clients were really guilty, I never doubted you believed they were innocent. Of course, it always seems to turn out you are right and I'm not."

"You were doing your job. As angry as I got with you sometimes, I never took it personally."

"I know. You wouldn't be here if you had." Lucas finished his drink. "This Edward Lydecker: he has ambitions."

"Ambitions?"

"He's probably going to run for a congressional seat next election cycle. He has his eyes on the White House. You understand what I'm telling you?"

Tracy gulped. "Yes. I do."

"I guess you can't tell me why you have Elias looking at an unsolved hit and run."

"Not at this point."

"Mm. Well this is the part where I become your confidential informant."

Tracy leaned in. "Okay."

"We talked to a lot of the people Cynthia Lydecker approached through the years. Have you heard of Y3D: Youth Against Drunk and Drugged Driving?"

"Sure."

"She was a big supporter of theirs. A personal one too — not just through her foundation."

"Okay."

"Funny thing though. We checked through her personal financial stuff just to see if there was anything there, you know?"

"Sure."

"She didn't take any of her donations to Y3D as deductions on her individual tax returns. Not one dollar. I mean in 2017 alone she donated $25,000 — personally."

Tracy just blinked. If Tracy had had any doubts about Cynthia Lydecker's involvement with Jeannine Acosta's death, they were now gone.

"And then Elias comes along looking at an old H&R where the victim was most likely hit by a drunk on his way to or from a party at Cynthia Lydecker's school. I looked into it myself."

"What did you find?"

"The investigating detective — Bujarki — hasn't returned my calls yet."

"Oh."

"I know what you're thinking."

"Because you're thinking it too."

"I wish I could find something tying your client to Ed Lydecker. Of course, maybe we just did."

"What?"

"Come on, Tracy. Isn't it possible that Keith Entwistle *was* having an affair with Cynthia Lydecker, and her ex-husband found about it?"

"And that's why he picked on Keith."

"Yes. It's pretty clear to me — as I'm sure it is to you — that whoever shot Cynthia wanted the gun to be found and traced back to your client. So, unless he had some bizarre reason for framing himself, I don't see him being the trigger man."

Tracy leaned back. "Does Ed Lydecker know anything about this — what you're thinking, I mean."

"He might. There's nothing official on-file about him other than confirming his alibi as a matter of procedure. But who knows?"

"His fiancée is his alibi, right?"

"You bet."

"Another Rum and Coke for you, sweetie?"

Both Lucas and Tracy looked at the smiling server who seemingly appeared out of nowhere. "How 'bout just a Coke?"

"Sure."

They watched her leave. Lucas then said, "I really should quit this drinking. I'm very close to becoming something I don't want to be." Lucas frowned. "Anyway, I suppose Debra Dooley could be lying. Or maybe she's a sound sleeper. I understand they're both early birds, so I doubt they'd both be up at two o'clock in the morning."

"And what about George Finnegan? Anything to tie him to Lydecker?"

"So far there's nothing."

Tracy sighed. "What are you going to do?"

"The orders from up on high right now are to connect your client to Finnegan. After Cheryl Whittaker's visit everyone thinks Cynthia's murder is a done deal. Your client will be convicted, Tracy."

"Jim—"

"If he doesn't take that plea offer then it won't be long before the affair is front page news. Alastair Conroy already knows what Cheryl said and is waiting for Pankow's call about your client's answer. He believes your client killed his daughter just like everyone else."

"Except you and me."

Lucas smiled. "Well, let's just say I'm open to alternate possibilities."

"I'll accept that," Tracy smiled in return.

"There is one odd thing that I don't quite understand yet that I have to work out."

"What's that?"

"You remember Cynthia's photo wall, right?"

"Sure. I took some photos of it."

"Oh right. Well, in every single picture, Cynthia and her companion appear to be at some gala function. They're all dressed up and maybe have a cocktail in their hands. And they are more or less facing the camera. That is, all except one."

"Oh?"

"Yeah. There's one where she's just talking to someone. It looks like it was taken at some meeting or something."

"Okay."

"Thing is the person she's talking to in that picture is someone from Y3D. It's curious."

"You think it means something?"

"I'm not sure. As I said, I want to work that out."

"Okay."

"In the meantime, you need to watch yourself. I mean it."

"Brian told me the same thing."

"Well, listen to him then. I'm getting those looks."

"Looks?"

"From other cops — the kind of looks you get when something's up. I got them sometimes on the murder cases *you* handled, usually after I had egg on my face. But this time, I'm getting them before I've even finished breakfast. You understand?"

"I think so," Tracy chuckled. "You've been hanging around me too long. You're making food metaphors."

"Maybe" Lucas grinned. "But my point remains that there's something going on here that people *other than me* seem to know about. Maybe it's just because of who Cynthia's father is. Or maybe it's something else. My partner — Bill Culpepper — doesn't seem to notice anything. But he's new. I don't know if I can trust him yet. I feel like I'm on my own here."

Tracy wanted to reach out for Lucas' hand, just as an expression of support and comfort. But given the circumstances she opted not to.

"I'm sorry, Jim. I guess I never appreciated your position in all of this."

"Forget it. I wouldn't really care except…Well…I don't want to see anything happen to you."

"Sorry it took so long, sweetie." The server placed the cold drink in front of Lucas. He and Tracy were just looking at each other.

"I don't really have anything else. But I think you're right to be looking into Jeannine Acosta's death. Maybe Elias will have better luck than I've had so far."

Tracy nodded. "Thank you, Jim. I mean it. Thank you."

"You can thank me by being paranoid. You may have reason to be. You may have…Well, just watch yourself."

Tracy slid to the end of the booth and then stood. "You be careful too, Jim. I don't want anything to happen to *you* either."

"Sure."

The attorney frowned. "Are you all right to drive? Do you need a ride a home?"

"I'm not leaving quite yet. I don't have a family awaiting my return. Don't worry about me."

Tracy forced a smile. "All right. Goodnight, Jim. And thank you again."

"You're welcome."

Tracy turned and exited the pub, while Lucas watched her. He wanted to walk her to her car. He wanted to do more than that. He had told her he loved her; probably a stupid thing to do. But he didn't care. In his secret fantasies she and Brian had a falling out, and he was there to catch her. Then they would be together. A woman like that…he bet she was very giving. And he wanted to receive. He let his thoughts travel a dirty road and now he wanted to stand up and go after her. Instead, he remained seated and motioned toward his server. He wanted at least one more Rum and Coke before the lonely trek home. At least…

Later that night in her home office, Tracy finished typing up her notes from her meeting with Jim Lucas. She listed the source as "confidential informant" for her own amusement. After emailing the report to her work address, she shut down her computer and went to her bedroom. She was already dressed in her nightwear.

"You okay?" Brian asked as she entered.

"Yeah, I guess."

"I don't like that answer, love. You shouldn't have to guess."

Tracy smiled. "I'm fine. It's just been a hell of a week, and there's still Friday left."

"Are you working this weekend?"

"I don't know yet. I guess it depends on when the news breaks about Cheryl Whittaker's claim. We'll have to come up with a statement for our journalist friends to nip the rumors in the bud."

"I see. Want a neck massage?"

"I'd *love* a neck massage," Tracy smiled.

"Then come over here and sit down."

Tracy sat on Brian's side of the bed with her back to her husband. As his hands started moving about her neck and shoulders she said, "I love you, Brian. You know that don't you?"

"Of course, I do," he answered, kissing her neck.

"I'd never cheat on you."

Brian stopped his massage. Tracy turned to look at him. "I know that, Tracy. You don't have to tell me."

"I wanted to, though."

"Why? What's going on?"

She sighed. "I guess I've been encountering infidelity a lot lately. It makes me sad. Why do people do it?"

"I don't know. People probably have all kinds of reasons."

"I guess."

"And for the record, I love you and would never cheat on you, either."

Tracy grinned. "Not with my mother watching over you, you sure won't."

They both laughed softly. Then Tracy turned her back again so Brian could continue practicing his art of stress relief. When he had finished, Tracy and he laid down so that Tracy could rest her head on his chest, a smile on her face. Brian had his arm around her. At least for now, she felt completely safe and secure. Sleep soon came to her.

The Shane's land line started ringing at 1:37 a.m. Tracy sat up and rubbed her eyes. Then she rolled over and grabbed the receiver. "Hello?"

"Tracy, it's Elias."

"Oh. El. What is it?"

There was a long pause. "Tracy…Tracy I…It's Jim Lucas."

Tracy could tell Tanner was upset. "What about Jim, El?"

"Jim's dead, Tracy. Somebody gunned him down tonight right outside his house."

"OH MY GOD!" Tracy cried out as she stood up, stirring Brian to consciousness.

"The investigating officer will want to talk to you."

"What is it?" Brian asked.

"Why, El?"

"Because he didn't die instantly, and the civilian who came to his aid said Jim said only one thing before he lost consciousness."

"What did he say?" Tracy asked, now in tears.

"He said your name, Tracy. The last thing he said was your name."

Chapter 10

The murder of Detective James Nathaniel Lucas was the dominant story Friday morning. How could it not be? The primary question being put to every live-at-the-scene correspondent by every news anchor was whether Lucas' murder was related to the death of Cynthia Lydecker. It was a question without, at present, a definite answer.

Tracy was seated in the office of Lieutenant Worth at the Northeastern District. She had been there since 4:00 a.m. It was now almost 6:00. Tracy had lost count how many times she'd been offered and turned down coffee. Caffeine was just one of the sacrifices this nursing mother had made.

"I'm really sorry to have kept you waiting all this time, Mrs. Shane," Worth said as he sat down in his chair.

"Please call me Tracy," she said quietly.

"All right," Worth responded. "Look. I know who you are. So, I'm just going to ask my questions and then you can go home. What were the phone calls you and Jim were exchanging yesterday about?"

Tracy gulped. "It's related to a case I'm working on. I'm afraid I can't go into details."

"You've got to be kidding me," Worth said sternly.

"I'm sorry."

"We know Jim was at Hooligan's House last night. We found a credit card receipt in his wallet, which helpfully included the name of his waitress. She told us he had someone with him — a woman. This woman matches your description. And his mobile phone shows calls to you."

"It was me."

"Why were the two you having dinner?"

"We weren't. I had a glass of water and that was it."

"Tracy, I'm very tired and upset. Can we please stop with the technical back and forth?"

"I'm tired and upset too. And I can't go into the nature of our meeting. It's work related. I'm sorry."

"You're sorry."

"Yes."

Worth stood up. "You are aware he said the name Tracy before he died?"

"Yes, I am."

"The only Tracy we know that he knew was you."

"Okay."

"So why did he say your name?"

Tracy gulped. She felt the tears were about to return. "I don't know," she fibbed. How Lucas felt about her was no one's business as far as Tracy was concerned.

"Forgive me, but I don't believe you."

"I'm sorry, Lieutenant."

"Yeah, I can tell."

"Look, sir. There's nothing I can tell you. I left Detective Lucas after our meeting and went home. It was probably 8:30 p.m. or so when I left. Maybe the waitress can confirm the time."

"That sounds right."

"I went home, had some warmed-up dinner, worked a little, and then went to bed. My husband will vouch for me."

"You're *not* a suspect, Tracy."

"Okay."

Worth sat back down. "Who knew about this meeting of yours?"

"Why do you think that had anything to do with what happened?"

"I don't know either way. Now can you please answer my question?"

"Okay. The only person besides Jim and me who knew I had a meeting last night was my husband, Brian. I called him to let him know I'd be home late. But I didn't tell him where the meeting was going to be or with whom I was meeting."

"And that's everyone."

"Yes."

"You're sure."

"*Yes*, Lieutenant. I didn't even tell anyone in my own firm what my plans were for the night, so they couldn't have in turn told anyone else. And Brian wouldn't have told anyone. Is that clear enough for you?"

Worth sighed. "All right."

"Was this person who found Jim able to tell you anything?"

Worth shook his head. "No. She heard the shots and looked out her window. She saw Jim lying there and that's it."

Tracy wiped her eyes. "I wish I could give you specifics, Lieutenant. But I can't, especially since I don't even know if what happened is related to my case."

"The one you were meeting with Jim about."

"Right."

"Listen. Somebody who guns down a cop in the middle of the night won't hesitate to do the same thing to a civilian. Do you understand what I'm telling you?"

"You're trying to scare me."

"Damn right I am! Now what were you and Jim meeting about?!"

"I'm sorry, Lieutenant. I can't."

"You can't huh? All right then. We're done. For now. Go home." Worth looked down at his desk.

Tracy stood up slowly, opened the door, and then navigated her way towards the exit doors. She should have been prepared for what awaited her on the other side, but she wasn't.

"Tracy! Tracy! Can you talk to us?"

Tracy wasn't sure who called out her name because there were suddenly too many people to count. The journalists moved with the urgency of a pack of piranhas that had just spotted their breakfast.

"Does Detective Lucas' death have anything to do with Cynthia Lydecker's murder?" someone shouted.

"Why did the police want to meet with you?" another voice called out.

"Is the rumor true the detective's dying words were your name?" still another asked.

"Were you and Detective Lucas having an affair?"

The last question caused Tracy to stop moving. She recognized the inquisitor's voice. She looked up and saw Shirley Hammersmith smiling at her.

"How 'bout it, Tracy?" Shirley chided. "You and Lucas have something going on?"

It was a rare thing that Tracy, as furious as she now was, could rein in her ire. She glared at the reporter and just said, "No." Then she continued moving through the crowd until she found her car — and freedom.

Everyone was awake when Tracy arrived home. It was now just past 7:00, and she was debating whether to take a power nap and go in late, or to say the hell with it and go in after taking a quick shower. The hugs she received from Nicole and the smiles bestowed on her by Peter moved her to tears again. She felt an impulse to call Rebecca and tell her to close the office forever.

Tracy managed to keep her emotions in check during breakfast. When she was finished, she headed towards the shower. Maybe it wouldn't be such a quick one after all; the hot water felt so damn good when it started hitting her bare skin. There were more tears to shed too. And when she finally did exit the stall, throw on her robe, and come into the bedroom, Brian was waiting for her.

"Are you okay?" he asked.

"No," she answered honestly.

They shared an embrace. "I'm sorry."

"Thank you." She squeezed him tightly.

"I saw some of the coverage."

Tracy released him and stepped back. "Coverage?"

"When you came out of the police station this morning. They had the thing subtitled and everything."

"That didn't take long, did it?" Tracy turned and moved towards her bureau.

"Is it true?"

Tracy turned back around. "Is what true?"

"That Jim Lucas said your name before he died. You were so upset after the call the only thing you told me was that someone had killed him."

Tracy sighed. "That's what they tell me."

"Why do you think he did?"

Tracy gulped. "What does it matter?" She folded her arms.

"Why are you so upset over his death? He arrested Crystal for murder in case you've forgotten."

"Of course, I haven't *forgotten*, Brian. But a man I knew is dead. *Murdered*. Forgive me if I can't just put on a happy face."

Brian folded his arms. "And he also arrested that kid for stabbing that bully. You liked that kid a lot and Lucas pissed you off. So, I don't…" Brian's expression changed. And then he knew. "My God, that was the case when…It was Lucas wasn't it? It was that goddamned Lucas who kissed you?! Wasn't it, Tracy? *Wasn't it?!*"

Tracy still had her arms folded. She tried to maintain a look of defiance at Brian's inopportune interrogation. But she couldn't keep it up. Her face turned red, and the tears returned with a vengeance.

"YES!" she finally screamed. "ARE YOU HAPPY NOW?! ARE YOU?! ARE YOU HAPPY THAT YOU KNOW NOW, BRIAN?!"

"Tracy I—"

"HOW DARE YOU?! HOW DARE YOU ASK ME ABOUT THIS NOW?!"

"I didn't mean to—"

"Are you glad he's dead, Brian? Do you think that's what he deserved for a few seconds of sin? Or maybe he deserves more! Maybe after he's buried, we can go dig up his body and you can *KICK IT AROUND A BIT*!"

"Jesus, Tracy, calm down—"

"DON'T you tell me to calm down, Brian! Don't you *dare*!" Tracy covered her face and sat down on the bed, sobbing.

Brian lowered his head in shame. Nice going, idiot. He went over to his wife, knelt in front of her, and embraced her firmly. She didn't resist.

"I'm sorry, Tracy. I'm a complete asshole. I'm sorry."

"I love you, Brian," she said, still sobbing.

"I know. And I know that accusation of an affair was total bullshit."

"I didn't—"

"I know you didn't. I'll never bring it up again. I promise. I won't say another word unless you want to talk about it."

"I can't now."

"I understand. I'm sorry. I really am. I guess you thought of him as a friend."

"He *was* a friend, Brian. And he was El's partner at one time. So, El is hurting too. And we're both thinking about my dad right now too."

"Because he was Elias' partner."

"I should try to call him and see how he's doing."

"Are you going to work?"

"Yes. I have my other family there. Some of them have resources I don't. And I don't want my babies to see me like this. They might get upset too. Kids notice that you know."

"Of course."

Tracy sighed and loosened her grip. Brian pulled back. They kissed. They looked into each other's eyes for several moments.

"I have to go clean up my face," Tracy said finally.

Brian nodded. "I'm sorry."

"I know. You don't have to say it anymore."

Tracy stood up and returned to the bathroom. Brian sat on the bed. He was now fighting an impulse of his own. He wanted to march into the bathroom and tear away that robe his wife was wearing. He suddenly wanted her so badly. It wasn't lost on him that some of their most intense sexual encounters had come after one of their fights. And this one, however brief, had been a doozy. He felt like a perverted variation of Pavlov's dog.

He stood up. He didn't think that's what Tracy wanted right now; it might even make her angry. But he couldn't stay where he was. Soon she'd be back and removing her robe, with no night shadows to obscure any detail. It didn't matter that she'd had two children: her naked body still excited him. *She* still excited him. He moved quickly towards the door.

"Poor Jim Lucas," Brian thought. At least he'd no longer be wondering about what he could never have had.

When Elias Tanner, Sr. arrived at Tracy's office it was almost lunchtime. The mood of the office was so somber that Tracy had Rebecca just order a tray of sandwiches and the relevant fixings. The office would serve as host to an unofficial wake.

Tracy and Tanner embraced much longer than usual. Tanner finally kissed her cheek and pulled away. They sat next to each other on the sofa that was in her office.

"I saw what happened after you left the precinct," Tanner began. He and Tracy were holding hands. "I can't tell you how sorry I am about that."

"I wasn't thinking, El. I should have gone out the back."

"That Shirley Hammersmith," Tanner said angrily.

"Don't worry about it, El. I kept my cool."

Tanner smiled. "You did. I'm very proud of you. I thought you were going to belt her one."

Tracy chuckled. "I gave myself a raincheck."

Tanner laughed. Then he bore a serious expression. "Tracy, what was going on between you and Jim? Will you tell me?"

Tracy sighed. "I don't know *how* to tell you, El. He was your friend."

Tanner nodded. "He was in love with you, wasn't he?"

Tracy blinked. "Well…"

"I knew it when he came to see you in the hospital after your car ordeal last year. I could tell."

"And how does that make you feel?"

"Feel?"

"You're not mad at him, are you? You still think of me as your daughter, right?"

Tanner smiled. "Of course, I do. And Jim's still my friend. He was never inappropriate with you, was he?"

Tracy squirmed a bit. "There was a very brief moment when he kissed me. But he was so sorry about it, El. And we put it behind us."

"I never knew that."

"Good; no one was *supposed* to know. I didn't even tell Brian. Well, I told him when it happened but left out Jim's name. But after this morning, Brian figured it out. And I'm glad he did. I didn't want it to come out this way of course. But..."

"Tracy," Tanner chuckled, "it's okay. You don't have to explain everything. I get it."

"Sorry."

"It's fine."

"I guess you want to know what Jim and I talked about last night."

"If you can tell me."

"Sure. It's related to Keith Entwistle's case." Tracy told Tanner everything about her and Lucas' conversation. Tanner's expression grew more infuriate with each new detail. "Now, I don't know if Jim's death is related to this. But I think it is."

"Yeah, it would seem so."

"Somebody must have been following him. And this person probably saw him with me — the defense for the very person this killer framed. I bet he panicked and followed Jim home."

"This coward shot him in the back. Jim never had a chance."

Tracy shook her head. "What do you think we should do?"

Tanner looked at her. "You're in danger. And don't you dare say something like 'We don't know that.' Because we do. Whoever's behind this couldn't have foreseen who the defense attorney would end up being. He's panicking."

"You think I should drop this case? How many times have we been through that before?"

"Too many. If this guy thinks Jim told you something, then..."

"I get it."

"So, since you're probably not going to drop this thing, just what are your plans?"

"Crys arranged a bodyguard for me once — after Brian got shot."

"Not a bad idea."

Tracy sighed and stood up. She folded her arms and started moving about the room. Tanner watched her. He watched the expression on her face change. Whatever she was thinking was making her very angry.

"You're right, El. This prick is a coward. When the car he was driving — or at least *in* — hit Jeannine Acosta: he ran. He used some low-life ex SA investigator to help frame Keith and then plugged *him*. He shot Jim in the back. He's a chicken shit."

"So?"

"He's afraid of being exposed, obviously. And Jim must have been close to exposing him."

"I get that."

"So, we need to put him in a position where he can't hide."

"Position?"

Tracy looked at Tanner. "In court El; on the stand."

"In court."

"Yes. Soon I'll be calling Art to turn down the plea offer. So, this thing is going to trial. Then we're going to build our case to tear down every piece of so-called evidence Art and his office has. I want you to do whatever you have to do to get a look at the hit and run file. Based on what Jim told me, I'll subpoena Cynthia's tax records so I can have proof she felt guilty about something involving drunk driving. Why else wouldn't she have deducted her donations? And Jim also mentioned something about one of the photos on the wall. I'll look into that too. And there are some other things brewing here as well. So, unless this piece of garbage kills everyone in this office, he's going down, El. And I'm taking him there."

Tanner stood up. He put his hands on his hips, smiled, and started shaking his head.

"What?" Tracy asked.

"You remind of your father when you get like this."

"Like what?"

"Defiant. Purposeful. Confident."

Tracy smiled. "You don't have a problem with that, do you?"

"No; not at all. Just be—"

"Careful. Yes, El."

There was a knock on Tracy's door.

"Entre vous," Tracy called out.

Tyler Wannamaker entered. "You two might want to come to the conference room. Cheryl Whittaker's claim just made the news."

Tracy shook her head. "Well, I guess I have no reason to put Art off any longer."

Shirley Hammersmith was summarizing the case against Keith Entwistle when Tracy, Tanner, and Tyler entered the conference room. Rebecca and Neal were there already. Everyone stared at the monitor.

"…Neither the police nor the State Attorney's office would confirm they now have evidence regarding an affair between Cynthia Lydecker and Keith Entwistle, the man accused of killing her. But WFFE's sources, who wish to remain unnamed, are telling us that someone *has* come forward with knowledge of such a relationship. And the mystery surrounding Cynthia Lydecker's death may just have gotten a little less mysterious. This is Shirley Hammersmith reporting live from the Northeastern District of the Baltimore City Police Department for WFFE News Watch."

"Mute this bitch," Tracy grunted. She turned to Tyler. "We need to get working on a statement refuting this."

"I started working on that already."

"And Katie's onboard?"

"Yes. For now, anyway. Let's just hope someone else doesn't make the same claim as Cheryl did."

Tracy grinned. "I already have some ideas about Cheryl Whittaker."

"Great!" Tyler enthused. "And I got that information from the chicken box numbers you wanted. I think you'll like it."

"Chicken box numbers?" Neal asked.

"Tracking code," Tracy answered. "Okay. I'll be making a list of things we need to do before the trial starts. I'll assign them as appropriate. In the meantime, everyone here, keep your eyes open. I don't want to scare anybody, but if Jim Lucas was killed by the person who killed Cynthia Lydecker and George Finnegan, then we shouldn't pretend he may not be finished."

"And let me get this out right now," Tyler added, "in case anyone was wondering: Katie assures me Keith was home with her last night when Detective Lucas was murdered."

Everyone looked at Tyler for a few moments. Then Tracy said, "The thought Keith did that never entered my mind, Ty."

"Well...I was just sayin'."

"Okay, then," Tracy continued, "Beck ordered this lovely food. I say we all eat. First though I'll call Art and tell him where he can file that plea offer."

Everyone chuckled. Tracy seemed determined as ever.

"Better make sure we save Tracy some pickle spears," Neal said after she'd left to make her call. "Or else..."

There was more laughter. Then everyone settled down to eat and quiet filled the room.

Rebecca Dietz was mildly shocked at the figure that approached her. He asked, "Is Tracy Shane available or has she left for the day?"

"She's here, Mr. Conroy."

"Oh, you know who I am then."

"Yes, sir. Let me call Tracy."

"Thank you, young lady."

It wasn't very long before Rebecca was showing Alastair Conroy to Tracy's private office.

"Mr. Conroy," Tracy said while coming from behind the desk with her hand ready to shake his, "it's a pleasure to meet you."

Conroy smiled as they shook. "And it's a pleasure to meet you too, Mrs. Shane."

"Please call me Tracy. And let me also say how sorry I am about your daughter. She did some amazing things. She must have been quite a person."

"Thank you, Tracy. She did and she was. But now...this news about an affair..."

"We don't believe it either, Mr. Conroy. Not for a second."

"Oh?"

"My client, as you know, has denied even knowing your daughter. His story hasn't changed."

"I see."

"Please sit down, Mr. Conroy. Would you like something to drink?"

"Oh, no. Your receptionist already offered."

"Very well. What can I do for you then?"

"What can you do? Get your client to take the plea offer."

"Mr. Conroy—"

"Now you listen. Today is just the beginning. They're going to spend the next few months tearing my daughter apart. My baby — who never hurt anybody. You yourself know what kind of person she was."

"Yes, sir; I do."

"Arthur Pankow assures me he has enough to convict that Keith Entwistle. That *murderer*!"

"He didn't do it, Mr. Conroy."

"Of course, he did!"

Tracy sighed. "My client insists he's innocent and therefore will not accept any plea offer. That's all there is to it, sir."

Conroy stood up. "I thought you were a person of character. I thought you didn't defend *murderers*!"

"I don't. Doesn't that tell you that maybe Arthur Pankow may not be right about this?"

Conroy looked at her. "Well…But the evidence…"

"Is all circumstantial, sir."

"Lawyer talk!"

Tracy stood up. "Mr. Conroy, if you're so concerned about what the press might say about your daughter, see if SA will push for a gag order. I'd support it. I don't want lies about this case spread about any more than you do."

"A gag order?"

"Yes."

"Mm."

"Is there anything else, Mr. Conroy? It's late and my people want to go home and enjoy the weekend."

Conroy blinked. "Your client had better be innocent just as you say."

Tracy didn't like the tone Conroy had just used. "What does that mean?"

"Whoever killed my daughter will not get away with it. Do you understand me?"

"Are you threatening my client, sir?"

"Not if he's innocent as you say he is. Goodbye, Tracy."

Conroy turned and left Tracy's office. And it wasn't long before Tray got the hell out of there too.

"Even though we were divorced, I still cared for Cynthia very much," Edward Lydecker was telling Shirley Hammersmith. "So, given everything that's happened, I think it only right to postpone our wedding until after the trial is over."

"Oh, good grief," Tracy groaned.

"And that's okay with you?" Shirley asked the woman seated next to Lydecker.

"Oh, I *completely* understand, Shirley," Debra Dooley answered. "Cindy and I were friends too. We all had lunch together on a regular basis. How can we truly enjoy what's supposed to be a special day with this awfulness all around us?"

"Blow it out your ass, lady!" Tracy shouted at the living room's television screen.

"Tracy!" Brian growled. "If I wanted to watch *Mystery Science Theater 3000,* I'd be watching it."

"What about these allegations of an affair with the accused? Do you really think Cynthia would do that, Edward?"

Lydecker sighed. "I am sure as I am sitting here that Cindy was faithful to our own marriage vows. But we did have our issues and she wasn't the same person after our marriage was over as she was before. I really can't answer that question one way or the other."

"Way to throw your ex under the bus, asshole!"

"Damn it, Tracy!"

Tracy stood up. "I don't even know why I'm watching this shit."

"Hey, easy on the language, okay?"

"The kids are asleep, Brian."

"But you shouldn't get in the habit."

"Fine!"

Brian took a deep breath and stood up. "Tracy, let's go to bed early. You didn't get very much sleep last night."

"Those two make me want to throw up. If they really cared so much, they wouldn't have waited until the plea offer was turned down to postpone. They would have done it months ago when the trial date was set. They hoped it would just all go away. But it didn't."

"I know. I agree with you a hundred percent."

"And as for the third stooge, you *know* how I feel about her. Shirley does like to toss accusations of infidelity around, doesn't she?"

"She does. But I told you I never for a second believed it."

"But somebody may have."

Brian's shoulders dropped. "So that's what's really bothering you. You think people out there think you and Lucas had something."

"Of course, some of them do. People will believe anything."

"Try not to worry about—"

"If Shirley Hammersmith says one more word; makes any kind of insinuation; does anything to impugn my character…I swear, Brian, I will go after her and that station of hers with every means at my disposal."

"I believe you; I do. Now try and relax."

"What?"

"You're tired. Let's go to bed."

"Oh. That's a good idea."

"You go on up. I'll take the dog out and join you soon."

"Okay," Tracy smiled, her equilibrium returning. "Make sure to be careful outside."

"Bonkers *does* bark at strangers."

"Oh. Well don't forget to lock everything up tight and set the alarm."

"Okay. Now go on upstairs and get into to bed. Clothing is optional."

Tracy chuckled. "Oh, it is, is it?"

"You have some energy left. Let's use it positively."

"Uh-huh. See you upstairs then."

Tracy gave Brian one of her infamous grins and then trotted up the steps. He was still looking upward when he heard Bonkers starting to whine. Brian looked and saw the pooch standing by the back door.

"Sorry, boy," Brian said.

He moved towards the sliding door and released the hound. The final potty break of the night went without incident. After Bonkers was done, he quickly came back in and made his own way to Nicole's room, where his sleeping-rug awaited him. Brian meanwhile secured the house, and then approached his bedroom with anticipation. The way his wife had grinned at him had told him what he could expect when he entered. He wasn't disappointed.

One of the elements that contributed to making sexual intimacy with Tracy continually exciting was the unpredictability of it. That is, Tracy was a woman of many moods. And they could manifest themselves in various ways in the bedroom. Today, she was overtired and irritated. This morning they had had a rather heated exchange. This all combined to make Tracy a very vigorous partner on this particular occasion. There had been little foreplay. But Brian hadn't minded, although it was all over much sooner than he would have liked. On the other hand, that meant there could be an encore later if they both could stay awake.

Tracy was on top of Brian, the side of her head resting on his chest. They were both covered with sweat so they were otherwise coverless. The air conditioning felt very good.

"Feeling a little better?" Brian asked while playing with her hair.

"*Mm hmm*," Tracy cooed.

"Peter didn't make a sound or budge an inch."

"He's a sound sleeper."

"Tomorrow we'll spend the day together doing fun family stuff. We can take Nicole to the park, and she can play on the swings while one of us pushes Peter in his stroller."

"And my mother can man the first aid kit just in case."

Brian chuckled. "And we can go to the pool."

"The water will still be cold though."

"Nicole won't mind."

"I guess I can just walk around with her and Peter in the baby pool."

"…Wearing that bikini you got last year."

"I don't know about that," Tracy chortled.

"Yeah: you might make all the other moms — and every other woman for that matter — jealous."

"Oh, good grief."

"I'm serious though. I see how happy you are when you're playing with the kids. So that's what you should do."

Tracy started kissing Brian's chest. "I like playing with my hubby too."

"Oh boy."

"Did you just call me a boy?"

"Oh woman."

"That's better."

"Let me see your face, Tracy. Let me look at you."

Tracy repositioned herself so the marrieds were face to face, eye to eye. They would take things slower this time. But they'd still arrive at the destination they wanted. *When* wasn't important.

After Brian had fallen asleep, Tracy pulled the covers over them. She kissed his back since he was on his side, and then she lay flat on her back. Sleep was trying to overtake her, but her mind wasn't quite ready. She thought about Jim Lucas and the warning he gave her but didn't heed himself. And she wondered why Cheryl Whittaker was lying about the affair. What did she hope to accomplish? She had a family of her own. Why would she risk perjury? Tracy also thought about Edward Lydecker and Debra Dooley, posturing for the camera. Tracy wasn't sure which one was the dog, and which one was the pony in that show they had put on tonight. Because that's what it was. There was no sincerity to it at all.

And what about Keith and Katie? How would they perform for the camera when they challenged the rumor of an affair? They would have to keep it short and simple. And then say nothing else about it. There would be no back and forth. If Alastair Conroy did put pressure on Arthur Pankow, maybe there wouldn't be any more press coverage anyway.

Conroy: a man with more money than he knew what to do with. He had threatened Keith Entwistle — *if* he got acquitted. What would he do? Destroy him financially, maybe. Drive him out of town, or at least turn him into a pariah. Or could it be something worse?

Tracy turned on her side. The trial was about a month and a half away. They had to keep it together until then. Watch their backs too. Because someone was watching them. They'd gather their evidence and build their case, but cautiously. And then they'd be ready. They'd have to be. This case was now more than just serving her client. She wanted to deliver Jim Lucas' killer to the police. If there was ever a case that she wanted to solve, this was it.

Well, except perhaps for the case involving the man sleeping next to her. Tracy moved towards the middle of the bed; reached over and grabbed Brian's hand; and managed to prod him so he turned and wrapped his arm around her. He kissed her neck and then rested his head against the top of her back. She felt safe now. She managed to clear her mind so that she could find rest too. The unrest could wait. There was plenty of *that* still to come.

Chapter 11

"I don't know about this," Katie Entwistle grumbled.

Tyler frowned. "Why now, all of a sudden? I thought you were fine with this."

"*Why not*? Jesus, Ty. People are dying, even so-called *confidential* informants. And now you want me to go out there and basically flip this guy off!"

Tracy sighed loudly. "Katie, I know this is scary. And if you don't want to do this, we won't. But the press is going to be bothering you and Keith, wanting a response. If you're proactive and you give them one right now, *you* control the situation."

"Listen, Katie," Tyler said angrily. "If you have such a problem with this, then how can you ask Tracy to continue to defend Keith, huh? Isn't *she* putting herself in danger too? Do you know how many times over the last five years or so someone has actually come after *her*? Do you, Katie?"

"Ty, you don't have to—"

Tracy's associate interrupted her. "Don't even say it, Tracy. Don't! I've had it! I've had it with this whole damn thing!" Tyler looked back at his sister. "I want to know once and for all if you believe in Keith's innocence. Do you?"

Katie Entwistle looked at the attorneys and then at her husband. Then she smiled weakly at her spouse. "Of course, I do."

"Fine," her brother said firmly. "Now, let's get this over with."

"Let's," Tracy agreed.

She moved quickly to her office door and was followed by Tyler and the Entwistles. The eager media members had gathered outside the law firm's office building where Tracy had instructed them to meet. Since it was a Saturday, she didn't think it would be a hindrance to her fellow lessees. Not too many people would be at their workplace on a beautiful Saturday in June.

Keith and Katie Entwistle, hand in hand, exited the building first. The attorneys were side by side and behind them. Soon however the quartet was all standing next to each other. As Tracy and company approached the gathered, the questions started. Tracy shook her head and waited for everyone to shut their damn mouths. When they did so, she began.

"Thank you all for coming here today. I promise this will be brief. Also, we will not be taking any questions afterwards. Now, my client is as shocked as anyone over the supposed confirmation of an alleged affair between him and Cynthia Lydecker. My client continues to deny such a relationship with the woman he is accused of killing. As to the motive or motives why someone would make such a claim, well…we won't comment on that right now. Instead, we will deal with that during the trial. Keith and Katie therefore would appreciate you respecting their privacy during the next several weeks as they continue to struggle with this nightmare they find themselves in. Again, thank you all for taking time out to be here. Good afternoon."

Tracy turned and then everyone in her party followed. As she had expected, questions were shouted. But she continued to move quickly towards the entranceway, doing her best to ignore what was being asked. Tyler and Keith entered last and made sure to pull the glass doors shut so the automatic locks would engage — such was one of the benefits of having the conference on a Saturday at a security-conscious office building.

Once the party had returned to the suite Tracy said, "I think that went rather well. Whether they'll respect my request to leave you guys alone, I can't say."

"I'm surprised you let WFFE know, Tracy," Tyler said. "After what that Hammersmith bitch did."

Tracy chuckled. "Come on, Ty. You've heard of keeping your enemies closer to you than your friends, right? If I had dissed her, it would have made matters worse. And you can bet Keith or Katie here would have had a WFFE microphone in their face at some point.”

“Well, is it true?” Katie asked.

“What?” Tracy returned.

“You and that cop were screwing.”

“NO!” Tyler answered emphatically. “What *is* your problem, Katie?”

“*My* problem? It’s *my* husband who goes to jail if you guys screw this up, *not* either of you!”

“It’s not true, Katie,” Tracy said softly. “And that’s all I’m ever going to say about it again.”

Katie looked at Tracy. She saw the hurt in the attorney’s eyes. “All right,” the worried wife said. “I’m sorry. I guess I’d be an incredible hypocrite if I didn’t believe you.”

“Thank you. Now, once things have cleared out down there, everyone should go home. That’s what I’m doing. I was supposed to be spending today with my family.”

“Yes,” Keith Entwistle said. “Go to your family, Tracy. It may not look like it, but both Katie and I appreciate all you’re doing for us. You *and* Tyler.”

Tracy smiled appreciatively. “Thanks, Keith.”

“I’ll look out a window and see if any of them are still hovering,” Tyler said. “I really could use a drink.”

Katie started laughing. “You can come with us then. That’s what we’ll be doing.”

It was another half hour before the office building’s parking lot looked empty and safe. Tracy debated staying around awhile longer to catch up on the work she had put on hold. Lucas’ murder and the public disclosure of Cheryl Whittaker’s claim had taken center stage Friday. But she decided not to do so. She’d go home and revisit everything Monday. She secured her office suite and then proceeded to her car, being very observant about her surroundings. Good Lord. Just how much longer would she feel the need to keep looking over shoulder?

Elias Tanner, Sr. was on the phone with Tracy early Monday morning.

"This Father Crowne is just a parish priest. So, it's just going to be guesswork about what the two of them talked about."

"I think Cynthia was seeking counseling. She needed to talk to *somebody*."

"I agree. But that's not evidence."

"I know."

"Detective Bujarski called me back finally. We're going to meet later today."

"Supreme! I am *so* hoping there's something in his report that can help us."

"*Her* report," Tanner corrected.

"Oh. Look at me. Guilty of sexism against my own gender."

"Forget it. Truth is the reason she called me back was because of Jim. He had contacted her too."

"I know," Tracy said quietly. "He told me."

"We might be getting a lot of unofficial help now, Tracy. The rules change when a cop gets killed. Not everyone liked Jim Lucas, but everyone respected the hell out of him."

Tracy gulped; her eyes were moistening. "I'm sorry, El. I don't know what else to say."

"I know. I'll let you know what Bujarski tells me."

"Call me right after your meeting; I want to know all the details *yesterday*."

"You got it. How are you doing otherwise?"

"Okay. You?"

"Working through it. I'll be in touch. You watch yourself."

"I will, El. Bye."

As soon as Tracy was done with Tanner, Rebecca, with obvious trepidation, told her, "Edward Lydecker is on line three Tracy. He's been holding pretty much the whole time you were on your call with Elias."

Tracy stiffened. She hadn't expected this, even though maybe she should have. She slowly reached for the receiver.

"Good morning, Mr. Lydecker," Tracy greeted somberly.

"Good morning, Tracy. May I call you Tracy?"

"Sure."

"How are you? I understand you and Detective Lucas were friends."

"You understand correctly. What can I do for you?"

"I saw your statement to the press. This whole thing has gotten so…so ugly."

"Yes."

"Even though we were divorced, I still loved Cynthia."

"Okay. What is it you want, Mr. Lydecker?"

"Please call me Ed."

"All right."

"I think we should meet; should talk."

Tracy gulped. Scenes from various *Godfather* films ran through her head: images of seemingly cordial phone calls summoning people to supposedly friendly sit-downs. And they sometimes didn't even live through the car ride. As much as she loved seafood, Tracy had no interest bedding down with the fishes.

"I don't know if I can do that anytime soon," Tracy answered finally.

"Please, Tracy. Just come to my office in Annapolis this afternoon. I just want to talk to you."

"Could I bring somebody with me?"

"If they wouldn't mind waiting outside while we talked. I really need your discretion here."

"Good Lord," Tracy thought.

Here was one of those possibly life-changing decisions. If she refused him, he might take that to mean she suspected him of being involved with the murders. Then what would he do? If she did accept the meeting, then he would probably come to the same conclusion.

"All right, Mr. Lydecker. I'll try to be there by 2:30 p.m."

"Excellent. Thank you, Tracy."

"Sure. Goodbye."

Tracy gulped again as she leaned towards her desk and replaced the receiver. She thought for a moment and decided she wouldn't be taking any chances. She buzzed Tyler. "Ty: can you go with me to a meeting this afternoon?"

Tracy Brubaker Shane had never been to the Casper R. Taylor, Jr. House Office Building in Annapolis, Maryland, which had been christened as such in early 2007. The three-story, red-bricked building encompassed over 90,000 square feet, and had offices for all 141 state delegates, including of course one for Edward Lydecker. After parking, Tracy and Tyler Wannamaker made their way to the building located on 6 Bladen Street. Soon the attorneys were being shown to Lydecker's third floor office.

"I'll be right outside," Tyler told Tracy.

She just smiled and followed Lydecker into his office.

"I really do appreciate you coming to see me," Lydecker said as they were both taking their seats. "I know you must be terribly busy."

"I'm sure you are too," Tracy said, attempting to sound pleasant.

He sighed. "This thing with Cindy…just awful."

"Yes, it is."

He looked at her. "I hear nothing but good things about you, Tracy. You're a credit to your profession."

"Thank you," she said uncomfortably. She was now feeling like a piece of freshly popped corn, and Lydecker was just starting to apply the butter.

"Your father: a real hero. I'm sure he'd be very proud of you."

Tracy wondered, "Did movie theaters use real butter anymore? No. That glop consisted mostly of oil. How appropriate." But she just forced a smile and said, "Thank you," again.

"I'd like to think your father and I would have worked together to make the state — the city — a safer place for everyone. The violence today is so pervasive; it seems an impossible war to win."

"You may be right."

"You know I'm an advocate of gun control, don't you?"

"Yes, I do."

"I really do think we need to get more guns off the streets. I realize that criminals will still find a way to get them if they want them. But we can still try to make it tougher for them to do so. Wouldn't you agree?"

Tracy sighed. "I suppose so. I'm no fan of guns but I'm not going to deny a person's right to own one."

"Neither would I."

"Look, Mr. Lydecker," Tracy said, getting impatient. "What did you want to see me about?"

Lydecker paused and covered the bottom part of his face with his hand. After rubbing his mouth and chin he said, "I understand Elias Tanner does work for your firm. He was your father's partner, wasn't he?"

"Yes, he was. And yes, he's a licensed PI now and does work for me occasionally."

"I understand he's looking into an almost 20-year-old hit and run."

Tracy gulped. Now it was beginning.

"I can't comment on any work he's doing in conjunction with my firm, sir."

"Uh-huh."

Tracy could see Lydecker's facial muscles tightening. "Anything else?" she asked matter-of-factly.

"Why are you looking into Jeannine Acosta's death, Tracy?" Lydecker asked emphatically.

"Why do you care?" Tracy narrowed her eyes.

Lydecker stood up. "If I'm honest with you, can I count on your discretion?"

"That would depend on what you tell me, sir. I can't really make any firm promises."

He shook his head. "You realize you could destroy a lot of people."

"*Excuse me*?" Tracy asked, beginning to lose her temper. "*I'm* not the one destroying lives, *sir*."

"You can't have any proof of anything."

"Are you so sure of that? I mean you practically begged me to come down here today."

Lydecker moved away from his desk and started pacing.

"I didn't kill Cindy. I loved her."

"So, you keep saying."

"Damn it, Tracy! How can you be so cold about this?"

"*Cold?*"

"There's no way what happened to her could be related to Jeannine Acosta. There's just no way!"

"And how can *you* be sure? What other reason might there be for someone to hurt her? And don't you dare insult me claiming my client killed her over some affair. We both know that's total crap."

After a few moments Lydecker shouted, "All right! I can't believe she'd have an affair either."

"Oh, good. We agree on something."

"But that's *all* we can agree on. This accident—"

Tracy came to her feet. "Accident?! Don't get me started, Mr. Lydecker. I am sick and tired of watching a drunk get a slap on the wrist for killing someone. People know when they start drinking what can happen. But do they give someone their keys to be on the safe side? No, they don't. They don't care. It's all about them and their next party. You and Cynthia killed Jeannine Acosta and then you just drove away."

"JESUS CHRIST!"

"I think *He'd* be on my side, sir."

"Tracy! *Please!* I have spent my entire adult life trying to make up for that; to do good. And I *have* done good. So did Cindy. I loved her but agreed that we should break up because she just couldn't look at me anymore. You understand? She thought about killing herself. Did you know *that?*"

"Of course not," Tracy answered, her tone revealing a tad of pity.

"Ever since she left me, she's done great things — wonderful things! You wouldn't deny that, would you?"

"No. I will not deny that."

"It was an *accident*, Tracy. I think *you* know that."

"Oh sure. And you talked Cindy out of saying anything about it. I can imagine the pitch: 'Why ruin two more lives over an accident; why not make something of our lives to right this wrong?' Something like that, right?"

Lydecker started shaking his head. "You'd really put all this out there if you could, wouldn't you?"

"Why is Cheryl Whittaker saying Cindy told her about an affair?"

"How should I know?"

"Maybe because she was asked to. Maybe because someone was afraid without a solid motive people would keep digging and digging like I and my firm did. Maybe Cheryl figured she'd rather have Cindy believed to be a cheater instead of known to be a *killer*!"

"*NO!*"

"But I bet it was you who was really driving the car that night. Cindy was just a passenger. Am I right?"

Lydecker was near tears, shaking his head. "*PLEASE* don't do this."

"Is that a threat, Mr. Lydecker? Are you going to try and kill me too?"

"*I HAVEN'T KILLED ANYBODY!*"

"Lots of people know my theory. You'd never be able to get all of us before the truth came out."

Lydecker made his way back to his chair and let his body fall into the seat. He was red-faced and looked like he could be physically ill at any moment.

"She forgave us," he muttered.

"What?"

"Kimberly Acosta. She forgave us."

Tracy sat back down. "So, I was right. That's the reason Cindy went to see her. She admitted what you two had done. I thought so."

"Cindy never told Kimberly who was with her; she told me I'd have to seek forgiveness in my own way. But apparently, I was forgiven anyway. The poor woman had made her own peace with things."

"I see. And Cindy made a promise to Jeannine's mother, and she kept it."

"Yes. Cindy told her that she wanted to start her own charity."

"And Father Crowne helped Cindy through all of this, right?"

Lydecker stared at the attorney. "How did you find out about *him*?"

"I can't say."

Lydecker's expression once again changed to anger. "If the victim's own *mother* could forgive and let this go, why can't *you*?!"

Tracy stood up. She was ready to leave.

"First of all, forgiveness of something doesn't negate punishment. I hope to go to heaven someday, but I'll be making a long stop in purgatory. Second — and being on the judiciary committee you of all people should know this — we don't get to make up our own punishments or whatever you want to call them. The law must be the same for everyone, regardless of how much money they have. And third, I'm not as convinced as you are that Cindy's murder isn't tied to this accident, as you keep calling it. Maybe somebody else knew about it. Maybe somebody was afraid Cindy might tell somebody about it." Tracy's eyes widened. "Tell me, Mr. Lydecker. Was it just you and Cindy in the car that night, or was someone else with you?"

"GET OUT!" Lydecker shouted. "JUST…"

"I'm leaving, Mr. Lydecker. If it makes you feel any better, I pretty much had put all of this together before I came here today. And I *am* really sorry things turned out as they did. But I have a duty to my client. He didn't kill Cynthia. Whoever did probably killed Detective Lucas — a friend of mine. And then there's this George Finnegan person. You see, Mr. Lydecker? Three people dead. Three people who might still be alive if it hadn't been for a 20-year-old accident you kept quiet about. You understand me, sir?"

Lydecker just glared at her. "I understand you. I understand you *perfectly*."

"Goodbye then."

Tracy turned and moved hurriedly toward the door. She made no comments as she passed Tyler Wannamaker, who was soon standing next to her, an eager expression on his face. All Tracy said to him as they left the House Office Building was, "Not now, Tyler." After they retrieved the auto from the garage, they headed back to their law office.

Neal and Tyler were in Tracy's office late Monday afternoon. Tracy had already told Tyler about the Lydecker meeting details and now she was telling Neal. She really wanted to tell the whole world.

"I don't get it," Neal said. "If he killed his ex-wife and the others, why would he essentially bare his soul to you?"

"Because…because maybe he's not guilty of the murders."

"What?" Neal asked incredulously.

"There may have been someone else in the car with him."

"Who?" Tyler asked.

"How about Cheryl Whittaker?" Tracy offered.

"Actually," Neal contemplated, "there could have been more than even three in the car."

Tracy leaned forward in her chair. "Tyler, how old is your brother-in-law?"

"35. Why?"

"How about his business partners? How old are they?"

Tyler started nodding. "I'm not sure."

"I know they all met while taking a cooking class, so they weren't high school buddies." Tracy slapped her head. "Why am I bothering you guys with this? El will have their ages in the background reports he ran for me months ago."

Tracy turned on her computer. Without thinking she opened her email as it was the first thing she always did. The email she had sent herself last Thursday about her meeting with Lucas was still in her inbox. She still hadn't moved it to the case file. She sighed.

"What's wrong?" Neal asked.

"Nothing," she said. "Just saw something that…it's nothing." Tracy next accessed the electronic file on the Keith Entwistle case, in search of the partner biographies. "Well, Barney is 39 and Ian is 38. But neither went to the same college as Cynthia."

"That doesn't mean anything," Neal said. "They could have been friends of friends or something."

"Did they go to an out-of-state school?" Tyler asked. "Some of us did that just to get away."

Tracy grinned. "No, both went to Maryland schools."

"You think that's really it, Tracy?" Tyler asked, sounding enthusiastic again. "You think Barney or Ian knew Cynthia via somebody else?"

"I think it's possible, Ty. We should consider it."

Tyler sighed. "Maybe Lydecker will admit if there was anyone else in the car. If you're right and he's innocent, then what's going to happen if this person finds out the secret is no longer a secret?"

Neal's eyes widened. "That's a *very* good question. If there were other people in that car, do you think Lydecker got on the phone with them as soon as you two left?"

Tracy and Tyler looked at each other. Tracy then looked at Neal. "I don't know. I got the impression it was just he and Cynthia in the car. But even if it was just them, it doesn't mean they didn't tell somebody else, making someone an accessory after the fact."

"Holy shit!" Tyler exclaimed while slamming his fist on Tracy's desk corner. "The car! There must have been damage to the car!"

Tracy snapped her fingers and pointed at Tyler. "Right! Once El tells us the car description we can see if it matches up with any auto of record tied to our ever-growing suspect pool."

"Cynthia Lydecker could have paid off some buddy of hers to fix up the car and keep his mouth shut," Neal said, also sounding excited.

Tracy looked at her watch. "God how I wish El would call. I can't stand it."

The attorney's comment served to break the tension. Everyone started laughing, just because they all felt like a good laugh was needed right about now. As the noise settled there was a knock on the door. Tracy knew it could be only one person.

"Come in, Beck," she called.

"You guys sound like you're working *so* hard in here," the secretary quipped.

Neal smirked. "What's up?"

"Well, I just heard something I think you'd all want to know."

She had their attention.

"What, Beck?" Tracy asked eagerly.

"I just heard that Edward Lydecker has scheduled a press conference for tomorrow at 11:00 a.m., subject unknown."

Everyone in the room looked at everyone else. But it was Tracy who made verbal what everyone was thinking.

"What in the hell is this about?"

Tyler shook his head. "Why do I have the feeling I'm not getting any sleep tonight?"

"You and me both, Ty" Tracy added. "You and me both."

Chapter 12

"I guess what I have to tell you is moot now," Elias Tanner, Sr. said.

"Don't be a silly head. There are still lots of unanswered questions here."

"I'm still putting my report together. I'll run the names of various witnesses and people the police talked to and see if I come up with anyone."

"How many names are you talking about?"

"Hundreds."

"Hundreds?"

"There were parties all over campus, not to mention parties that were taking place *off* campus. The investigators talked to everyone they could, looking for potential witnesses."

"Wow. I should have realized that. What about the description of the car?"

"Bad news there. There are conflicting statements, which isn't surprising considering most of the witnesses were probably drunk."

"Too true."

"But you *will* find this very interesting. One of the witnesses to the accident was Cheryl Shiflit. You know her as Cheryl Whittaker."

"AH-HAH!" Tracy shouted. "She lied!"

"What?"

"I bet she gave a bogus description of the car to help her friend. Thank you, El! I'll look forward to your report. Oh, see if any other so-called witnesses described the same vehicle Cheryl did."

"Gotcha. And I'll move them to the top of the list."

"Supreme! It's late, El. I should let you go."

"You don't sound tired," Tanner chuckled.

"There's a press conference tomorrow that could blow this whole thing open. It's Christmas Eve as far as I'm concerned."

"Well then you better go to bed, little girl, if you want Santa to come."

"Oh, you're cute," Tracy giggled. "Goodnight, *Dad*."

"'Night, Tracy," Tanner responded pleasantly. Their call had ended.

Tracy came skipping down the steps. "MOMMY HERE!" Nicole shouted joyfully. Peter squealed a delighted squeal. The children were both secured for dinner. Tracy kissed and hugged each of them multiple times.

"How about a little sugar for Daddy?" Brian asked while bringing in the chicken breast.

"You'll get *yours* later," Tracy grinned.

"Lord, have mercy," Brian murmured. Euphoric Tracy was one of his favorite moods.

"Sit down and eat," Violetta ordered. But she was smiling. Tracy's happiness was contagious. When Tracy took her seat, Bonkers came over to get his lovin'. Tracy obliged.

There was much silliness during the bedtime preparations. Nicole and Peter shared bath time with their mother, who tonight joined them in the tub. Afterwards Tracy read three storybooks, each with more enthusiasm than the last. Tracy then handed Peter to Brian, so she could tuck in Nicole.

"You have to go to sleep now," Tracy whispered. The child's bedroom was dark except for the nightlight's gentle beam.

"You stay home tomorrow to play?" Nicole asked.

Tracy sighed. "I'm sorry, sweetheart. Mommy has to work tomorrow."

"Why?"

"I have to because people need my help. My job is helping people."

"But you always work."

"Not always, darling."

Nicole put her arms around Tracy's neck. "I love you, Mommy."

"I love you too," Tracy whispered. Nicole however wouldn't let her go. She started giggling. Tracy did too. "Okay, Nicole. Bedtime."

After the mother broke her little one's grip, she covered her with the bed's linens. Tracy then gave Nicole another kiss and another smile before leaving.

Tracy next went to say goodnight to her mother, and then to take Peter so Brian could in turn take Bonkers outside. Once Bonkers was with Nicole and the house safe and secure for the night, Brian returned to his bedroom, where Tracy was still nursing his son. Brian quickly closed the door behind him and readied himself for a long summer's nap. He eschewed his pajama top, however.

"You've been smiling practically all night," Brian said, rubbing his wife's shoulder.

Tracy was gazing at Peter, who was sucking gently. "He's so adorable, isn't he?"

"Sure, he is."

"I think he looks more and more like you every day."

"I think he looks like both of us. He has your nose."

"I think when this case is done, I'm taking a vacation. All of us should go to the beach. And we can ask Crys and El-J if they could join us. It would be so much fun to watch Nicole and Ken play in the sand."

Brian smiled. "Just tell me when, love. I'll arrange it."

"I think he's done," Tracy said as she started shifting in the bed. When Peter was resting comfortably in his crib, Tracy retuned to Brian's side and said, "You have to watch Ed Lydecker's press conference tomorrow, Brian. It's at 11:00."

"I think you mentioned that a couple of times. You even told Nicole."

"Did I?" Tracy chuckled.

"Yes. Now, can you tell me what it's all about?"

"I'm not exactly sure. But I met with him today and he wasn't a happy man when I left. So, I'm pretty sure it will impact my case. How exactly, I don't know."

"Mm."

Tracy rolled onto her back. "I wonder what he and Debra Dooley are talking about right now."

"I don't know."

"I think the statute of limitations for a hit and run fatality back in 2000 was three years. I'd have to check on that."

"Uh-huh."

Tracy turned her head and grinned. "What are you thinking, Brian?"

"Thinking? I was promised sugar earlier."

"Sugar's not good for you."

"The kind *I'm* talking about is."

Tracy turned the rest of her body towards her spouse. "Well, I am a little too wired to get to sleep. Maybe…" She started rubbing his bare chest. "Maybe you could do something to tire me out."

"Exercise..." Brian said softly as he moved towards her. *"That's* good for you…better than sugar…"

"I don't care what you call it."

Tracy started giggling. Then they started their workout.

The entire staff of Tracy Brubaker Shane & Associates: Attorneys-at-Law was in the conference room Tuesday morning impatiently awaiting the promised conference to start. It was already five past 11:00 a.m. and Tracy was ready to start tearing her hair out. Neal didn't resist the chance to needle her.

"Why don't you go use the bathroom?" he kidded.

"No way," Tracy said quickly. "As soon as my butt hit the seat this conference would start."

Everyone started laughing. "This is just nuts," the pacing Tyler Wannamaker murmured.

"You don't think they'll cancel it, do you?" Rebecca asked.

"Silence!" Tracy ordered. "You're not helping matters." Everyone laughed again.

Finally, at 11:09 a.m., Edward Lydecker and Debra Dooley, hand in hand, approached the podium that had been set up near the former's Annapolis office. The familiarity of the sight caused Tyler and Tracy to exchange a quick glance. As the attending journalists started quieting down, a very nervous looking Edward Lydecker adjusted the microphone.

"Good morning," Lydecker began.

He pulled out what appeared to be several pages of script. His hands were slightly shaking. His fiancée put her hand on his forearm in an attempt to relax him. It seemed to work. Tracy was holding her breath.

"As you all know, my former wife, Cynthia Conroy Lydecker, was murdered earlier this year. As I have said before, I still loved Cindy and am heartbroken over her death, especially the horrific circumstances surrounding it. And as you also are already aware, her murderer's trial begins in about five weeks. Of course, he and his attorney continue to maintain his innocence. But I will not comment on that. I will leave that to the jury to decide."

Lydecker took a deep breath, as Debra's grip got even tighter.

"However, during the course of Cindy's murder investigation, something from her past was discovered — from *our* past. And while I have no doubt this has nothing to do with her murder, I understand that what I think means little when an attorney is zealously representing her client."

"That shit!" Rebecca exclaimed. "Trying to dump this—"

"Easy there, Beck," Tracy admonished quietly.

"In other words, ladies and gentlemen, I would rather make this public now, than wait until the trial. Please bear with me." Lydecker paused to a take a gulp from the water glass that had been considerately placed on the podium in advance. "On the night of Saturday, April 8, 2000, Cindy and I had left the party of a friend of ours at Riegert University. I was driving. I was distracted. And I hit…and I hit and killed a woman who I would later learn was named Jeannine Acosta. I did not stop. Cindy begged me to, but I didn't."

There were some murmurs amongst the attendees. And those gathered in the conference room exchanged knowing glances. But as Tracy watched Lydecker, she couldn't help but be filled with sympathy for him. Yes, he had done a horrible thing. And yes, she still believed this incident was in some way the reason behind Cynthia's murder. But still. Edward Lydecker did not appear to be the person who pulled the trigger last January. She was sure of it.

"Therefore," Lydecker continued after finishing his water glass, "I will be resigning from my positions effective end of business today. I have tried to serve the people of this great state for the last 13 years. It has been my honor and privilege to do so. I believe I have served the state honorably. I wanted to do so to somehow make amends for the terrible wrong that I did. I beg your forgiveness."

Lydecker turned to look at his teary-eyed fiancée. She smiled at him and nodded. He looked back at his audience.

"My beautiful Debra has forgiven me. Jeannine's own mother, who is no longer with us, forgave me. I am truly sorry for all of this. I ask forgiveness from the people I've hurt; from the people I've let down; and most especially from anyone who knew and cared about Jeannine Acosta. I have not forgotten her. I never will. Thank you, ladies and gentlemen."

As the noise erupted and the engaged couple turned from the stage, it was then that Tracy noticed the line of officers that were now in place to protect Lydecker from being mobbed. Some people were more aggressive than others in their attempt to break through the police line. But Tracy had seen enough. She told Neal to shut off the monitor. The conference room was thundering with quiet.

Tracy shook her head. "It's not him," she said. "No way it's him."

"It could be," Neal said. "After you gave your own press conference Saturday, he realized he couldn't stop the truth from coming out. He couldn't just keep on shooting people. Now he's playing the sympathy card. I mean they can't touch him over the hit and run, can they?"

Tracy looked at Neal. "I was only 17 in 2000, Neal. Maryland laws have changed over the years. But since they could never prove he was drunk at the time he hit Jeannine, and he didn't say he was during that speech, the most they have is him leaving the scene. And the statute of limitations has run out on that. Or are the new laws retroactive?"

Tyler shook his head. "I'm not sure either. But I'm sure he's been checking into this. I bet nothing happens to him."

"They'll forgive him," Neal said. "You just watch. In another year or so he'll be right back in the spotlight with his beautiful, supportive bride by his side."

"All right," Tracy said. "Enough of this right now. Tyler, where did you leave things with Keith and Katie?"

"I told them I'd meet them for lunch."

"Okay. Do that. I'm going to start pestering Art."

"What?" Neal asked.

"If Art doesn't start looking at Lydecker as a suspect, I'm going to give *another* press conference."

"But I thought you just said you didn't think he killed her," Neal countered.

"I don't, exactly. But he knows a lot more details about that night than he's told everyone today. He may even know…Well, you see my point, right?"

"Yeah," Neal nodded. "You're right."

"I wanted to cry," Rebecca added. "It was such a sad thing what just happened."

Tracy nodded. "Yes, Beck. It was." She sighed. "Let me go update the case file for all of this."

"I can do that," Rebecca said.

"That's okay, Beck. I want to reorganize too. I need to rethink some things."

"Okay then."

"If you want, Beck, you can take an early lunch today. Neal can man the phones."

"Sure," Neal said sincerely.

"Thank you both," Rebecca smiled. "I think I will."

With both Rebecca and Tyler leaving, Tracy went back to her office while Neal arranged to switch incoming calls to his personal office. But before she laid one finger on her keyboard, she left the first of many messages she'd be leaving for the day for Arthur Pankow. She had no intention of being patient.

The State Attorney for Baltimore City called Tracy back at 5:57 p.m. that same afternoon.

"I think you set a record today," he told attorney after a quick hello.

"Excuse me?"

"For number of messages left over a six-hour period."

"Oh. Well, you can understand why, can't you?"

"Sure, I can."

"So, what's going on?"

"Pandemonium. It's pretty ugly here, Tracy. A lot of people like Ed Lydecker."

"Yeah. And?" There was no enthusiasm to be found in her tone.

Pankow sighed. "Fine. You'll be happy to know that people seem to suddenly like Jim Lucas more. Bill Culpepper — Jim's partner — was on this thing fast. If they haven't already, they'll be serving a search warrant any time now."

"Ah. They never did find Cynthia's key ring, did they?"

"No. I've always wondered if there was a key to something on that ring that the killer wanted — safe-deposit box, filing cabinet, locker…"

"Mm. But I doubt you'll find anything. He'd have to be pretty stupid to keep anything at his place or office."

"You're probably right. But honestly, we were lucky to get our warrants for Lydecker. All we have is a possible motive, no physical evidence really. But the personal calendars show they kept in touch. And he certainly knew his way around the neighborhood. Plus, his alibi is weak."

"Yeah. Did you get a warrant for Debra Dooley's place?"

"No. How could we? She's not implicated in this yet."

"As you just indicated, she alibied him. If he did this that means she lied."

Pankow sighed. "Technically, of course, you're correct. And if we *do* find something from the Lydecker warrants then we may be able to revisit getting one for her place."

"I see. Yeah, that makes sense. But I still doubt you'll find anything."

"What else are we supposed to do?"

"Oh, I didn't mean that as a knock at you guys. I'm sorry if it sounded that way."

"No problem. I *am* rather punchy."

"I can understand why."

"As far as your client goes though, the charges still stand."

"Uh-huh. I'm working on that. I have my own ideas."

"I bet you do. But now I need to go."

"Sure. I really do appreciate the call. I'll try to leave you alone unless something else dramatic happens."

"Don't even joke about that."

"Who's joking, Art? Goodnight."

"Goodnight."

Tyler Wannamaker entered Tracy's office as she put down her smartphone.

"Was that Pankow?"

Tracy gave him the executive summary. "I'm going to the conference room to pump and watch TV."

"Um…"

"I'll cover myself. Just give me a couple minutes if you want to join me. If the police descend on Ed Lydecker's house in the next hour or so it will be on the news. And I want to be watching."

"All right."

Tracy chuckled as she reached for her breast pump and then headed to where the monitor awaited her. Not surprisingly the news of Ed Lydecker's mea culpa was now national. But Tracy knew where she'd find the most salacious coverage. She tuned into WFFE. Shirley Hammersmith was already standing outside the Lydecker home and speaking to the camera. It had already begun.

"…. earlier today. We understand that Mr. Lydecker has been very cooperative and allowed the police entry when they served the warrant not half hour ago."

"That was fast," the handsome male news anchor commented.

"They no doubt want to avoid accusations of preferential treatment," the pretty female anchor offered.

"Of course, Ed Lydecker is one of the State's most respected delegates," Shirley continued. "He says he has nothing to hide and will do whatever he can to help."

By now Tyler had joined Tracy in the meeting room.

"Just how long are they going to drag out their conversation?" he wondered aloud.

Tracy chuckled. "As long as they can, I guess."

He shook his head. "You realize this could take hours and they're not going to find anything. No way he'd be dumb enough to keep anything incriminating at his own house."

"I agree. But what else am I gonna do when I'm immobilized like this? You men are so lucky."

Tyler cleared his throat. "What do you do with that milk? Does the little guy really go through all that as quickly as you pump it?"

"No," Tracy smiled. "I freeze it and we rotate the stock. I feed him in the morning, as soon as I get home, and just before bed, unless of course I get home too late. If I didn't pump though, I'd dry out. My girls have to be reminded Peter needs their services."

Tyler started laughing. "You know, I don't know what's going to happen with the Lydecker business and the case against Keith. But I really do want to thank you for all you've done."

"It's okay, Ty."

"Katie appreciates it too. I know she may not seem to."

"That's all right, Ty. I'll just bill her extra."

The associate laughed. "Call it a nuisance fee. I'd love to see the expression on her face."

Tracy nodded. "My husband and his sister are always giving each other a hard time. And it usually is Crys who starts things. But they're pretty close in age. You guys go at it a lot?"

"No, not really. She can be stuck up and standoffish sometimes. But she's a good person. And Keith is good for her. As far as brothers-in-law go, I could have done worse."

Tracy laughed.

"...don't know if the police are looking for anything in particular. We also don't know if Mr. Lydecker is a suspect in the murder of Detective James Lucas, who, as you no doubt recall, was fatally shot outside his own home late last Thursday."

Pretty Anchor commented, "It hasn't been determined if his murder is connected with Cynthia Lydecker's, has it Shirley?"

"No, Wendy. There has been no official word either way. We only know the detective's murder is classified as an ongoing investigation."

"You and Lucas must have been pretty tight," Tyler commented. "I could tell his death upset you."

"Yeah," Tracy sighed. "We had our differences, but he was a good detective."

"I don't know if I could be as big as you."

"What?"

"Didn't Lucas arrest your sister-in-law for murder?"

"Yes. But Crys was framed. And it almost worked."

"Still. I've seen how cops can berate the suspects they interview. If they did that to someone I cared about…"

"Like Keith?"

"Sure." Tyler gulped. "Of course, I won't have that problem with Lucas anymore."

Tracy sighed. "No, you won't."

Tyler stood. "Going after a cop…God I hope they find *something* there. Maybe they could check his phone records and see if he called any college buddies of his."

"Actually, he was a few years older than Cynthia. He wasn't in school when the—"

The sudden activity on the monitor stopped Tracy's discourse. Shirley Hammersmith was suddenly moving haphazardly, trying to get closer to the Lydecker driveway. Additional uniformed officers were arriving. It appeared they were trying to secure a clear path from the house's doorway to the street.

"What the hell?" Tyler wondered aloud.

"What's going on, Shirley?" Wendy asked intently.

"I can only go by what's been overheard on the officer's radios. But it appears the police did find *something*."

Tracy wanted to stand up. But that would have made for an uncomfortable scene. Not that Tyler would have noticed. His eyes were glued to the screen.

"Wendy, it appears that Ed Lydecker has just been placed under arrest."

"Why?" the male asked, not wanting to be left out.

"We don't know. But I can confirm he's been read his rights."

The hell with it. Tracy terminated her pumping session, thankfully succeeding in preserving her modesty. She then moved closer to the monitor and turned up the volume.

"Oh my God," Tyler whispered at the next image, that of a handcuffed Ed Lydecker being escorted out of his house, his hysterical fiancée behind him. Tyler and Tracy exchanged glances.

"A gun, Wendy. I believe they found a gun in Lydecker's garage!"

Tracy started shaking her head. "No…It can't be."

"But they have the gun that killed Cynthia so that means…"

The events that followed would never be clearly known, because the frenzy would obfuscate any clear pictures despite the numerous cameras present. But the exact details hardly mattered. As the media representatives started staking out their places against the manmade barricade of blue, and as Edward Lydecker was being led to an awaiting, marked police car, a voice was suddenly heard screaming from somewhere near the house. And it was Shirley Hammersmith's camera operator who decided to break away from the main event to see who was crying out.

"Jesus *CHRIST*!" Tyler shouted.

Alastair Conroy, red-faced and unkempt, was moving towards the driveway. If he had been imitating a deranged vagrant, he couldn't have done a better job. Suddenly Shirley's visage again appeared on the screen. She started moving towards Conroy.

Tracy shook her head. "Oh, you gotta be kid—"

But the loud popping sound froze Tracy's tongue and blood. Shirley Hammersmith went down fast. Her camera operator started moving backward looking around, revealing that numerous other cameras were trying to see what was happening. By the time officers realized what had occurred, Conroy was close enough so that he was able to fire three bullets into Edward Lydecker before being subdued. Tracy, by now, had both hands pressed against either side her face.

"MURDERER!" she could hear Conroy crying out. "YOU KILLED MY BABY! YOU KILLED MY BABY! YOU KILL…YOU…"

Conroy's hands were now being shackled as other officers were demanding emergency vehicles. It wasn't long before the screams of Debra Dooley could be heard too. And with Conroy now handcuffed, people were refocusing their attentions.

"Eddie. Oh my God, Eddie," Debra sobbed as she embraced the immobile body of her beloved, rocking him as he stared upwards at her with unblinking eyes.

"SHIRLEY!" Wendy was shouting with tears streaking down. "SHIRLEY! SHIRLEY! TALK TO US!"

Tracy started crying too. She couldn't help herself. It was all too much. Before she decided she didn't want to watch anymore, she knew of only one certainty: Edward Lydecker was dead. The 20-year-old hit and run of Jeannine Acosta had apparently claimed at least one more victim.

Chapter 13

Thursday morning Tracy was seated in Arthur Pankow's office. But this visit was initiated by Pankow, as a courtesy to the person who exposed the Jeannine Acosta connection as well as the lawyer whose client was most likely now in the clear.

"It's just the damndest thing," Pankow was muttering. "Conroy was getting information from one of the uniforms — who will remain nameless for now — helping with the search. That dumb son of a bitch will only lose his job — if he's lucky."

"He told Conroy about the gun?"

"Actually, we also found Cynthia Lydecker's key ring as well as her alarm code."

"Oh, that's what did it."

"The gun we found of course was the one that killed Jim. And the paper with Cynthia's alarm code had George Finnegan's prints on it."

"So, you just tied Ed Lydecker to Finnegan, Jim, as well as his ex-wife. What about Keith Entwistle?"

"Nothing solid. But we did find a brochure from your client's catering company with some carryout menus in the kitchen."

"But Keith's business isn't a carryout place."

"I realize that."

Tracy sighed. "You didn't find a key to Keith's place, did you? How about *his* alarm code?"

Pankow shook his head. "No. But I didn't expect to. If George Finnegan was the one who stole your client's gun, then most likely Lydecker killed George before getting Entwistle's key and code. That's why Lydecker had to break in that night to plant the key — he didn't have what he needed. So, he made it look like a burglary to cover himself."

"Mm. You didn't find the stolen movie player, did you?"

"No."

"And what about Cheryl Whittaker? Have you had a chance to follow up with her?"

Pankow cleared his throat. "She's basically recanted. She said she got scared when Finnegan's body was found. She thought that Entwistle might go after her, so she wanted to make sure he went to jail. But given all that's happened: I doubt we'll charge her with anything."

"Uh-huh. Well, I think she's lying to you, Art. I think she was scared her role in the Acosta hit and run might come to light because she knew I was interested in Cynthia's past."

"What role?"

"I think she intentionally gave an incorrect description of the car. She's on record as one of the witnesses. But we were just getting started looking into all of that when…Well, I guess the point is moot now."

"You think she knew it was Cynthia and Ed who hit Jeannine Acosta?"

"Yes, I do. They were friends and she knew them well enough to know what Ed's car looked like. There's no doubt anymore about who was driving."

"Yeah, I can't argue any of that." Pankow grinned. "You know, when we were looking into Jim's death, we did note he made a call to her the day he died."

"He did? I didn't know that. Can I ask why he called Cheryl?"

"He wanted to know if she had any pictures of inside Cynthia Lydecker's house. But as to why, we don't know."

"Pictures?"

"Photographs. I guess he wanted to confirm nothing was missing or got moved around or something."

"Oh, that was a good thought. Maybe he thought something was stolen after all."

"Maybe." Pankow leaned back in his chair. "All right, just for fun, how were you planning to handle the frozen food box? *That* had your client's prints on it."

"Are you dismissing the charges against him, then?"

Pankow nodded. "It may take another day or two to push the paperwork through. But yeah, Tracy. Keith Entwistle is in the clear. You have my word. I mean, how could I hope to get a conviction after all that's happened?"

Tracy smiled appreciatively. "Okay then. Did you notice that set of numbers and letters on the flap of the frozen chicken box?"

"I guess."

"Well, that's part of the company's inventory tracking system. With that code, combined with the UPC number, they can tell you exactly where that food was delivered. And the store it was delivered to was neither close to Keith nor Justin Wilmont, whose trash can it was found in. The store it was delivered is in…want to guess?"

"No."

"Annapolis."

Pankow rolled his eyes. "Marvelous. But how did Keith's prints get on it?"

"Not sure. But since you found a brochure from his business, maybe Lydecker showed up and got Keith to touch it without Keith realizing what he was touching. Something like that."

"Mm. We did find his prints *only* on the flap."

"Right."

"Good Lord. For each piece of evidence we had, you had your explanation ready, didn't you."

"That's my job, Art."

"Yeah, so it is."

Tracy sat quietly for few moments, and then she started shaking her head. "No, Art. This just doesn't feel right."

"I know it doesn't. Lydecker would have had to have been a complete imbecile to keep that evidence at his place."

"Exactly. I'm sure he denied ever seeing the gun and all that."

"Sure, he did."

Tracy looked at her folded hands that were resting on her lap. "What's going to happen to Conroy?"

Pankow started rubbing his eyes. "He killed two people, Tracy. For the life of me I don't know why he shot Shirley Hammersmith. I guess he just totally snapped. And I should have seen it coming."

"Poor Shirley. I didn't like her but…Well, it's just awful."

"After that press conference, Conroy was on the phone to the governor yelling and screaming, saying there was no way Cynthia would ever do something like that. And this was on top of him already being on the edge because he didn't think we were going to win at trial. I was seriously contemplating having officers at the ready the day the verdict would have been read. I blew it."

"Come on, Art. How could you have known Conroy had reached out to that officer you referred to?"

"True. And you know what this idiot would have gotten for helping Conroy?"

"No, Art."

"Conroy promised him two season tickets to the Jolts. One ticket for each life Conroy took. This world…"

Tracy sighed heavily. "So, what is going to happen with all this, Art? Are all the cases considered closed?"

"Everybody wants them to be. *I* want them to be. And we have the evidence to do it, too."

"Isn't the fact the Debra Dooley was with Lydecker the night Cynthia was killed giving anyone pause? And what about the night Jim was killed?"

"She could have been asleep and not even noticed he was gone."

Tracy frowned. "Has it been *that* long, Art?"

"What?"

"How long have you been married?"

"Jeez, Tracy. I guess 23 years this September. Why?"

"Don't you remember those early days of starting to live together, sharing the same bed?"

"What the heck are you talking about?"

Tracy grinned. "Debra and Ed were in love and engaged and excited about getting married. I bet they went to bed at the same time and got up at the same time. If one of them got up to use the bathroom or get a late-night snack, the other was wondering where they went. If one of them sneezed funny the other would ask if they were all right. Remember those days, Art?"

Pankow laughed softly. "Okay, Tracy. You don't think Lydecker could have been gone from the house for any lengthy period without Debra realizing it."

"A-plus. So, either's she lying…or she's not. You get me?"

"I get you. But I don't think your romantic theory will sway people to think as you do."

"*Umpf.* Philistines."

Pankow chuckled. "You know, this is the first time I laughed during the workday since all this happened. Thank you, Tracy."

"Shucks."

"But to get back to the real question here. I don't know if anyone has any reason not to close everything down. Believe me. I don't relish the thought Jim's killer is still out there. But you know all too well we have to go where the evidence takes us. And our instincts will give us only so much leeway. So, we'll try to follow through on some things over the next few days. But if nothing turns up…"

"Yeah, Art. I hear you." Tracy twisted her lips. "I'll look at what I have too. Maybe there's something there."

"Wouldn't telling me anything you have get you in trouble?"

"I would clear it with my client first. Once you officially dismiss the charges and he's in the clear, he would probably let me share some things with you if they might be helpful. He was the one who was framed, after all. I'm sure if he thought whoever did that was still out there, he'd want to help. I'm *sure* his wife would."

"All right."

Tracy smiled as she stood. Then she frowned. "You know, if I am right about this, then whoever's really behind this couldn't have predicted that Cheryl Whittaker would have lied about the affair. And he certainly couldn't have foreseen Ed Lydecker's public confession and his death."

Pankow, now also standing, folded his arms. "Okay. But what's your point?"

"Nothing, I guess. I'm just once again wondering what the endgame here was. I guess I'm just thinking out loud. Sorry."

"Sure," Pankow smiled. "Go tell your client the good news. At least somebody has something to be happy about."

"Yeah. Thanks, Art."

"No problem."

The attorneys shook hands and then Tracy went in search of her auto. Once there she called Tyler Wannamaker to tell him his brother-in-law's life would soon be back to normal.

"Thank God," Tyler said. "Tracy, I don't know how to thank you for everything. Really—"

"Forget it, Ty. I know this is good news, but I really don't feel like feeling good right now. You know what I mean?"

"Sure. This whole thing… Just awful."

"It's amazing, isn't it? 20 years ago, Ed Lydecker is careless for a few seconds. Look what it led to; look at how many people got hurt in so many different ways. It's horrible."

Tyler was silent a few seconds. "Yeah. I see your point. Okay, I'll let Keith and Katie know. Are you coming back to the office or are you going home for the day?"

"I'll be back soon enough. I need to grab something to eat. I missed lunch. Peter will not be happy if Mommy starts skipping meals."

"All right," Tyler chuckled. "See you then."

Tracy remained seated, her car immobile, for several minutes. Just why did someone think Detective Jim Lucas was such a threat that he had to die? What did he find out? The only thing Tracy knew was bugging him was that photograph on the wall — the one with the representative from Youths Against Drunk and Drugged Driving. Photographs. Lucas wanted to see photographs of inside Cynthia's house. Was that it? Did Cheryl tell somebody about Lucas' request? Tracy frowned. Then her belly started growling at her. She would have to save any further reflections until after her stomach was satisfied. She started her vehicle's engine and went in search of sustenance.

"A party, Tyler?" Tracy asked skeptically.

"Not a party, really. Keith's co-workers are just putting something together for tonight — a late dinner, consisting mostly of hors d'oeuvres. And they'll be drinking of course — not that that matters to you. Neal and Rebecca were invited too. But they already have plans they can't cancel."

"I don't know if I'm up for it."

"Just stop in for a few minutes. They'll be making those mushrooms you like. Keith would really like you there so he can thank you."

"He hasn't seen the bill yet," Tracy murmured.

Tyler started laughing. "I know this whole thing took a lot out of you. And that you lost a friend. But you did help save an innocent man's life, right? Focus on that. At least, let yourself focus on that for a little while tonight. Please?"

Tracy couldn't help but smile. "All right, Ty. I'll stop by for a little bit."

"Terrific! And you'll see that Katie's not so bad either. I think she was crying when I told her the news."

"Okay. I'll be there. Promise."

"Things start around 8:00 p.m. You show up whenever you feel like it. I'm going to be leaving the office promptly at 5:00 if that's okay."

"You can leave now if you want to. I don't mind."

"You're too good to me, boss. I'll finish what I'm working on first though."

"All right." Tracy grinned as Tyler left her office. He was right. There *was* some good on which she could focus. What would be wrong with that?

Tracy entered Whistler's Cooking at 8:15 p.m. The mood was merry. Keith Entwistle was smiling and engaged in conversation with both Ian Tapper and Barney Schultz. Katie was holding her husband's arm. Vanessa — who had delivered the magnificent morsels last time Tracy was here — smiled when she saw the attorney and approached her, serving tray in hand.

"Hello, Mrs. Shane," Vanessa grinned. "These scallops and bacon just came from the kitchen."

"God bless you, Vanessa," Tracy smiled as she picked up a loaded toothpick. She instantly devoured the attached food.

Keith Entwistle managed to hear Tracy's voice through the jubilant noise. He immediately approached her.

"I am *so* glad you could make it, Tracy," he smiled. "If it hadn't been for you…" Perhaps it was the alcohol Entwistle had been imbibing for the last few hours that gave him the courage. He embraced Tracy firmly. He had no more words.

When the client released Tracy, the attorney saw Katie had joined them.

"Don't suffocate the poor woman," Katie told her husband teasingly.

"Oh, I think I'm a little drunk," Entwistle responded, a tad embarrassed.

"That's why I'm doing the driving tonight," Katie said.

Entwistle just nodded and then turned. Katie looked at Tracy.

"Look, Tracy. I know I gave you a lot of grief. And I'm really sorry about all of that."

"Don't worry about all of that," Tracy said sincerely. "I'm just happy it's over for you guys."

Tyler Wannamaker, a wide smile on his face, approached the women.

"So great you could stop by," he said.

"You guaranteed my attendance when you reminded me of the mushrooms," Tracy chuckled.

Katie grabbed her brother. "Thank you, Tyler. Thank you for helping us. I knew you could do it."

Tyler smiled at his sister. "What else was I gonna do?"

Tracy smiled at the siblings. But then…then something changed. The smile left Tracy's face. And when Katie Wannamaker Entwistle finally released her brother and went in search of her husband, Tracy's eyes followed her. The attorney continued staring until she realized Tyler was talking to her.

"…for me to go," Tyler was saying.

"What?" Tracy asked, now looking at her associate.

"I said I think it's time for me to leave. This thing started too early. And I couldn't eat anything else. Besides, Keith and Katie will want to be alone at some point anyway."

"All right, Ty. I may stick around here for a little bit though."

"Oh, please do. There're all kinds of food here with your name on it."

Tracy smiled weakly. "You going home then?"

He sighed. "I think I'll go back to the office, actually. I may do some work. I'm a little wired."

"All right. I'll see you tomorrow then."

"Thanks, Tracy. I mean it."

"It was a group effort. Everyone helped."

Tyler nodded and then sighed. Soon Tracy was watching him leave. Again, the attorney found herself looking at Katie Entwistle, who was behind Keith with her arms wrapped around his waist. When Tracy had entered the catering established mere moments ago, she was famished. Now she wanted to throw up. Her mental chain reaction had started. And she didn't like the fence it was building.

Tyler Wannamaker was seated at his desk. There was half a bottle of J&B Scotch resting on the blotter, and a glass in his hand. Normally, he liked his liquor on the rocks. But he didn't really care this particular night. His goal was to just keep on drinking until he couldn't anymore. There was a sudden light rapping on his office door. He looked in its direction.

"Tracy…" he said, his surprise to see her obvious. "What are you doing here? You have a family to go home to."

Tracy smiled and entered. "I'll be headed there soon enough. Can I join you?"

"Of course, you can. I'd offer you a drink but…" Tyler was now staring at her breasts. They were plenty attractive when they *weren't* storing nourishment. But now…Tyler looked away, embarrassed.

Tracy sat down, seemingly not offended. "Even if I weren't nursing, I'd still pass. I need my head to be clear right now."

"All right," Tyler sighed. "I do most of my drinking alone these days anyway. I'm used to it."

Tracy cleared her throat. "I was surprised you left the party so early. I was kind of worried about you. This case — so much ugliness about it; so much pain."

"Yeah."

"But you know what I keep thinking about?"

"No. What?"

"Kimberly Acosta. She must have been a very special person."

Tyler blinked at her. "Why would you say that?"

"She forgave Cindy and Ed Lydecker; she forgave them before she even knew who they were. Ed Lydecker said as much in his press conference."

"Mm. I guess he did."

"I don't know, Tyler. I don't know if I could forgive someone if they hurt Nicole or Peter. I don't know if I'm a strong enough person to do that."

Tyler smiled. "I bet you are. You always put yourself down. I still haven't figured out if it's false modesty or if you really don't realize how highly people think of you." Tyler poured from his bottle.

"I don't know how much you know about Brian and me. But while were dating in college, we had a terrible fight one night. His drinking had gotten out of hand, and I told him it was me or the bottle. I thought his choice would be a no-brainer. I was wrong."

Tyler was just staring at her. Just what in the hell was this all about?

"I still remember the banging of my parents' screen door and turning around to see he'd left. Later I would find out he intended to quit on his own terms. But he couldn't. We spent 10 years apart. And as much as I wanted to just forget about him and find someone else, I couldn't. I couldn't because I knew who he really was. And I still loved him. I never stopped loving him, Tyler. Weird, huh?"

"I couldn't say."

"When he did come back into my life, he wanted a second chance. But for me to be able to give him that, I had to forgive him. I had to forgive him for all the hurt he had caused me. And he had caused me a lot of hurt, Tyler. A lot."

"I'm sure he did."

"But I did it just the same. I forgave him. And I promised him I wouldn't bring up the past. I would never use it against him if he were sincere in wanting us to be together." Tracy smiled. "And now look at us: married, with two incredible, beautiful children. You see what I mean?"

"Not exactly."

"That forgiveness can bring happiness, Tyler. As hard as it may be to do, sometimes forgiving someone is the only way you can be happy again. And that's what Kimberly Acosta must have realized too. Instead of letting her pain eat away at her, she chose to forgive and move on. So when — all those years later — Cynthia showed up, she had already made peace. And that's why Cynthia too was able to move on. You see what I'm saying now?"

Tyler sighed; drank some more; and said, "I guess."

"Of course, it's not always easy to forget, even if you forgive. And that goes for the forgiven person too. Brian felt awful about that fight, and he needed to forgive himself. And — if I'm totally honest — there are times when I wonder about those lost 10 years. I still find myself thinking about it. And it hurts."

"I'm sure it does."

Tracy took a deep breath. "When Ed Lydecker was making his speech, he talked about forgiveness. And I remember him apologizing to the people he hurt. And he also apologized to everyone who ever knew or loved Jeannine Acosta. Remember that, Ty?"

"Sure," Tyler grunted.

"I started wondering if there was someone out there who loved Jeannine Acosta the way that I love Brian, or that your sister loves Keith. I wonder what such a person — if he exists — would have felt when he got the news of what happened to Jeannine. Would he have been able to forgive? Or would he have started rotting inside?"

Tyler Wannamaker put his glass on the table. He stared at the attorney across from him. "Is there something you want to ask me, Tracy?"

Tracy gulped. "At the party tonight, I saw Katie hug you. And she said how she knew you would help her. And, as I was watching the two of you, I remembered something. I should have realized it at the time, but I guess I was just too upset to be thinking clearly."

"And what is it you remembered?"

"The morning we were preparing for that little press conference to deny the affair — the Saturday after Jim Lucas was killed — Katie was understandably upset. She was losing confidence in me. She said something to the effect that I couldn't even protect my confidential informant. You remember that?"

"I guess."

"But the thing is, that meant she knew Jim Lucas was in fact a confidential informant. But how could she? It was Jim who came up with that description. And the only place *I* used it was in that memo I wrote up Thursday night. I emailed it to myself. And I didn't make it part of the official file until Monday. So, my question is how did Katie know Jim was a confidential informant?"

Tyler leaned back in his chair; his glassy eyes were still locked on Tracy. "And what, pray tell, do you think is the answer to your question?"

Tracy's heart started beating faster. "Well, I know she and Keith were together on Thursday. So, *she* couldn't have killed Jim. That means the mostly likely answer is that somebody she had spoken with Friday or Saturday referred to Jim that way. And there's only person who that could be."

"And who might that be?"

"Tell me, Tyler. If we were to keep digging around in Jeannine Acosta's past, would we find *your* name among all the others? I know you said you went to an out-of-state college. But that doesn't mean you couldn't have been having a long-distance relationship."

The room was now deathly quiet. Tyler Wannamaker was considering how to answer her. He wasn't particularly sober and therefore his tongue wasn't as tight as it may otherwise have been. Suddenly he was smiling.

"And how did I supposedly learn about your confidential informant?"

Tracy should have known better. She should have shut up and left. But she couldn't. Maybe she didn't want to believe what she had been thinking the last hour or so and wanted to be proved wrong. But now…Now she knew she was right.

"Well, if someone's been planning a murder as long as you have, Tyler, I think it's a good bet you managed to learn my password during the two years you've been here. I think you saw my report. I think somehow you learned Jim and I were meeting. Maybe you even overheard the phone call we had before you left that day, and left Keith and Katie as soon as you could so you could be at Hooligan's House. And when you realized I was going home, you came back to the office and started going through my files. You must have been doing that when my email came through and you read the report. Is that more or less how it happened?"

Tyler was grinning at her. Then he shook his head. "Do you really think I'm going to answer that?"

"It must have been the picture. Jim told me something about one of the pictures that bothered him, and I put that in my notes. And now I realize why that was such a threat to you."

"You do, do you?"

"Yes. The killer switched photographs. He couldn't have known about Cynthia's old calendar books, which is how we found Kimberly Acosta. He couldn't have known about Cynthia not deducting those contributions to Y3D on her tax returns. But he would have needed a legitimate reason to pursue the whole drunk driving thing. And putting a picture on her wall showing she was involved with that charity would have given us a reason to look into her association with it. With Ed and Cindy going from hard partiers to being teetotalers right after college, you would have found a way to move our investigation in the way you wanted it to go. I mean this was all about framing Ed Lydecker after all. Keith was just a means to an end. You knew that if he were accused of murder, he'd come running to you — or rather, his wife would."

Tyler made himself comfortable as he said, "You really are something, Tracy. Please, continue."

"You knew about George Finnegan. Maybe you even worked with him at some point. You used him to get the alarm codes and key copies to not only Cynthia Lydecker's home, but also Ed Lydecker's. I'm sure you already knew the code to your sister's house and had a key copy. It never occurred to me to ask her about it since I was sure the key at least was planted during that burglary farce. So why would someone trying to frame Keith and having access to his house have to break in? Why would they provide a possible explanation as to how the gun went missing and the key was planted? Unless, of course, that's *exactly* what they wanted."

"Really."

"Each piece of evidence in this case had a problem with it, a way for any decent defense attorney to counter it. The gun had no prints. The food box was from a store not even close to the accused. The break-in could explain the gun being missing — at least, initially. And so on. You must have been really pissed when Cheryl suddenly provided the motive. You couldn't have seen *that* coming."

"No plan is perfect."

"No, it isn't. And I'm guessing you didn't want Lydecker dead, either. You could have done that yourself once you figured out he was Cynthia's companion that night. So, you must have wanted him to be exposed on the stand. You *wanted* this to go to trial. You *wanted* Lydecker put on the stand where his past crime would be made public. That's the only way this all makes any sense, as if it ever truly would.

"But that didn't work for you either, did it Tyler? He confessed and resigned. And then Alastair Conroy totally lost it. And Ed Lydecker and Shirley Hammersmith lost their lives."

Tyler smacked his lips. "Good riddance to Shirley. Thank you, Alastair."

"I guess when you felt the time was right you alerted the police to where they could find George Finnegan. His body would need to be found because you had to provide Lydecker with a means of getting his ex-wife's code. Where did you keep poor George all that time? Was his car in your garage? Do you have one of the freezers that can keep a body nice and cold?"

"You sure have a grisly imagination."

Tracy shook her head. "You got what you needed from Finnegan and then you killed him. The only thing I'm not sure about is if you offered him money to kill Cynthia and he turned you down. Is that why you killed him? Or did you always want to handle the murder yourself and knew George couldn't be around to tell anyone what he'd done for you?"

"Another question you know I won't answer."

"Of course, you probably wanted to make sure George had given you the right information and that the keys worked. Sometime before the murder you visited Cynthia's house while she was otherwise occupied. That's when you noticed the wall photos and came up with your idea about the photograph. So, when you returned to her house to kill her, you brought that picture with you. I guess you must have attended one of those Y3D meetings and snapped that picture yourself. Cynthia wouldn't have posed for it. It would have made her uncomfortable. She wanted no glory or attention for her work when it came to drunk driving. She would never have put that picture on her wall."

"Good luck proving *that*."

"I guess the only other question was how you found out about her. And I guess the only possible answer is that Kimberly Acosta told you. She must have told you a woman named Cynthia Lydecker came to her house and confessed. But she must also have insisted you move on. She had no idea what you really had in your heart and mind — the desire for revenge and the willingness to carry it out. I remember during our initial interview that you told me you thought about being a cop before starting law school. I mean if you knew you someday wanted to find and kill the person or people who killed the woman you loved, being in law enforcement would be the perfect way to do that. You'd have access to information and of course firearms. But of course, you have to pass a psych exam. Maybe you thought you wouldn't be able to. So, you opted for being a lawyer instead — a criminal lawyer. One who would hobnob with killers and learn the dos and don'ts of getting away with murder. I bet you've been taking notes since day one, haven't you, Tyler?"

Tyler was now covering his eyes and shaking his head. When would this woman finally just shut up?

"So, after Kimberly told you about Cynthia, you did your research, and you came to the same conclusion we all did about Ed Lydecker. You waited until Kimberly died, and then you put your plan into action — and that included leaving your big law firm, because you wouldn't necessarily have the control over things you would at a much smaller place. And that's when I came into the picture: bad timing for me, perfect timing for you. And after you earned my trust and friendship, you began things in earnest."

Tracy stood up; she couldn't hold back the tears the anymore. It wasn't helping matters that Tyler Wannamaker was just sitting there in silence. He didn't even have the courtesy to deny anything, like an innocent person would. But Tyler wasn't innocent; he was the furthest thing from it.

"I have to admit, Tyler, you gave a brilliant performance. Every feigned outrage, every phony surprised look, and every pretend reaction to the latest discovery: flawless. I even thought that Katie might be the killer at one point. I thought maybe Keith *was* having an affair and Katie found out about it. Clients have lied to me before. Her conference was just in Virginia. She could have driven into the city, killed Cynthia, and then returned. And then she turned to you to defend her husband, knowing if you did find out the truth, you'd let Keith go down for it before you'd expose her. But I had that wrong didn't I, Tyler?

"It would seem so."

"How could you, Tyler?" Tracy asked, crying. "How could you hurt all those people over what was an *accident*? How could you drag your own family into it? How could you hurt your sister like that? How could have hurt Jim...*HOW COULD YOU*?"

Tyler Wannamaker, not in complete control of his faculties, couldn't keep his mouth shut anymore. He stood up.

"How could I? Listen, Tracy, if the police had done their job 20 years ago then none of this would have been necessary! Is it so hard to believe at least one of them had to be sacrificed because of their, at best, incompetence, or, at worst, helping cover up what happened?

You don't think Alastair Conroy might have known what happened but made sure no one else did?! Please. The Conroys and Lydeckers of the world think they can do whatever they want. They *deserved* what they got! They didn't do the right thing, so they deserved it!"

"And what about *you*, Tyler?! Huh?! What do *you* deserve for all that you've done? Are you above the law?!"

"I righted the scales! Things are as they should be now. You should be thanking me. You hated that Hammersmith bitch more than I did."

"I never wished her *dead*, Tyler! I would never have wanted that! So don't you *dare* think I'm *ANYTHING* like you!"

They were now positioned on opposite sides of the room, red-faced and glaring at each other. And then, out of the blue, Tyler Wannamaker started laughing, laughing so hard he had to sit down. Tracy's jaw dropped as she bore witness.

"You know what's so funny, Tracy?" he finally was able to ask. "I think you'll appreciate the answer."

"What's so funny, Tyler?" Tracy asked angrily as she wiped the tears from her cheeks.

"I feel nothing; absolutely *nothing*. I thought I'd feel a sense of victory, or at least satisfaction. Despite all the complications, it all worked out, more or less. Everyone knows what they did; it's part of their legacy now — their forever *tainted* legacy. But I feel nothing. Isn't that the damndest thing?"

Tracy gulped and looked at her soon-to-be former associate intently.

"Well, it's like I told you at the beginning. If you want to be happy, you must forgive and let go, otherwise it will eat you up inside until you can't feel anything anymore. You'll never be happy. And you're living proof of that, Tyler. You couldn't move on and now look at you. I guess you're a bachelor because Jeannine is still with you. But she's not in your heart, Tyler. If she were there you never would have done what you did. You let the love she may have had for you turn into a cancer and it has left you hollow. Is it really any surprise you feel nothing?"

Tyler by now had stopped laughing. He was more concerned over what he had just more or less admitted. He never would have done such a stupid thing sober. But Tracy was sober, and how stupid was *she* allowing herself to be alone with a multiple murderer? What was *her* excuse?

"What you did Tyler, is unforgivable. Not only is Cindy Lydecker, Jim Lucas, and George Finnegan's blood on your hands, but so are Ed Lydecker and Shirley Hammersmith's. And then there are poor Debra Dooley and Alastair Conroy's lives you've destroyed. And no matter how you try to justify things, what you put your sister and brother-in-law through will haunt them forever."

Tracy shook her head. "God forgive me for saying this, but you're *evil* Tyler! You're inhuman. I've met some pretty despicable killers over the last five years, but you're the…I just can't believe what you did."

Tracy shook her head again. She had said all she had wanted to say — more than that. She couldn't remember the last time she had felt so indescribably awful. If she had to rank it, it would fall in third place, behind the night her father died — which would always be the worst night of her life — and the night Brian broke her heart.

Tyler Wannamaker was now looking at her. He could sense she was finished. And he didn't feel like laughing anymore.

"You really do have guts, Tracy. Saying these things to someone you think killed a cop. That's either gutsy or stupid, and I know you're not stupid."

"Just get out Tyler," Tracy said quietly. "Get out, and never come back."

"What a coincidence. I was just sitting here — before you showed up — wondering how I was going to give you my notice. I've enjoyed it here of course. But I miss the courtroom. You know. The excitement of cross examining a witness you figure is telling the truth but making it sound like they aren't. The satisfaction you get when you hear a not guilty verdict when you know damn well the opposite is true."

"Jesus, Tyler…"

"What, Tracy? You don't feel the same way? All I have is my work. And I'm good at it. I'm very good at it. What's wrong in taking pride in it?"

"Just leave, Tyler. I don't want to talk to you anymore, or to look at you."

"Mm. You sound angry. I would think you'd be scared."

She looked at Tyler defiantly. "I'm not scared of you. You can't kill me too. Brian knows I'm here and Art Pankow knows there's something off about this whole thing too."

Tyler laughed. "I don't want to kill you, Tracy. Really, I don't. In fact, if you were available, I would love to take you to bed. A woman with your passion and intelligence…Well, there's just something about making a smart and beautiful woman cry out in pleasure. It's one of the few times she behaves like the animal she really is."

Tracy covered her mouth. She could taste bile. And Tyler Wannamaker was going to have his turn.

"That Brian is sure a lucky man. I envy him. I sure had a hard time restraining myself from sneaking a peek at those incredible breasts of yours when you were pumping. Mm mm mm…"

The tears returned to her eyes. What was it with these men — Jim Lucas and Tyler Wannamaker — who looked at her as some object to be desired? Is this really how all men ultimately saw her? Even Brian at times made her feel like his main interest in her was physical. She wanted to protest. Instead, she bit her lip. And she put her hand in her suit jacket pocket feeling for the pepper spray.

"But alas, I know I will never know such pleasures," he continued. "And since we both know what I will never do, let's talk about what *you* will never do. There is absolutely no proof against me. None. This little meeting tonight never happened. Even if you do manage to find someone from all those years ago who can put me and Jeannine together, it proves nothing. You have no witnesses. You have no physical evidence. All you have is an imagination. That's all.

"And let's not forget about ethics here. You found out what you found out via that calendar book. No book, no Kimberly Acosta to interview. And that book was discovered as part of your — of *our* — defense of Keith. It's privileged. Your whole case against me hinges on the case against Keith. No way can you go to the cops with what you're thinking. You'd lose your law license. You might lose more than that."

Wannamaker let his words hang in the air a few moments.

"But as I told you, I like you and don't wish any harm on you, despite you thinking I'm some kind of monster. I wish you well. And it's in your best interest to wish me well, too. Take satisfaction in that you figured most everything out — or at least think you did. And leave it at that. Okay?" He smiled at her.

"Goodbye, Tyler," Tracy mumbled.

"Goodbye, Tracy. I will trust you with my final paycheck, which should include some much earned but untaken vacation. I've already been in discussions with my next place of employment. So, no one should be bothering you for references. I think that's it unless you want to help with my personal things. It won't take me too long to gather them up."

"Go ahead. Empty out a box of copy paper if you need a box."

"Thank you. I'll do that."

And he did. He removed his framed certificates and whatnot from the wall. He removed some personal magazines and journals and tossed them in too. The last thing was his unfinished bottle of J&B, which was soon stored securely. It took both hands to balance the container given the size of the picture frames. Tracy stepped aside and let Tyler pass. Then she followed him to the door. He put the box down and withdrew his keys. Without a word he removed the office door key and handed it to Tracy. Then he picked up his belongings as Tracy opened the door for him. Tracy watched as he eventually boarded an elevator car. She watched him smile at her one last time before the doors closed. And then Tyler Wannamaker was gone.

The first thing Tracy did was change all the passwords to the various office computers. She also contacted her alarm company's emergency number and changed the code to the office's alarm. And then she called a 24-hour locksmith and had the locks changed on the main entrance door. She'd deal with the building's management later. Tracy figured she'd just have to be in the office early tomorrow to give Rebecca and Neal their new keys and pass codes. But now she had to get home to do the same thing for her personal residence that she had just done for her office. She had no way of being certain that George Finnegan hadn't provided Tyler Wannamaker with someone else's information. Tomorrow she would advise Neal, Rebecca, and Elias Tanner, Sr. to do the same.

It was almost 1:00 a.m. when Tracy finally got home. While she and Brian waited for the arrival of the locksmith, she told him everything. She cried during most of the telling. Brian held her, listening, occasionally nodding or shaking his head. He made no comments since Tracy wasn't quite yet looking for feedback. Right now, she was a wife telling a husband what was eating away at her.

When she had finished, she wiped her eyes and blew her nose. She looked at Brian.

"What am I going to do, Brian? I don't know what I'm going to do."

He shook his head. "But we have to do something. He might change his mind about you."

Tracy nodded. "That's what I'm afraid of. He's so sick in the head, so twisted. One day he may decide he doesn't want me around anymore."

"Any ideas?"

"In a few minutes I'm going to write down everything I just told you. And then I'm going to make copies of it. You ever see in the movies where someone arranges correspondence to be opened in the event of their death?"

"Jesus…" Brian grumbled.

"Art will get a copy; so, will El. I'm afraid if Tyler does try something, he's not …He might not just go after me."

Brian blew out a sigh. He couldn't argue with her. And such a person might not stop at him and Tracy. Such a person might go after their children.

"I have to talk to El about this. He'll have some ideas."

"Do *you* have any?" Brian asked, sounding desperate.

"Yes. Jim Lucas. I haven't quite figured out just exactly what Tyler did the night he killed Jim Lucas. I have a general idea. But there might be something to find. He'll never go down for Cynthia Lydecker's death. And George Finnegan is just as unlikely. So, my best bet is helping the police any way I can with Jim."

"Without getting yourself in trouble, you mean."

"Jim wasn't a client. But, if, at the end of it all, it's a question of either keeping my license or helping nail that monster, I'll choose the latter. I mean it."

"Okay, Tracy."

"And we can't tell anyone about this, Brian. Not my mother, not Crys and El-J, not anybody. He's going to be watching me — watching us. I know it. I can't be vigilant 24/7 and I don't want to live like that. So, I must get him first. I have to figure out how to get him first. And if he knows me as much as he thinks he does, then he'll know I won't leave things as they are."

"And you tell me what you need *me* to do, and I'll do it, love."

Tracy smiled. "I'm going to want to run scans on all of our computers, home and office, just in case Tyler put some spyware on them or something. But for right now just hold me. Make me feel safe for a few hours. Help me pretend there really aren't monsters hiding in the shadows."

Brian pressed his forehead against Tracy's temple. The two of them sat together until the locksmith came and went. And then they sat together again. They would be next to each other on the couch for the rest of the early morning. Tracy's eyes were closed but her mind wouldn't follow their example. There had to be something; there had to be something out there Tyler Wannamaker hadn't counted on. He had to have erred somewhere. No murder was perfect. Tyler's plan hadn't gone as he had originally intended, had it? No one has the ability to properly predict every person's actions and reactions. That was impossible. And it could be the key to Tyler's undoing.

Tracy started thinking about the monsters from her childhood: the black and white images of Dracula, the Wolf Man, and the Frankenstein monster that she had seen on the Brubaker family's television screen. When she was a child, her father had shown her the classic horror movies and she never particularly liked them. As she grew older though she had revisited them and grown to at least appreciate them. She especially liked the fact that in those old movies, good always triumphed. The monster could be destroyed: a stake or ray of sun would take care of a vampire; a silver bullet would stop a werewolf; and very few monsters — especially manmade ones —

could withstand fire. So, Tracy would find out what it took to dispose of one Tyler Wannamaker — metaphorically speaking, of course. Right now, he was a monster among us, living in the sunlight. And Tracy was fully prepared to go monster hunting, in the hopes of sending him back into the shadows — the ones protected by very real iron bars.

PART II: …BUT DELIVER US FROM EVIL

Chapter 14

As much as she didn't want to, Tracy nevertheless told her horror story to Neal Bennett, Elias Tanner, Sr., and Rebecca Dietz. She even got upset enough, once again, where she had to pause. Neal was the first to comment after she had finished.

"I say we have him killed," Neal hissed.

"Not funny," Tracy responded.

"Who said I was trying to be funny? Do I look or sound like I find *any* of this the least bit amusing?"

Tracy just looked at her associate. Then she looked at Elias Tanner, Sr.

"What are *your* thoughts, El?"

"Right now, disbelief."

"You don't believe me?"

"Oh, I believe you all right. I just meant that during my almost 30 years on the job I thought I'd seen it all — or at least heard about it. I was wrong."

"You look so tired, Tracy," Rebecca said sympathetically. "Why don't you lie down on your sofa for a little while?"

"I'll be fine, thanks. I may have circles under my eyes, but my mind is spinning."

The secretary chuckled lightly. "And then some, I bet."

Tracy again looked at Tanner. "Do you think you can reach out to Jim's partner, Bill Culpepper?"

"And tell him what?"

"Just ask to see the reports on Jim's death. I'm curious if he went directly home from Hooligan's House that night or if he made a stop somewhere."

"A stop? What kind of stop?"

"I don't know exactly. I know he tried getting a hold of Cheryl Whittaker about any pictures she may have taken at Cindy's house. What I don't know is if or how she responded. Art didn't tell me that. And the fact is I'm not sure when and where Tyler picked up Jim's trail that night. It seems awfully tight for Tyler to have followed me to the pub, gone back to my office to read my report, and then go to Jim's place to wait for him. There must be something about that night I haven't figured out. The answer could be in the report. Plus, Jim's death probably wasn't planned out like Cynthia's was. Tyler had years to think about that. But killing Jim was a panic kill, in a manner of speaking. If Tyler screwed up, it's likely going to be related to Jim."

Tanner was nodding. "All right; you've convinced me. I'm sure Culpepper will cooperate. The poor son of a bitch was still inside Lydecker's house when Conroy started shooting. He's battling his own demons right now."

"Guilt over not being there to protect Lydecker? He'd most likely be dead too."

"I agree."

"What do you want *me* to do?" Neal asked.

"Nothing right now except to be careful and watchful. Tyler's probably sober right now and wondering what the hell is going on *here* today. For the time being I want all of us leaving together. We'll order our lunches in. We'll *all* be careful."

"Great," Neal muttered.

"You can't tell Sara about this, Neal. If she asks, just say your current case is very stressful. You wouldn't be lying."

"Yeah; sure."

"And El, Tyler may have some pals at the Northeastern district. Be careful how you approach Detective Culpepper. I know you can't discuss all the details with him. But I'm sure once he understands that Lydecker may not have killed Jim, he'll want to help."

"You better hope Culpepper isn't one of Tyler's 'pals'," Neal grunted.

Tracy stared at her associate. Then she looked back at Tanner.

"Jeez. Neal has a point. I never considered that. Just how well do you know Bill Culpepper, El?"

"I don't. He recently transferred into the unit. Before that he was with computer crimes in the Southwest District. But I hear good things."

"Still, you should talk to someone you trust and who would be discreet. As few people as possible should know what we're doing."

"All right," Tanner agreed.

"Tracy," Neal said. "Have you considered talking to Keith Entwistle?"

"No," was the emphatic answer. "Not at this point anyway. It would do no good. He was charged only with Cynthia's murder. And there's no way Tyler is ever going down for that."

"But didn't you say Tyler was with Keith and Katie for some part of that Thursday night?"

"Yes, I did — and he was. But I don't know exactly what time he left. And asking Keith about that now is dangerous. I thought of asking them last night before I left to confront Tyler. But I was afraid Tyler would ask them if *I* asked them any questions. I guess I was worried about putting Keith — maybe even Katie — in any danger. Personally, I think Tyler is a ticking time bomb."

"Neal's right though," Tanner offered. "It would help things if we knew what time he left them. And I think Keith could be of further help to us too."

"I don't want to pull him into this yet, if at all. Any contact we have with him is likely to get back to Tyler somehow. It's too risky."

"All right then," Tanner sighed. "We start with Culpepper and see where that takes us. But Tracy, Jim was my partner for four years. If I decide Keith Entwistle needs to be talked to, I'm talking to him."

Tracy nodded. "All right, El. But please warn me ahead of time. Okay?"

"Okay. Now let me start my background on Culpepper. I'll keep you guys in the loop."

Tracy moved towards Tanner and hugged him.

"And don't forget to be careful, El."

"I plan to be. But to be honest I almost wish Wannamaker would try something. I've still got most of my wits about me. I just need an excuse to use them for battle."

Tracy released Tanner and smiled. Then she watched him leave. Soon Neal and Rebecca were returning to their familiar places in the law office. Tracy closed her private office's door, kicked off her shoes, and laid down on her sofa. Soon she was asleep. She just couldn't fight it off anymore.

Detective William Culpepper had always enjoyed cloak and dagger movies. He liked play acting too. He and his older brother would sometimes play hide and seek when their mom dragged them to the grocery store with her. They would pretend to be opposing spies trying to hide from their mutual nemesis, codename: Mother. Now he was standing in a Safeway looking at various flavors of tortilla chips, having been summoned for some top-secret meeting. And soon his company arrived.

"Hi, Bill," Elias Tanner, Sr. said as he approached.

"Elias." They shook hands. "Forgive the lack of small talk, but what is this all about?"

"No one knows you're seeing me, right?"

"Nope. And I didn't notice anyone following me either. What's got you so daggone paranoid?"

"I can't explain everything. But I will tell you this. It's quite possible — I'd even go as far as to say it's a certainty — that Edward Lydecker did *not* kill Jim Lucas."

Culpepper at first remained quiet. He reached for the spicy chili-flavored snacks. "Jim knew, you know?"

"He knew what?"

"Right from the beginning he knew there was something wrong about this case. That first night. I mean he just *knew* it."

"You'll develop those kinds of instincts the longer you stay on the job."

"Will I? I hope so. So, I take it you can't give me all of the details."

"No. I'm sorry. It's very complicated."

"I'll bet. I know you do work for Tracy Shane. I've heard Pankow talk about her before. I swear he thinks she's his kid sister or something. He'll complain about her sometimes but the minute someone says something against her he'll jump down their throat. It's bizarre."

"Tracy's special. Take my word for it."

"Sure. Jim liked her too. Some even say they had a date the night he died."

"Not *that* kind of date. Just a meeting. She's happily married. Just take my word for that too."

"Uh-huh. So, what is it Tracy found out that she can't tell the police?"

Tanner looked at Culpepper. The people he'd reached out to this afternoon had said Culpepper was a sharp one, and not to be fooled by his boyish face or seeming lack of experience in homicide. He was good at playing the deferential new guy out of respect to those with more years on the job than he had. But he was always thinking. Tanner concluded they had been right.

"All right. I won't jerk you around. But I also am not going to get Tracy into any trouble. So, for now, I'd just like to look at the file you have on Jim's murder. I'm especially interested in the time from when he left the restaurant to when he was shot."

"You just want the report?"

"Yes, for now. It's the only thing Tracy hasn't seen."

"And she wants to see it, huh?"

"Yes."

Culpepper nodded. "You know, I heard the craziest rumor today."

"You did? What's that?"

"Tyler Wannamaker is no longer with Tracy. Is that true?"

Tanner hesitated before answering, "It is."

"I guess the case really got to him, being it was his brother-in-law who was accused."

"Sure."

"You know Wannamaker very well?"

"Not really. He worked for Tracy a little over two years, but I never really got to know him."

"Mm. Well, I know *about* him. I hear he's an asshole."

Tanner couldn't help but chuckle. "Why do you say that?"

"Heard about how he would treat us in court. And if the public were going through one of their 'hate all police' phases, he'd never fail to take advantage. Quite honestly, from what I've heard about him and what I've learned about Tracy, I have no idea why the two of them joined forces."

"Well, maybe that's why he left."

"Uh-huh. I also heard something else."

"Really?"

Culpepper turned and was now meeting Tanner's eyes. "Wannamaker knew Finnegan. Some of the guys from IA said his name came up when they were looking at George for taking bribes. Nothing was ever proven though. I gotta tell you, this case is chock full of coincidences, isn't it?"

"Were you thinking Entwistle hooked up with Finnegan through his brother-in-law?"

"I really don't see how that works. Why would Wannamaker ever have reason to introduce George to some cook? It doesn't make sense."

"Not really."

"Besides, we're not looking at Entwistle as a killer anymore. Right?"

"Right."

Culpepper looked around and started nodding.

"I'll get you the file, Elias. And I'll get you anything else I can. You just ask. Now I must go home. My wife's making her meatloaf and I promised I'd be home to read our two-year-old his bedtime stories. I'll be in touch."

Culpepper patted Tanner on the shoulder before grabbing his selection — Monterey Jack-flavored chips — from the shelf. Tanner watched him walk towards the register. Then Culpepper grabbed a chocolate bar from the impulse-buy offerings. Tanner suddenly liked Detective William Culpepper — a lot.

"Petaw wants this one, Mommy," Nicole said while handing Tracy *The Cat in the Hat*. "It's his most favorite."

Tracy chuckled. "Peter likes Thomas stories, sweetie. *You* like cats."

The light haired, blue-eyed tyke climbed onto her mother's lap. "It's okay Mommy. Read." Mommy obliged.

Bonkers was lying at Tracy's feet, waiting for Brian to be finished with changing Peter into his nighttime onesie. Then it would be time to go outside and exercise a bit. When Brian came down holding his son, he whistled and Bonkers came running. Brian went outside with both Bonkers and Peter. Peter enjoyed watching the dog running about. And Brian liked looking at his son looking at Bonkers.

Violetta sat down on the couch next to her daughter and granddaughter. Nicole decided she wanted to sit in Grammaw's lap for the rest of the cat's tale. Violetta though was more interested in how Tracy was doing. She knew her daughter *very* well. And she knew something was *very* wrong. But Tracy wouldn't share any details.

After Nicole and Bonkers had been tucked in for the evening, the attorney retreated to her bedroom to nurse Peter to sleep. Violetta confronted her son-in-law.

"I can't get into it, Mom," Brian told her. "It's work-related and confidential. Tracy will be fine."

"That's what you always tell me. If her job keeps doing this to her, she should quit and stay home."

Brian sighed. "I'll be talking to Tracy about that very thing in the near future. But right now, she needs our support. So please, try and go easy on her. I think being with her family like this is what is keeping her together."

"I knew it," Violetta said, tears now in her eyes. "Something's wrong."

"It will be fine," Brian tried to say convincingly. He hugged Violetta, who just waved a hand and then retreated to her bedroom. With particular vigilance Brian secured the first floor. He almost goofed when he nearly entered their old alarm code. Soon however he was on his way upstairs.

Tracy was under the covers when he entered. He soon joined her and then realized she had nothing on underneath. Without a word she started kissing him. He responded in kind. She wanted Brian close to her right now and for him to feel close to her. And she knew for a certainty that making love with him would make Brian feel that way.

The experience was an intense one. They were both sweating by its conclusion. Tracy was now looking in Brian's eyes, saying nothing. She didn't have to. The silence was noisy enough. Eventually Tracy rolled onto to her back and was staring at the ceiling. She started smiling.

"Want to hear something funny?" she asked.

Brian turned his head so he could look at her. "Sure."

"It's the very first piece of marital advice my mother ever gave me." She looked at him. "In fact, she gave it to me the night you met her and Dad."

Brian turned over, reached his arm across Tracy's waist, and pulled her towards him. "What did she say?"

"She told me the way she held onto my father was by keeping his stomach full and his bed warm."

Brian let out a guffaw. "She really said that?"

"Yup. Shocked me to my innermost core, she did."

He laughed again. "Well, you didn't get here via a stork."

"I didn't?"

"No.

"Mm. You think Nicole and Peter will be horrified one day to consider what you and I do in here on occasion?"

"Of course, they will be. It's the way things are."

"Mm. I don't know if I'd share what my mother said with Nicole, though. I mean it's not really me who's keeping your belly full now is it."

Brian started moving his hand over her stomach. "Don't worry. You *more* than make up for it with that other thing."

Tracy chuckled. "Oh, do I?"

"Sizzling."

She grinned. "I know it makes you happy and I want to keep you happy."

"I *am* happy, Tracy. Even on the nights when the oven is off."

"Oh, you're cute."

"Do I keep *you* happy, Tracy?"

Tracy took Brian's hand. "Yes, Brian. If I didn't have you in my life right now, I don't think I could handle what just happened. I'm so happy you're here waiting for me every day."

"I always will be."

"When this is over, Brian…" Tracy looked back at the ceiling.

"What is it?"

"Nothing really. I just mean when this is over, we're going to have that long family vacation that keeps getting messed with. I promise."

Brian kissed her cheek. "I'll look forward to it. But right now, I'm perfectly content just having you here."

"Beats that picture I had taken for you, huh?"

"No contest. Besides, you have a bikini on in that photo. I like you *much* better like this."

"Uh-huh," Tracy grinned.

Then she kissed him. She next positioned herself so his arm could be wrapped around her shoulder, and she could lean her head against his. He had such strong shoulders. She gently ran her fingers across his chest before giving him one last kiss and smile for the night. It was this type of moment that she wanted to remember as sleep overtook her. Moments like this helped keep the monsters at bay.

Elias Tanner, Sr. and his wife Rita were lunch guests at the Shane household on Saturday. Nicole and Bonkers seemed the most excited to see them. Tracy's daughter, like Tracy herself when she was little, called the visitors Aunt Rita and Uncle El. There were hugs and kisses to spare. Rita brought treats, even some for Bonkers. As a result, the canine rarely left Rita's side the entire visit.

After the noontime meal, Tracy and Tanner moved stealthily upstairs to the home office, where Tracy secured the door. Tanner pulled out a flash drive and soon its contents were uploaded on Tracy's computer.

"Bill scanned everything he could find," Tanner said. "Technically this isn't public-accessible yet, so Bill is taking a risk here."

"I hope he feels it's worth it down the line."

"He will. You help put Wannamaker away, you'll have a new best friend."

"Mm. Detective Culpepper already had his suspicions, huh?"

"Something like that. But he has no idea of the reasons behind it."

"No." Tracy took a deep breath. "All right, let's look at this thing. We'll start with making a timeline."

The two did so. And it was puzzling. Jim Lucas' receipt from Hooligan's House had him paying his bill at 9:38 p.m. So that meant he was there about an hour after Tracy had left. A discussion with the waitress had confirmed he left very shortly after paying. Witnesses place the gunshots at having been fired at 12:16 a.m.

"Two and a half hours," Tanner muttered. "It's 20 minutes from Hooligan's to Jim's house. So that still leaves more than two hours."

"I wonder where he went," Tracy mused. "Is there anything about Cheryl Whittaker's whereabouts in here?"

"She went to dinner and the movies with her family. Bill checked. He knew Jim had called Cheryl too."

"Mm. Jim didn't have a lady friend, did he?"

Tanner looked at Tracy. "Not that anyone could find."

Tracy just sighed. "I think he may still have been in love with his ex. But he hated himself for it."

Tanner grinned. "Know about such things, do you?"

"Both men and women pine away for lost loves, El. There's this thing call the Miss Havisham effect when referring to someone who becomes addicted to the grief over losing someone."

"Uh-huh."

Tracy frowned. "Forget it, then. But where did he go—" Tracy stopped talking.

"What? What is it?"

"He said my name."

"That's right. The witness said all Jim said was 'Tracy'."

"But why? Why did he say my name?"

Tanner sighed. "Don't you know?"

"That he was in love with me? Come on, El. That wasn't love. He may have been attracted to me. But why would he let himself get hung up on someone he could never have?"

"People do it all the time."

"I think I was just a female that was showing him kindness. So, he was drawn to that. But my point is maybe he wanted a message delivered to me or something. But he passed out before he could say what it was."

"…Which means will never know *what it was*."

Tracy started scanning the file, looking for something to indicate where Lucas had spent the missing two hours.

"I think I may have things mixed up. Maybe Tyler didn't read my report until *after* he killed Jim. Maybe Jim went someplace that alarmed Tyler, and then Tyler went looking to see if Jim told me anything about it. You see why it's so important we know what Jim did?"

"Of course, I do. But the investigators have been trying to find that out for a week now."

Tracy continued scanning the images. Then suddenly she sat up straight.

"Crap! I'm such an *idiot*!"

"What?" Tanner asked, mildly alarmed.

"He told me; he sat there and told me."

"Told you what?"

"The picture, El. He wanted to find out about the picture. And he was drinking that night and feeling bad about it. He knew he was drinking too much. What if he went to try and see someone from Y3D?"

"…To follow up on the picture."

"Yes!"

"But that late at night?"

"When do you think young people meet, El, during normal business hours? They'd be in school. It's at night they'd hang out together."

"I guess you have a point there."

"Let's find out everything we can about Y3D. And then we should talk to the people in charge of it; see if they remember Jim being there or at least asking questions. Detective Culpepper might be able to help with that."

"All right; it's something."

"We can still keep looking of course. But I bet Jim was bent on figuring out who took the picture and when it was taken and why it was on Cynthia's wall. I think I've already answered the first and last questions. The middle one though…"

"Okay. I'm with you."

Tracy smiled. "Are you doing okay, El?"

"I am. You?"

"Still a little shaky. But I'm all right."

"How can you be shaky *and* all right?" Tanner grinned.

"Fine. I'm *mostly* all right."

"You saved a copy of the file, right?"

"Oh sure." Tracy removed the flash drive and handed it to Tanner. "He you go."

He took it and thanked her. "You know, if all else fails, there is something we could try."

Tracy nodded. "You mean try and set Tyler up using me as bait?"

Tanner sighed. "You thought about that too, huh?"

"Of course, I did. But he wouldn't fall for something like that. He might even be expecting it."

"But he's also probably nervous and jumpy. That will make him more likely to make a mistake."

"You have any ideas?"

"I have some; one in particular. And the beauty of it is you'd be totally protected."

Tracy smirked. "I'd have to be, otherwise you'd never let me do it."

Tanner smirked back. "You have me there."

"Let's revisit this later. I'm not feeling very brave right now."

"Of course. I just meant that we have other options if this picture thing doesn't work out. But I'll look into it just like I promised."

"All right. We better go back downstairs. I'll look at this some more later."

"I'll do the same."

The two exchanged smiles before they left the office. The smiles were hopeful ones. They had to remain hopeful. The other option was just too depressing. Who wanted to feel defeated?

Tracy and Tanner rejoined their family. Their business was done so they'd indulge in pleasure for the remainder of the Tanners' visit. And then they could resume their hunt. Their prey was certainly a wily individual. But he still may have left some tracks behind. And maybe — just maybe — Tracy and Tanner had discovered a place where some could be found.

Chapter 15

Elias Tanner, Sr. was pleased to learn that Youth Against Drunk and Drugged Driving had their weekly meetings on Sunday nights, sometimes more often than that if necessary. Sadly, there was a seemingly never-ending stream of new faces that would attend. They could be loved ones who lost someone; a survivor of an accident; a friend to a person who habitually drank; or just someone who wanted to learn more about what the organization did. But Tanner figured his reason for being here was rather unique. He sighed as he pulled into the parking lot of the building.

The charity operated out of a Baptist church. Signs had been placed along the lawn so there would be no problem for a newbie to find his or her way. When Tanner entered the medium-sized room, he immediately smelled the coffee and moved in its direction. Several homemade items were also available: breads, cookies, and muffins. Tanner passed on those. He filled a Styrofoam cup and took his first sip as he looked around the room. Wow — the coffee was pretty dang good.

The attendees were, as expected, a mix of all types since drunk drivers didn't discriminate based on race, religion, social class, or anything else. Some here appeared to be from well-to-do families. Others had holes in their shoes. But what they all had in common was a hurt in their eyes that was unique. The only other place he'd seen such a look was in the eyes of parents who'd just lost a child to violence. The look would never really go away.

The person that Tanner was looking for, however, was the one whose photograph he had, the one Tracy had forwarded to him from the phone snapshots she had taken at Cynthia Lydecker's house. And Tanner saw him too. He was near the front, dressed in a polo shirt and jeans, and rather unkempt looking with a scraggly beard that seemed poised to devour his face. He was speaking with — or rather listening to — someone and nodding occasionally. Tanner suddenly had an eerie feeling. If he swapped out the person doing the talking and replaced her with Cynthia, Tanner could have replicated the photograph he was looking at. There was no doubt about it. That image Cynthia had on her wall was captured right here. As to the when it was taken, Tanner hoped the young man up front would be able to help.

Tanner moved towards one of the empty metal chairs and sat down. It wasn't long before everyone else was following his example. The bearded man hopped up on the stage and greeted everyone, encouraging them to grab whatever refreshments they desired and then to have a seat.

"For those among us who don't know me," the host began, "My name is Bobby Swinton and I'm the executive director of Y3D. 14 years ago, on my way home from a party, I killed someone. I was 17 years old, and I was drunk. It was my first offense. I lost my license for a few months and was fined. That was it. I didn't spend one day in jail. I guess I should have been happy. But I wasn't. The person whose life I took would never feel anything again.

"To make a long story short, I decided that I needed to do *something*. With my family and friends' support, we launched the Youth Against Drunk and Drugged Driving initiative nine years ago. What makes us different from similar organizations is that we target teenagers and preteens. We want to educate them *now*, not later. Later is always too late. And the one thing I've found when talking to young people is that they don't want to hear bullshit. They don't want catchphrases. So, when I sit down and talk to a group of people, I can speak from personal experience and tragedy. So can other people who volunteer their time. So, if there's anyone out there tonight who would like to do that, I'd love to talk to with you sometime."

Swinton cleared his throat. "Now to follow up on some old business. On Friday, the Pastor told me he had received the formal approval to rename this room we're all in right now Cynthia Lydecker Hall."

The crowd started applauding. Swinton was visibly moved; he made no effort to hide his tears. Tanner clapped his hands also. Swinton held up a hand in hopes the gathered would let him continue.

"We were worried after what was said about her that this might not happen. But we needn't have. Thank you to everyone who helped support our wish to honor this woman who worked behind the scenes and helped us in so, so many ways — a woman who wanted no recognition. I will miss Cynthia more than most people because I knew her. So again, I thank everyone for their support.

"Now, there's someone here tonight who I would like to give the opportunity to speak. Two Saturdays ago, her parents were coming home from a date when they were sideswiped by a drunk driver. Her father lost control of the car and was hit by multiple vehicles. Both her parents died. The person who caused all of this was unharmed. And he's 18 years old. The young lady you're about to meet is 15. And she needs to know she's not alone. Please welcome Lacey."

As the applause resumed, although much more restrained, Tanner looked about. Most attendees had already started weeping. By the end of Lacey's tale, they were doing more than that. Tanner had a lump in his throat. He wanted to leave. But he needed to remain. And when the meeting had officially ended, he wiped his eyes and blew his nose. Then he rose to stand in line to speak with Bob Swinton.

Tanner introduced himself as he and Swinton shook hands. The latter had a warm grip and genuine smile. But Tanner could see the hurt in Swinton's eyes too.

"Can I show you a picture, Bobby?" Tanner asked after the brief self-introduction. "It's of you and Cynthia. I'm wondering if you might remember when it was taken."

"Sure," Swinton nodded. Tanner showed the image that was on his smartphone. Swinton studied it a moment. "Oh," he said finally. "I'm wearing my new sweatshirt — the one my girlfriend got me for Christmas. I think that was taken in January."

"This past January?"

"Right," Swinton confirmed.

Tanner nodded. That made sense. Tracy had told him her theory that Tyler Wannamaker obtained the key and code from George Finnegan in November — right before he killed him — and that he probably visited Cynthia's house in advance. That would have been when he saw the picture wall. It was probably Finnegan also who told Wannamaker about Cynthia's attendance at these meetings. And that led to Tanner's next question, which was also accompanied by a photograph, this one being of Tracy's former associate.

"Can you tell me if you recognize this man?" Tanner asked.

Swinton again studied the photo. "I don't think so."

"He was at the January meeting when this picture was taken. He was the one who took it."

"Oh," Swinton murmured. "Hm. I really can't say he's familiar. Sorry."

Tanner smiled. Swinton's answer hadn't surprised him. Wannamaker wouldn't just show up without some disguise, maybe a hat and probably dark glasses. Somebody wanting to remain anonymous was probably a common occurrence here and wouldn't raise an eyebrow.

"Okay, Bobby. Just a couple more questions. I believe you spoke previously to a Detective Jim Lucas."

Swinton sighed loudly and nodded. "Yeah. I heard what happened."

"He talked to you about Cynthia, right?"

"Yeah. He wanted to know if anyone ever had any problems with her or anything. There was nothing I could tell him. We didn't talk long."

"Mm," Tanner said, scratching his chin. "And he didn't try to follow up with you at any point?"

"No."

"Were you here the Thursday he was killed?"

Swinton started shaking his head. "I'm not here on Thursdays. Letty's here then."

"Do you know if she saw Detective Lucas that night by any chance?"

"I don't know. I haven't talked to her since that night. She's not always here Sundays. And she's not here tonight."

"I'd really like to talk to her. But I understand you may not want to give any personal information. If I left you my card, would see that she gets it and calls me?"

"Sure, I'll do that for you. I'll call her right now if you want."

Tanner smiled. "I'd really appreciate that."

"All right."

Swinton pulled out his phone, scrolled through his phone book, and found the number he was looking for. Soon he was talking to his associate. And then he was handing his phone to Tanner.

"I'm working right now," Letty told Tanner after he introduced himself. "I have two more hours to go. Maybe you come and see me, huh? We're not that busy."

Tanner couldn't help but chuckle at the very friendly tone. Because he heard the clinking of what sounded like dishes he answered, "If you have coffee where you are, I'll visit you."

Swinton smiled and laughed gently too. After the call was over, he told Tanner, "Letty's a real sweetheart. You'll like her."

"I already do," Tanner grinned. "Do me a favor please, Bobby. If you see this guy and he tries striking up a seemingly casual conversation, don't let on that you recognize him. I'd like to keep my inquiries about him quiet for now."

Swinton nodded. "I guess that's why they call you a *private* detective, huh?"

"Exactly. I doubt you'll see him. But just in case."

"I got it."

"All right. Thanks, Bobby. You've been quite a help."

"Sure. Say 'hi' to Letty for me."

"Will do."

Tanner smiled. Now it was time to try *Letty's* coffee.

The coffee shop where Letty Hernandez worked wasn't too far from the church. Tanner was walking through the eatery's door 15 minutes later. Since there were only two waitresses visible, and one was Asian, Tanner immediately sat at the counter near the attractive, perky young woman who was chatting with a customer while topping off his coffee mug. It wasn't long before the smiling server was approaching him.

"Can I get you something to drink?" she asked.

Tanner grinned. "If you're name's Letty I'd like to try your coffee."

"Oh, it's *you*," she said, starting to whisper. "I'll be right back."

Tanner chuckled. He looked around. There were only a few customers, and all were minding their own business. When Letty returned, she placed a mat and mug in front of him.

"Thanks, Letty."

"You want cream?"

"Black is fine."

"Okay. So, what you want again?"

"You're at the church on Thursdays?"

"That's right. We try to have the place open a few nights a week for people who need to talk to someone."

"You know who Detective Jim Lucas is?"

Her eyes widened. "Sure. The cop that got shot."

"Yes. Do you remember if he stopped by the church the night he got shot?"

Letty nodded. "Yeah, he stopped by. But he was looking for Bobby." She started giggling. "I think he was a little drunk."

Tanner nodded. That made perfect sense since it was Swinton in the picture with Cynthia.

"Do you remember what time he got there and how long he was there?"

"I think it was around 9:00 or so he showed up. He didn't stay long though. He asked if I knew where Bobby was, and I told him I didn't. Then he showed me some pictures, but I couldn't help him."

Tanner furrowed his eyebrows. "Pictures?" Tanner showed her the one of Cynthia and Swinton.

"That was one of them," Letty confirmed.

"Do you remember anything about the other pictures?"

"It was just one other one. Some guy."

"What guy?"

"I didn't know him."

Tanner found his picture of Wannamaker and showed it to Letty. "Is this the guy?"

Letty bit her bottom lip. "I think so. It wasn't that picture exactly but I'm pretty sure it's the same guy. Who is he anyway? Cop wouldn't tell me."

"Damn!" Tanner thought. He looked at the waitress. "Letty, if you see this guy, don't engage him. If you see him, make sure you act like it's the first time you've ever laid eyes on him."

Letty's own eyes were wide at this point. Again, she was whispering. "What this guy do? He's real bad, huh?"

"We think he is. I don't think you'll ever see him, but if you do…Understand?"

"Sure. I understand. I'll be right back." Letty moved quickly to check on the few customers she had and added some fresh brew to select mugs. Then, as promised, she was back. "So, you have any more pictures for me to look at?"

"Not right now. But, if possible, can you tell anything about the photo Detective Lucas showed you of the bad man? For example, do remember what he was wearing or doing, or any details like that?"

Letty took a deep breath and sighed. "No. It was just mostly a face. Oh, I think he was eating something."

"Why do you say that?"

"He had something on the side of his face — sauce or something. You know, like you get when you're dipping something."

"Oh."

"Or it could have been lipstick."

"Lipstick?"

"I don't know. It was hard to make out what it was, really."

"All right. Thank you. And watch out for this guy."

"You don't have to tell me twice."

Tanner grinned. He handed her a five-dollar bill and then left. During his journey home he tried to try figure out what everything he had just learned tonight meant. He now knew Lucas went to the church right after leaving the pub. And then he must have gone somewhere else too. But where? The most important point, though, was that Lucas already seemed to be on Wannamaker's trail. But if he thought Wannamaker was a threat, why didn't he warn Tracy? Unless he hadn't realized yet just what Wannamaker's role in all this was. He cursed internally. What was going through Lucas' inebriated mind? Tanner decided another look at the file was in order. But that would have to wait until tomorrow. As much coffee as he had had tonight, he was still having a hard time keeping his eyes open. And he was also frequently checking his rearview mirror. He didn't think anyone was following him. But he wasn't taking any chances.

After Tanner parallel parked his auto, he didn't immediately exit. Letty thought it might have been lipstick. That could imply Wannamaker had a woman in his life after all. Just because he may still have loved the late Jeannine Acosta — or whatever it was he was feeling — didn't mean he was a monk. His heart started beating faster. The caffeine may have had something to do with it. But it was more likely because Tanner thought there could be someone else out there who could help them. And with all the deaths connected with this case, Tyler Wannamaker would be a fool to attempt to eliminate anyone right now. So that meant — if Tanner was right — this woman was safe. For now.

Tanner decided to deliver his report to Tracy in person Monday morning. It was just the two of them in her office. He couldn't have had a more attentive audience.

"Tyler always did make it sound like he had lady friends," Tracy said. "A guy has needs, right?"

"I plead the fifth."

"But he never mentioned any names. And I never knew him to make or receive personal calls. But I can understand why, now."

"I'm wondering if she has any idea what he's done. Is she totally ignorant? Is she scared? Is she part of it?"

Tracy nodded. "All good questions, El. But I think we're hopping to conclusions. It may have been sauce, not lipstick."

"So, the picture would have been taken at a restaurant."

Tracy looked at Tanner. "Or a catering company."

He nodded. "But what would be the big deal about that? What's so incriminating about a picture taken at the place his brother-in-law works?"

Tracy started feeling uneasy. "Wouldn't that depend on where Jim got that picture he showed Letty?" Tracy stood up, folded her arms, and started pacing. "I'm starting to get creeped out again, El. If Jim Lucas had gotten close enough to Tyler Wannamaker to snap such a candid photo, he would have to have had a very good reason. And he either would have said something to me about it or it would have been in the police investigation records."

"You don't think it was Jim who took the picture of Wannamaker, then. He got it from somewhere else. But where?"

"Well, I'm thinking from someone's phone."

"Someone connected to this case — maybe someone who had no apparent reason for having such a picture."

Tracy froze. She covered her mouth. She then looked at Tanner. "Dear God, El. What if it's from Cynthia Lydecker's phone?"

Tanner blinked. "Tyler put the moves on Cynthia? Why?"

"He didn't necessarily make moves. Maybe he just wanted to get to know her a little bit before he did what he did. Who else's phone would Jim have been able to pull pictures from in this case other than Keith Entwistle's?"

"All right. I follow you."

"We never considered the most obvious possibility here. Jim was frustrated and he knew something was wrong about the whole thing. He finds Tyler's picture on Cynthia's phone and wonders if it means anything. And that night he was drunk. So, he tries to get some information from Bobby Swinton, but he isn't at the church and Letty's no help. And he's had it. What if...what if the place he went next was Tyler's apartment?"

Tanner gulped. "And asked him about the picture directly."

"Yes. And Tyler plays it cool but after Jim leaves, he follows him; maybe even manages to beat him home by a few minutes."

"And then comes back here to dig around your files, notes, and personal emails."

"Exactly. He reads my notes but sees the only mention of a photo is regarding the one found on the wall. He's so relieved that later he slips when talking with Katie and mentions Jim being an informant."

"If you're right about this, then Cynthia Lydecker's phone could still be in evidence. And that picture could still be on it."

Tracy became even more agitated. "But that doesn't prove anything, El! It isn't proof of anything except Tyler and Cynthia may have known each other for a spell. *GOD!*"

Tanner approached the frustrated attorney and put his hands on her shoulders. "Tracy, I appreciate that this is very difficult for you. But Tyler has been planning this for a very long time and been very attentive to covering his tracks. We're not just going to find all we need in a couple of days. We have to take this one step at a time while keeping our heads."

Tracy was nodding while looking at the floor, her right index and middle fingers pressed against the center of her head. "You're right, El. I'm sorry."

"It's okay; I understand — completely." They embraced, and then Tanner said, "I'll get in touch with Culpepper. If he has access to Cynthia's phone, I'll have him check it for pictures. If he does find that picture Letty described, we'll go from there. Bill will help us."

"Okay, El. Okay." They released each other. Tracy returned to her seat. "So just what shenanigans have you and Detective Culpepper worked out to contact each other?"

Tanner grinned. "I'll just text him. I know you think Tyler's some super villain or something, but I doubt he can intercept text messages."

Tracy frowned. "I know he's no super villain. But I do think he has to be sweating right now. And that, to me, makes him dangerous."

"I know that."

Tracy stood up and moved towards Tanner. "Just be careful. I know we keep telling each other that but…"

"I understand. I'll let you know what Bill finds out."

Instinctively they embraced again. Then Tanner left her. She sat this time on her couch and rested her elbows on her knees while her hands covered her face. She wasn't sure how much more waiting she could take.

Late that Monday afternoon Rebecca told Tracy, "Karen Purl is on line one."

Tracy smiled broadly. "Oh my God: Karen!" Tracy responded. "I'll take it, Beck."

Karen Purl had been Tracy's client just over four years ago. She had been accused of murdering the man she was having an affair with and loved — and whose child she was carrying at the time. And it was this case that resulted in Tracy and Brian expediting their exchange of wedding vows. It was also the case that led to Brian being shot. Despite it all though, Tracy and Karen had become friends. In fact, Karen had named her daughter after the attorney — the person who did more than just defend her.

"Hi, Karen!" Tracy greeted enthusiastically.

"Hi, Tracy!" Karen greeted in the same manner.

Tracy heard a high-pitched voice ask, "What Mommy?"

Karen laughed. "Not you, short stuff. This is a friend of Mommy's also named Tracy."

Tracy chuckled. "Just call me T-1."

"Great idea," Karen agreed. "So how have you been? It's been over a year since we've talked."

"Oh, I know. Time can be so mean sometimes. I was sorry you couldn't come to Peter's baptism."

"I'm sorry, too. This thing I do has me working almost every weekend."

"Is the song writing still your passion?"

"Oh, yes. And Tr— I mean T-2 here makes up songs too. She's actually very good. I sense a mother-daughter team when she's old enough."

"That's just great. I'm so happy to hear you're doing so well."

"And you're doing well too, aren't you? I saw you on the news not too long ago."

"Oh. That."

"I'd call that woman a bad word except... Well, I think that would be in poor taste."

"It was awful, I will say that."

"How's Brian?"

"He's great. He loves being a stay-at-home dad. And my mom's there to help if he needs it. It's pretty nice actually."

"Yeah. We should set up a play date with T-2 and yours. And your sister-in-law has a son, right?"

"Yes; Kenneth."

"She was so nice to me too. You all were. We should all get together."

"I'd love that. If you really want to go crazy, my husband has a beach house in Ocean City that he shares with his sister. Maybe we could all meet down the ocean, hon."

Karen laughed. "T-2 is pretty fair skinned. But I'd love to do that. Let me check my calendar and let you know what weekends I have free."

"Supreme! My email hasn't changed."

"Good. I'm *so* glad I called."

"Me too. Was it just to catch up or did you need to talk to me about something?"

"Oh. Well, I *have* been meaning to call. And then I ran into your friend, and he said it would do you good to hear a friendly voice."

"My friend?"

"Yeah. Tyler."

Tracy's face went pale. Her good mood did a one-eighty.

"When did you see Tyler?" Tracy asked somberly.

"Yesterday. He came up to me in the store and said he recognized me. I thought he was just trying to hit on me at first, but he turned out to be really nice."

Tracy pursed her lips and tried to remain as calm as she could.

"Karen, I need you to listen to me and take what I say seriously, okay?"

"Sure. What is it?"

"Tyler and I are *not* friends. He used to work for me and now he doesn't. Stay away from him. And if you see him again, avoid him. And call me if you do — immediately."

Karen was breathing heavily. "God, Tracy. What's wrong? Who is this guy?"

"Someone you don't want to get involved with. He didn't ask you out, did he?"

Karen gulped. "Uh…well…he did ask if he could call me some time."

Tracy started shaking her head. "Screen your calls, Karen. Have a headache until I let you know you don't have one anymore. Okay?"

"Tracy, you're scaring me."

"I'm sorry. But I'm serious about everything I just said."

"All right. Is he…is he some kind of stalker?"

"Let's just say he's not the nice person he pretends to be. I really don't want to say anymore. My guess is you'll never see or hear from him again. But just in case…"

"Okay. Well, I'll send you those dates."

"Great, Karen. I really do think it would be a lot of fun if we all got together."

"Me too. I…I hope whatever is going on works itself out."

"Me too."

"Bye T-1."

"Bye. And give T-2 a kiss for me."

Karen laughed. "Gladly."

Tracy covered her mouth as soon as the call had ended. So, Tyler Wannamaker was going to take advantage of everything he had learned over the two years he was here. And who knows how much information he had gathered. How many nights had he been here late, probably doing more than just working a case? He had just sent Tracy a warning. Tracy didn't truly think that Karen or her child were in any immediate danger. But they might be eventually. If Tyler thought he had nothing to lose, he might not hesitate to hurt someone truly innocent.

Tracy was in tears now. This was now officially a race. She had to get *him* before he got someone she cared about. He understood that about her — that she cared very deeply for those she called friend or family. And he was prepared to take every advantage of it. Had he found out what she and Tanner and Culpepper had been doing? Hopefully not. Hopefully, this was just a warning that a now-sober Wannamaker was sending — a desperate move by someone who was afraid that Tracy might go after him. And he knew going after her directly would be dangerous. So, he'd try a different approach. That's what people like him did.

Tracy's fear however slowly morphed into anger. Some of it was directed towards herself. How did she allow herself to be taken in by him all this time? Just how much time did he put into figuring the kind of person she was and what kind of person he had to appear to be so that she'd hire him? No wonder he was such a good criminal attorney, something Tracy never really wanted to be. But here she was. And up until last week she had a criminal several times over in her midst. And he was still out there.

Tracy, now trying to contain her fury, stood up. She shoved some papers and files, along with her laptop, into her briefcase and then exited her office. Rebecca was just switching the phones to the night service.

"I'll walk you down, Beck. Neal's going home directly from court."

"Sure, Tracy. You okay?"

"Of course not. And I won't be until Tyler Wannamaker is behind bars or six feet under."

Rebecca stared at her red-faced employer. She said nothing further on the matter. Once the office was secured, the women went to their cars and then to their homes. Tracy was still angry when she arrived. She marched upstairs with barely a hello to her family members and found herself dialing Elias Tanner, Sr.

"What is it, Tracy?" he asked with great concern.

"It's time to go on the offensive, El. You said you had some ideas about using me as bait. Tell me about them. Tell me all about them right now."

Chapter 16

"You keep interfering with my dinner," Detective Culpepper told the former Detective Tanner Tuesday evening. "Next time let's meet in the morning."

"Sure," Tanner agreed. He looked around the electronics section where he and Culpepper were standing. He saw no familiar faces. "You hearing anything?"

"No. Whatever Pankow's thinking, he's keeping his lips closed tight."

"Mm."

Culpepper sighed. "There was no photo like the one you described on Cynthia Lydecker's phone. In fact, there really weren't too many pictures at all."

"That's too bad," Tanner murmured. "Tracy's going to be disappointed. She thought she was onto something."

"She could be. I'm working on trying to get access to Jim's phone. It's in evidence. If I can somehow get to it without people knowing it, I'll forward the picture to you. You can take it from there."

"That'd be great. Tyler worked for Tracy long enough so that she might pick up on something."

"That's what I'm hoping; that's *why* I'm helping."

Tanner sighed. "I should tell you something else."

"What's that?"

"Tyler arranged to bump into an old friend of Tracy's. He may have spent the last couple of years going through the company records gathering information. Now he's using it. And he made certain Tracy found this out."

"Did he hurt this friend?"

"No. It was probably just a warning for Tracy to keep her mouth shut."

Culpepper sighed. "Elias…Elias if this gets any worse, I may do something I shouldn't but still won't regret. No way am I letting Wannamaker take another life."

"I hear you."

"Maybe I should pay him a visit."

"What does that mean?" Tanner asked, mildly alarmed.

"I'd tell him Jim had his suspicions and that I found some things going through Jim's stuff."

"You mean you'll pretend to blackmail him?"

"If he knows someone else knows what he did, maybe he won't be so damn cocky."

"That's risky."

"I realize that. But I'll put that on hold until we know if the picture will help us."

"All right. We should probably break this up."

"Yeah. See ya."

Culpepper quickly turned and left Tanner standing in front of the higher-priced laptops. But the former detective wasn't there much longer. He had supper waiting for him too.

Tracy put her smartphone on her the kitchen counter. Brian was staring at her, trying to figure out whether the news she'd just received was good or bad. She gave him a weak smile, which he took to mean it was the latter kind. But she did manage to put on a happy face the rest of the night for the benefit of her children. But once she returned to her bed after laying Peter in his crib, the bad mood returned too.

"Where the hell did Jim get that picture?" she asked rhetorically. "Why was he showing it to people? What does it all mean?"

Brian remained silent. He wasn't sure if she was looking for his input or venting her frustrations. She had so many right now.

"Any ideas, Brian?" she finally asked.

"Sorry, Tracy. I'm not sure."

"It had to be something that didn't appear to be too incriminating on the surface. If it were, Jim would probably have told Detective Culpepper about it or at least put it in his report. So, he was probably merely curious. But maybe it *was* incriminating. Maybe Jim went to Tyler's and asked him about it."

"Right, you told me this theory."

"Oh, I did? Sorry, honey."

"No problem."

Tracy sighed. "I swear it's like I have a stone in my shoe, or a gnat that won't leave me alone. You know what I'm saying?"

"Perfectly."

Tracy continued staring at the ceiling. "I can't get to sleep, Brian. I think I'm going to do some work."

"You can stay here," Brian said suggestively.

"I'm not in the mood." She sat up straight, pulled back the covers, and swung her legs over the side of the bed. Then she marched out of the bedroom and into the home office.

After a few hours of re-reviewing the Jim Lucas murder investigation file, Tracy's eyes were finally getting tired. The only thing she decided as a result of her seemingly futile exercise was that she'd re-check the evidence the state's attorney had turned over for their case against Keith Entwistle. Specifically, she wanted to see just whom Lucas had interviewed. Maybe there was something to find there. At almost two in the morning Tracy crawled back into bed and joined her deep-sleeping husband.

Tracy learned one thing Tuesday morning. Detective Bill Culpepper was efficient. He must have gone to where the evidence in the Lucas murder was being stored very early, because before Tracy even left her house Elias Tanner, Sr. had forwarded her what Culpepper had sent *him* at 7:22 a.m. She immediately returned to her home office, where she could bring up the photo on her monitor and take a very close look at it. Brian joined her.

"I think that was taken at Whistler's Cooking," Tracy said soon after a quick scan. "The background — the wall — looks like the same design."

"Okay," Brian said.

Tracy looked at few moments longer, and then her eyes widened. She smiled at Brian.

"Look at his shoulder," she told him. "Someone is touching it."

"Yeah," Brian nodded. "And judging by that bracelet it's a woman."

"A woman named Vanessa," Tracy added quickly. "She was wearing that same bracelet when I first met her. Now, I know who took this picture."

"Who?"

"Keith. It *has* to be him. But why Jim thought it meant something, I'm not sure."

"Can we ask Keith about it?"

Tracy shook her head. "That'd be risky. Besides, I'd rather talk to Vanessa."

"You think she and Tyler were…"

"You know, I should have considered this possibility before. Tyler had to have a way of knowing the Entwistle's schedules so he could coordinate everything. But if he was asking questions all the time about what their plans were, they may have gotten suspicious when the poo started hitting the fan. He may have befriended Vanessa to get the information he needed."

"I wonder just how friendly they are."

Tracy sighed and looked at Brian. "I guess he still had 'needs,' huh? Vanessa is very pretty and seemed very nice."

"Should we ask her?"

"Again, risky. And I don't want to get her into any trouble."

"She may *already* be in trouble."

Tracy looked at her spouse quizzically. "You think she was in on it?"

"I don't mean that. But if she has feelings for the guy and he's done with her now, that could be a potential problem for him."

Tracy shook her head. "I wonder just what Tyler has told everyone about our 'divorce.' I might be persona non grata."

"After what you did for Keith? I doubt it. Bad-mouthing you after singing your praises for two years would be a very dumb move on his part."

Tracy smiled. "Thank you, honey. That's a very good point. But my window of opportunity could still be closing." She sighed loudly. "I guess it's time then."

"Time for what?"

"To make a risky move. Let's face it. For us to move forward, either Keith or Vanessa needs talking to. I think I'll run all this by El; see what he thinks. I don't recall anything showing up on Vanessa's background check that El did."

"Whether it did or didn't might not mean anything," Brian countered.

"True. But I will go through the State's evidence against Keith and see if Jim Lucas interviewed Vanessa. *That* I can do safely. Speaking of which…" Tracy stood up and embraced Brian. "I'm off."

Brian kissed her. "You call me later and tell me what's going on."

"I will, Brian. Promise."

They exchanged some additional words of affection before Tracy left her home. Now Brian had to pretend he wasn't as nervous as he truly was. Nicole had an early tea party with Daddy planned.

Lucas had talked to Vanessa. Tracy was reading Vanessa's official statement concerning when Keith Entwistle had left Whistler's Cooking the night Cynthia Lydecker was murdered. She put the time at close to 11:30. A quick check of other statements taken seemed to confirm the time. All right. So, the police wanted to trace Keith Entwistle's movements for the night, and after 11:30 he had no alibi. So, what was it about Vanessa then?

Tracy slammed the folder on her desk, frustrated. Maybe Vanessa has nothing to do with this. Okay, so she was friendly with Tyler at some party and Keith took a picture. Maybe Jim wanted to ask about Tyler and that picture of him was the best he could do. Vanessa being off to the side may not mean anything. Maybe Tracy was wrong about Tyler having a connection within Whistler's Cooking. But that's how he seemed to operate. He had buddies on the police force who might give him some information now and again. He positioned himself so he'd be on his brother-in-law's defense team when the time came. So, didn't it make sense to think he got friendly with someone at his brother-in-law's business? It did to Tracy. But damned if she could really find anything to support her belief.

When Tanner called her later, he could offer nothing about Vanessa Yeardly worth raising an eyebrow. Single; 31 years old; lived in an apartment in Anne Arundel County, not too far from where she'd been working for three years. She'd never been in any trouble with the law or anyone else for that matter.

"I'm going to talk to her," Tracy said finally. "I can't stand this anymore."

"I'll come with you," Tanner volunteered.

"No, El. I think one-on-one is my best bet here."

Tanner sighed. "I don't like it."

"Listen. If you want to be a lookout that's fine. You can meet me there. It's early. I doubt she's at work yet."

"I will. And don't you try and see her until you know I'm there. Understand?"

"Yes, El. I'll be good."

Tanner sighed. "All right. I'm leaving now."

"Me too. See you soon."

Vanessa's apartment complex was located near the Marley Station Mall in Pasadena, Maryland. Tracy didn't frequent this area too much. The one thing she knew about Anne Arundel County was that when it snowed, their schools always seemed to close. She'd get angry as a child when *she* had to go to school, and *they* didn't. City schools rarely canceled classes unless a blizzard hit. So, while she trounced off to school all the other kids were building snowmen and tossing snowballs. She had resented "them" ever since.

Tanner had beaten her there. He exited his auto when he saw Tracy's car pull into the complex's parking lot. He was standing by her door as she opened it.

"Since I had time, I checked the lot. No sign of Wannamaker's car."

"Ah," Tracy responded. "Okay. I'm off then."

"You be careful. If you get a bad vibe, you get the hell out of there."

"Sure."

"Once you do this, Tracy, Wannamaker is likely to find out we're going after him. If Vanessa is completely innocent, she's going to be upset after your talk. Somebody could notice that, and she might say something. You understand?"

"Yes, El. But what else can we do at this point?"

Tanner sighed. "All right. Go ahead then. I'll be here. I may even be closer than that."

Tracy managed a smile. Then she was climbing the steps to the building entranceway and pushing the buzzer assigned to unit 2-C.

"Hello?" A voice asked.

"Vanessa?"

"Yes."

"This is Tracy Brubaker Shane, Keith's attorney. Remember me?"

"Oh sure!" Vanessa answered quickly and pleasantly. "Come on up."

Tracy pulled on the door as the buzzer buzzed. She looked at Tanner and smiled. Then she let the door close behind her as Tanner watched anxiously.

Tracy was about to knock on Vanessa's door when it opened. Vanessa was dressed in a t-shirt and jeans, and her hair looked slightly damp. But she had a smile on her face and welcomed the attorney inside. Soon the women were seated next to each on a beige sofa.

"How have you been?" Tracy asked, trying to ease into things.

"Just great! Things are so much better now that it's all over."

"Supreme! I'm glad Keith is doing all right."

"Yeah. So, what did you want to see me about?"

Tracy gulped. "Before I begin, I need to warn you. This will probably get uncomfortable for you."

Vanessa stared at her guest. "Oh, okay."

"First, have you seen Tyler Wannamaker lately?"

"Not since Keith's victory party last week. You were there for a while, remember?"

"Right. Had you heard that Tyler no longer works for me?"

Vanessa nodded. "I did. I heard he got an offer too good to pass up."

"Who told you that?"

"Keith did."

"Ah. What else did Keith tell you?"

"Not much. He said you understood about the whole thing and that you and Tyler were cool."

Tracy felt relieved. This was good news as far as she was concerned.

"And now the part where it might get uncomfortable. Just how close are you and Tyler?"

Vanessa Yeardly blinked a few times and then looked away from Tracy. "What does that have to do with anything? Why do people think it's their business?"

Tracy raised an eyebrow. "Somebody else asked you about it already?"

"Yeah, the cops."

"Which cop?"

"The one who investigated Keith; the one got killed by that Lydecker guy."

"Detective Jim Lucas."

"Yeah. Him."

"When did he ask you about you and Tyler?"

Vanessa scratched her head. "As a matter of fact, it was the night he got killed. It was so weird."

"What was weird?"

"He just suddenly showed up at the office. I think he was even drunk. I was in the kitchen cleaning up and he just shows up."

"Anyone else see Detective Lucas there?"

"I'm not sure. Keith wasn't there and the other guys were in their offices. Georgina was cleaning up in the storeroom."

"Okay. What did Jim do and say?"

"Well, he showed me this picture of Tyler. I think he pulled it off Keith's phone or something. He wanted to know just how close Tyler and Keith were."

"Did he say why he was asking *you* this?"

"Keith told him it was me standing next to Tyler in the picture, I think. I guess Keith gave him the impression Tyler and I were…close."

"And are you, Vanessa?"

"What does it matter?"

"Vanessa, it matters. Please just trust me for now. I'm not here to hurt you. Can you please answer my question?"

Vanessa remained quiet a few moments. Then she nodded.

"All right. Tyler and I have been seeing each other off and on; more 'off' lately, though. I knew from the beginning he wasn't looking for anything…I'd guess the word is permanent."

"He romanced you?"

"Yeah."

"Anyone else know about this?"

"No one's supposed to. He was afraid it might piss off Keith."

"Why?"

"I…I don't think Keith likes Tyler very much. You'd never know it though. Anytime he'd show up for one reason or another Keith acted pleased as punch to see him."

"Maybe he acted like that for his sister's sake. Keeping the peace."

"Maybe."

"So, you and Tyler had a secret fling. Did he ask you questions about Keith and his plans; stuff like that?"

"Sometimes. He was always talking about planning surprise parties or buying cruise tickets for them as a gift. So of course, he had to know when they were available. And asking them directly might spoil the surprise."

Tracy couldn't help from smiling. She'd been right about things after all.

"Okay. Back to the night Detective Lucas asked you his questions. Please tell me everything that happened after he found you in the kitchen."

"Well as I said, he showed me the picture and I could tell he was in no condition to mess with. He was mad about something, and he was drunk. So, I told him pretty much what I just told you."

"Did he say why he wanted to know these things about you and Tyler, other than because of the picture, I mean?"

Vanessa was starting to get nervous. "Look, has Tyler done something? What is going on?"

"Did you get the impression Detective Lucas thought Tyler may have done something wrong?"

"What? I don't know."

"Okay. Please try and stay calm, Vanessa. I just have a few more questions and then I'll tell you what I can. Okay?"

"Okay."

"Do you know why specifically Jim was asking about Tyler?"

"Not really. I think Keith may have made some comments. I remember that cop saying that Tyler was a...well, it wasn't a nice word he used. Anyway, I think Keith noticed the cop's dislike for Tyler and maybe let his own true feelings be known."

Tracy furrowed her brow. Lucas shouldn't have talked to Keith without his attorney present, and Tracy didn't remember being party to any such discussion. Had Lucas approached Entwistle behind her back? If he had become convinced that someone close to Entwistle had set him up, then maybe he thought an official meeting with Entwistle meant Tyler would be there, which is exactly why Tyler had arranged things like he had. He hadn't counted on a cop undertaking his own unofficial investigation.

"Okay, Vanessa, what happened after the detective was done asking his questions?"

"He just grunted 'thank you' at me and left. And then — as if I couldn't have been any more upset — Tyler called."

"*Tyler called?*"

"He was just leaving Keith and Katie and was close by; wanted to know if we could hook up."

"And you told him about your talk with Detective Lucas."

"Sure."

"Did Lucas also show you another picture, Vanessa? It would have been of Cynthia Lydecker and a man you probably didn't know."

"Yeah, he did. He asked if I knew either person in the picture. Of course, I recognized Cynthia since she'd been all over the news. I didn't know the other guy."

"And you told Tyler about that too, right?"

"I think so."

"And what did Tyler say?"

"Nothing really. He said this Lucas was just doing his job and not to worry about anything."

"I see. And *did* you and Tyler hook up?"

"Maybe."

"*Please*, Vanessa."

The anxious woman sighed. "Yes! Okay? He got to my place a little after one."

"How did he seem to you?"

"What?"

"What was his mood: was he happy, anxious…what?"

Vanessa grinned. "He was happy to see me. Okay?"

"Okay. What time did he leave?"

"About three maybe; he rarely stays all night."

Tracy nodded. So, after Tyler left Vanessa's, he must have gone to Tracy's office to see what he could find. And he found her report.

"What did you think when you heard about the shooting?"

Vanessa again paused. Her face now was showing anger. "What's that supposed to mean?"

Tracy decided on a different approach. "Never mind then. I guess Tyler thought it would be best if you didn't say anything to anybody about Jim's visit. That would have meant all kinds of additional questions and all that. Am I right?"

There was another sigh. "Yeah, pretty much."

Tracy took a deep breath. "Okay, Vanessa. You've answered my questions and so I will keep my earlier promise to you. I can't tell you everything yet, because *I* don't know everything yet, but you need to stay away from Tyler Wannamaker."

The color drained from Vanessa's face. "Why? What's going on? Are you telling me…? But…I mean…That Lydecker guy did all this. It's all over."

Tracy put her hand on Vanessa's shoulder; the woman was near tears. It was clear to the attorney Vanessa had suspected something was wrong herself.

"I can tell you this: Tyler and I did not leave on amicable terms. But that's all I can say on that point. The investigation into Detective Lucas' murder is not officially closed. And while I completely understand that you're very upset right now, I suggest you keep my visit a secret too. Don't say anything to Keith. And if Tyler calls, don't say anything to him either. If he wants to see you, make up a reason why that's not possible. Do you think you can handle all of that, Vanessa?"

Vanessa shook her head. "I don't know. You're telling me Tyler killed this cop, aren't you? Did he also kill that woman?"

Tracy sighed. "If that's what you think I'm telling you, then act accordingly. Do you understand, Vanessa?"

There was a gulp and a nod. "Okay. I understand. But I have to admit I'm scared."

Tracy instinctively embraced Vanessa. "I am too, for lots of reasons. But I promise you I'm doing everything I can so we both can stop being scared." Tracy felt a nod on her shoulder. "If you need to talk to somebody about this, just call me. But do it privately. We need to keep this quiet for now. I think you understand why."

Tracy pulled away and watched Vanessa wipe water from her eyes. Tracy rose and left the now-frightened cook. Tracy felt bad about doing what she had done, bringing Vanessa into this. But as upset as Tracy had made Vanessa, the attorney knew it was ultimately unavoidable. It had been a necessary evil. And there may be more such evils to come.

Tanner and Tracy were seated in the former's car, which was still parked outside of Vanessa Yeardly's apartment building.

"Jim was starting to make connections. He knew Tyler had prior business with George Finnegan. Detective Culpepper told us as much. He knew something was wrong with the picture of Cynthia and Bobby Swinton. His gut was telling him Keith was innocent and was set up by someone who had to be close to him. And I think Jim approached

Keith at some point — without clearing it with me — and started asking him about Tyler.

"I was too close to Tyler to see it. But Jim and Bill and who knows how many other people never liked Tyler, and Jim at least started acting on those feelings, probably helped by alcohol."

"Dumb son of a bitch," Tanner said angrily, pounding his fist against the steering wheel. "He got sloppy and screwed up. He shouldn't have just showed up to question Vanessa like that."

Tracy nodded. "I'm sorry, El. Jim was struggling. He meant to do the right thing, though. Everyone was telling him they had the right man, but he knew in his gut they didn't. I feel so awful about this."

Tanner gulped. "All right. What next? We know Jim talked to Vanessa and that Vanessa talked to Wannamaker right afterwards. We can assume that he then went after Jim and then went back to the county for his date with Vanessa."

"Yes. And he later planted the gun at Lydecker's house. After that news conference, Tyler left to have lunch with Keith and Katie. But either before or after he made a stop at Ed Lydecker's place. I'm sure Finnegan secured a key and code for there too. And Tyler knew that with the admission to the hit and run, the police would very soon be looking at Lydecker. So, Tyler took the opportunity while Ed and Debra where still at Ed's office to plant the evidence that was found. He put the stuff in the garage and placed a brochure from Keith's business in the kitchen. I'm sure all that stuff wasn't in the home this whole time. Certainly, the gun that killed Jim couldn't have been."

"True."

"Well then I see only one next course of action."

"Entwistle…"

"Yes, El. It's time to tell Keith Entwistle what his brother-in-law has done. And God help us if he doesn't believe it."

Chapter 17

Neither Tracy nor Tanner could tell what was going through Keith Entwistle's mind at the present moment. He was taking turns staring at each of them. But he remained silent. He offered no protestations, no utterances of disbelief. When his former defenders had finished, he mulled everything over quietly for what seemed like hours. Finally, he gulped, sighed, and started walking about his basement, where the secret meeting was taking place.

"This is…This is just so…" He shook his head. "I should be saying I can't believe it. I should be angry you'd even suggest such a thing."

"But you *aren't* saying that, are you Keith?" Tracy asked quietly. "You're *not* angry with us."

He shook his head. "No. I think I knew; part of me did anyway. He was just so damn nice and understanding. I knew something was off since that first day he told me not to worry. But this?"

"We're past the tipping point now," Tanner began. "Vanessa Yeardly knows; I personally think she did already and just couldn't face it. And Detective Bill Culpepper knows too. And now you do. Eventually someone is going to say or do something and then Tyler Wannamaker is going to be more desperate than he already is. So, what do we do now?"

Entwistle was rubbing his eyes. "This is going to destroy Katie when she finds out. I don't know if she'll ever believe it. You've seen how she can be when she gets bad news. And this is much worse than bad news."

"I don't care about your wife right now," Tanner said tersely. "Tell me and Tracy about that conversation you had with Jim, the one where you identified Vanessa as being the owner of that bracelet."

Entwistle blinked. "That picture was taken at the holiday party we had last December. It was the first Saturday after Thanksgiving, I think. Ty got a little drunk and was obviously into Vanessa. It was a side of Tyler I rarely saw, so I captured the moment. I didn't realize at the time they had been seeing each other for a while."

"Did Jim tell you why he was so interested in that picture?" Tracy asked.

"He just found the picture on my phone when they were going through it looking for evidence against me. Then one night he just shows up at the office and asks how Tyler and I got along. The man clearly had had a few. I wanted to call you Tracy, but he said he was there unofficially and that he might be able to help me. He didn't want me calling you. I didn't feel like arguing."

"It's okay, Keith," Tracy offered.

"Well, I told him that Ty was okay, but he was full of himself. He was good at what he did, and he knew it. He liked helping Katie all the time because he liked having control over her."

"What do you mean 'all the time'?" Tanner asked.

"Oh, good Lord. Before she and I started dating Tyler was her go-to guy. Car trouble? She called Tyler. Needed an escort to something? She called Tyler. Needed help with something around the house? She dialed 1-800-Tyler."

Tracy chuckled. "That's cute. So, when you came along Tyler wasn't getting those calls anymore."

"No. So *he* started calling *her*. He wanted to see her more often than you'd think someone like him would. I never understood it. I mean he's a good-looking guy with more money than he knows what to do with. He talks about what a ladies' man he is, but I swear he'd rather be with Katie. Now, I think I understand why."

"He's not well," Tracy said. "His grief over Jeannine Acosta's death took him over and he let it turn into something rotten. I'm not sure what his feelings towards anyone really are."

"Yeah. I guess things kind of make sense now. Anyway, I tell Detective Lucas about Tyler and that even though we get along, he doesn't think much of me. And I'm pretty sure the only reason he tried to get along with me at all was because Katie told him to stop putting me down. Otherwise, he'd not see her very often."

Tracy nodded. "She's the only one he really has to care about. He lost his girl; his parents are tucked away in assisted care; and he must have a tough time finding another person to care about. And it just keeps getting worse as he gets older."

"I don't like the sound of that," Entwistle mumbled.

"So how did Detective Lucas leave things with you?" Tanner asked.

"Leave things? I don't know. I told him about Tyler and me, and I told him who belonged to the bracelet. And I did tell him I thought Vanessa and he might have hooked up that night. But he never asked the question if I thought Tyler set me up. In fact, what I remember thinking is that maybe Tyler would try and lose the case."

"You thought Tyler would talk me into losing the case?" Tracy asked, mildly annoyed.

Keith looked at her sheepishly. "I told you Tyler was a snob. And then one day he starts complimenting you, talking about his great new job and his great new boss, and all of that. He never complimented *anyone* in his *life*. So, when all this started to happen, and that detective showed up…Well, I guess I got suspicious of you too. I'm really sorry."

Tracy smiled. "Okay. It's fine."

"And Jim asked you not to mention his visit, right?" Tanner asked.

"Yeah. He thought Tracy would get angry with him." Everyone laughed gently. "Then a few days later, he's dead. But before I even had a chance to consider Tyler being involved the whole Ed Lydecker business came out. I thought it was over."

The room was now quiet. Everyone was debating what to say next. Entwistle broke the silence when he asked the obvious question.

"What do we do now?"

"It's a problem of evidence," Tanner answered. "We don't have any. Tyler's motive for killing Jim is tied to a murder the evidence says someone else committed. No witnesses can put him at the scene, and while he doesn't have an alibi, neither you nor Vanessa can offer anything that Tyler has done or said that can help us."

"But Tyler is still nervous, El. Why else would have visited Karen Purl? We should use that."

"Use that?" Entwistle asked.

"El here has some thoughts about using me as bait."

Tanner frowned. "…As a last resort."

"We have some more resorts to visit, El? I think Keith here is our last one."

"I'll help," Entwistle volunteered. "I'll do anything."

"The problem is," Tracy continued, "Tyler is probably expecting somebody to do something. So, we'd have to be very sneaky."

Entwistle shook his head. "I wish you had recorded that talk with him the night you fired him."

Tracy folded her arms. "Sorry. Hindsight may be perfect, but my 20/20 vision doesn't arrive until next year. I don't carry a tape recorder around with me and everything I knew derived from the case I was working on. Even if I had managed to record something, in all likelihood it would have been tossed out anyway. And if he had suspected I was doing such a thing, pepper spray may not have stopped him from killing me right then and there. Any more criticisms you have on your mind, Keith?"

Tanner frowned. "Let's focus on the here and now, shall we?"

Tracy was still irked at Entwistle's comment. "You want to get at Tyler? You tell Katie what he did."

Tanner and Entwistle looked at her. The latter said, "She won't believe me."

"That's not the point. The point is that she will tell Tyler what you accused him of."

"And then what?"

"Then El here is watching Tyler from that moment on."

"What? You think he'll go after somebody, and the cops can catch him in the act?"

"Not exactly, Keith. I don't want him for attempted murder. I want him charged with Jim Lucas' murder. That's our best shot right now.

If that sticks, then maybe they go after him for the other ones. What I'm hoping is that Tyler panics and tries to start covering his tracks. By that I mean maybe he'll incriminate himself."

"How?"

"I don't know. Revisit the crime scene. Call or try to see Vanessa. Confront *you*, Keith."

"Sounds awful vague to me."

Tanner snapped, "Got any better ideas, Keith? I'm all ears."

Entwistle sighed loudly. "I'm sorry. I am. But you guys dumped all this on me out of the blue. How can you expect me to be thinking clearly?"

Tracy glared at Entwistle. "We didn't *dump* anything. This is how it is, Keith. I and El — especially El — lost a friend. We're just telling you the truth here. Deal with it."

Entwistle put up his hands. "Sorry. I didn't mean to sound like a dick. Sorry."

"I think we're all feeling it," Tanner said. "But I think Tracy may be right. Tell Katie what we just told you. Put Tyler on the defensive."

The former client shook his head. "I don't like that idea."

"I repeat," Tanner responded. "If you have another one, let's hear it."

Then the room went silent again.

"I wish you had consulted me first," Culpepper told Tanner. "You have no idea how his sister is going to respond to the news."

"We can't just sit around hoping evidence suddenly pops up. We need to make something happen."

Culpepper sighed. "So that's why you're calling me instead of arranging a rendezvous, huh? You hope someone is listening to my phone calls, do you?"

"Something like that."

"Mm. Too bad. I needed to visit a shoe store. My kid's outgrown his sneakers already."

Tanner laughed softly. "Keith said he still has to think about it. That's where we left things. But his wife is going to know something's bothering him and according to Keith, Tyler's been calling a least once a day to check on how they're doing. If Katie tells her brother that she thinks Keith's upset about something…"

"Uh-huh. What am I supposed to do in the meantime? I shouldn't have been doing what I've been doing to begin with."

"I'll keep you in the loop. My guess is that once Keith tells Katie, she'll call Tyler. And I'll be right outside Tyler's door waiting to see what he does. If he goes after anyone, I'll be *right* there."

"You're not a young fella anymore, Elias."

"Thank you so much."

"You might not be able to handle Tyler on your own was all I meant."

"I can handle him."

Culpepper sighed. "Elias, don't get yourself into trouble over this."

"If he comes after me Bill, I have to defend myself."

"Yeah. I know exactly what you're telling me. But this way…Would you be able to live with yourself?"

"If it comes down to me or him? Damn right I could live with myself. I'd be dead otherwise."

Culpepper sighed. "All right. You keep me posted. As soon as Tyler starts moving you let me know. Agreed?"

"Sure."

"Talk to you soon then, Elias."

"Soon," Tanner said. Then he sighed. Tyler Wannamaker might not even get a chance to go after Tanner. The waiting might be the death of Tanner first.

"Vanessa, it's Tracy."

"Hi, Tracy."

"Is it a good time to talk?"

"I have a couple of minutes. What is it?"

"Has Tyler been in touch?"

"No."

"Good. How are you holding up?"

"Okay, I guess. But I'm nervous."

"Of course. Have you seen Keith?"

"Yeah; we talked a bit."

"And how did *he* seem to you?"

"I guess okay. He's been rather cross with people today though. Twice he's complained about the food. He hardly ever does that."

"When this is all over, people will understand."

"I think everyone thinks it's some delayed reaction to what he just went through."

"Oh, that's actually a good thing then."

"I guess. Was there anything else?"

"Not really. I feel bad about upsetting you this morning and just wanted to check in. We're kind of in a holding pattern right now. This is the worst of it."

"I can believe that."

"You and Keith try to be there for each other today. That would be the best thing."

"Okay. I really need to go now."

"Sure. Good luck."

Tracy put her phone down. That was another benefit of telling Entwistle right after speaking with Vanessa. They wouldn't feel alone with what they knew. That just might help them survive the workday.

What to tell Brian about everything is what Tracy struggled with the rest of *her* workday. She didn't want to keep things from him, and she didn't want to lie to him. But she also didn't feel like dealing with the tantrum he'd most definitely throw. She wasn't up for it. Maybe she could work late and then just go right to bed when she got home. That might work since she had plenty to do to fill the time. Entwistle wouldn't be having his conversation with his wife until after he and Katie were home together. Then he'd call and tell Tracy how it went. *That* would be the time to start worrying. Besides, maybe Entwistle would lose his nerve. She had the feeling his wife intimidated him. Tracy had seen how Katie Entwistle could be when she got upset. So maybe her husband would decide he didn't want to tell her what was *really* bothering him.

Tracy just continued staring at her computer screen. She didn't like being at the mercy of others. She liked having control. That's part of the reason she started her own firm. She wanted to do things *her* way, take on the clients *she* wanted to take on. She didn't want to be told who she'd be representing. And it had worked out for her. She was doing well — *very* well. Things could get tough emotionally from time to time but she always came out wearing the victory medal. Well, most always. But this was one of those times when she just *had* to prevail. The other option was too disturbing to contemplate. Yet she contemplated it, nonetheless.

She stared at her phone. She looked back at the monitor. Tyler Wannamaker. Asshole. Maybe he'd get run over by a very large construction vehicle in the near future. God, that wasn't very nice, was it? What he had done would be with her for a very, very long time. How was she going to hire his replacement? How could she be sure she wasn't getting charmed by a snake again? A woman. Maybe she should hire another woman. Neal wouldn't like it but tough ducks.

Tracy shook her head. That was a stupid thought. Women committed murder too. Tracy had run into several female killers over the last five years herself. You can just never tell. That was another thing she'd never be able to control. She wasn't psychic. All she could do was the best she could do. But that was not always going to be good enough.

The time continued to pass slowly. It was 8:00 p.m. when Neal entered her office. "How late are you staying?" he asked.

"You don't have to wait up for me."

"Like hell I don't."

Tracy chuckled. "All right. How about another half hour then?"

"All right. I'll stop by to get you. I need to clean up and shutdown the coffee station anyway."

"Well go to it then," Tracy grinned. Neal grinned back. Then she was alone again.

Tracy's phone started ringing at 8:19.

"Katie just came in," Entwistle began. "She's upstairs getting changed. I don't know if I can do this."

"You have to tell her, Keith," Tracy said forcefully. "Once she realizes you're upset it's only a matter of time before Tyler learns about it. He'll suspect the right reason. Tell her."

Entwistle sighed. "I'll try."

"Keith, 'There is no try,' a wise, pointy-eared green fella once said. You get me?"

"How can you make jokes at a time like this?"

"Because this is the best time to make them. Tell her, Keith."

"Here she comes."

"Goodbye, Keith."

Tracy didn't wait for Entwistle's response. She dialed Tanner.

"You outside Tyler's, El? Keith should be having his conversation with Katie starting just about now."

"He called you?"

"Yup. He tried to back out of it, but Yoda set him straight."

"Yoda?"

"Yeah. Is Tyler home?"

"His car's here. He got back from dinner about half an hour ago. He kept looking over his shoulder, but I don't think he spotted me."

"Mm. I wish you had an associate he'd never laid his eyes on that you could use."

"If that's a hint, consider it ignored."

"Hey, that wasn't very nice. I'm just thinking of your safety, El."

"Uh-huh. You should hang up in case he calls you again."

"Good point. Okay, El. Be vigilant. But more importantly, be safe."

"The same goes for you 10 times over."

"So just how late are you going to be then?" Brian asked.

"I'm waiting for a call from a client. Once I get it and know what's what, I'll head home."

"Wait for the call here."

Tracy sighed. "You don't have to worry about me, Brian. El is keeping watch over Tyler Wannamaker. If he makes a move, El will let me know. I'm fine."

"Mm. I still don't like it."

"It's an important call. It may help end the very thing you're worrying about right now."

Tracy heard Brian grunt. "When is this call supposed to come?"

"Any time now. He'll be calling on my office line. I wanted to keep my smartphone free for other calls."

"Mm."

"Don't worry, honey."

"The more you keep telling me not to do that the more I will."

Tracy sighed. "I have to go. I'll be home as soon as I can."

"Yeah; sure."

"I love you, Brian. Give my love to Nicole, Peter, and Mom."

"I love you too, Tracy. Remember that."

"Always. Goodnight, Brian."

At 8:30 p.m. Neal was again in Tracy's private office.

"I can't leave yet, Neal. But you go ahead."

"No."

"Neal, El is watching over Tyler. I'll be fine here."

"Tracy—"

"No arguments. I'll walk you to your car if you'd like though."

"Uh-huh."

"I don't mind."

Neal shook his head. "I can't believe this call is *that* important."

"It is. Now you go home to that family of yours."

"All right." He frowned. "When are you going to start interviewing again?"

"…Because the last time turned out so well for us, right?"

"I wasn't going to say anything like that. The works piling up and I don't want to work my summer away."

Tracy nodded. "I hear you. Rebecca has already put the word out. As soon as the resumes start coming in, you can run with it."

"Mm." Neal paused. "When this whole thing with Tyler finally comes out, do you think it will hurt us?"

Tracy looked at the floor. "I don't really know. I don't think so. Our clients aren't typically the kind who have dark secrets that someone like Tyler might try and use. I'm more worried about their safety."

"Like Karen Purl."

"Yes."

Neal sighed. "Well, I'll head downstairs and check out the parking lot. But if I see anything suspicious, I'll be coming right back."

"Want me to walk out with you?"

"And risk missing that call you're so desperate to get? No thank you."

Tracy chuckled. "Okay."

The impulse seemed to hit them simultaneously. Tracy rose and moved towards Neal, and they embraced each other tightly. Then without another word Neal turned and left, making sure to lock the office doors behind him. He also studied the parking lot carefully before he left it. If anything happened to Tracy tonight, he'd never be able to forgive himself.

It was just past 10:00 when Tracy shut down her computer. As she did every night before leaving, she packed her notepad and laptop into her briefcase and then pushed her chair in. Then she made sure all the lights were turned off before turning on the alarm. She locked the doors behind her and moved towards the elevator. She pressed the down button. She was pulling out her phone when the doors opened. She entered. But the elevator car was not empty. It had an unexpected passenger.

"I didn't feel like waiting for you outside," Katie Entwistle said.

The doors closed behind Tracy. Katie then opened her purse and allowed Tracy to see its contents. Tracy looked inside. It appeared to be a Glock 42 handgun that Katie wanted the attorney to see. Then Katie Entwistle removed it so Tracy could have a closer look.

Chapter 18

Tyler Wannamaker entered his sister's home agitated and seemingly out of breath.

"Bolt the door," Katie barked. "I don't want Tracy trying to leave us until we're ready for her to do so."

Wannamaker shook his head. But did as his sister had instructed.

"What the hell's the matter with you, Katie?" he asked her.

"You made sure that cop didn't follow you, right?"

"My car is still at my place. I caught a cab."

"Good. Very good. Keith can give you a ride home when this is all over."

"When *what* is all over?"

"What do you think, Ty? They're onto you and you need my help."

"Katie, I don't know what you're talking about."

"Fine. Play dumb. I don't really care. Besides, it's too late now."

Wannamaker stared at Tracy. She didn't meet his eyes. She was standing near the Entwistle couch, and it looked like she had been crying. He looked back at his sister.

"What are you going to do?"

"The only thing we *can* do. We need to make it, so everyone thinks the cops are out to get you — you, an innocent man. And it starts with her."

"Can I sit down?" Tracy asked, shaking with tears in her eyes.

"Sure. Sit down. Sit down all you like."

"What do you mean 'starts with her'?"

"It's simple. She got so mad at you for quitting on her that she plotted revenge. She got that old cop friend of hers to start the story about you killing people. But when things weren't going her way, she showed up here. She tried to get Keith to lie about you. She brought this gun. There was a struggle. She got killed."

"That will *never* work!" Wannamaker shouted.

"Sure, it will. Keith and I will get our story straight. Everyone knows what a temper little Tracy has. It won't be hard to convince them she has an ego to match her hot head."

"No," Wannamaker grunted.

"Yes, Ty, yes. I planned this out. I showed up at her office and made her drive us here. I knew she wouldn't just come over if I asked her to. And I didn't want to be the one doing the driving and trying to keep an eye on her. So, Keith will just take me to pick up my car when this is all done. Then he'll drop you off at your place. Easy."

"Oh right, and let the body cool for an hour or so while you make that trip."

"I'll cover her with an electric blanket; that will keep the body warm. Trust me, Ty. I've given this *a lot* of thought."

Wannamaker looked at Keith. And while he was doing so, Tracy's phone started buzzing.

"SHIT!" Wannamaker yelled.

"Answer it," Katie ordered glaring at Tracy.

Tracy glared back at the woman holding the gun.

"No!" she answered defiantly.

Katie moved the gun a few inches to the right of where Tracy was seated and pulled the trigger. The sofa now had a hole in it. The noise made Keith Entwistle cover his ears.

"JESUS!" Entwistle shouted. "*What the hell, Katie*?!"

"The next one goes into you, Tracy," Katie growled. "And be nice. If you say anything I don't like, Ty or I will pay a call on a couple of cute kids before your cop friends have a chance to do anything about it. NOW ANSWER THE GODDAMNED PHONE!"

Tracy looked at the read out. "It's El," she announced somberly.

"Talk to him," Katie ordered. "And Ty, get nice and close so you can hear what's being said." He obeyed.

"Hi, El," Tracy said quietly after accepting the call.

"Are you all right? I thought you'd have picked up first ring."

"Uh…ladies' room."

"Oh. Sorry."

"Is Tyler still there?"

"Yes. I have the perfect view of his car and his apartment."

"What's he doing?"

"Not sure. Watching TV maybe."

"Okay."

"You hear anything from Keith?"

"Not since he called about having his doubts. Maybe he couldn't go through with it or is still working up the nerve."

"Possibly. But he should have called by now."

Tracy looked at Keith Entwistle. "Do you think I should call *him* and see what's going on?"

"A late-night call from you, Tracy? I don't think that's a good idea. What if his wife answers? What would you tell her was the reason for your call?"

"Good point."

"I'll stay here as long as Tyler's light is on. I doubt he'll be staying up all night. But it's almost midnight as it is."

"Yeah."

"Are you okay, Tracy? You sound…"

"I'm just tired, El. I want this to be over."

"Well just go home then. You're safe. If Tyler makes a move, I'm right there."

Katie Entwistle grinned. She covered her mouth with her free hand as if she had to stifle laughter.

"I'll talk to you tomorrow, El."

"All right. Goodnight."

"Bye, El."

Wannamaker grabbed the phone so he could personally terminate the call.

"Very good, Tracy," Katie told her. "Very nice indeed."

"That ex-cop isn't an idiot," Wannamaker growled. "He's probably on his way to Tracy's office right now!"

Katie just smiled at her brother. "And he'll see that her car is gone and then give her enough time to get home before calling her husband. We have *plenty* of time, Ty."

"I'm going to be sick," Entwistle said suddenly.

"Grow a pair," Katie told him. "You asked me what we should do about this, and this is my answer. What did you think I would do, Keith?"

"But why did you have to shoot the couch?" he whined. "How can we explain *that*?"

"It will go with the struggle story. Tracy here pulled the gun; there was a struggle; you didn't mean to do it. Then we'll tell everyone who'll listen how crazy she'd gotten. We'll make it seem like she and this Elias person were out to get us. Maybe I can even say both you and I grabbed for the gun, so we're not even sure which one of us actually pulled the trigger. That will muddy the waters even more."

Tyler Wannamaker was standing in front of his sister shaking his head.

"No one will ever believe the things you're saying about Tracy, Katie. There's just no way. She has friends on the force and even the SA likes her. Their mission will be to break your story. You'll *never* get away with it."

Katie looked at Wannamaker and tiled her head. And then she started laughing.

"My God, Ty: are you in love with her or something?"

"Of course not!"

"You are, aren't you? I should have suspected because of the way you always talked about her. Maybe it wasn't all about getting us to trust her."

"Stop it!"

"Hey! I have an idea. Maybe we could say the reason you left was because you two were having an affair and you wanted to end it. She didn't want to, and it led to this. Yeah — I think that's even *better*. What do you say, Tyler?"

"Katie: no one would—"

"You want to screw her, Ty? You can use the upstairs bedroom."

"KATIE!" her husband yelled.

"*What?*" Katie barked.

Tyler glared at his sister. "And what, Katie, give her the chance to pull out my hair and scratch me? That's a real great criminal mind you got working right there."

Katie frowned. "Mm. Hey, I know. Keith I will help. Keith can hold her wrists and I can grab her ankles."

"JESUS CHRIST!" Entwistle shouted. "I'LL *NEVER* HELP YOU DO SOMETHING LIKE THAT! NEVER!"

"What Keith? We're just paying Ty here back in kind. He screwed us, didn't he? Now we can help *him* get screwed!"

"ENOUGH!" Wannamaker shouted. "Give me the gun, Katie! NOW!"

"No. No way, brother dear. *I'm* in control now. NOT you."

"We *can't* hurt her. Don't you understand that?"

"It's too late. You thought you could get away with what you did. You dragged us into it. And now *I* have to drag us out."

"I didn't do anything."

"Oh *puh-leeze*, Ty. You think I didn't know; that I didn't *suspect*?"

Wannamaker blinked. "What are you talking about?"

"You've never liked Keith. And then all of a sudden you were the best brother-in-law the world had ever seen. I *knew* something was wrong."

"I wanted to help him!"

"Bullshit, Tyler! Just stop it. But it's okay. I understand. I feel bad for you, big brother. I know all about Jeannine Acosta. I talked to Mom."

"You *what*?"

"She doesn't have Alzheimer's, Ty. And she can still speak on a telephone. She remembered her more or less."

Tracy looked up momentarily and could see the rage on her former employee's face. She wondered if she could say anything to ease the mounting tension, given that Wannamaker might grab for that gun any moment. Then what would happen?

"Look," Tracy said finally, trying to compose herself, "there's no real evidence against Ty, Katie. You and Keith were our last hope. I thought you loved your husband more than your brother. I was wrong."

"A little late for mea culpas, wouldn't you say?" Katie snapped.

"My point is, Katie, there's no proof. Even tonight, no one would ever be able to prove what just happened here. It would be your three's words against mine."

"Wait," Katie said. "Are you seriously suggesting we just let you go?"

"Sure!" Entwistle interjected. "She's right! We all stick together, and we'll be okay. She has kids. She wouldn't dare risk something happening to them."

"And what about the hole in the couch, Keith dear? How would we explain *that*?"

"You wouldn't have to," Tracy said, continuing to speak softly. "I won't go to the police. I'll just go home. I just want to go home."

She couldn't keep her feelings in check anymore. She started crying.

Entwistle moved from his position and stood between Tracy and the gun.

"I believe her. We should let her go."

"No," Katie said firmly. "This is a trick. I've done my research on her. She likes trying to trick people. Those tears are just to get your sympathy. Even you, Keith, said she would try and be 'sneaky' when going after my brother. We let her go, she'll come up with some plan. I'm not willing to risk it. I don't want to be worrying about when she'll make her move. This woman is too self-righteous to just forget about all of this. Can you *grasp* all of that?"

"We're not *killers*, Katie. We're not like...." Entwistle looked at his brother-in-law.

Tyler Wannamaker stared at the weeping attorney. He didn't want this. He never wanted Tracy to find out what he had done much less see her hurt. In a way, she had been a very good — if unaware — accomplice after the fact. He had nothing against her — not like he had against the murderers of Jeannine Acosta, or the people who might have ruined his plan. Despite everything he genuinely felt great sadness looking at Tracy Brubaker Shane at this moment. Tyler looked at his sister.

"You really think you can pull the trigger huh? You think it that's easy, do you?"

Katie snuffed. "You want to do the honors, Ty? Or if I gave the gun to you, would you just send her home?"

"I won't let you do this," Entwistle said.

"Keith, I am perfectly willing to shoot you in the leg if I have to, or maybe in the foot or something. That would go even further to support our story. Wouldn't you agree?"

Entwistle put his head down. After a few moments, he stepped aside.

"That's better," Katie said. "Tyler — while a total shit — is my family, Keith. My parents are on their last legs. You didn't want to have kids. And you're working all the time. What does that leave me with? I have to protect what family I have." She looked at her brother. "Now, we need to get this done with, just in case that cop didn't believe her." She narrowed her eyes. "And then, dear brother, you and I are going to have a little talk, ourselves."

"Oh really?"

"You set up Keith. You put me through hell. I owe you. I owe you *a lot.*"

Wannamaker noticed how his sister now had her gun aimed at his chest. But instead of being frightened but what she may have been thinking, he smiled.

"You think you have the guts to pull that trigger, Katie? Go ahead. Shoot me. Do it."

"I should," Katie said, starting to show cracks in her stone-faced front. "You were supposed to *protect* me, *not* throw my life into the shitter!"

"*Your* life? My life's been in the shitter for 20 years!"

"Oh, you *poor* baby. You must be the only person who's ever lived that lost a loved one! Jesus, Ty."

"She was my life!"

"She didn't even care about you!"

"What? How dare you!"

"Mom told me all about it. That girl *dumped* your ass!"

"Stop it!"

"You're *so* smart Ty except when it comes to women."

"I said *shut up*!"

"You killed all those people over a woman who didn't even give a *SHIT* about you! It would be funny if it weren't so *pathetic*!"

"They killed her! They deserved it!"

"You should have left *us* out of it! You *SON OF A BITCH*!"

Bad enough Tracy would no longer be in his life. Now Katie too was showing how she truly felt about him. And he didn't want to lose her too.

"I'm sorry!" he shouted. "If I could have done it any other way I would have! I never meant to hurt you!"

Katie was in tears now. "Never meant to *hurt* me?! Do you realize how goddamned stupid that sounds? And then you kill a cop? If Keith had gone to jail that guy's cop buddies would have made sure he died in prison! Did you ever think of that, Tyler?!"

"I had to! You just have to believe that! Would you have wanted *me* to go to jail?! You keep putting Tracy down, but she did just what I said she would do. I was right about her, wasn't I? I knew Keith would be okay. He *is* okay!"

"No, Tyler. Keith is not 'okay.' He will never be 'okay' again. Neither of us will. And we have *you* to thank for it. And I *will* thank you for it, Tyler. I promise you that!"

Tracy's heart was beating faster than it ever had. And she had heard enough. Tyler Wannamaker was probably going to make a move for the gun any moment now. So now the moment was hers. She sprang up from the sofa and moved quickly towards the front door.

"HEY!" Wannamaker shouted.

Katie just froze. Tyler grabbed the gun from his sister and rushed towards the attorney. Tracy was pounding on the door as Wanamaker grabbed her around the throat and pulled her backwards.

And then there was a booming knock at the door. "DETECTIVE CULPEPPER, POLICE! OPEN THIS DOOR NOW!"

Wannamaker pulled Tracy towards him and wrapped his arm her waist. He pressed the gun against her temple. But as he did so the front door swung open, and both Culpepper and Elias Tanner, Sr. entered.

"ONE MOVE AND TRACY DIES!" he screamed.

"It's not loaded," Tracy said calmly.

"What?" Wannamaker asked.

"It's not loaded, Ty. There was only one live round. And *that* went into the couch for the convincer."

"Bullshit!"

"Ty, how did those two police officers manage to just enter here when the door was bolted shut? Does the door look broken to you? Think about it."

Tyler Wannamaker thought about it. Then his jaw dropped. He looked at his sister Katie, who was crying, her husband by her side with his arm around her. And then he understood. Tracy took advantage of the moment and broke free of his grip.

"YOU TRAITOROUS BITCH!" Wannamaker screamed as he started moving towards his sister. But Tracy had anticipated this possibility. She lifted her leg so that her foot got caught up in Wannamaker's legs and he lost his balance, landing face down on the floor with a loud thud. Tanner and Culpepper were soon on top of him, the latter putting a different kind of bracelet — a pair in fact — on his wrists. Then the uninvited guests lifted Wannamaker to his feet.

Katie Entwistle glared at her brother, her expression one of both great hurt and greater anger.

"When Keith told me everything, I didn't believe it. And yet I did believe it at the same time; all of it. And then I called Mom. She remembered how you wept over some girl who died. And then I knew it was the truth." Katie Entwistle next tore herself from her husband's gentle hold and started pounding Tyler Wannamaker with her fists. "YOU MONSTER! YOU EVIL MONSTER! I HOPE THEY EAT YOU ALIVE WHERE YOU'RE GOING! I HOPE I NEVER SEE YOU AGAIN! MOM AND DAD WILL DIE WHEN THEY FIND OUT! YOU *MURDERER!*"

Tracy just stood and watched. In this moment Katie Entwistle reminded her of Alastair Conroy. The difference was of course that

Conroy had been wrong; Katie wasn't. Keith Entwistle was finally able to pull his wife off her brother. But she wasn't finished yet.

"You call *me* a traitor? After what *you* did? I don't know who you are, Ty. I can't..." Katie relaxed her fists and turned to embrace her husband. Meanwhile Wannamaker said nothing. He just stood there, looking stunned.

"The biggest mistake you made tonight, Tyler," Tracy began, "was thinking I was right when I said Katie loved you more than she did her husband. She doesn't."

"You got nothing!" Wannamaker hollered.

"You confessed, Tyler. You said 'I had to' when Katie talked about you killing Jim Lucas. Everyone heard it. And you put a gun to my head. You're done."

"I think I should read this guy his rights," Culpepper interrupted. "Not that I think he doesn't know what they are. But I wouldn't want him getting off on a technicality."

"By all means," Tracy said flatly. "See you in court, Ty — if you're foolish enough to let this go to trial, that is. If I said it once, I've said it a single time: Never screw with the Bru."

Wannamaker just looked at her. And this time he wasn't smiling. He then looked to the front door where two other officers were now standing. He pursed his lips tightly and decided against further comment. Then Culpepper nodded at Tracy as those officers came to assist taking Tyler Wannamaker to the place where monsters are consigned after they're caught.

Tracy looked at Katie. "*YOU* were amazing!"

"I told you," Entwistle said, forcing a smile. "I don't call her my drama queen for nothing."

Katie shook her head. "I can't believe I did it."

"I just gave you the beats to hit; I had no idea what a musician you were."

"Thanks," Katie said gloomily.

"For a minute there I thought you changed your mind. When it came time for you to fire that shot, I was really feeling nervous."

"Let's sit down, dear," Entwistle said, easing his wife onto the couch.

"You were good too, Keith," Tracy said.

"I wasn't doing much acting. When she got to the part of taking you upstairs… God, Katie, where did *that* come from?"

Katie shook her head. "It's just how I was feeling over what he'd done. He violated Tracy and he had *us* help him."

"Katie," Tracy said, putting her hand on the amateur thespian's knee, "don't think for a second I hold you or Keith in any way responsible for what your brother did."

"*I* do," Katie whispered. "I wasn't lying when I said part of me knew the truth. I felt guilty. There was a moment when I thought I'd shoot Tyler with that bullet."

Entwistle hugged his wife. "You were incredible," he whispered. "You did the right thing tonight."

"Keith's right," Tracy agreed. "I wish there had been another way to do this. But none of us could think of one. I guess you might say it was a necessary evil. Tyler's only possible weakness was you. You're the only one he ever would have admitted the truth to. There was no real evidence against him. Even your mother's confirmation of some kind of relationship with Jeannine Acosta wouldn't have meant much at this point. I'm really sorry, Katie."

"You don't owe anyone anything, Tracy," the woman responded. Then Katie sighed. "I just unleashed tonight, didn't I? I still can't believe I did it."

Tracy stood up. "I think I'll leave you two alone now. I think they'll have the surveillance devices out of here soon so I'm sure any statement-taking can be done later. I'll insist on it."

The Entwistles smiled and nodded. "I guess you'll have your own statement to give," the husband said.

"Maybe I'll see you there."

Tracy smiled again and then headed towards the door. An officer was just bringing Katie Entwistle's car back from where it had been left. It was the least they could do for her. Tyler Wannamaker, on the other hand, was no longer in the area. And Tracy was glad. She had said all she ever wanted to say to him, seen all she ever wanted to see of him, again.

Elias Tanner, Sr. was speaking with Arthur Pankow in the driveway. Tracy smiled. She hadn't expected the cameo.

"Hi Art!" Tracy said as she came skipping towards him. The sight caused Tanner to laugh. Pankow just grinned.

"I can't believe you pulled this off," he told her.

"Don't thank *me*. Thank Katie Entwistle in there. She was supreme."

"I thought I did pretty well, myself," Tanner offered.

"Oh, you were good too, El. Tyler really thought you were still outside his apartment."

"You weren't?" Pankow asked.

"Not after Tyler left. His sister called him insisting he come over. Then Keith called me to say Tyler was on his way. I waited a few minutes and then made my way here. Bill had already arrived."

"Watched Tyler Wannamaker pull in, myself," Culpepper said as he joined the gathering.

"And we got all of this?" Pankow asked.

Culpepper nodded. "State of the art recordings and three witnesses. He's done."

"I already said that," Tracy grinned. "Tyler started panicking when he realized his relationship with his sister could be forever ruined. He didn't want that. She was really the only person he cared about. When Katie had finally said enough to frighten him, he felt he had to explain himself in hopes she would forgive him. And that's when he truly screwed up."

"And *that's* what you were counting on, huh Tracy?" Culpepper asked.

"Something like that," Tracy admitted.

"You got a lot of guts there, missy," Culpepper smiled. "If Katie had accidentally fired at you…"

"If I didn't see the gun moving from my direction when the phone started buzzing, I'd have hit the floor." Her companions started laughing.

"What's the deal with that car Officer Corey was driving?" Pankow asked.

"That's Katie's," Tracy explained. "She left it at my office."

"Why?"

"Didn't anyone fill you in on the plan, Art?"

"No one ever fills me in on anything, Tracy. You should know that by now."

She chuckled. "To give this story any credence, I couldn't have driven here myself. I had to be — shall we say — kidnapped. So, when Keith called me back saying Katie had talked to her mother and was on board, I asked that she come and pick me up. Then I waited for another 30 or 40 minutes and headed to meet her in the parking lot. But she had made better time than I thought she would and decided to meet me inside. We ended up meeting at the elevator. Then she showed me the gun Detective Culpepper provided. And on the way back to her place I explained what needed to happen. I gave her the basic story to tell but she basically wrote the script. She was brilliant at improvising. But you'll hear what I mean when you listen to the recording."

"I guess I will."

"If Tyler had checked to make sure his sister's car wasn't in the driveway or garage, we were covered. Turns out I could have just driven here myself. But I wasn't leaving anything to chance."

"Of course not," Pankow chuckled.

Tracy paused a few moments and then said, "Vanessa Yeardly might still be awake. Someone should call her to let her know she can rest easy now."

"I just got off the phone with her," Culpepper said.

"Oh," Tracy smiled. "You *are* super-efficient, Detective. I think I like you." Everyone laughed again.

"And I think I like you too, Tracy. You helped do what I thought might be impossible. But I have no doubt Tyler Wannamaker will spend the rest of his life in jail." Culpepper looked at Tanner, who nodded. Then he looked back at the attorney. "Now I have to get to the station and start the damned paperwork on this thing. I wish you could help me with *that* too, Tracy."

She chuckled. "*I* have to go home to a husband who's going to be very upset with me. Luckily, he'll know about the happy ending in advance. But he'll still give me what for."

"Then he's a fool," Culpepper grunted. Then he turned and headed towards his vehicle. Tracy just watched him. A famous line about a beautiful friendship beginning came to her mind.

"I need to go too," Pankow said. "I have some calls to make about what's coming in the next few hours. I'll see you *thespians* later." Pankow left and it was now just Tracy and Tanner.

"You broke my heart when I heard you crying," Tanner said as he rubbed Tracy's shoulder. "Are you okay now?"

"I'm fine El. I guess I used what they call method acting. I just imagined never seeing my family again. Plus, the hell we've all been through helped. I needed a good cry anyway."

Tanner nodded. "You're going right home then?"

"Yes. Are you?"

"Yes."

"Then I'll see you later. Thanks for everything."

Tanner just nodded. Then they embraced. Soon Tracy was en route to her home. She had debated making one more check on the Entwistles but decided against it. They needed their alone time now. They deserved it. Tracy deserved some R&R too. But first she would have to recount the night's events to a sure-to-be irate husband. But he'd forgive her. He had to. Or *he'd* be dealing with an irate wife. Tracy smiled. She didn't care if the face she saw when she entered her home would be an angry one. As long as it was Brian's, she wouldn't care at all.

Chapter 19

"What do you have there?" Neal Bennett asked his employer.

"It's note — a thank you card more or less — from Debra Dooley."

"Really?"

"It's to thank us for clearing Ed Lydecker's name — at least as a murderer."

"*Us*? I think you mean *you*, Tracy."

"Neal, I couldn't do what I do without the support of my office family. So, it is 'us'."

He smiled. "You're the boss."

"It's a hand-written note, too. Not too many people these days take the time to hand-write anything. They text or email instead. So, this is special. I'm going to keep this. And the next time I'm wondering if what we do around here is worth it all, I'm going to pull this out and read it. This was just such an awful thing to be involved with. I needed this."

"What does it say?"

Tracy looked at the paper and started reading aloud.

Dear Tracy:

I know we've never met but I wanted to say thank you for all the hard work you and your firm did with respect to Cynthia Lydecker's death. I have learned over the last several days just exactly what you did — and this coming after your client was, for all intents and purposes, cleared. Most people would have just kept their mouths shut and went on with their lives. That's how most people are today it seems. So, to take all the risks you did makes you someone very special in my eyes. And I'm sure all of Eddie's friends — and he had many of them — would want to thank you too if they knew all the facts. I hope now to continue both Eddie and Cynthia's work in some way. But that might have been impossible if it weren't for what you and your firm did. I will be forever grateful.

Sincerely,
Debbie Dooley

Tracy lifted her head. "You see, Neal. You can never go wrong with doing the right thing."

Neal came towards Tracy's desk and sat down in front of it.

"I should call her and thank her for this. I prejudged her at one point during all of this and I'm feeling guilty about it."

Neal looked around the office and then he said, "Tyler's picked his attorney. Danny Gabin."

Tracy rolled her eyes. "The diminished capacity guru, huh?"

"That's him."

"Mm. I'm not worried."

"He may have a shot at getting Tyler acquitted."

"I doubt it. Gabin has two options as I see it. The first one is to plead not guilty hoping the fact that both Keith and Ed Lydecker were arrested for the same crime will create doubt. But Tyler's own sister is going to testify against him, and I'll be telling the jury how I had a gun to my head that Tyler thought was loaded. I don't see how a jury will come up with a reasonable explanation for all of that.

"The other option is to plead temporary insanity, diminished capacity, or something similar on account of extreme grief over Jeannine Acosta's death. The problem with that argument is that he planned the whole thing over a very long period of time. Plus, he didn't just kill the people who ran down his beloved. He murdered George Finnegan and Jim Lucas for the very *sane* motive of self-protection. He knew the whole time what he was doing was wrong. So, I'm confident at the end of the day Tyler ain't goin' home."

Neal grinned and nodded. "You offer to make Arthur Pankow's opening statement for him?"

"I'm available for consultations for the right price," Tracy winked. "But I think Art will do just fine without my help."

"Probably."

"Now, follow me."

Tracy stood up, came around her desk, and headed towards her doorway. Neal, a little perplexed, followed. Tracy stopped at Rebecca Dietz's desk.

"I have some good news for you and Neal," Tracy told the secretary.

"What's that, Tracerino?"

As both Neal and Rebecca looked at her, she said, "I'm closing down the office the last week of July. You guys have the week off — paid, of course. And that's in addition to your normal vacation."

"But Tracy," Neal started to stay before he was shushed.

"No 'buts' Neal. I've checked the calendar and that week is clear for right now and we're going to keep it that way. We'll bust our collective butts over the next several weeks to keep up and advise our clients. When we get back, we'll start interviewing to fill our recently vacated position. So, we won't be taking on any additional work until that happens. We *all* need this. Tyler was with us for two years and we each need to deal with our feelings about what happened. I know I do. So, you both do what you need to do. I'm going to do what *I* need to do at the beach. That is all."

Neal and Rebecca just looked at Tracy in disbelief. She never ceased to surprise them. All they could offer in return were "thank yous." They continued staring at their employer as she returned to her office. Then they looked at each other. Neal finally left to resume his duties and so Rebecca resumed hers. She was soon back to answering calls. When she said, "Tracy Brubaker Shane and Associates," she couldn't have felt any prouder.

"But the most bizarre aspect of this," Tracy was telling her sister-in-law, Crystal Shane, "is that Jeannine Acosta had broken up with Tyler a year or so before this all happened. They started dating in high school but went to different colleges. At some point she dumped him, but he was sure he'd win her back. That's what Katie told me based on her talk with her mother."

Crystal shook her head. "You never can tell about people, can you sis?"

"No. I've never been so wrong about a person."

"Well. you never really *knew* him, did you? He was play-acting the first time you met him."

"That's true. He had his own agenda from the moment he sent us his resume."

"BABY BAD! BABY BAD!" Nicole Shane shouted as she came running towards her mother. Her father was right behind her. He was holding Peter. Peter, in turn, immediately reached for his mother when he saw her.

"Baby isn't bad," Brian told Nicole firmly as he handed Tracy her son.

"What happened?" Tracy asked.

"Kenny—"

"Ken!" Crystal corrected sternly.

"Fine. Ken was playing with a fire truck and went to get some Little People to put inside it. Peter crawled over and started moving the truck back and forth and Ken got upset."

"Ken had first!" Nicole said forcefully.

Tracy shook her head. "Your brother is just a baby, Nicole. He didn't know what he was doing. He doesn't understand sharing yet. He's not bad, just like Daddy said."

"Everything is okay," Brian continued. "Elias calmed Ken down and he's fine now." Brian picked up Nicole. "Let's go back and see Ken," he smiled. "I bet he misses you."

"OKAY!" Nicole shouted happily. She wriggled until her father put her down and then she moved quickly towards the playroom.

"I've got him," Tracy told Brian. "I think he's hungry anyway."

"Sorry, love. I know you wanted some time alone with Crystal."

Tracy smiled. "It's fine. Peter won't reveal our darkest thoughts."

He grinned and then followed the path his daughter had taken. Tracy started nursing the eager Peter Shane.

Crystal twisted her lips. "I don't know how you do it. I tried that with Ken for like a day. It just wasn't for me."

Tracy chuckled as she stroked Peter's light brown hair. "I do it more for the bonding than anything else," Tracy said softly. "I don't see him as much as I want to."

"You're a born mother," Crystal sighed. "So, we're all set for the big trip, right?"

"Yes. Karen won't be able to join us for the whole week, but she'll be there for most of it."

"Great! Two little girls and two little guys. Could be interesting."

Tracy chuckled. "I think it will be a great time."

"So do I."

Peter had drifted off to sleep. Tracy looked at Crystal.

"Tyler and Katie's parents seem like good people from all I've heard. And Katie is really something given what she was able to do."

"Sure."

"But look how Tyler turned out."

Crystal frowned. "Tracy, that guy had mental problems. If you're worrying about one of ours turning out like that, don't. That *is* where you were headed with that, right?"

"I don't know."

"I'll take that as a yes. Good gravy, Tracy, stop adding things to the worry list."

"Don't you worry about Ken?"

"Sure, but not like *that*. I worry about normal stuff: dealing with a cold, is he doing everything he should be doing for a 19-month-old. I'm *not* worrying that because I punished him for back-talking me that he'll someday want to hurt people."

"Yeah, you're right."

"Tracy, the line of work you've chosen is going to put you in contact with bad people. It just is. But most people aren't like that. You're dealing with a skewed sample. Know what I mean, sis?"

Tracy smiled and nodded. "I know you're right. I'm just so worried I'm not being a good mother sometimes."

"Nonsense."

"I was so late home so many nights over the last few weeks that I didn't get to put my children to bed. I don't want them to think I love my work more than them. That would kill me."

"When they get older, and see what it is you do, I'm sure they'll understand. Hell, if I were you, I'd be making a scrapbook of all those articles that have your name in it. You weren't home late because you were knocking down a few brews with the girlfriends."

Tracy smiled gratefully. "Thanks, Crys."

"…Not that anything I just said will matter…"

"It matters." Tracy looked at the snoozing infant. "I'm going to put him in his bassinet. Then I want something sweet."

Crystal chuckled. "Banana split?"

"Good choice."

The sister-in-law grinned and headed towards the kitchen where she'd wait for Tracy. But it wasn't long before Crystal's son came looking for his mother, wrapping his arms around her legs giggling. Crystal picked him up and kissed him.

"Do you want to share some ice cream with me?" she asked him. His lips formed an "O" and his eyes widened. "I'll take that as a yes. We better let your cousin know, too. Or she'll be calling *all* of us bad."

And while the kitchen was soon noisy because of clinking dishes and excited youngsters, it was just as quickly quiet again when the eating began. Ice cream was a very potent silencer.

It was a subject that had been broached several times over the last several years. And Brian felt the need to broach it again. He had kept his mouth shut until now. He wanted some time to pass before he entered tricky territory. But enter it he would, nevertheless.

With their guests now gone, and Violetta Brubaker retired for the evening, Brian took Bonkers out as he normally did. Tracy was cleaning up the playroom, which the trio of tykes had severely messed. And Nicole balked at having to clean everything up by herself. She was only two and a half, after all. After Brian returned with Bonkers — who quickly bolted up the steps to join Nicole — he joined Tracy in the playroom. She was sitting crisscross on the floor paging through a Dr. Seuss classic. She looked up when she heard Brian enter.

"Amazing, isn't it?" she asked him. "These books are timeless. They're over 50 years old and are just as fresh and original as they must have been when they were written."

Brian sat down next to her. "Yes, they are."

"I wonder how he felt about what he had accomplished."

"Proud I guess."

"Yeah." Tracy sighed. "I want to do something that matters."

"What?" Brian asked, sounding surprised.

She looked at him. "Why don't you just say what you've been wanting to say for the last week or so? I know something's been on your mind."

"I guess it has."

"So, tell me."

"I think you know."

"Tell me anyway."

Brian gulped. He took Tracy's hands in his and looked into her eyes. "Do you remember when we first met?"

"Of course, I do."

"And you remember at that time you thought you were going to be a detective like your father?"

"Yes," she answered slowly.

"And do you remember what I said in response to that?"

She smiled. "Of course. You said you didn't think you could be married to a cop."

"...Because it takes a very strong person to be a cop's husband or wife. They have extra worries on top of everything else."

"Sure, Brian. I always wondered why you said that though."

"I would think by now you could guess the answer."

Tracy grinned. "Are you *really* saying you were thinking about us getting married just moments after we met?"

"I don't know exactly. Let's just say I immediately saw you as someone I could see myself falling in love with and wanting to marry."

"I'll accept that."

Brian sighed. "Tracy, I feel like I married a cop."

Tracy looked down at her crossed legs. "It's not really that bad, is it?"

"Yes, it is. It's been five years since you came to my rescue, but I feel 10 years older sometimes."

"Oh, Brian…"

"I mean it. I can't take this anymore."

Tracy looked up. "So, what are you saying? You want to leave me?"

"Of course not! Never! That's not what I'm saying at all."

"Then what *are* you saying?"

"If you don't think you can take on a murder case without approaching it strictly from a legal sense, then I don't want you take on any more murder cases. In fact, I'd rather you just didn't take any on from this day forward. *That's* what I'm saying."

Tracy sighed heavily and looked downward again. "I see," she said quietly.

"You have two kids. Your situation isn't like it used to be. You have people who *need* you. And to tell you the truth, it only adds to my frustration when you get so flip about things. Remember hiding my pajamas that one time so I couldn't go after you?"

"I apologized for that."

"I know. But my point is you get so caught up in things you don't take time to think what might happen. You may have had most of your bases covered on this Tyler thing, but something could still have gone wrong. What if Tyler had brought a gun with him? What would you have done then?"

"There was a contingency for that."

Brian snorted. "I'll bet. But you still could have been hurt — or worse. And telling me about everything *after* the fact tells me you knew how I'd react if you told me ahead of time. Admit it."

"I don't deny that."

"I love you, Tracy. I love you more than you can understand. I know our life isn't perfect, but I feel like I'm living a fairy tale sometimes being with you. I never thought that would happen for me.

But it has. And I'm scared to death of losing it — of losing you. Can't you understand that?"

"Of course, I can."

"You…." Brian shook his head. "I don't know if I can handle things the way they are. I'm not as strong as you are, as your mother must have been. I think I've really come to understand her these last few years."

"What does *that* mean?"

"She had to find a way to deal with her worries. She didn't want her daughter knowing how she felt every second her husband wasn't home with them. So, she decided to make it seem like she was naturally a…well, a sour puss, I guess. She pretended so long to be this firm, seemingly hard-hearted person that that's what she became. But I've seen the pictures of her with you and heard some of the stories you've told. And now I understand."

Tracy released one of Brian's hands so she could wipe the water that was streaking down from his left eye.

"Mom might be interested to hear your opinion."

"Yeah…well…that was for your ears only. And I don't want to become like that. I have to play bad cop here at home enough as it is. Nicole still thinks she should get her way all of the time."

Tracy sighed. "Brian…Brian, I…I can't."

"What do you mean you can't?"

"I've thought about doing just what you're asking me to do so many times over the last five years more than I can count. In fact, at one point I told myself, 'No more murder cases.' But I was just lying to myself."

Brian shook his head. "I don't accept that."

"Brian, the night my father died, he had a choice. When the killers made their move, he could have turned and ran. But he didn't. He decided to help. It cost him his life. But if didn't do what he did, someone else would have died that night. And he probably wouldn't have been able to live with himself."

"Tracy, he was a cop. He was doing what—"

"*What he was being paid to do*? Is that what you were going to say? You think because he got a paycheck that meant what he did was easy to do — or that it should have been?"

Brian snorted. "My point is he knew the dangers when he chose his profession."

"So what? You don't think he got scared sometimes?"

"I didn't say that."

Tracy sighed. "Brian, can you sit here now and look me in the eye, and tell me that you truly believe every one of my clients who faced a murder charge in the last five years would have been cleared if they went to someone else? If you can say 'yes' to that question, I'll do as you ask."

They were looking into each other's eyes once again. He wanted to lie to her — one harmless lie to bring him and the children untold comfort for the rest of their lives. Surely Brian could be forgiven for such a deception. It wasn't *just* for his sake. And this was the opportunity he'd been waiting for. He knew if said "yes" she'd be true to her word. That's just who she was. So, he started to answer her. Then he stopped. And then he sighed loudly. Damn her, this fairy tale princess of his.

"No," he answered honestly. "I'd say the odds were against *that*."

Tracy placed her hand on her husband's cheek. "Thank you, Brian. Thank you for being honest."

"I wish I could say you're welcome."

"I don't mean to drive you crazy with this. I don't go looking to get myself into trouble. I really don't."

"I know that."

"But when it comes to those moments when it's time to move forward or turn back, I always think of my father. *He* moved forward. And if I don't do that too, and an innocent person paid the price because of it, then I would feel worse than you do. I can promise you that."

"You can't know that."

"Brian, you say that you love me. You say you love me more than I can understand. Well, if you love me then you'll be strong for me, because this is important to me. I need you to support me and believe in me. I told Neal not too long ago that I can do what I do because I know people have my back. I don't feel alone. And if there's one person whose support I need more than anyone, it's you. I love you too. I've loved you for such a long time. So please be strong for me. Please don't ask me to stop doing what I sometimes do. I think it's important. And I want to do something important. But I won't be able to if you won't support me."

Brian remained quiet for a few moments. Then he said, "What you're asking isn't easy for me."

"To support me?"

"To pretend it doesn't get to me."

She smiled again. "I never asked you to pretend it doesn't get to you. That would be a ridiculous thing to ask. What I want is for you to tell me that, even though it's hard for you, you'll try and be understanding; that you understand I think I'm doing the right thing."

Brian started nodding slowly. "I know you're doing the right thing already. But I'm selfish. I'm afraid for you sometimes."

"I'm afraid too. And there may come a time when I change my mind about things and decide, 'enough with the right thing crap'." Brian laughed softly. "That's better," Tracy smiled.

"I can't promise I won't bring this up again, Tracy."

"And we'll talk about it then just like we are now."

He sighed. "I guess that's it then."

Tracy stood up and extended her arms and hands downward. "Come on, Brian. Let's go to bed."

Brian let Tracy help pull him up. "All right."

"Carry me?"

"Don't push it."

She grinned. "I'm not *that* much heavier since the babies came."

"No. But my back isn't what it used to be."

"Oh. I guess I'll have to take your word for it then."

"Would I lie to you, Tracy?" he grinned.

She didn't answer. She started her exit from the toy room and Brian had no choice to follow her since their hands were clasped together. Upstairs, as he watched his wife undress, he asked, "Tracy: can I ask you something?"

"Sure, Brian."

"I know you think sometimes I'm only interested in one thing."

Tracy paused a moment. Did she not have this very same thought not too long ago when Tyler Wannamaker was deliberately provoking her? Did she really think Brian's only interest in her was a physical one? After a quick deliberation, Tracy grinned and climbed onto the bed.

"Not really, Brian. I'm just teasing you most of the time."

"But there are probably times you and I have made love when you really didn't want to. Right?"

Tracy put her face directly in front of his. "Sure, Brian. But I know it's important for you. And it's not like I was miserable doing it. If I really am not in the mood, I will tell you. I *have* told you."

"And tonight? Are we going to make love just because you know I'm upset?"

Tracy kissed him. "No, Brian. Tonight is one of those nights when I have no reservations. When my husband shares his feelings with me like you did, that's a turn on. So, I'm on."

"So am I."

"You're never 'off,' Brian — except of course when you have to reload."

He started laughing. "You may be right. But I can't help it. I'm just wired like that."

"I know. I think I've figured that out by now."

"I'm sure I won't always be this way. You know age and the march of time and all of that."

"Don't talk like that. This is fairy tale time, remember? This is when we remind ourselves, we'll live happily ever after. And I *know* some things I can do to make you happy."

They smiled at each other and kissed. And they were happy. Soon they were even more than that. Afterwards Tracy was running her finger down, and then back up, the middle of Brian's face.

"What are you doing?" he asked.

"You have a small nose," she answered.

"O-kay."

"You know I've never seen you with a mustache or beard. Did you ever grow one or the other?"

"No. I never cared for either."

"I like a moustache — if it's not too bushy."

Brian chuckled. "Is that a hint?"

"No. Just sayin'. Besides: it might tickle when we lock lips."

"You mean like this?" Brian kissed her.

"Smooth move, Brian."

"I could imagine Peter or Nicole pulling on it."

Tracy chuckled. "Oh, that would be adorable."

"I think not."

Tracy rolled onto to her back. "Do you believe in hell, Brian?"

"What? What just happened?"

"I mean the hell of pitchforks and fire pits."

"You…I hate when you do this."

"File a complaint later. In the meantime, what do you think?"

"I don't know. It sounds kind of silly to me that there's a bunch of people with horns and tails managing a place like that."

"Mm. You know what I think?"

"No."

"I think hell is loneliness. I imagine hell is just a really big room. And maybe there's a stool in there. And the person who's been damned has to spend eternity sitting on that stool with no one else there; complete solitude. As far as their eyes or whatever can see, there's nothing *to* see. That's what I think hell is like."

Brian frowned. "You think Tyler Wannamaker is going to hell, Tracy?"

"I think he already *is* in hell. But in terms of an afterlife, I can't say. One day he could genuinely be sorry for what he did and seek forgiveness from someone far wiser than anyone who inhabits this planet. And if he's truly sorry he *will* be forgiven."

"I guess."

"To get by in this life you need other people. And I think if you demonstrate while you're here that you don't think that you do, you'll spend forever alone. What do *you* think?"

"I think — for some bizarre reason only you understand — you're trying to depress me."

"I'm not trying to depress you."

"Oh, right. Hell and death and loneliness are such wonderfully uplifting nighttime topics. Would it cheer you up if I grew that moustache?"

Tracy started laughing gently. "Never mind then, my horny little devil."

"Who are you calling little?"

Tracy just frowned. "Good grief. It's not the size that counts, Brian."

"But it couldn't hurt."

She grinned at him. "Goodnight then, big boy."

"Goodnight…girl."

She chuckled as they kissed. He was *so* lucky he remembered to drop the "big" from his retort.

With the couple having shared their final thoughts for evening, Tracy hoped she could now officially put the strange case of Tyler Wannamaker behind her. It had truly been a hellish six months. But other people involved in the affair had experienced much worse than she had. Some were even no longer alive to deal with the aftermath. Tracy would always feel tremendous sympathy for Detective Jim Lucas. He never did get the chance to master his inner demons before another type of demon caught up with him. And as much as she disliked Shirley Hammersmith, Tracy still felt awful about the reporter's fate. She had died just doing her job, hadn't she? She had friends and family too, hadn't she?

Okay, so maybe Tracy would never *truly* be able to put these events behind her. It was hard sometimes to forget even if one sincerely wanted to move on. Forgive and forget was such a bizarre saying — a stupid one really. Forgiveness comes from the heart. A memory gets filed in the brain. Those two organs don't always see eye to eye. Despite a certain popular song, you can't always "simply chose to forget." There was nothing "simple" about it.

Damn him! Damn Tyler Wannamaker for insinuating himself into her life for his evil purposes. And that's what they were: evil. When it came to Wannamaker Tracy had no qualms about using such a term, despite what the political correctness police might say about it. He hurt so many people in so many ways — and he really didn't care. At no point had even genuinely shown remorse. His apologies to his sister were insincere — desperate lies so she wouldn't hate him. They hadn't worked.

Now, Tracy was worried what the lasting effects of this ordeal would be. How would she treat the next candidate vying for a place by her side? Would she have trust issues with *anyone* new that came into her life? Forgive Tyler for what he had done? She would have to; someway, somehow, she would have to. She'd have to try. But truly forget? That was a totally different proposition.

But that upcoming week at the beach was a step in the right direction. Heck, it was probably a leap. Just watching the children play together — and fight, and then make up — would be good for her soul. Children were the best at forgiving — and maybe even forgetting. And in return, her job as parent to Nicole and Peter was to protect them from the monsters as long as she could. Tracy had met far too many monsters over the last five years to think she could let her guard down for even one second. She would have to remain ever vigilant. And she truly believed doing what she was doing now was the best way to do that.

Of course, even the vigilant need to close their eyes and rest on occasion. And so, Tracy closed her eyes. She suddenly had the desire to pray. And so, she did — the Lord's Prayer to be exact. "...but deliver us from evil. Amen." Yes. Save and protect her children and everyone else from evil. And if Tracy Brubaker Shane was put on this earth to help do that, then she would do it. She already had, and successfully at that. And that's one thing — especially in the most difficult of situations — she must never let herself forget.